SPECIMEN DAYS

Michael Cunningham

SPECIMEN DAYS

FARRAR, STRAUS AND GIROUX   *New York*

Farrar, Straus and Giroux
19 Union Square West, New York 10003

ISBN 0-7394-6266-0

Designed by Jonathan D. Lippincott

This novel is dedicated to the memory of my mother, Dorothy

Fear not O Muse! truly new ways and days receive, surround you,
I candidly confess a queer, queer race, of novel fashion,
And yet the same old human race, the same within, without,
Faces and hearts the same, feelings the same, yearnings the same,
The same old love, beauty and use the same.

—Walt Whitman

Author's Note

Any writer who sets part or all of a novel in an identifiable time and place faces the question of veracity. The simplest answer is also the most severe—historic events must be rendered with absolute precision. Battles must be fought where and when they were actually fought; zeppelins may not appear in the sky a moment before they were invented; a great artist cannot appear at a masked ball in New Orleans when he is known, on that particular evening, to have been recuperating from gout in Baton Rouge.

The strict sequence of historical events, however, tends to run counter to the needs of the storyteller. Biographers and historians may be required to account for all those missed trains, canceled engagements, and long periods of lassitude; the fiction writer is not necessarily so constrained. Novelists must usually decide what degree of slavish accuracy would make their stories more alive, and what degree would make them less. We seem to fall along a broad spectrum in this regard. I know novelists who wouldn't think of tampering with recorded fact, and I know—and greatly admire—a certain writer who invents everything, from habits and customs during the time of Christ to botany and the workings of the human body. When questioned about it, he simply says, "It's fiction."

Specimen Days falls somewhere between those two poles. It's semi-accurate. To the best of my ability, I've been true to historic particulars in the scenes I've set in the past. But it would be a mistake on the reader's part to accept any of it as literal fact. I've taken especial liberty with chronology and have juxtaposed events, people, buildings, and monuments that may in fact have been separated by twenty years or more. Anyone interested in the absolute truth about New York in the mid to late nineteenth century would be well advised to consult *Gotham* by Edwin G. Burrows and Mike Wallace, which was the primary source from which I spun my own variations.

IN THE MACHINE

W alt said that the dead turned into grass, but there was no grass where they'd buried Simon. He was with the other Irish on the far side of the river, where it was only dirt and gravel and names on stones.

Catherine believed Simon had gone to heaven. She had a locket with his picture and a bit of his hair inside.

"Heaven's the place for him," she said. "He was too good for this world." She looked uncertainly out the parlor window and into the street, as if she expected a glittering carriage to wheel along with Simon on board, serene in his heedless milk-white beauty, waving and grinning, going gladly to the place where he had always belonged.

"If you think so," Lucas answered. Catherine fingered the locket. Her hands were tapered and precise. She could sew stitches too fine to see.

"And yet he's with us still," she said. "Don't you feel it?" She worried the locket chain as if it were a rosary.

"I suppose so," Lucas said. Catherine thought Simon was in the locket, and in heaven, and with them still. Lucas hoped she didn't expect him to be happy about having so many Simons to contend with.

The guests had departed, and Lucas's father and mother had gone to bed. It was only Lucas and Catherine in the parlor, with what had been left behind. Empty plates, the rind of a ham. The ham had been meant for Catherine's and Simon's wedding. It was lucky, then, to have it for the wake instead.

Lucas said, "I have heard what the talkers were talking, the talk of the beginning and the end. But I do not talk of the beginning or the end."

He hadn't meant to speak as the book. He never did, but when he was excited he couldn't help himself.

She said, "Oh, Lucas."

His heart fluttered and thumped against the bone.

"I worry for you," she said. "You're so young."

"I'm almost thirteen," he said.

"It's a terrible place. It's such hard work."

"I'm lucky. It's a kindness of them, to give me Simon's job."

"And no more school."

"I don't need school. I have Walt's book."

"You know the whole thing, don't you?"

"Oh no. There's much more, it will take me years."

"You must be careful at the works," she said. "You must—" She stopped speaking, though her face didn't change. She continued offering her profile, which was as gravely beautiful as that of a woman on a coin. She continued looking out at the street below, waiting for the heavenly entourage to parade by with Simon up top, the pride of the family, a new prince of the dead.

Lucas said, "You must be careful, too."

"There's nothing for me to be careful about, my dear. For me it's just tomorrow and the next day."

She slipped the locket chain back over her head. The locket vanished into her dress. Lucas wanted to tell her—what? He wanted to tell her that he was inspired and vigilant and recklessly alone, that his body contained his unsteady heart and something else, something he felt but could not describe: porous and spiky, shifting with flecks of thought, with urge and memory; salted with brightness, flickerings of white and green and pale gold, like stars; something that loved stars because it was made of the same substance. He needed to tell her it was impossible, it was unbearable, to be so continually mistaken for a misshapen boy with a walleye and a pumpkin head and a habit of speaking in fits.

He said, "I celebrate myself, and what I assume you shall assume." It was not what he'd hoped to tell her.

She smiled. At least she wasn't angry with him. She said, "I should go now. Will you walk me home?"

"Yes," he said. "Yes."

Outside, on the street, Catherine slipped her hand into the crook of his elbow. He tried to steady himself, to stride manfully, though what he wanted most was to stop striding altogether, to rise up like smoke and float above the street, which was filled with its evening people, workingmen returning, newsboys hawking their papers. Mad Mr. Cain paced on his corner, dressed in his dust-colored coat, snatching distractedly at whatever crawled in his beard, shouting, "Mischief, gone and forgotten, what have ye done with the shattered hearts?" The street was full of its smell, dung and kerosene, acrid smoke— something somewhere was always burning. If Lucas could rise out of his body, he would become what he saw and heard and smelled. He would gather around Catherine as the air did, touch her everywhere. He would be drawn into her when she breathed.

He said, "The smallest sprout shows there is really no death."

"Just as you say, my dear," Catherine said.

A newsboy shouted, "Woman brutally murdered, read all about it!" Lucas thought he could be a newsboy, but the pay was too low, and he couldn't be trusted to call the news, could he? He might lose track of himself and walk the streets shouting, "Every atom belonging to me as good belongs to you." He'd do better at the works. If the impulse overcame him, he could shout into Simon's machine. The machine wouldn't know or care, any more than Simon had.

Catherine didn't speak as they walked. Lucas forced himself to remain silent as well. Her building was three blocks to the north, on Fifth Street. He walked her up onto the stoop, and they stood there a moment together, before the battered door.

Catherine said, "Here we are."

A cart rolled by with a golden landscape painted on its side: two cows grazing among stunted trees and a third cow looking up at the name of a dairy, which floated in the golden sky. Was it meant to be heaven? Would Simon want to be there? If Simon went to heaven and it proved to be a field filled with reverent cows, which Simon would he be when he got there? Would he be the whole one, or the crushed?

A silence gathered between Lucas and Catherine, different from the quiet in which they'd walked. It was time, Lucas thought, to say something, and not as the book. He said, "Will you be all right?"

She laughed, a low murmuring laugh he felt in the hairs on his forearms. "It is I who should ask you that question. Will you be all right?"

"Yes, yes, I'll be fine."

She glanced at a place just above Lucas's head and settled herself, a small shifting within her dark dress. It seemed for a moment as if her dress, with its high collar, its whisper of hidden silk, had a separate life. It seemed as if Catherine, having briefly considered rising up out of her dress, had decided instead to remain, to give herself back to her clothes.

She said, "Had it happened a week later, I'd be a widow, wouldn't I? I'm nothing now."

"No, no. You are wonderful, you are beautiful."

She laughed again. He looked down at the stoop, noticed that it contained specks of brightness. Mica? He went briefly into the stone. He was cold and sparkling, immutable, glad to be walked on.

"I'm an old woman," she said.

He hesitated. Catherine was well past twenty-five. It had been talked about when the marriage was announced, for Simon had been barely twenty. But she was not old in the way she meant. She was not soured or evacuated, she was not dimmed.

He said, "You are not guilty to me, nor stale nor discarded."

She put her fingertips to his cheek. "Sweet boy," she said.

He said, "Will I see you again?"

"Of course you will. I shall be right here."

"But it will not be the same."

"No. It will not be quite the same, I'm afraid."

"If only . . ."

She waited to hear what he would say. He waited, too. If only the machine hadn't taken Simon. If only he, Lucas, were older and healthier, with a sounder heart. If only he could marry Catherine himself. If only he could leave his body and become the dress she wore.

A silence passed, and she kissed him. She put her lips on his.

When she withdrew he said, "The atmosphere is not a perfume, it has no taste of the distillation, it is odorless, it is for my mouth forever, I am in love with it."

She said, "You must go home and sleep now."

It was time to leave her. There was nothing more to do or say. Still, he lingered. He felt as he sometimes did in dreams, that he was on a stage before an audience, expected to sing or recite.

She turned, took her key from her reticule, put it in the lock. "Good night," she said.

"Good night."

He stepped down. From the sidewalk he said to her retreating form, "I am of old and young, of the foolish as much as the wise."

"Good night," she said again. And she was gone.

He didn't go home, though home was the rightful place for him. He went instead to Broadway, where the living walked.

Broadway was itself, always itself, a river of light and life that flowed through the shades and little fires of the city. Lucas felt, as he always did when he walked there, a queasy, subvert exaltation, as if he were a spy sent to another country, a realm of riches. He walked with elaborate nonchalance, hoping to be as invisible to others as they were visible to him.

On the sidewalk around him, the last of the shoppers were relinquishing the street to the first of the revelers. Ladies in dresses the color of pigeons' breasts, the color of rain, swished along bearing parcels, speaking softly to one another from under their feathered hats. Men in topcoats strode confidently, spreading the bleak perfume of their cigars, flashing their teeth, slapping the stone with their licorice boots. Carriages rolled by bearing their mistresses home, and the newsboys called out, "Woman murdered in Five Points, read all about it!" Red curtains billowed in the windows of the hotels, under a sky going a deeper red with the night. Somewhere someone played

"Lilith" on a calliope, though it seemed that the street itself emanated music, as if by walking with such certainty, such satisfaction, the people summoned music out of the pavement.

If Simon was in heaven, it might be this. Lucas could imagine the souls of the departed walking eternally, with music rising from the cobblestones and curtains putting out their light. But would this be a heaven for Simon? His brother was (had been) loud and rampant, glad of his songs and his meals. What else had made him happy? He hadn't cared for curtains or dresses. He hadn't cared about Walt or the book. What had he wanted that this heaven could provide?

Broadway would be Lucas's heaven, Broadway and Catherine and the book. In his heaven he would be everything he saw and heard. He would be himself and Catherine; he would be the calliope and the lamps; he would be shoes striking pavement, and he would be the pavement under the shoes. He would ride with Catherine on the toy horse from Niedermeyer's window, which would be the size of an actual horse but perfect in the way of toys, moving serenely over the cobblestones on its bright red wheels.

He said, "I am large, I contain multitudes." A man in a topcoat, passing by, glanced at him strangely, as people did. The man would be among the angels in Lucas's heaven, just as plump and prosperous as he was on earth, but in the next world he would not consider Lucas strange. In heaven, Lucas would be beautiful. He'd speak a language everyone understood.

The rooms when he returned to them were dim and silent. Here were the stove and the chairs and the carpet, its pattern ghostly in the dark. Here on the table was the music box that had ruined the family. It still stood cheerfully on the tabletop, a little casket with a rose carved into its lid. It could still play "Blow the Candle Out" and "Oh, Breathe Not His Name" as well as it did the day Mother bought it.

Here, too, were the faces, looking down from the walls, revered and consulted, dusted regularly: Matthew at the center, six years old, dark-eyed and primly serious, rehearsing for the influenza that would make a picture of him a year later. Here was sly Uncle Ian, who found it humorous that he would one day be only a face on a wall; here the round satisfied countenance of Grandmother Aileen, who believed that living was a temporary inconvenience and death her true and only home. They were all, according to Mother, in heaven, though what she meant by heaven was an Ireland where no one starved.

Mother would have to make room for Simon's picture, but the wall was full. Lucas wondered if one of the older dead would have to be taken away.

He paused before the door to his parents' bedroom. He felt their breathing on the other side, wondered over their dreams. He stood for a moment, alone in the slumbering darkness, before going into his and Simon's room.

Here was their bed, and above the bed the oval from which St. Brigid looked out, suffering and ecstatic, crowned by a fiery circle that Lucas had thought, when he was younger, represented her headache. Here were the pegs on which the clothes were hung, his and Simon's. St. Brigid looked sorrowfully at the empty clothes as she would at the vacant bodies of the faithful after their souls had gone. She seemed to be wondering, from under her circle of light, Where were the mechanisms of wish and need that had once worn shirts and trousers? Gone to heaven. Would it be like Broadway or Ireland? Gone to boxes in the earth. Gone into pictures and lockets, into rooms that refused to shed their memories of those who had eaten and argued and dreamed there.

Lucas undressed and got into the bed on Simon's side. Simon's pillow still smelled of Simon. Lucas inhaled. Here were Simon's humors: oil and sweat. Here was his undercurrent of tallow and his other smell, which Lucas could think of only as Simon, a smell that resembled bread but was not that, was merely the smell of Simon's body as it moved and breathed.

And there, visible through the window, were the lighted curtains of Emily Hoefstaedler across the air shaft. Emily worked with Catherine at Mannahatta, sewing sleeves onto bodices. She ate Turkish delight privately, from a silver tin she kept hidden in her room. She would be eating it now, Lucas thought, over there, behind the curtain. What would heaven be for Emily, who loved candy and had hungered for Simon? Would there be a Simon she could eat?

He lit the lamp, took the book from its place under the mattress. He began reading.

> A *child said* What is the grass? *fetching it to me with full hands;*
> *How could I answer the child? I do not know what it is any more*
> *than he.*

> *I guess it must be the flag of my disposition, out of hopeful green*
> *stuff woven.*

> *Or I guess it is the handkerchief of the Lord,*
> *A scented gift and remembrancer designedly dropt,*
> *Bearing the owner's name someway in the corners, that we may see*
> *and remark, and say* Whose?

He read it again and again. Then he closed the book and held it up, looking at Walt's likeness, the small bearded face that gazed out from the paper. Although it was wicked to think so, he could not help believing that God must resemble Walt, with his shrewd, benevolent eyes and the edible-looking spill of his beard. He had seen Walt twice, walking in the streets, and he thought he had seen St. Brigid once, cloaked and melancholy, slipping into a doorway, wearing a hat to conceal her circle of light. He liked knowing they were in the world but preferred them as they resided here, on the paper and on the wall.

Lucas put the book back under the mattress. He extinguished the lamp. Across the air shaft, he could see the light of Emily's curtains. He buried his face in Simon's pillow. Simon was with them still. His pillow still smelled of him.

Lucas whispered into the pillow, "You should go away now. I really think it's time."

In the morning he made tea for himself and his father and put out some bread. His father sat at table with his breathing machine, a tube and a bellows on a metal pole, with three square, delicate feet. His mother hadn't risen yet.

When Lucas had eaten his bread and drunk his tea, he said, "Goodbye, Father."

His father looked at him, startled. He had been turned to leather by his years in the tannery. His burnished skin, fine-grained, fit perfectly on his big-jawed skull. His dark eyes were set like jewels. Simon's beauty, his large and defiant features, came mostly from their father. No one knew how Lucas had come to look as he did.

"G'bye, then," his father said. He raised the tube to his lips, drew in a mouthful of air. The little bellows rose and fell. Now that he was leather, with jewels for eyes, the machine did his breathing for him.

"Will you see to Mother?" Lucas asked.

"Aye," his father said.

Lucas put his small hand on his father's brown one. He loved himself for loving his father. It was the best he could do.

"I'm off to the works," he said.

"Aye," his father answered, and took another breath from the tube. The machine was a gift from the tannery. They had given him the machine, and some money. There had been no money for Simon, because dying was his own fault.

Lucas kissed his father's forehead. His father's mind was leather now, too, but his goodness remained. All he had lost were his complications. He could still do what he needed to do. He could still love Lucas's mother and tend to her. Lucas hoped he could still do that.

He said, "I'll see you tonight, then."

"Aye," his father answered.

On his way to the works, Lucas stopped at the school. He didn't enter. He went around to the side and looked through the window. He could see Mr. Mulchady frowning at his desk, the little flames from the lamps dancing on his spectacles. He could see the others hunched over their lessons. School would go on without him. Here as always were the desks and slates. Here were the two maps on the wall, the world and the stars. Lucas had only lately understood (he could be slow in some things) that the two were different. He'd believed, and had not thought to ask otherwise, that the stars were a version of the world, that they mirrored its countries and oceans. Why else would they be mounted side by side? When he was younger he had found New York on the map of the world and found its counterpart on the map of the stars, the Pleiades.

It was Mr. Mulchady who'd given Walt's book to Lucas, on loan. Mr. Mulchady said Lucas had the soul of a poet, which was kind of him but wrong. Lucas had no soul at all. He was a stranger, a citizen of no place, come from County Kerry but planted in New York, where he grew like a blighted potato; where he didn't sing or shout as the other Irish did; where he harbored not soul but an emptiness sparked here and there with painful shocks of love, for the map of the stars and the answering flames on Mr. Mulchady's spectacles; for Catherine and his mother and a horse on wheels. He did not mourn Simon; he had no convictions about heaven, no thirst for Christ's revivifying blood. What he wanted was the raucousness of the city, where people hauled their loads of corn or coal, where they danced to fiddles, wept or laughed, sold and begged and bartered, not always happily but always with a vigor that was what he meant, privately, by soul. It was a defiant, uncrushable aliveness. He hoped the book could instill that in him.

Now, abruptly, he was finished with school. He would have liked to say goodbye to Mr. Mulchady, but if he did Mr. Mulchady would ask him to return the book, and Lucas couldn't do that, not yet. He was still an empty suit of clothes. He hoped Mr. Mulchady wouldn't mind waiting.

He said goodbye, silently, to the classroom, to the maps and Mr. Mulchady.

The works was like a city unto itself. It was red brick walls and red brick towers, a gate big enough for six horses walking abreast. Lucas entered through the gate, among a crowd of boys and men. Some went quietly. Some spoke to one another, laughed. One said, "Fat, you never seen one as fat as her," and another said, "I like 'em fat." The boys and the younger men were pale. The older men had darkened.

Lucas, uncertain, walked with the others into a cobbled courtyard where stacks of brown-black iron, dusky as great bars of chocolate, stood against the red brick walls. He went with the others to a doorway at the courtyard's opposite end, an arched entrance with flickering dark inside.

He stopped there. The others moved around him. A man in a blue cap jostled him, cursed, walked on. The man would be eaten as Simon had been. What the machine did not care for would be put in a box and taken across the river.

Lucas couldn't tell whether he was meant to go in or to wait here. He thought it might be foolish to wait. The others were so certain, so loud but steady, like unruly soldiers on parade. He hated drawing attention to himself. But he thought, too, that if he went on he might be drawn forward into some error, obscure but irredeemable. He stood in an agony of doubt with the others flowing around him.

Soon Lucas was alone save for a few stragglers who hurried by him without seeming to see him at all. Finally—it seemed an unspeakable mercy—a man came from the building into the courtyard and said, "Are you Lucas?"

He was an immense gray-skinned man whose face, wide as a shovel, didn't move when he talked. Only his mouth moved, as if by magic a man made of iron had been given the power of speech.

"Yes," Lucas said.

The man looked at him skeptically. "What's the matter with you?" he asked. As he spoke, his mouth showed flashes of pink, livid in the gray face.

"I'm sound, sir. I can work as well as anybody."

"And how old are you?"

"Thirteen, sir," Lucas answered.

"You're not thirteen."

"I'm thirteen in another month."

The man shook his iron head. "This isn't work for a child."

"Please, sir. I'm stronger than I seem." Lucas settled his shoulders, striving to look sturdier.

"Well, they've given you the job. We'll see how you do."

Before he could stop himself, Lucas said, "Miserable! I do not laugh at your oaths nor jeer you."

"What?"

"Please, sir," Lucas said. "I'll work hard. I can do anything."

"We'll see. I'm Jack Walsh."

Lucas held out his hand. Jack looked at it as if Lucas had offered him a lily. He took it in his own, pressed it hard enough to put the sting of tears in Lucas's eyes. If Walt was the book, Jack was the works. He was made of iron, with a living mouth.

"Come on," Jack said. "Let's get you started."

Lucas followed him through the entranceway, into a hall where men behind wire cages scowled over papers. Beyond the hall, they came to an enormous room lined with furnaces. Where the light from the furnaces didn't reach, it was twilight, a dull orange twilight that faded, in its remoter parts, to a bruised, furtive undark. The room reeked of heat and coal, of creosote. It rang and wheezed. Furies of sparks swirled up, skittish as flies. Among the sparks, men stood before the furnaces, stoking the fires with long black poles.

"This is coking," Jack said, and said no more. Did he mean "cooking"? Lucas thought he would ask his questions later.

Jack escorted him past the row of furnaces, under a chaos of black hooks and leather pulleys that depended from the high ceiling, touched here and there by small incidences of orange firelight. A portal that opened from the room where the coking (the cooking?) was done led onto another room, equally large but dimmer, lined on either side by the gray-brown bulks of machines as preposterous and grand as elephants, machines made up of belts and beams and wheels turning with sharp squeals and groans. The room was like a stable or a dairy. It was full of steady, creaturely life.

"Cutting and stamping," Jack said. "This is where you'll be."

The atmosphere of the cutting-and-stamping room was dust, but bright dust, drifting silvery particles that winked and glimmered in the sluggish light. Men stood at the machines engaged in mysterious efforts, bent over, straining with their shoulders and thighs. Lucas saw that the men, like Jack, had taken on the color of the room. Were they dying or just becoming more like the air?

Jack led him to a machine at the far end. Yet another room opened off this one, though Lucas could discern only a sepulchral stillness and what appeared to be stacks of vaults, like catacombs, filled with silver canisters. It seemed there must be another room after that and then another and another. The works might extend for miles, like a series of caverns. It seemed that it would be possible to walk through them for hours and finally reach—what? Lucas didn't fully understand what it was that the works produced. Simon had never spoken of it. Lucas had imagined some treasure, a living jewel, a ball of green fire, infinitely precious, the making of which required unstinting effort. He wondered now why he had never thought to ask. His brother's labors had always seemed a mystery, to be respected and revered.

"Here," Jack said, stopping before a machine. "You work here."

"This is where my brother worked."

"It is."

Lucas stood before the machine that had taken Simon. It was a toothed wheel, like a titanic piano roll, set over a broad belt bordered by clamps.

Jack said, "You must be more careful than your brother was."

Lucas understood from Jack's voice that the machine was not to blame. He stared at the machine as he'd stared once at the gorilla at Barnum's. It was immense and stolid. It wore its wheel as a snail wears its shell, with a languid and inscrutable pride. Like a snail with its shell, the machine contained a quicker, more liquid life in its nether parts. Under the wheel, which snagged flecks of orange light on its square teeth, were the rows of clamps, the pale, naked-looking leather of the belt, the slender stalks of the levers. The wheel harbored a shifting shadow of brownish-black. The machine was at once formidable and tender-looking. It offered its belt like a tentative promise of kindness.

Jack said, "Tom Clare, over there" (he nodded at a young man laboring at the next machine), "stacks plates in the bin here. Tom, this is Lucas, the new man."

Tom Clare, sharp-faced, whiskered, looked up. "Sorry about your loss," he said. He would have seen Simon eaten by the machine. Was it his fault, then? Could he have acted more quickly, been more brave?

"Thank you," Lucas answered.

Jack lifted from the bin a flat rectangle of iron, the size of an oven door, and laid it on the belt. "You fasten it tight," he said. He screwed clamps down onto the iron plate, three on each side. "See the lines on the belt?"

The belt was marked with white lines, each drawn several inches above one of the clamps. "The top edge," Jack said, "has to be lined up exactly. Do you understand? It has to be right up on this line."

"I see," Lucas said.

"When it's even with the line and when the clamps are secure, you pull this lever first."

He pulled a lever to the right of the belt. The wheel awakened and began, with a sigh, to turn. Its teeth came to within an inch of the belt.

"When the drum is turning, you pull the other lever."

He pulled a second lever that stood beside the first. The belt slowly began to move. Lucas watched the belt bear the iron plate forward until it met with the teeth of the wheel. The teeth, impressing into the iron, sounded like hammers banging on glass that wouldn't break.

"Now. Follow me." Jack led Lucas to the back of the machine, where the plate was beginning to emerge, full of shallow, square impressions.

"When it's come through," he said, "you go back and pull the levers again. First the second one, then the first. Understand?"

"Yes," Lucas said.

Jack pulled the levers and stopped the machine, first the belt and then the wheel. He released the clamps from the plate of iron.

"Then you inspect it," he said. "You make sure it's taken a complete impression. Four across, six down. They must all be perfect. Look into every square. This is important. If it isn't perfect you take it over there" (he pointed across the room) "to Will O'Hara, for resmelting. If you have any doubts, show it to Will. If you're satisfied that the impressions are perfect, if you're sure, take it to Dan Heaney over there. Any questions?"

"No, sir," Lucas said. "I don't think so."

"All right, then. You try it."

Lucas took a new plate from the bin. It was heavier than he'd expected but not too heavy to manage. He hoisted it onto the belt, pushed it carefully up to the white line, and attached the clamps. "Is that right?" he asked.

"What do you think?"

He tested the clamps. "Should I pull the lever now?" he asked.

"Yes. Pull the lever."

Lucas pulled the first lever, which started the wheel turning. He was briefly exultant. He pulled the second lever, and the belt moved forward. To his relief, the clamps held tight.

"That's all right," Jack said.

Lucas watched the teeth bite into the iron. Simon would have been pulled under the wheel, first his arm and then the rest. The machine would have ground him in its teeth with the same serenity it brought to the iron. It would have believed—if machines could believe—it had simply produced another iron plate. After it had crushed Simon it would have waited patiently for the next plate.

"Now," Jack said, "let's go and inspect the piece."

Lucas went with him to the machine's far end, and saw what he had made. A plate of iron with square impressions, four across and six down.

Jack said, "Does it look all right to you?"

Lucas looked closely. It was difficult to see in the dimness. He ran a finger into each impression. He said, "I think so."

"Are you sure?"

"I think so."

"All right, then. What do you do now?"

"I take it to Dan Heaney."

"That's right."

Lucas lifted the stamped iron, carried it to Dan Heaney's machine. Dan, bulbous and lion-headed, nodded. After a hesitation, Lucas placed the plate carefully in a bin that stood beside Dan's machine.

"Fine, then," Jack said.

He had pleased Jack.

Jack said, "Do another one."

"Sir," Lucas asked, "what are these things I'm making?"

"They're housings," Jack said. "Let me watch you do another one."

"Yes, sir."

Lucas did another one. Jack said it was all right and went off to attend to other things.

Time passed. Lucas couldn't have said how much. There were no clocks. There was no daylight. He loaded a plate onto the belt, lined it up, sent it through, and inspected the impressions. Four across, six down. He began trying to drop each plate onto the belt so that its upper edge fell as close to the white line as possible and needed only the slightest nudge to put it in place. For a while he hoped the impressions made by the wheel would be perfect, and after what seemed hours of that he began hoping for minor imperfections, a blunted corner or a slight cant that would have been invisible to eyes less diligent than his. He found only one flawed impression, and that debatable. One of the squares seemed less deep than the others, though he could not be entirely sure. Still, he took the plate proudly over to Will for resmelting and felt strong and capable after.

When he had tired of trying to hit the line on his first try, and when he had grown indifferent to the question of whether he was searching for flaws or searching for perfection, he tried thinking of other things. He tried thinking of Catherine, of his mother and father. Had his mother awakened? Was she herself again, ready to cook and argue? He tried thinking of Simon. The work, however, didn't permit such thoughts. The work demanded attention. He entered a state of waking sleep, an ongoing singularity of purpose, in which his mind was filled with that which must fill it, to the exclusion of all else. Align, clamp, pull, pull again, inspect.

It was after the lunch hour when his sleeve caught in a clamp. He'd allowed his mind to drift. The tug was gentle and insistent as an infant's grip. He was already reaching for another clamp and saw that a corner of his shirtsleeve was in the serrated mouth of the first, pinched tight between clamp and plate. He pulled instinctively away, but the clamp held the fabric with steady assurance. It was singular and passionate as a rat with a scrap of gristle. Lucas thought for a moment how well the machine was made—the jaws of the clamps were so strong and sure. He tugged again. The clamp didn't yield. Only when he turned the pin, awkwardly, with his left hand, did the clamp relax itself and give up the corner of his sleeve. The cloth still bore the imprint of the clamp's tiny toothmarks.

Lucas looked with mute wonder at the end of his sleeve. This was how. You allowed your attention to wander, you thought of other things, and the clamp took whatever was offered it. That was the clamp's nature. Lucas looked around guiltily, wondering if Tom or Will or Dan had noticed. They had not noticed. Dan tapped with a wrench on his machine. He struck it firmly but kindly on the flank of the box that held its workings. The wrench rang on the metal like a church bell.

Lucas rolled his sleeves to his elbows. He went on working.

It seemed, as he loaded the plates onto the belt, that the machines were not inanimate; not quite inanimate. They were part of a continuum: machines, then grass and trees, then horses and dogs, then human beings. He wondered if the machine had loved Simon, in its serene and unthinking way. He wondered if all the machines at the works, all the furnaces and hooks and belts, mutely admired their men, as horses admired their masters. He wondered if they waited with their immense patience for the moment their men would lose track of themselves, let their caution lapse so the machines could take their hands with loving firmness and pull them in.

He lifted another plate from the bin, lined it up, fastened the clamps, and sent it under the teeth of the wheel.

Where was Jack? Didn't he want to know how well Lucas was doing his work? Lucas said, as the plate went under the wheel, "Urge and urge and urge, always the procreant urge of the world."

Jack didn't come to him until the workday's end. Jack looked at Lucas, looked at the machine, nodded, and looked at Lucas again.

"You've done all right," he said.

"Thank you, sir."

"You'll be back tomorrow, then."

"Yes, sir. Thank you, sir."

Lucas extended his hand to Jack and was surprised to see that it shook. He had known his fingers were bleeding; he hadn't known about the shaking. Still, Jack took his hand. He didn't appear to mind about the shaking or the blood.

"Prodigal," Lucas said, "you have given me love—therefore I to you give love!"

Jack paused. His iron face took on three creases across the expanse of its forehead.

"What was that?"

"Good night," Lucas said.

"Good night," Jack replied doubtfully.

Lucas hurried away, passed with the others through the cooking room, where the men with the black poles were shutting down their furnaces. He found that he could not quite remember having been anywhere but the works. Or rather, he remembered his life before coming to the works as a dream, watery and insubstantial. It faded as dreams fade on waking. None of it was as actual as this. None of it was so true. Align, clamp, pull, pull again, inspect.

A woman in a light blue dress waited outside the entrance to the works. Lucas took a moment in recognizing her. He saw first that a woman stood at the entrance and thought that the works had summoned an angel to bid the men goodbye, to remind them that work would end someday and a longer dream begin. Then he understood. Catherine had come. She was waiting for him.

He recognized her a moment before she recognized him. He looked at her face and saw that she had forgotten him, too.

He called out, "Catherine."

"Lucas?" she said.

He ran to her. She inhabited a sphere of scented and cleansed air. He was gladdened. He was furious. How could she come here? Why would she embarrass him so?

She said, "Look at you. You're all grime. I didn't know you at first."

"It's me," he said.

"You're shaking all over."

"I'm all right. I'm well."

"I thought you shouldn't walk home alone. Not after your first day."

He said, "This isn't a fit place for a woman on her own."

"Poor boy, just look at you."

He bristled. He had set the wheel turning. He had inspected every plate.

"I'm fine," he said, more forcefully than he'd meant to.

"Well, let's take you home. You must be starving."

They walked up Rivington Street together. She did not put her hand on his elbow. He was too dirty for that. A fitful breeze blew in from the East River and along the street, stirring up miniature dust storms with scraps of paper caught in them. The dark facades of brick houses rose on either side, the lid of the sky clamped down tightly overhead. The sidewalk was crowded, all the more so because those who walked there shared the pavement with heaps of refuse that lay in drifts against the sides of the buildings, darkly massed, wet and shiny in their recesses.

Lucas and Catherine walked with difficulty on the narrow paved trail between the housefronts and the piles of trash. They fell in behind a woman and a child who moved with agonizing slowness. The woman—was she old or young? It was impossible to tell from behind—favored her left leg, and the child, a girl in a long, ragged skirt, seemed not to walk at all but to be conveyed along by her mother's hand as if she were a piece of furniture that must be dragged home. Ahead of the woman and child walked a large bald man in what appeared to be a woman's coat, worn shiny in spots, far too small for him, the sleeves ripped at the shoulders, showing gashes of pink satin lining. Lucas could not help imagining this procession of walkers, all of them poor and battered, wearing old coats too small or too large for them, dragging children who could not or would not walk, all marching along Rivington Street, impelled by someone or something that pushed them steadily forward, slowly but inexorably, so it only seemed as if they moved of their own will; all of them walking on, past the houses and stables, past the taverns, past the works and into the river, where they would fall, one after another after another, and continue to walk, drowned but animate, on the bottom, until the street was finally empty and the people were all in the river, trudging along its silty bed, through its drifts of brown and sulfur, into its deeper darks, until they reached the ocean, this multitude of walkers, until they were nudged into open water where silver fish swam silently past, where the ocher of the river gave over to inky blue, where clouds floated on the surface, far, far above, and they were free, all of them, to drift away, their coats billowing like wings, their children flying effortlessly, a whole nation of the dead, dispersing, buoyant, faintly illuminated, spreading out like constellations into the blue immensity.

He and Catherine reached the Bowery, where the rowdies strutted together, brightly clad, past the taverns and oyster houses. They swaggered and shouted, chewing cigars fat as sausages. One tipped his stovepipe to Catherine, began to speak, but was pulled onward by his laughing companions. The Bowery was Broadway's lesser twin, a minor star in the constellation, though no less bright and loud. Still, there was more room to walk here. The truly poor were more numerous.

Catherine said, "Was it dreadful there?"

Lucas answered, "The machinist rolls up his sleeves, the policeman travels his beat, the gate-keeper marks who pass."

"Please, Lucas," she said, "speak to me in plain English."

"The foreman said I did well," he told her.

"Will you promise me something?"

"Yes."

"Promise that as long as you must work there you will be very, very careful."

Lucas thought guiltily of the clamp. He had not been careful. He had allowed himself to dream and drift.

He said, "I know I am deathless, I know this orbit of mine cannot be swept by a carpenter's compass."

"And promise me that as soon as you can, you will leave that place and find other work."

"I will."

"You are . . ."

He waited. What would she tell him he was?

She said, "You are meant for other things."

He was happy to hear it, happy enough. And yet he'd hoped for more. He'd wanted her to reveal something, though he couldn't say what. He'd wanted a wonderful lie that would become true the moment she said it.

He said, "I promise." What exactly was he meant for? He couldn't bring himself to ask.

"It's hard," she said.

"And you? Were you all right at work today?"

"I was. I sewed and sewed. It was a relief, really, to work."

"Were you . . ."

She waited. What did he mean to ask her?

He asked, "Were you careful?"

She laughed. His face burned. Had it been a ridiculous question? She seemed always so available to harm, as if someone as kind as she, as sweet-smelling, could only be hurt, either now or later.

"I was," she said. "Do you worry about me?"

"Yes," he said. He hoped it was not a foolish assertion. He waited nervously to see if she'd laugh again.

"You mustn't," she said. "You must think only of yourself. Promise me."

He said, "Every atom belonging to me as good belongs to you."

"Thank you, my dear," she answered, and she said no more.

He took her to her door, on Fifth Street. They stood together on the stoop that was specked with brightness.

"You will go home now," she said, "and have your supper."

"May I ask you something?" he said.

"Ask me anything."

"I wonder what it is I'm making at the works."

"Well, the works produces many things, I think."

"What things?"

"Parts of larger things. Gears and bolts and . . . other parts."

"They told me I make housings."

"There you are, then. That's what you make."

"I see," he said. He didn't see, but it seemed better to let the subject pass. It seemed better to be someone who knew what a housing was.

Catherine looked at him tenderly. Would she kiss him again?

She said, "I want to give you something."

He trembled. He kept his jaws clamped shut. He would not speak, not as the book or as himself.

She unfastened the collar of her dress and reached inside. She drew out the locket. She pulled its chain up over her head, held locket and chain in her palm.

She said, "I want you to wear this."

"I can't," he said.

"It has a lock of your brother's hair inside."

"I know. I know that."

"Do you know," she said, "that Simon wore its twin, with my picture inside?"

"Yes."

"I was not allowed to see him," she said.

"None of us was."

"But the undertaker told me the locket was with him still. He said Simon wore it in his casket."

Simon had Catherine with him, then. He had something of Catherine in the box across the river. Did that make her an honorary member of the dead?

Catherine said, "I'll feel better if you wear it when you go to the works."

"It's yours," he said.

"Call it ours. Yours and mine. Will you do it, to please me?"

He couldn't protest, then. How could he refuse to do anything that would please her?

He said, "If you like."

She put the chain over his head. The locket hung on his chest, a little golden orb. She had worn it next to her skin.

"Good night," she said. "Have your supper and go straight to bed."

"Good night."

She kissed him then, not on his lips but on his cheek. She turned away, put her key in the lock. He felt the kiss still on his skin after she'd withdrawn.

"Good night," he said. "Good night, good night."

"Go," she commanded him. "Do what you must for your mother and father, and rest."

He said, "I ascend from the moon . . . I ascend from the night."

She glanced at him from her doorway. She had been someone

who laughed easily, who was always the first to dance. She looked at him now with such sorrow. Had he disappointed her? Had he deepened her sadness? He stood helplessly, pinned by her gaze. She turned and went inside.

At home, he fixed what supper he could for himself and his father. There were bits, still, from what had been brought for after the burial. A scrap of fatty ham, a jelly, the last of the bread. He laid it before his father, who blinked, said, "Thank you," and ate. Between mouthfuls, he breathed from the machine.

Lucas's mother was still in bed. How would they manage about food if she didn't rise soon?

As his father ate and breathed, Lucas went to his parents' bedroom. Softly, uncertainly, he pushed open the door. The bedroom was dark, full of its varnish and wool. Over the bed the crucifix hung, black in the sable air.

He said, "Mother?"

He heard the bedclothes stirring. He heard the whisper of her breath.

She said, "Who's there?"

"It's only me," he answered. "Only Lucas."

"Lucas. M'love."

His heart shivered. It seemed for a moment that he could abide with his mother in the sweet, warm darkness. He could stay here with her and tell her the book.

"Did I wake you?" he asked.

"I'm ever awake. Come."

He sat on the edge of the mattress. He could see the sprawl of her hair on the pillow. He could see her nose and chin, the dark places where her eyes were. He touched her face. It was hot and powdery, dry as chalk.

"Are you thirsty, are you hungry?" he asked. "Can I bring you something?"

She said, "What's happened to ye? How have they darkened ye so?"

"I've been to work, Mother. It's only dust."

"Where's Lucas, then?"

"I'm here, Mother."

"Of course you are. I'm not quite right, am I?"

"Let me bring you some water."

"The hens need looking after. Have ye seen to the hens?"

"The hens, Mother?"

"Yes, child. It's gone late, hasn't it? I think it's very late indeed."

"We haven't any hens."

"We haven't?"

"No."

"Forgive me. We did have hens."

"Don't worry, Mother."

"Oh, it's fine to say don't worry, with the hens gone and the pota-toes, too."

Lucas stroked her hair. He said, "Divine am I inside and out, and I make holy whatever I touch or am touch'd from."

"That's right, m'dear."

Lucas sat quietly with her, stroking her hair. She had been nervous and quick, prone to argument, easily angered and slow to laugh. (Only Simon could make her laugh.) She'd been vanishing gradually for a year or longer, always more eager to be done with her work and off to bed, but still herself, still dutiful and fitfully affectionate, still alert to slights and hidden insults. Now that Simon was dead she'd turned into this, a face on a pillow, asking after hens.

He said, "Should I bring you the music box?"

"That'd be nice."

He went to the parlor and returned with the box. He held it up for her to see.

"Ah, yes," she said. Did she know that the box had ruined them? She never spoke of it. She seemed to love the music box as dearly as she would have if it had caused no damage at all.

Lucas turned the crank. Within the confines of the box, the brass spool revolved under the tiny hammers. It played "Forget Not the Field" in its little way, bright metallic notes that spangled in the close air of the bedroom. Lucas sang along with the tune.

Forget not the field where they perish'd,
The truest, the last of the brave,
All gone—and the bright hope we cherish'd
Gone with them, and quench'd in their grave.

His mother put a hand over his. "That's enough," she said.

"It's only the first verse."

"It's enough, Lucas. Take it away."

He did as she asked. He returned the music box to its place on the parlor table, where it continued playing "Forget Not the Field." Once wound, it would not stop except by its own accord.

His father had moved from his place at the table to his chair by the window. He nodded gravely, as if agreeing with something the music said.

"Do you like the music?" Lucas asked him.

"Can't be stopped," his father said in his new voice, which was all but indistinguishable from his breathing, as if his machine's bellows were whispering language as they blew.

"It'll stop soon."

"That's good."

Lucas said, "Good night, Father," because he could not think of anything else to say.

His father nodded. Could he get himself to bed? Lucas thought he could. He hoped so.

He went to his own room, his and Simon's. Emily's window was lit. She was faithfully eating her candy, just as Lucas faithfully read his book.

He undressed. He did not remove the locket. If he removed the locket, if he ever removed the locket, it would no longer be something Catherine had put on him. It would become something he put upon himself.

Carefully, he found the locket's catch and opened it. Here was the black curl of Simon's hair, tied with a piece of purple thread. Here, under the curl, was Simon's face, obscured by the hair. Lucas knew the picture: Simon two years ago, frowning for the photographer, his eyes narrow and his jaw set. Simon's face in the locket was pale brown, like turned cream. His eyes (one was partially visible through the strands of hair) were black. It was like seeing Simon in his casket, which no one had been allowed to do. What the machine had done had rendered him too extraordinary. Now, in the quiet of the room, the Simon who was with them still met the Simon who was in the locket, and here he was, doubled; here was the smell and heft of him; here his habit, on the drinking nights, of slapping Lucas playfully. Lucas closed the locket. It made a small metallic snap.

He got into bed, on his own side. He read the evening's passage.

I guess the grass is itself a child, the produced babe of the
   vegetation,

Or I guess it is a uniform hieroglyphic,
And it means, Sprouting alike in broad zones and narrow zones,
Growing among black folks as among white,
Kanuck, Tuckahoe, Congressman, Cuff, I give them the same,
   I receive them the same.

When he had finished it he put out the lamp. He could feel Simon in the locket and Simon in the box in the earth, so changed that the lid had been nailed shut. Lucas determined never to open the locket again. He would wear it always but keep it forever sealed.

He slept, and woke again. He rose to dress for work and get breakfast for his father, feeling the locket's unfamiliar weight on his neck, the circle of it bouncing gently on his breastbone. Here was the memento of Simon's ongoing death for him to wear close to his heart, because Catherine had put it on him.

He gave his father the last of the jelly for breakfast. There was no food after that.

As his father ate, Lucas paused beside the door to his parents' bedroom. He heard no sound from within. What would happen if his mother never came out again? He got the music box from the table and crept into the room with it, as quietly as he could. His mother was a shape, snoring softly. He set the music box on the table at her bedside. She might want to listen to it when she awoke. If she didn't want to listen to it, she'd still know Lucas had thought of her by putting it there.

Jack wasn't there to greet him when he arrived at the works. Lucas paused at the entrance, among the others, but didn't linger. Jack would most likely be waiting for him at the machine, to tell him he had done well yesterday, to encourage him about today. He passed through the vestibule, with its caged men scowling at their papers. He passed through the cooking room and went to his machine. Tom and Will and Dan all said good-morning to him, as if he had been there a long time, which pleased him. But there was no Jack Walsh.

Lucas got to work. Jack would be glad of that when he came by. Lucas steadied himself before the machine. He took the first of the plates from Tom's bin. Align, clamp, pull, pull again, inspect.

He inspected every plate. An hour passed, or what seemed like an hour. Another hour passed. His fingers started bleeding again. Smears of his blood were on the plates as they went under the wheel. He wiped the plates clean with his sleeve before conveying them to Dan.

He began to see that the days at the works were so long, so entirely composed of the one act, performed over and over and over again, that they made of themselves a world within the world, and that those who lived in that world, all the men of the works, lived primarily there and paid brief visits to the other world, where they ate and rested and made ready to return again. The men of the works had relinquished their citizenship; they had immigrated to the works as his parents had immigrated to New York from County Kerry. Their former lives were dreams they had each night, from which they awakened each morning at the works.

It was only at day's end, when the whistle blew, that Jack appeared. Lucas expected—what? A reunion. An explanation. He thought Jack would tell him apologetically of a sick child or a lame horse. Jack would squeeze his bleeding hand (which Lucas feared and longed for). Jack would tell Lucas he had done well. Lucas had aligned each plate perfectly. He'd inspected every one.

Instead, Jack stood beside him and said, "All right, then."

There was no tone of congratulation in his voice. Lucas thought for a moment that Jack had confused him with someone else. (Catherine hadn't known him at first, his mother hadn't known him.) He almost said but did not say, It's me. It's Lucas.

Jack departed. He went to Dan, spoke to him briefly, and went into the next chamber, the room of the vaults.

Lucas remained at his machine, though it was time to go. The machine stood as it always did, belt and levers, row upon row of teeth.

He said, "Who need be afraid of the merge?"

He was afraid, though. He feared the machine's endurance, its capacity to be here, always here, and his own obligation to return to it after a short interlude of feeding and sleep. He worried that one day he would forget himself again. One day he would forget himself and be drawn through the machine as Simon had. He would be stamped (four across, six down) and expelled; he would be put in a box and carried across the river. He would be so changed that no one would know him, not the living or the dead.

Where would he go after that? He didn't think he had soul enough for heaven. He'd be in a box across the river. He wondered if his face would be hung on the parlor wall, though there were no pictures of him, and even if there had been, he couldn't think of who might be taken away to make room.

Catherine wasn't waiting for him tonight. Lucas stood briefly outside the gate, searching for her, though of course she would not have come again. It had been only the once, when he was new, that she was worried for him. What he had to do was go home and see about getting supper for his parents.

He left among the others and made his way up Rivington and then the Bowery. He passed by Second Street and went to Catherine's building on Fifth.

He knocked on the street door, tentatively at first, then harder. He stood waiting on the glittering stoop. Finally, the door was opened by an ancient woman. She was white-haired, small as a dwarf, as wide as she was tall. She might have been the spirit of the building itself, pocked and stolid, peevish about being roused.

"What is it?" she asked. "What do you want?"

"Please, missus. I'm here to see Catherine Fitzhugh. May I come in?"

"Who are you?"

"I'm Lucas. I'm the brother of Simon, who she was to marry."

"What do you want?"

"I want to see her. Please. I mean no harm."

"You're up to no mischief?"

"No. None. Please."

"Very well, then. She's on the third floor. Number nineteen."

"Thank you."

The woman opened the door slowly, as if it required all her strength. Lucas struggled to enter in a civil manner, to refrain from rushing past her and knocking her down.

"Thank you," he said again.

He stepped around her, went up the stairs. He was aware of her eyes on his back as he ascended, and he forced himself to go slowly until he had reached the second floor. Then he raced up the next staircase, ran down the hall. He found number nineteen and knocked.

Alma opened the door. Alma was the loudest of them. Her face had a boiled look, peppered with brown freckles.

"What's this here?" she said. "A goblin or an elf?"

"It's Lucas," he answered. "Simon's brother."

"I *know* that, child. To what do we owe the pleasure?"

"I've come to see Catherine, please."

She shook her large, feverish head. "You all want Catherine, don't you? Did y'ever think we others might have a thing or two to offer?"

"Please, is Catherine at home?"

"Come on in, then." She turned and shouted into the room. "Catherine, there's a fella here to see ye."

Alma allowed Lucas into the parlor. It was identical to the apartment he lived in with his family, though Catherine and Alma and Sarah had left the dead out of theirs. They'd hung pictures of flowers on the walls instead. They'd covered their table with a purple cloth.

Sarah stood at the stove, stirring something in a pot. A lamb's neck, Lucas thought, and cabbage. Sarah's face was round and white as a saucer, and almost as still.

"H'lo," she said. She was small and pretty, childlike, though she was at least as old as Catherine. She wore a tangerine-colored dressing gown. She might have been something you could win at a carnival.

Catherine emerged from what would have been her bedroom, still wearing her blue dress from work. "Well, hello, Lucas," she said. For a moment she wore her former face, the face she'd had before the machine took Simon. She seemed, as she once had, to know a joke that was not yet apparent to anyone else.

"Hello," Lucas said. "I'm sorry if I'm disturbing you."

"I'm glad to see you. Have you had supper?"

He knew he mustn't accept. "Yes, I have, thank you," he said.

"Such a strange-lookin' thing," Alma said. "What's the matter with ye?"

"Alma," Catherine said sternly.

"It's a question, is all. Do y' think he don't know?"

Lucas struggled to answer. He liked Alma and Sarah, though they weren't kind. They were raucous and brightly colored, heedless, like parrots. They had a shine about them.

"I was born this way," he said. It seemed insufficient. He might have told them that between himself and Simon there'd been Matthew, dead at seven, and Brendan, dead before he was born. Now they'd lost Simon and it was somehow, miraculously, only he, Lucas, the changeling child, goblin-faced, with frail heart and mismatched eyes. He should have been the first to die but had somehow outlived them all. He was proud of that. He'd have liked to declare it to Alma and Sarah.

"Well, I never thought you'd decided on it," Alma said.

"Alma, that's enough," Catherine said. "Lucas, surely you'll have something with us. Just a bite."

Lucas saw Sarah shift her weight to shield the pot. He said quietly to Catherine, "May I speak to you for a moment?"

"Of course."

He paused, in an agony of confusion. Catherine said, "Why don't we go out into the hallway?"

There would be nowhere else for them to go. There would be only the parlor, and the two bedrooms.

"Yes. Thank you." As he followed Catherine out he said good-night to Alma and Sarah.

"Even the goblins prefers Catherine," Alma said.

Sarah answered from the stove. "You should watch that mouth of yours, some goblin'll fix it one day."

Lucas stood with Catherine in the hall. It was like his own. A lamp flickered at one end, by the stairwell. Near the lamp, piles of paper, empty bottles, and a sack (what must it contain?) were visible in the semidark. At the hallway's farther end, the refuse was only shadows. Halfway down, in the direction of the true dark, something lay atop a discarded oil can. Did it have teeth? Yes. It was a goat's skull, boiled clean.

Catherine said, "I'm happy to see you again."

Speak as Lucas, he bade himself. Don't speak as the book.

He said, "I'm happy to see you, too. I wanted you to know that I'm well."

"I'm glad of that."

"And you're well, too?"

"Yes. I'm fine, my dear."

"And you're careful?"

"Why, yes, Lucas. I am."

"Does someone walk with you? In the dark, when you come home?"

"My friend Kate does, as far as the Bowery. Really, you mustn't worry about me. You have so much to attend to."

Lucas said, "My voice goes after what my eyes cannot reach."

"Wait here a moment," she said. "I have something for you."

She went back into the apartment. Lucas touched the locket at his breast. His mind was a chaos of urges. What would she have for him? He wanted it, whatever it might be. He wanted so much. He watched the goat's skull as he waited for Catherine. He went into the skull. He became that, a bone grinning in the dark.

Catherine returned with a plate covered by a cloth. She said, "Here's a little food for you and your parents."

This was what she had for him. She gave him the plate. He accepted mutely and held it.

He was a beggar, then.

He said, "Thank you."

"Good night, my dear."

"Good night."

She retreated and closed the door. She did not kiss him again.

He remained for a while before the door, holding the plate as if he had brought it and not received it. He heard the murmur of the women's voices, couldn't make out their words. Then, because there was nothing else for him to do, he went back down the corridor, carefully holding the plate. His father and mother would want it. He wanted it.

The old woman was waiting on the ground floor to see him out. "No mischief, then," she said.

"No, ma'am. No mischief."

Lucas went into his building, carrying the plate. He went up the stairs. He was aware of a subtle wrongness, as if this most familiar of places (the stairwell, with its gas smell and its flickering lamps, the rats busy among the scraps) were altered, as if it had become, overnight, an imperfect copy of itself, in contrast to his day at the works, which was perfect in every regard.

But the parlor was itself. His father sat as he did, in his chair by the window, with the machine at his side. Lucas said, "Good evening, Father."

"Hello," his father replied. His work was breathing and looking out the window. It had been for more than a year.

Lucas took three plates from the cupboard, divided the food among them. He put a plate on the table for his father and said, "Here's your supper."

His father nodded and continued looking out the window. Lucas took his mother's plate into the bedroom.

She was in bed, as she'd been when he left in the morning, as she'd been the night before. Her breathing, the gauzy rasp of it, filled the dark. It seemed for a moment that the rooms were like the works and his parents like machinery—they were always as they were, always waiting for Lucas to come and go and come back again.

From the doorway he said, "Mother? I've brought you some supper."

"Thank you, m'love."

He brought her plate and set it on the bedside table. He sat gently on the edge of the mattress, beside the shape she made.

"Should I cut it up?" he asked. "Should I feed it to you?"

"You're so good. You're a good boy. Look what they done to you."

"It's just the dust, Mother. It'll wash off."

"No, m'love, I don't think it will."

He cut off a bit of potato with the fork, held it close to her mouth. "Eat, now," he said.

She made no response. A silence passed. Lucas found, to his surprise, that he was embarrassed by it. He put the fork down and said, "Should we hear some music, then?"

"If ye like."

He took the music box from the bedside table, wound the little crank. He sang softly along.

Oh! could we from death but recover
These hearts they bounded before
In the face of high heav'n to fight over
That combat for freedom once more.

"Don't be angry," his mother said.

"I'm not angry. Have you slept today?"

She said, "How can I sleep, with your brother making such noise?"

"What noise does he make?" Lucas asked.

"His singing. Should someone tell him his voice ain't as much like an angel's as he seems to think?"

"Has Simon been singing to you?"

"Aye, but I canna understand the words."

"Eat a little, all right? You must eat."

"Has he learned some other language, do ye think?"

"You were dreaming, Mother."

He took up the fork again, pressed the bit of potato against her lips. She turned her mouth away.

"He's been like that since he was a babe. Always crying or singing just when you think you've earned a bit of rest."

"Please, Mother."

She opened her mouth, and he slipped the fork in as gently as he could. She spoke through the mouthful of potato. She said, "I'm sorry."

"Chew. Chew and swallow."

"If I understood what he wanted of me, I might be able to give it."

Soon he could tell from her breathing that she slept again. He listened nervously for the sound of Simon's voice, but the room remained silent. He wondered, Would his mother choke on the bit of potato? Gathering his nerve (it seemed so wrong, but what else could he do?), he slipped his fingers into her mouth. It was warm and wet. He found the bit of potato, the mush of it, on her tongue. He took it out. He put it in his own mouth. He ate the rest of her supper, ravenously, then went back into the parlor and ate his own. His father had not moved from the window. Lucas ate his father's portion as well, and went to bed.

And now it seems to me the beautiful uncut hair of graves.

Tenderly will I use you curling grass,
It may be you transpire from the breasts of young men,
It may be if I had known them I would have loved them,
It may be you are from old people, or from offspring taken soon out
*   of their mothers' laps,*
And here you are the mothers' laps.

There was nothing for breakfast, though his father sat at table, waiting. Lucas said, "Father, will you get food for Mother and yourself while I'm at work?"

His father nodded. Lucas took the last ten pennies from the tin in the cupboard. He saved three for himself, for his lunch, and put the other seven on the table for his father. He thought his father could go out and buy something to eat. He thought his father could do that.

He would find out today when he was to be paid. He was sure Jack had meant to tell him but had been too taken up with managing the works. He resolved as well to ask Jack about the nature of what the machines were making, what the housings housed. He wondered if he would find the courage to ask so many questions all at once.

The workday passed. Align, clamp, pull, pull again, inspect. In the afternoon Lucas began to discern a faint sound as the teeth of the machine bit down, a lesser noise within the machine's greater one. He wondered if it was a new sound or simply an aspect of the machine's usual noise, inaudible to him until he'd grown accustomed to the machine's complexities of being. He listened more carefully. Yes, there it was—amid the crunching of the metal teeth into the softer metal of the plate, all but lost in the slalom of the rollers, the swish of the belt—there was another sound, barely more than a whisper. Lucas leaned in close. The whisper seemed to emanate from deep within, from the dark place under the turning wheel, just past the point at which teeth embedded themselves in iron.

He leaned in closer still. He could hear it but not quite hear it. From behind him, Tom said, "Somethin' wrong with yer machine, there?"

Lucas righted himself. He hadn't thought Tom noticed him at all. It was surprising to know he was so visible.

"No, sir," he said. Quickly, with a show of diligence, he loaded another plate.

He didn't see Jack until day's end, when Jack came to him, said, "All right, then," spoke to Dan, and went into the chamber of the vaults. Lucas passed through a moment of dreamlike confusion—he thought he had reentered the previous day, had only imagined it was Thursday and not Wednesday. In his bafflement he forgot to ask Jack when he would be paid. He resolved to ask tomorrow.

He left the works and made his way home. On Rivington he passed a madman who screamed about a rain (or was it a reign?) of fire. He passed a bone that lay in the gutter, knobbed at either end, ivory-colored, offering itself like something precious.

He wanted to go to Catherine again but forced himself home instead. When he let himself into the apartment, he found his mother standing in the middle of the parlor, on the carpet she had paid too much for. It seemed for a moment—only a moment—that she was herself again, that she had made supper and put the kettle on.

She stood transfixed in her nightgown. Her hair flowed to her shoulders; wisps of it stood around her head in wiry confusion. He had never seen her so, in the parlor with her hair undone. He remained dumbly at the entrance, uncertain of what to do or say. He saw that his father stood at the window with his breathing machine, looking not out at the street but into the room. He saw that his father was frightened and confused.

He said, "Mother?"

She stared at him. Her eyes were not her own.

"It's Lucas," he said. "It's only Lucas."

Her voice, when she spoke, was low. She might have feared being overheard. She said, "He mustn't sing to me no more."

Lucas glanced helplessly at his father, who remained standing at the window, looking into the room, watching intently the empty air before his eyes.

His mother hesitated, searching Lucas's face. She seemed to be struggling to remember him. Then, abruptly, as if pushed from behind, she fell forward. Lucas caught her in his arms and held her as best he could, awkwardly, with one hand under her left arm and the other on her right shoulder. He could feel the weight of her breasts. They were like old plums loosely held in sacks.

"It's all right," he said to her. "Don't worry, it's all right."

He got a better purchase on her limp form. He worked his right arm around her waist.

She said, "I know what language you sing in now."

"Come back to bed. Come along, now."

"It isn't right. It isn't fair."

"Hush. Hush."

"We done what we could. We didn't know what'd happen."

"Come, now."

Lucas snaked his arm farther around her, supporting her under her opposite armpit. At his direction, she walked unsteadily with him into the bedroom. He set her down on the bed. He pulled her legs up, arranged her as best he could, with her head on the pillow. He drew the counterpane over her.

"You'll feel better if you sleep," he said.

"I can't sleep, I never will. Not with that voice in my ears."

"Lie quietly, then. Nothing will happen."

"Something will. Something does."

He stroked her hot, dry forehead. It was as impossible to tell time in the bedroom as it was at the works. When she was quiet, when she slept or did not sleep but was quiet and breathing steadily, he went out of the room.

His father hadn't moved. Lucas went to the window and stood beside him. His father continued staring at the empty air. Lucas saw that the seven pennies still lay on the tabletop, untouched.

He said, "Father, are you hungry?"

His father nodded, breathed, and nodded again.

Lucas stood with his father at the window. The ashman ambled by, dragging his bin. Mr. Cain shouted, "No place, everyplace, where's the string of pearls?"

"I'll get you something," Lucas said.

He took the pennies, went out, and found a man selling a cabbage for three cents, and a woman selling a hen's egg that, after some argument, she let him have for four. It seemed it might be propitious that his mother had asked after chickens and he had gone out and found an egg.

He cooked the egg and boiled the cabbage, and set a plate before his father. He was seized by an urge to take his father's head in his hands and knock it sharply against the table's edge, as Dan did with his machine at the works, knocking it when it threatened to seize up, ringing his wrench against its side. Lucas imagined that if he tapped his father's head against the wood with precisely the correct force he might jar him back to himself. It would be not violence but kindness. It would be a cure. He laid one hand on his father's smooth head but only caressed it. His father made noises when he ate, ordinary slurpings combined with low moans, as if feeding were painful to him. He lifted a spoonful of cabbage to his mouth. A pallid green string dangled from the spoon. He slurped, moaned, and swallowed. He took a breath, then ate again. Lucas thought, Four across, six down.

This grass is very dark to be from the white heads of old mothers,
Darker than the colorless beards of old men,
Dark to come from under the faint red roofs of mouths.

O I perceive after all so many uttering tongues,
And I perceive they do not come from the roofs of mouths for
nothing.

Lucas read his passage. He put out the lamp but could not sleep. He lay awake in the room. There were the walls. There was the ceiling, with its black triangles of missing plaster and its stain in the shape of a chrysanthemum. There were the pegs on which the clothes hung, his and Simon's.

He rose and went to the window. Emily's light was on. Emily was lazy and cross, Catherine said so. Her stitches had sometimes to be resewn, but she remained sullen, unrepentant.

And still, Simon had gone to her. Only Lucas knew. Once, a month or more ago, he had looked out the window and seen Simon there, with Emily, who'd left her curtains open. It had seemed impossible at first. Simon had said he was going out for his pint. He was promised to Catherine. How could he be in Emily's room? For a moment Lucas had thought that some other Simon, his living ghost, had gone there to haunt Emily, because she was lazy and cross, because her stitches were sloppy. He'd watched as Emily stood slightly apart from that other Simon and removed her bodice. He'd watched her breasts tumble out, huge and lax, with aureoles the color of lilacs going dark with age. He'd seen Simon reach for her.

Emily had gone to the window then, to draw the curtains, and seen Lucas watching her. They'd regarded each other across the empty air. She had nodded to him. She had smiled lewdly. Then she'd closed the curtains.

Lucas had wished Simon dead that night. No, not dead. Brought low. Brought to justice. He'd imagined consoling Catherine. He hadn't asked for what happened to Simon. He hadn't meant to ask for that.

He stood now at the window. Behind her curtains Emily was still alive, still fat and lewd, still eating Turkish delight from the tin. Lucas wondered why he'd wished harm to Simon and not to Emily, who was more at fault, who had surely lured Simon with some trick. Lucas struggled now to wish her well, or at any rate to wish her no ill fortune. He stood for a while at the window, wishing her a long and uneventful life.

In the morning, there was nothing to give his father for breakfast. His father sat at table, waiting. Lucas didn't speak to him about food. He kissed his father's forehead and went into the bedroom to see how his mother had passed the night.

He found her sitting up in bed, holding the music box on her lap.

"Good morning, Mother," Lucas said.

"Oh, Simon," she said. "We're sorry."

"It's Lucas, Mother. Only Lucas."

"I was speakin' to your brother, dear. In the box."

For a moment Lucas thought she meant the box that was in the earth across the river, until she looked wistfully down at her lap. She meant the music box.

He said, "Simon isn't there, Mother."

She lifted the box in both hands and held it out to him. "You listen," she said. "Listen to what he says."

"You haven't wound it."

"Listen," she said again.

Lucas turned the crank. The small music started up from within the box. It was "Oh, Breathe Not His Name."

"There he is," Mother said. "Do you hear him now?"

"It's only the music, Mother."

"Oh, sweet child, ye don't know, do ye?"

Lucas was all but overcome by a weariness that struck him like fever. He wanted only to sleep. The music box, playing its little tune, felt impossibly heavy. He thought he would sink to the floor and lie there, curled up like a dog, so fast asleep that no one and nothing could wake him.

He was responsible for the music box, because he had so wanted the horse on wheels. He'd lost himself, contemplating it. The horse was white. Where must it be now? It was long gone from Niedermeyer's window. It looked steadily forward with round black eyes. Its face bore an expression of stately gravity. Its wheels were red. He'd

gazed at it every day, until one afternoon, passing Niedermeyer's with
his mother, he gave over to his desire for the horse as he gave himself
over to the book, and wept like a lover. His mother had put her arm
tenderly over his shoulders; she'd held him close. They'd stood there
together as they might on a train platform, watching a locomotive bear
its travelers away. Lucas's mother had stood patiently with him, holding him as he wept for the horse. The next day she'd gone out and
bought the music box, an extravagance his father said would be the
ruin of them. His mother had laughed bitterly, told him he was
miserly and fearful, insisted that they needed music, they deserved a
bit of cheer every now and then, and a music box would not spell the
end of the world no matter what it cost. Later, Father turned to
leather, and the machine took Simon, and Mother went into her
room.

Lucas said, "It's only music, Mother."

"I know what he's saying now. I know the language he speaks."

"You should go back to sleep," Lucas told her. "I'm going to put
the music box in the parlor for a while."

"He's all alone in a strange land."

"I must go. I can't be late for work."

"We brung him here from Dingle. It's only right we should go to
him where he is now."

"Goodbye, Mother. I'm off."

"Farewell."

"Farewell."

He left the bedroom and put the music box on the parlor table,
where his father still sat, awaiting breakfast. "Goodbye, Father," he
said.

His father nodded. He had acquired an infinite patience. He
would come to table at the appointed hours, eat if food was offered
him, not eat if food was not.

At the works, Lucas had to struggle to pay proper attention. His
mind wanted to wander. He aligned a plate, pulled the lever, and then
was at the back of the machine, inspecting the impressions, with no
memory of having gotten there. It was dangerous, a dangerous condition to bring to the machine, and yet he could not seem to do other-

wise. Trying to think only of his work—align, clamp, pull, pull again, inspect—was like trying to remain awake when sleep was overwhelming. Inattention took him like dreams.

To steady himself he set his mind to the whisper in the machine. He listened carefully. It might have been the squeak of an unoiled bearing, but it sounded more like a voice, a tiny voice, though its words were indistinguishable. It had the rhythm of a voice, the rise and fall and rise again suggesting intention rather than accident, the tone implying a certain urgency more human than mechanical, as if the sound were being made by some entity struggling to be heard. Lucas knew well enough what it was to speak a language no one understood.

He fed it another plate and another and another.

The nature of the machine's song didn't disclose itself until afternoon. The song wasn't sung in language, not in a language Lucas recognized, but gradually, over time, the song began making itself clear, even though its words remained obscure.

It was Simon's voice.

Could it be? Lucas listened more carefully. Simon's voice had been deep and raucous. He had sung not well but with bravado, with the rampant soaring tunelessness of someone who cared less about sounding beautiful than about creating a sound big enough to reach the sky. This seemed, in fact, to be Simon's voice, rendered mechanical. It had that reckless, unapologetic atonality.

The song was familiar. Lucas had heard it elsewhere, at a time and place that hovered on the outer edge of memory. It was a song of melancholy and yearning, a sad song, full of loneliness and a thread of hope. It was one of the old ballads. Simon had known hundreds of them.

Simon was imprisoned in the machine. It made sudden, dreadful sense. He was not in heaven or in the pillow; he was not in the grass or in the locket. His ghost had snagged on the machine's inner workings; the machine held it as a dog might hold a man's coat in its jaws after the man himself had escaped. Simon's flesh had been stamped and expelled, but his invisible part remained, trapped among the gears and teeth.

Lucas stood dumb before the singing wheel. Then, because he must not stop working, he loaded another plate. He aligned, clamped, pulled, pulled again, and inspected. In his mind he sang a duet with Simon, matched him note for note, as the hours passed.

At day's end, Jack came to say, "All right, then." Lucas desperately wanted to ask him if he knew about the dead in the machines, but he couldn't seem to manage a question as large as that, not right away. He began by asking instead, "Please, sir, when do we get paid?" It seemed better to say "we" than "I."

Jack said, "You get paid today. Go to accounting after you've shut down."

Lucas could scarcely believe it. It seemed he had produced his pay by asking for it; that if he had failed to ask he'd have worked on and on for nothing, and no one would have remembered. He said, "Thank you, sir," but Jack had already left him, to say "All right, then" to Dan. Lucas hadn't had time to ask anything more. Still, he was glad to know there'd be money tonight. Tomorrow he would ask Jack the other, more difficult question.

Lucas shut down his machine. He said good-night to Simon and went with the others to receive his pay from the men in the cages. With money in his pocket, he set out for home.

When he arrived, all was as ever. His father sat in his chair, his mother dreamed or did not dream behind the closed door. Lucas said to his father, "I have money. I can buy us a proper supper. What do you think you'd like?"

"Ask your mother," he said.

That was an answer from former times, when his mother was herself. Lucas said, "I'll go see what I can get, then."

His father nodded agreeably. Lucas leaned over to kiss him.

It was then that he heard it. The same song, steady, pining, the little song of love and yearning.

It came from his father's breathing machine.

Lucas put his ear closer to the mouth of the tube. It was there, softer than soft, inaudible to anyone who didn't seek it. It was the same song, sung in the same way, but by a voice gentler and breathier, more like a woman's. It came, he thought, from the little bladder at the machine's base, rose up through the tube, and issued from the opening, the slender oval of horn, where his father put his mouth.

It was the song Lucas had heard at the works. It was lower and more sibilant, it was more difficult to detect, but it was that song, sung in that voice.

And so he knew: Simon was not caught in the machine at the works; he had passed over into a world of machinery. Machines were his portals, the windows he whispered through. He sang to the living through the mouths of machines. Every time his father put his lips to the breathing machine, it filled him with Simon's song.

Lucas understood now that Mother was not dreaming, not deranged; she heard more clearly than anyone. Simon wanted his people with him. He was alone in a strange land. Hadn't the Simon-machine taken his sleeve when he was distracted? Hadn't it tried to pull him from this world into the other?

The dead returned in machinery. They sang seductively to the living as mermaids sang to sailors from the bottom of the sea.

He thought of Catherine.

She would be the main prize. She was Simon's bride-to-be; he'd want to marry her in his new world if he could no longer do so in the old. He was singing to her, searching for her, hoping she might go to him just as everyone had left Ireland to come to New York.

He ran from the apartment, raced down the stairs. He had to warn her. He had to tell her the nature of the threat.

When he reached the steps of Catherine's building he stopped. His heart fluttered and raged. He needed to knock at the door, to beg admittance from the tiny woman and see Catherine. But he knew—he knew—that what he'd come to tell her she would not immediately believe. He understood the strangeness of his news, and he understood that he of all people was suspect, he who was known to be frail and odd, who suffered fits in which he could speak only as the book.

He hesitated. He couldn't bear, even now, the prospect of going to Catherine, telling her what he knew, and finding her merely remote and kind. If she treated him as a sad, addled boy, if she gave him more food to take to his family, he would fall into a shame so deep he might never return from it.

He stood on the stoop in an agony of unresolve. It came to him that he might bring her something. He need not arrive at her door desperate and penurious. He could come to her with an offering. He could say, I have a present for you. He could give her something rare and wonderful. And then, as she exclaimed over the gift, he could broach his true purpose.

He couldn't take her the music box, not when it had proved itself a window into the world of the dead. He couldn't give her the book, either. It wasn't his to give. Beyond the book and the music box, everything he had, everything his family had, was worn and plain.

He had money, though. He could buy her something.

But all the shops were closed. He went along Fifth Street, past the darkened windows that offered nothing to give as a present even when the shops were open. Behind these windows were meat and bread, dry goods, a cobbler's stall. Passing the shops, Lucas was aware of their slumbering contents, their beef and boots. He looked through the glass past his own dimly reflected face at the red-and-white haunches hanging against the tiles, at the shelves of silent shoes, at the bottles upon which a mustached man in spectacles was expressing his gratitude for the tonic the bottles held, the same man over and over again, expressing the same pleasure.

Lucas went to Broadway. Something there might be open still.

Broadway might have been a toy for a giant child. It was like a gift to lay before a sultan, a turbaned invader who had refused all other offerings, who had been indifferent to a forest full of mechanical nightingales, who had yawned over golden slippers that danced on their own.

But the shops on Broadway were closed, too. At this hour it was only cafés and taverns and the lobbies of the hotels. He went down Broadway as far as Prince Street, and saw a boy standing at the corner, offering something to those who passed. The boy was ragged, older than Lucas. He wore breeches half again too large for him, cinched with a rope. A limp felt hat, the color of a rat's pelt, was pulled down over his head. From it a single lock of lank orange hair protruded like a secret he couldn't keep.

He held in his hand a small white bowl. He displayed it to

passersby, who ignored him. Was it an alms bowl? No, it seemed that he was offering it for sale.

Lucas stopped near the ragged boy, who had of course stolen the bowl and was trying to sell it, as people did. Lucas knew how it must be for him. His bowl was a prize, and it was a burden. Something more common would be easier to sell; a turnip, in its way, would be more valuable. The people of the boy's neighborhood wouldn't want a thing like the bowl, and those who walked on Broadway might want it but wouldn't buy it from a boy like this. He extended the bowl to passersby in his outstretched hands with weary hopefulness, like a priest offering the holy cup. Lucas thought the boy had been here a long time, had begun by shouting out a price and had declined, as the hours passed, to this condition of mute resignation.

He approached the boy, looked more closely at the bowl. The boy drew away from Lucas, cradled his prize to his breast. Lucas could see it well enough, though. It was a white china bowl, undamaged. It bore along its rim a band of pale blue figures.

Lucas said, "How much?"

The boy regarded him nervously. He would naturally suspect a trick.

To allay him Lucas said, "I want it for my sister. How much?"

The boy's eyes were as shrewd and avid as a cat's. He said, "A dollar."

A dollar and three pennies was what Lucas had in his pocket. It seemed for a moment that the boy somehow knew that, that he was a sprite who haunted Broadway with his treasure and asked in payment all that everyone had.

Lucas said, "That's too much."

The boy compressed his lips. The bowl was worth more than a dollar, and he might get a dollar if he stayed longer on the street, but he was tired, he was hungry, he wanted to go home. Lucas felt a pang of sympathy for the boy, who was wily and cunning, a thief, but who wanted, as everyone did, to be finished with his work, to be restored to himself, to rest.

The boy said, "You can have it for seventy-five cents."

"That's still too much."

The boy settled his mouth. Lucas knew: he would go no further. He was a thief, but he was someone; he had a private realm inside him, and he would not let himself be any poorer than this.

He said, "That's the last price. Take it or leave it."

Lucas was filled with sympathy and rage. He knew how much seventy-five cents would mean to the boy. But the bowl had cost him nothing. He could give it to Lucas, who needed it, and in so doing be no worse off than he'd been before. Lucas felt, briefly, the turning of the inscrutable world, in which a bowl that had cost nothing, a bowl he might have stolen himself (though he never stole; he was too nervous for that), would cost him most of what he'd earned by a week's labor.

He glanced up and down the street, as if he hoped another bowl, or something better, might lie ahead or behind. There was nothing. He might walk all night to find only someone selling a few leeks or a half bottle of ale.

He said, "All right, then."

He took the money from his pocket and counted out seventy-five cents. He and the boy paused over who would relinquish first and found a way to exchange bowl for coins so that neither was empty-handed. Lucas felt the money taken from him by the boy's calloused fingers. He felt the bowl settle into his palm.

The boy ran off, fearful that Lucas might change his mind. In a panic, Lucas examined the bowl. Was it false? Had it turned to wood? No, it was in fact a bit of finery. It seemed, in his hands, to emit a faint white light. The figures inscribed along its rim were mysterious. They appeared to be tiny blue suns, icy disks from which rays emanated, finer than hairs.

The bowl was good, then. But he had only twenty-eight cents left, which was not enough for a week's food for three. Still, he had a gift to take to Catherine. He would think about food and money later.

He returned to Fifth Street and knocked at the door until the tiny woman opened it. She wondered that he was back again but admitted him more easily, because he was becoming visible to her. She warned him again that there was to be no mischief. He agreed and mounted the stairs to Catherine's apartment.

Catherine answered the door. She seemed neither pleased nor

sorry to see him. He wondered if he'd changed again, if he was unrec-
ognizable to her again, though he wore the same clothes and the same
dirt he'd worn yesterday.

He said, before he could help himself, "Alone far in the wilds and
mountains I hunt."

She said, "Hello, my dear. How are you?" Tonight she wore her
new face, the wearied one.

Lucas heard a sound from within the apartment, a strange sort of
wailing laughter that sounded like Alma's. It was followed by a man's
voice, deep and urgent, saying something undecipherable.

Catherine stepped out into the hallway, closed the door behind
her. "Lucas," she said, "it's not a good time to call, just now."

"But I've brought you something," he answered.

He produced the bowl. He extended it toward her on outstretched
palms.

She looked at it uncertainly, as if she could not quite discern its nature. Lucas found he couldn't speak, not as himself or as the book. He
was the bowl and his hands. He was only that.

Presently she said, "Oh, Lucas."

Still he couldn't speak. He was a bowl and a pair of hands offering
a bowl.

"You mustn't," she said.

He answered, "Please." It was what he had to say.

"How have you come by this?"

"I bought it. For you. I was paid today."

It was not as he'd expected. He had imagined her glad and grateful.

She bent toward him. She said, "It's sweet of you. But you must return it."

"I can't," he said.

"Did you pay for it? Truly?"

She suspected he'd stolen it, then. He could think of nothing to
tell her but the truth.

"I bought it from a man on Broadway," he said. "He was selling
them from a tray." It seemed better to have bought it from a man with
a tray. It seemed truth enough.

"My dear. You can't afford this."

He trembled, filled with rage and confusion and blind, desperate hope. Somehow he'd made himself poorer by bringing her a gift.

"Please," he said again.

"You're the sweetest boy in the world. You truly are. And tomorrow you must return it to the man on Broadway and get your money back."

"I can't," he said.

"Would you like me to go with you?"

"What is a man anyhow? What am I? And what are you?"

"Please, Lucas. I'm touched, I truly am. But I can't accept it."

"The man is gone."

"He'll return tomorrow."

"No. This was his last bowl. He said he was going away."

"Oh, poor boy."

How could he tell her, what could he say, here in the dark of the hallway (where the goat's skull still grinned), holding out to her the only treasure he could find, a treasure she didn't want?

He said, "The spinning-girl retreats and advances to the hum of the big wheel."

"Hush. Hush, now. You'll disturb the neighbors."

He hadn't meant to speak so loudly. He didn't mean to speak again, more loudly still.

"The bride unrumples her white dress, the minute-hand of the clock moves slowly."

"Stop. Please. Come inside, you mustn't rant like this in the hall-way."

"The prostitute draggles her shawl, her bonnet bobs on her tipsy and pimpled neck. The nine months' gone is in the parturition chamber, her faintness and pains are advancing."

Catherine paused. She looked at him with a new recognition.

"What did you say?"

He didn't know. She had never before seemed to hear him when he spoke as the book.

"Lucas, please repeat what you just said."

"I've forgotten."

"You spoke of a spinning-girl. You spoke of a bride, and . . . a prostitute. And a woman about to give birth."

"It was the book."

"But why did you say it?"

"The words come through me. I never know."

She leaned closer, gazing into his face as if words were written there, faint but discernible, difficult to read.

She said, "You really don't know, do you? Oh, Lucas. I fear for you."

"No. Please. You mustn't fear for me. You must fear for yourself."

"You have some gift," she said softly. "You have some terrible gift, do you know that?"

He thought for a moment that she meant the bowl. It was in fact a terrible gift. It should have cost nothing, but he'd paid for it with money meant for food. And what use did Catherine have for a bowl like this? Lucas stood with his blood racketing and his hands outstretched. He was the boy who had bought the bowl, and he was the boy who had sold it. Would that boy, the other, be now returning to his own family with food? Lucas could be only this, the one who had bought it. He could only stand before Catherine with a terrible gift in his hands.

Gently (he thought he had never known such gentleness) she took the bowl from him. She held it in her own hand.

"What are we to do with you?" she said. "How will your mother and father live?"

He said, "This hour I tell you things in confidence, things I might not tell everybody, but I will tell you."

"Hush, hush."

"The dead sing to us through machinery. They are with us still."

"Stop. Speak as yourself."

"Simon wants to marry you in the land of the dead. He wants you there with him."

Sadly, she shook her head. "Listen to me," she said. "It's wonderful of you to want to buy me a gift like this. You are a sweet, generous boy. I'm going to keep the bowl safe tonight, and tomorrow I am going to sell it and give you the money. Please, don't be offended."

"You must not trust your sewing machine. You must not listen if it sings to you."

"Shh. If we make such a racket every night, we'll be thrown out."

"Do you take it I would astonish? Does the daylight astonish? Or the early redstart twittering through the woods?"

"Go home now. Come to me tomorrow, after work."

"I cannot leave you. I will not."

She put her hand on his head. "I'll see you tomorrow. Be careful until then."

"It's you who must be careful."

She seemed not to hear or understand. With a rueful smile she opened the door and went back inside.

Lucas remained for a while before the door, like a dog waiting to be let in. Then, because he could not bear being like a dog, he went away. He passed the tiny woman, who said, "No mischief, then?" He told her there had been no mischief. But there had been mischief, hadn't there? There was the bowl and what the bowl had cost. There were other crimes.

He made his way home, because he had money now (he had some left), and his mother and father must eat. He bought a sausage from the butcher and a potato from an old woman on the street.

The apartment was as always. His mother slept behind her door. His father sat at table, because it was time to do so. He put his lips to the machine, breathed Simon's ghost song into his lungs.

"Hello," Lucas said. His voice was strange in the quiet room, like a bean rattling in a jar.

"Hello," his father said. Had his voice changed slightly, from his chest being filled with Simon? It might have. Lucas could not be sure. Was his father turning into a machine, with Simon inside him?

Lucas cooked the sausage and the potato. He gave some to his father, took some in to his mother, who slept fitfully but slept. He decided it was best not to disturb her. He left the food on the bedside table, for when she awoke and wanted it.

After his father had finished, Lucas said, "Father, it's time for bed."

His father nodded, breathed, nodded again. He rose. He took the machine with him.

Lucas left his father in the doorway to the bedroom. His mother murmured within. His father said, "She cannot stop dreaming."

"She sleeps. It's what's best for her."

"She doesn't sleep. She only dreams."

"Hush. Go to sleep now. Good night, Father."

His father went into the dark. The machine's little feet scraped on the floorboards after him.

I wish I could translate the hints about the dead young men and
*   women,*
And the hints about old men and mothers, and the offspring taken
*   soon out of their laps.*

What do you think has become of the young and old men?
And what do you think has become of the women and children?

Lucas read his passage. He put out the light and went to sleep.

He dreamed he was in a room, an enormous room and clangorous. It was the works but not the works. It was full of silvery dusk like the works but empty of all save the noise, a deafening sound, not like what the machines produced, not quite that sound, though it resembled it. Lucas understood that the machines were gone but would return soon, as cattle return to a barn. He was to wait here. He was to see them home. He looked up—something told him to look up—and saw that the ceiling was covered in stars. There were the Great Horse, the Hunter, the Pleiades. He knew then that the stars were machinery, too. There was nowhere to go that was not the world, that was not the room. The stars moved mechanically, and something was descending, a dark shape from high in the night sky . . .

He turned and looked into a face. Its eyes were black pools. Its skin was stretched taut over its skull. It said, "My boy, my boy."

His mother's face was pressed to his. He was dreaming of his mother. He struggled to speak, but couldn't speak.

The face said again, "My poor boy, what they done to ye."

He was awake. His mother crouched beside his bed, with her face to his face. He felt her breath on his lips.

"I'm all right, Mother," he said. "Nothing's been done to me."

She held the music box, cradled close. She said, "Poor child."

"You're dreaming," Lucas told her.

"My poor, poor boys. One and then another and another."

"Let me take you back to bed."

"It's greed that done it. Greed and weakness."

"Come. Come back to bed."

He rose and took her arm. She yielded, or did not resist. He led her out of the bedroom and through the parlor, where the faces watched. Her feet shuffled on the floor. He took her into the other bedroom. His father wheezed and gagged in his sleep.

Lucas helped his mother into bed, pulled the blanket up. Her hair was spread over the pillow. In the fan of dark hair her face was impossibly small, no bigger than his fist.

She said, "I should be dead with him."

Lucas thought—he could not help thinking—of the bowl he'd bought. There were nineteen cents now, to keep them until Friday next. There wouldn't be food for the week.

He said, "You're safe. I'm here."

"Oh, safe. If anyone were safe."

"You must sleep now."

"Do ye think sleeping is safe?"

"Shh. Just be quiet."

He sat with her. He couldn't tell if it was better to stroke her hand or refrain from stroking her hand. He rocked slightly, to calm himself. There was nothing so frightful as this. There was nothing, had been nothing, as terrible as sitting on his parents' mattress, wondering if he should or should not touch his mother's hand.

He knew he had to take the music box away. But what of Simon's other point of ingress, their father's breathing machine? Father needed the machine. Or did he?

Lucas didn't know if the machine was crucial to his father or merely helpful. He hadn't been told. It was possible, it was not impossible, that the breathing apparatus, which had been given as a gift, was in fact a bane. Could it be sucking his father's life away, when it pretended to help him? Did any machine seem to want the good of its people?

Lucas stood, went as quietly as he could to his father's side of the bed, and took up the machine. Its iron pole was cool to his touch. It was full of its song, as steady and unmistakable as the mice inside the walls. Gingerly, as he would take up a mouse by its tail, he carried the machine through the parlor and put it in the hallway. Was that far enough away? He hoped it was. In the twilight of the hall the machine was as indistinct as the goat's skull. Its bladder, the size and shape of a turnip, was gray but subtly luminous. Its tube and mouthpiece dangled.

He would leave it there overnight. He would bring it back in the morning, when he'd seen how his father fared without.

He went into the parlor for the music box. He took it and put it in the hallway, beside his father's machine, then returned to the parlor and locked the door. He checked to make sure it was fast.

When sleep found him again, it brought its dreams, though he recalled upon awakening only that they had involved children and a needle and a woman who stood far away, calling out across a river.

In the morning his father had not yet risen. Lucas went to his parents' bedroom and cautiously opened the door. They were quieter than usual. His mother murmured over her dreams, but his father, who was ordinarily given to deep snorts and coughings, was silent.

He must need the machine. Lucas must hurry and bring it back.

When he went into the hallway to retrieve it, it was gone. Breathing machine and music box had vanished entirely.

He stood for a moment, confused. Had he dreamed of putting them there? He searched up and down the hall, wondering if they were only farther away. Perhaps he had gotten up during the night and moved them, somnambulistically. No. They were nowhere. He thought briefly that the mechanisms were more alive than he'd imagined, that they walked. Would they have found their way back into his parents' bedroom? Would the music box be sitting at his mother's side, singing a song she couldn't bear to hear?

He summoned himself. He was agitated, but he was not insane. Someone had taken the machine and the music box, as people did. Nothing of any value could be left unattended. He had thought they'd be all right for those nocturnal hours, but someone had carried them off. Someone would be trying to sell them, as the boy had sold the china bowl.

Lucas returned to the parlor. What could he say to his father that his father would understand? He could think of nothing, and so he said nothing. He left his father and mother in their bedroom together. He hoped that when he returned from work, they might be restored to themselves.

Here it was, then: his own machine. He stood before it in the enormous room. Dan and Will and Tom were at theirs, tending them as they ever did, with the steady dispassionate attention of farmers.

Lucas whispered, "You were unworthy, you must admit it. You were untrue. I'm sorry you're dead, but you can't have Catherine with you. You must stop singing to Mother about your sorrows."

The machine sang on. Its song didn't vary. Lucas still couldn't decipher the words, but he knew they were all about love and longing. Simon wanted more than he should rightfully have. Why would he be different dead than he was alive?

Lucas loaded a plate and fed it in. The machine took the plate as it always did. It made the impressions, four across, six down. As Lucas carried the first of the day's plates to Dan, he wondered if his machine spoke to the others at night, when the men were gone and the machines lived here alone. He could imagine it easily enough, the machines murmuring in the darkened rooms, singing the songs of their men, praising their men, dreaming of them, singing each to the others, He is mine, he is my only love, how I long for the day when he allows me to have him completely. Lucas thought he should warn Dan, he should warn Tom and Will. But how could he tell them?

Dan was bent over his machine. He said, "Good morning, Lucas," without looking up.

"Good morning, sir."

Lucas lingered after he had dropped the plate in Dan's bin. Dan was the biggest man in cutting and stamping. He was massive and stooped. He carried his immense round shoulders like burdens; upon his shoulders, partly buried in them, his head looked out with drowned blue eyes. Lucas knew nothing of his life but could imagine it. He would have a wife and children. He would have a parlor with a bedroom on one side and a bedroom on the other.

Dan turned from his machine. He said, "Something wrong?"

"No, sir."

Dan took a kerchief from his pocket, wiped the sweat from the gleaming red dome of his brow.

He was missing the first and second fingers of his right hand. Lucas hadn't noticed it before.

Lucas said, "Please, sir. What happened to your fingers?"

Dan lowered the kerchief and looked at his hand as if he expected to see something surprising there.

"Lost 'em," he said.

"How did you lose them?"

"Accident."

"Was it here? At the works?"

Dan paused. He seemed to wonder whether or not to reveal a secret.

"Sawmill," he said.

"You worked in a sawmill, before you came here?"

"That's right."

Dan wiped his brow again and returned to his work. Idling so, talking, wasn't permitted. Lucas returned to his own machine and loaded another plate.

A different machine had eaten Dan's fingers. That machine, one that split logs, contained a fragment of Dan's ghost, though the rest of Dan lived on. Would this new machine know of that? Could it hear that other machine, singing from far away in a sawmill, happy to have had Dan's fingers but lamenting the loss of the rest of him, wishing the new machine better luck?

Catherine must be sewing now. Lucas couldn't think how a sewing machine might take her. It would be an arm with a needle, ratcheting. It might prick her, it could do that, but it couldn't harm her truly.

There must be other machines at her work, though, machines that could maim. He struggled to picture it. He could imagine presses and rollers through which the garments must be passed. Did she go near those machines during her day? She might. He couldn't know. She might be asked to take bodices and shirts to be sent through a larger apparatus. It would be big as a carriage, he thought; white, not black; it would have a mouth through which the freshly made shirts and dresses were fed, to be smoothed and folded. It would exhale torrents of steam.

Finally, the whistle blew. Lucas waited for Jack Walsh to pass and say, "All right, then." He shut down his machine. He hurried away. He ran up Rivington, keeping to the street, dodging the carts and carriages.

A river of girls and women was already streaming out of the Mannahatta Company when he got there, and they showed no signs of having seen a calamity that day. He searched for Catherine among the crowd. He saw any number who might have been her. They were so alike, in their blue dresses. As more and more of them passed by, in twos and threes, talking low, stretching their spines and flexing their fingers, he finally made bold enough to ask one of them, and then another, if she had seen Catherine Fitzhugh. Neither of them knew who she was. There were hundreds of girls in the sewing room; Catherine would be known only to the few who worked near her. From a distance Lucas saw Emily Hoefstaedler walking among the many, plump and serene, laughing lewdly with another girl, but he didn't speak to her. He would never speak to her about anything, certainly not about Catherine. He asked another girl and another. Several smiled and shrugged, several scowled, and one, a young dark-haired girl, said, "Won't I do instead?" and was pulled away, laughing, by her friends.

And then he saw her. She was near the end, with an older woman who had drawn her thin gray hair severely back and walked with her neck craned forward, as if her face were more eager to go forth than her body was.

Lucas approached them. "Catherine," he cried.

"Hello, Lucas," she said. She looked at him with exquisite patience.

"Are you well?"

"Quite well. And you?"

How could he say what he was? He said, "Shall I pray? Shall I venerate and be ceremonious?"

"Lucas, this is my friend Kate."

The older woman dipped her head.

"Kate, this is Lucas. He is Simon's brother."

Kate said, "I am sorry for your loss."

"Thank you, ma'am."

"Have you come to see me home?" Catherine asked.

"Yes. Please." He struggled not to snatch at her hand.

"Kate, it seems I am escorted. I'll see you tomorrow, then."

The older woman dipped her head again. "Goodbye," she said. Her face led her onward, and her body followed.

Catherine placed her hands upon her hips. "Lucas, my dear," she said.

"You are well."

"As you can see."

"Will you let me walk with you?"

"I have to sell the bowl."

"Where is it?"

"In my reticule."

"Don't sell the bowl. Keep it. Please."

"Come with me, if you like."

She walked on. He went beside her.

How could he tell her? How could he make her see?

He said, "Catherine, the machines are dangerous."

"They can be. That's why you must be careful."

"Even if you are careful."

"Well, being careful is the best we can do, isn't it?"

"You mustn't go to work anymore."

"Where should I go, then, my darling?"

"You could sew at home, couldn't you? You could take in piecework."

"Do you know what that pays?"

He didn't know what anything paid except his own work, and he had learned that only by being paid. He walked on beside her. They passed together through Washington Square. He didn't come often to the square. It lay beyond the limits of his realm; it wasn't meant for a boy like him. Washington Square, like Broadway, was part of the city within the city, cupping its green and dappled quietude, ringed by the remoter fires—a place where men and women strolled in dresses and greatcoats, where a lame beggar played on a flute; where the leaves of the trees cut shapes out of the sky and an old woman sold ices from a wooden cart; where a child waved a scarlet pennant that snapped and rippled in countertime to the flute player, who in his turn produced a little point of ginger-colored beard as answer to the pennant. Lucas tried not to be distracted by the beauty of the square. He tried to remain himself.

He asked Catherine, "Where are we going?"

"To someone I know of."

He went with her through the square, to a shop on Eighth Street. It was a modest place, half below the street, called Gaya's Emporium. Its window showed two hats floating on poles. One was pink satin, the other stiff black brocade. Under the hats were bracelets and earrings, arranged on a swatch of faded blue velvet, gleaming like brave little gestures of defeat.

Catherine said, "Wait here."

"Can't I come in with you?"

"No. It's best if I go in alone."

"Catherine?"

"Yes?"

"May I see the bowl again, first?"

"Of course you may."

She opened her reticule and removed the bowl. It was bright in the evening light, almost unnaturally so. It might have been carved from pearl. Its line of strange symbols, its blue curls and circles, stood out boldly, like a language that insisted on its own cogency in a world that had lost the skill to decipher its message.

"You mustn't sell it." Lucas was briefly host to an urge to snatch it away from her, to hold it to his breast. It seemed for a moment that if the bowl was lost something else would be lost as well, something he and Catherine needed and would not be offered again.

She said, "Sell it is exactly what I must do. I won't be long."

She went inside. Lucas waited. What else could he do? He stood before the shop window, watching the hats and jewelry live their silent lives.

Presently, Catherine returned. She wearily mounted the stairs to the street. Lucas thought of his mother's weariness. He wondered if she would improve, with the music box gone.

Catherine said, "I could get fifty cents. It's all she would give me."

She held out the coins to him. He wanted the money, he needed the money, but he couldn't bring himself to take it. He stood dumb, with his hands at his sides.

Catherine said, "It can't be what you paid for it. It's the best I could do."

He couldn't move or speak.

"Don't reproach me," she said. "Please. Take the money."

He stood helpless. His ears roared.

"Lucas, you begin to try my patience," she said. "It was difficult in there. I don't like being treated as a thief."

So he had done that to her. He had forced her to demean herself. He imagined Gaya of the emporium. He thought she'd be skeletally thin, with skin the color of candle wax. He thought—he knew—she'd have taken the bowl and examined it greedily and disdainfully. She'd have named her price with the superior finality of those accustomed to dealing in stolen goods.

He said, "The spinning-girl retreats and advances to the hum of the big wheel." He could not be certain how loudly he'd spoken.

Catherine faltered. She said, "You've never repeated yourself before."

How could she know that? Had she been listening to him, all this time, when he spoke as the book? If so, she'd given no sign.

He couldn't control himself. He said, "The bride unrumples her white dress, the minute-hand of the clock moves slowly."

Catherine blinked. Her eyes were bright.

She asked, "What did Simon tell you?"

What had Simon told him? Nothing. Simon sang the old songs, teased Lucas for being small, went to Emily's room in secret.

Lucas said, "The nine months' gone is in the parturition chamber."

Catherine dropped the money at Lucas's feet. One of the coins rolled and stopped against the toe of his boot.

"Pick it up and take it home," she said. "I have no more patience for you."

He said, "The prostitute draggles her shawl, her bonnet bobs on her tipsy and pimpled neck."

Catherine began to weep. It took her like a spasm. She stood one moment erect, with a single tear meandering down her cheek, and the next moment her face sagged, and the tears came coursing out. She put her face into her hands.

He couldn't think what to do or say. He put his fingers gently on her shoulder. She shrugged him away.

"Leave me alone, Lucas," she sobbed. "Please, just leave me alone."

He couldn't leave her weeping on Eighth Street, with people passing by. He said, "Come with me. You must sit down."

To his surprise, she obeyed. She had lost herself to weeping. She had become someone who wept and walked with him as he led her back to Washington Square, where the child's pennant snapped against the sky and the flute player hopped nimbly from foot to foot.

He found a bench and sat on it. She sat beside him. Timidly, he put his arm over her shaking shoulders. She didn't seem to mind.

He said, "I'm sorry. I didn't mean to upset you. I don't know what I said."

Her weeping diminished. She raised her head. Her face was red and haggard. He had never seen her so.

"Would you like to know something?" she said. "Would you?"

"Yes. Oh, yes."

"I'm going to have a baby."

Again he paused in confusion over something that was true but could not be true. She hadn't married.

He said, "I see," because it seemed what he ought to say.

"They won't keep me at work. I'll be too big to hide it in a month or so."

"How could you get too big to go to work?"

"You don't know *anything*, you're a child. Why am I talking to you?"

She made as if to rise but sank down again on the bench. Lucas said, "I want you to talk to me. I'll try to understand."

She went away again, into her weeping. Lucas put his arm again across her shoulders, which shook violently. The people who passed looked at them and then looked politely away, to help deliver Lucas and Catherine from their own shamefulness. The people who passed were intricately made, with gold buckles and little clocks on chains. Lucas and Catherine were made of cruder stuff. If they lingered on the bench, a policeman would come and send them along.

At length Catherine was able to say, "I've spoken to no one of this. It isn't fair, saying it to you."

"It is fair," he said. "You could never be anything but fair."

She gathered herself. She wasn't through crying, but her aspect changed. Something new took hold of her, a rage with grief caught up in it.

She said, "All right, then. I'm going to teach you something."

"Please."

Her voice when she spoke was like a wire, thin but strong.

She said, "I told your brother he must marry me. I don't know if the child is his. It probably isn't. But Simon was willing. Would you like to know something else?"

"Yes," Lucas said.

"I suspect. He had his accident because he was unhappy. He may have been so distracted by the thought of our wedding that he allowed it to happen. Think of it. He'd been in the works for years. He knew better than to let his sleeve get caught."

Lucas said, "Simon loved you."

"Did he tell you that?"

"Yes," Lucas said, though Simon had never said the words. How could he help loving her? Not everything needed to be said in words.

Catherine said, "I'm a whore, Lucas. I tried to force myself on your brother."

"Simon loved you," he said again. He couldn't think of anything else.

Catherine said, "I'm going to have the baby. It's what I can do for poor Simon."

Lucas could not think of an answer. How could she do anything but have the baby?

She said at length, "I told him he'd taken advantage, I told him he must make it right. I told him he'd come to love me, in time. So there you are. I'm a whore and a liar and I'm going to give birth to your brother's bastard. You mustn't come to see me anymore. You mustn't buy me things with the money you need for food."

Her face took on a new form. It grew older; its flesh sagged. She became a statue of herself, an effigy. She was not who she'd been. She was going somewhere.

Lucas said, "I can help you."

She stood with grave finality. She was formal now.

"No one can help me," she said.

She walked resolutely eastward, toward home. Lucas went alongside her.

"You are in danger," he said.

"I'm in the same danger as every woman who draggles her shawl, neither more nor less."

"Don't go to work anymore. Please."

"Soon enough I won't be going to work anymore. That will happen regardless."

"No. Tomorrow. Don't go tomorrow, you're in danger."

"I'll need every penny I can get, won't I?"

"The dead search for us through machinery. When we stand at a machine, we make ourselves known to the dead."

"Your precious book."

"It isn't the book. It's true."

He confused himself. The book was true. What he was trying to tell her was differently true.

She walked on. Her new face, reddened and ravaged, cut through the air. She might have been the carved woman at the prow of a ship.

She said, "I can't worry about you anymore. I'm sorry, but I can't. I have too much else to think about."

"You don't need to worry about me. Let me worry about you. Let me help you. Let me care for you."

She laughed bitterly. "What a good idea," she said. "I'll come live with you and your parents. We'll live, all four of us, on what you make at the works. No, there will be five. That shouldn't be a problem, should it?"

For a moment, Lucas could see her as she'd said she was: a whore and a liar, a woman of the street, hard and calculating, naming her price.

He said, "I'll find a way."

She stopped, so abruptly that Lucas went on several paces ahead. Foolish, he was a foolish thing.

She said, "Forget me. I'm lost."

He said, "Undrape! you are not guilty to me, nor stale nor discarded."

She emitted a small, muffled cry and continued walking. He stood watching the back of her blue dress, the pile of her copper-colored hair, as she passed out of the square.

Always, then, it—everything—made a more complete and sickening sense. Simon would want her and the child as well. He sought to marry her in the realm of the dead, to live there with her and his child.

She must be prevented from going to work tomorrow.

Lucas couldn't think what to do, yet he must do so much. He must keep her from her machinery. He must find money for her.

He remembered the money she'd thrown at his feet. He hadn't picked it up. He ran back to Eighth Street for it, but of course it was gone.

He walked east on Eighth Street. He thought perhaps he could find the money again, if not the coins Catherine had tossed at his feet then some other money, some equivalent sum that might be out there, sent by a heavenly agency that forgave and abetted foolish hearts. He thought that if he scoured the city, if he went high and low in it, he might happen onto some money that was not being watched, that belonged to someone but was unattended, dropped on the pavement or otherwise misplaced, as his own coins had been. He didn't propose to steal, any more than whoever had found his money had stolen it from him. He hoped rather to take his place on a chain of losses and gains, an ongoing mystery of payments made and payments received, money given from hand to hand, to satisfy an ancient debt that had always existed and might be finally repaid in some unforeseeable future. He hoped the city might produce help through incomprehensible means, just as his stamping of iron plates produced housings.

He would search for whatever might be there.

He went along Eighth Street to Broadway. If there was money overlooked, if there were coins carelessly dropped, it was likeliest to happen there.

Broadway was filled with its lights and music, its departing shoppers and its glad men in hats, laughing, blowing smoke from the bellows of their chests. Lucas walked among them, looking attentively downward. He saw the tips of boots, the cuffs of trousers, the hems of skirts. He saw the little leavings that were trod upon: a cigar end, a curl of twine, a canary-colored pamphlet announcing "Land in Colorado."

He'd gone along for several blocks, twice incurring the muttered indignations of citizens who had to step out of his way, when he came upon a pair of boots that seemed familiar, though he knew he had never seen them before. They were workingman's boots, dun-colored, stoutly laced. They stopped before him.

He looked up and beheld Walt's face.

Here was his gray-white cascade of beard, here his broad-brimmed hat and the kerchief knotted at his neck. He was utterly like his likeness. He smiled bemusedly at Lucas. His face was like brown paper that had been crushed and smoothed again. His eyes were bright as silver nails.

"Hello," he said. "Lost something?"

Lucas had gone searching for money and found Walt. A vast possibility trembled in the air.

He answered, "Stout as a horse, affectionate, haughty, electrical, I and this mystery, here we stand."

Walt expelled a peal of laughter. "What's this?" he said. "You quote me to myself?"

His voice was clear and deep, penetrating; it was not loud, but it was everywhere. It might have been the voice of a rainstorm, if rain could speak.

Lucas struggled to answer as himself. What he said was, "The earth, that is sufficient, I do not want the constellations any nearer, I

know they are very well where they are, I know they suffice for those
who belong to them."

"How extraordinary," Walt said. "Who are you, then?"

Lucas was unable to tell him. He stood quivering and small at
Walt's feet. His heart thumped painfully against his ribs.

Walt squatted before Lucas. His knees cracked softly, like damp
twigs.

"What's your name?" he asked.

"Lucas."

"Lucas. How do you come to know my verse so well?"

Lucas said, "I am the mate and companion of people, all just as
immortal and fathomless as myself; they do not know how immortal,
but I know."

Walt laughed again. Lucas felt the laughter along his own frame,
in his skeleton, as an electrified quake, as if Walt were not only laughing himself but summoning laughter up out of the earth, to rise
through the pavement and enter Lucas by the soles of his feet.

"What a remarkable boy you are," Walt said. "How remarkable to
find you here."

Lucas gathered himself. He said, "I wonder if I might ask a question, sir?"

"Of course you may. Ask away. I'll answer if I'm able."

"Sir, do the dead return in the grass?"

"They do, my boy. They are in the grass and the trees."

"Only there?"

"No, not only there. They are all around us. They are in the air
and the water. They are in the earth and sky. They are in our minds
and hearts."

"And in the machines?"

"Well, yes. They are in machinery, too. They are everywhere."

Lucas had been right, then. If he'd harbored any doubts, here was
the answer.

"Thank you, sir."

"Tell me of yourself," Walt said. "Where do you come from? Are
you in school?"

Lucas couldn't find a way to answer plainly. What could he tell
Walt, how account for himself?

He said at length, "I'm searching for something, sir."

"What are you searching for, lad?"

He could not say money. Money was vital, and yet now, standing before Walt's face and beard, under the curve of his hat, it seemed so little. Saying "money" to Walt would be like standing in Catherine's hallway, blazing with love, and receiving a lamb's neck and a bit of potato. He would have to say what the money was for, why he needed it so, and that task, that long explanation, was more than he could manage.

He could say only, "Something important, sir."

"Well, then. We are all searching for something important, I suppose. Can you tell me more exactly what it is you seek?"

"Something necessary."

"Do you think I could be of any help?"

Lucas said, "You help me always."

"I'm glad of that. Do you hope to find this precious thing on Broadway?"

"I've found you, sir."

Walt drew up more laughter from the earth. Lucas felt it throughout his body. Walt said, "I'm hardly precious, my boy. I'm an old servant, is all I am. I'm a vagrant and a mischief-maker. Do you know what I think?"

"What, sir?"

"I think you should walk far and wide. I think you should search Broadway and beyond. I think you should search the entire world."

"That would be hard for me, sir."

"Not all at once, not in a single night. I suspect you're something of a poet yourself. I suspect you'll spend your life searching."

Lucas's heart caught. He needed the money now. He said, "Oh, I hope not, sir."

"You'll see, you'll see. The search is also the object. Do you know what I mean by that?"

"No, sir."

"You will, I think. When you're older, you will."

"I need, sir—"

"What do you need?"

IN THE MACHINE   69

"I need to know which way to go."

"Go where your heart bids you."

"My heart is defective, sir."

"It's not in the least defective. You can believe me on that account."

Lucas flinched. He thought he might weep. He hoped Walt couldn't see the tears rising in his face.

Walt said softly, "Would you like me to give you a direction?"

"Oh, yes, sir. Please."

"All right, then. Go north. Go up to the edges of the city and beyond. Go see where the buildings diminish and the grass begins."

"Should I?"

"It's as good a way as any. If you want instructions, I give them to you. I hereby tell you to walk north."

"Thank you, sir."

"Will you come here tomorrow?" Walt asked. "Will you meet me here at the same time tomorrow night and tell me what you've found?"

"Yes, sir. If you'd like."

"I'd like it very much. I don't meet someone like you every day."

Lucas said, "A child said—"

Walt joined him, and they spoke together. They said, "*What is the grass?* fetching it to me with full hands; how could I answer the child? I do not know what it is any more than he."

"Good night, sir."

"Good night, Lucas. I hope you'll come back tomorrow. I'll be here, waiting."

"Thank you, sir."

Lucas turned and walked away. He went north, as Walt had told him to. He strode up Broadway, past the stores and hotels. Presently he turned and saw that Walt stood watching him. Lucas raised his hand in salute. Walt returned the gesture.

He had gone looking for money and found Walt instead. Walt had sent him north.

Lucas continued up Broadway. He went past Union Square and farther, until the grand buildings dwindled and there were fewer and fewer people, until fields spread out around him, lit here and there by the lights of farmers' cottages and more brightly by the windows of important houses, houses of brick and limestone, that stood proudly in the flatness and quiet. He passed like a ghost along the road, which was sometimes paved and sometimes not. He passed a house of particular grandeur, with a stone front and a white portico. He saw within (they did not draw their curtains, so far away) a regal woman in a white gown, lifting a goblet of ruby wine, standing before a portrait of herself in the same gown. A man came and stood beside her, a man in a waistcoat. His chin came to a sharp point—no, his beard was the color of his skin, and the hair on his head was the color of his skin. Lucas thought the man would appear in the portrait, too, but he did not. The man spoke to the woman, who laughed and gave him her goblet to drink from. In the portrait, she continued looking out serenely.

Lucas watched them. The dead might be present and absent like this, in the world but not of the world. The dead might wander as Lucas wandered, past the windows of strangers, looking in at a woman and a picture of a woman.

He left the man and the woman and the woman's picture. He passed other houses. Through another window he saw the crown of a chair and a framed mirror that showed him the crystal drippings of a chandelier. He saw a farmer's wife pass out of her door and pause, gathering her shawl. He saw an opossum that walked as he did, along the road. The opossum went alongside him with her quick, humping gait, unafraid, like a companion, for fifty or more paces, then slipped away, pausing to show him the pale, articulate line of her tail.

Lucas went as far as Fifty-ninth Street, and stopped before the gates of the Central Park. He had heard about the park but had never been there before. Behind the low stone wall were trees and blackness and the sound trees made. He lingered outside, and then, hesitantly, as if he might be trespassing, he went in.

The park was faintly lit near the gates, by the streetlamps of Fifty-ninth Street, but beyond that it rolled on into deep shadow. Here by the entrance were grass and the trunks of the nearest trees, which were small, newly planted. They might have been men transformed into trees, lifting their wooden arms, displaying the leaves that had burst forth from their slowed and altered flesh. Farther in, the grass went from bright green to deep jade, and the trunks of the remoter trees were pewter, then iron, then black. Beyond the jade-black grass and the black trees it was pure dark, as if the entrance to the park were a ring of forest that surrounded a lake of black, filled with the rustle of leaves and an unnameable, underlying sound that must have been insects and something else. Beyond the visible woods lay the sound of some limitless attention.

Lucas wondered if this might be where the dead resided, the dead who were not caught up in machinery. Here was grass, here were trees. Here was a rustling, alert silence far from the world of the living, with its lights and its music, its windows full of goods. Lucas gathered his courage and went forward, as he might have dived into water of uncertain depth and coldness, water that might or might not harbor fish and creatures that were not fish but lived in water, creatures that would be eyes and teeth and sudden movement. He had never seen such dark. It was never so, not even in the bedroom with the lamp extinguished, not even when he closed his eyes.

The park as Lucas walked into it, however, was not as dark as it had appeared. It was not pitch-dark. The grass beneath his feet was impenetrably black but steady; the trees were black but lesser black, their shapes discernible against a field of blackness. He felt as if he carried with him some faint illumination, a candle that was his own seeing and hearing, his human presence.

Something was here, among the trees. It deepened as he walked into it.

Presently he arrived at a stone balustrade, with a broad, curving staircase descending on either end. He went down the stairs. And there, in the middle of a dark plaza, stood an enormous figure. It spread its wings, touched faintly by moonglow. Its face was canted down, toward Lucas. It seemed for a moment that he had found the park's avenging mother, the entity that waited, watching and listening, that had dreamed the park into being and did not like to have its sleep interrupted. Lucas trembled. He made as if to turn and run, though he thought that if he did, the figure would stir its wings, take flight, and snatch him up as easily as a terrier takes a rat.

In another moment, he understood that it was a statue, only a statue. He drew nearer. It was a stone angel, standing on a pedestal above an immense stone bowl of water. He saw that the angel was severe and contemplative, that she had blank and sorrowful eyes, that she had turned from heaven and looked down at the earth.

He looked up. There, beyond the angel's arm, were the stars.

He had reached the heart of the park, and what the angel guarded—what she had wanted to show him, what Walt had sent him to find—was stars. Then he understood that here, so far from the city proper, the smoke was dispersed, and the stars were visible. He nearly lost his balance, looking up. The stars sparked, brilliant and unsteady on a field of ebony. There were thousands of them.

He knew them, some of them, from the map in the schoolroom. There was the Great Horse. There was the Hunter. There, so faint he could not be sure, but there, he thought, were the Pleiades, a cluster of minor stars, the seven, a circle of phosphorescence.

He stood for some time, watching. He had never imagined this star-specked stillness. Had the farm in Dingle been like this? He couldn't know, for the farm was the past; it·had existed before he was born. He knew it from his parents' memories as the place where the hens had died, where the potatoes had died. It was what his mother meant by heaven: Dingle with the hunger removed. He wondered now if it had stood under stars like this. If it had, she would naturally believe that the dead went there.

A sensation rose in him, a high tingling of his blood. There came a wave, a wind, that recognized him, that did not love him or hate him. He felt what he knew as the rising of his self, the shifting innerness that yearned and feared, that was more familiar to him than anything could ever be. He knew that an answering substance gathered around him, emanating from the trees and the stars.

He stood staring at the constellations. Walt had sent him here, to find this, and he understood. He thought he understood. This was his heaven. It was not Broadway or the horse on wheels. It was grass and silence; it was a field of stars. It was what the book told him, night after night. When he died he would leave his defective body and turn into grass. He would be here like this, forever. There was no reason to

fear it, because it was part of him. What he'd thought of as his emptiness, his absence of soul, was only a yearning for this.

At the apartment, his parents remained behind their door. Lucas
didn't venture in. He thought it would be better to let them rest. With
rest, they might yet become themselves again.

He went into his bedroom and read the book.

What do you think has become of the young and old men?
And what do you think has become of the women and children?

They are alive and well somewhere,
The smallest sprout shows there is really no death,
And if ever there was it led forward life, and does not wait at the
*   end to arrest it,*
And ceas'd the moment life appear'd.

All goes onward and outward, nothing collapses,
And to die is different from what anyone supposed, and luckier.

Lucas lay in his bed with St. Brigid above him and Emily across
the way, eating behind her curtain. He slept. If he dreamed, his
dreams were lost upon awakening.

His parents were still quiet behind their door. He decided it was
better to leave them. He couldn't help them anymore. He could help
only Catherine.

He was waiting before her building when she emerged in her blue
dress. She was not glad to see him. Her face settled into an expression
of sorrowful blankness, like the angel's in the park. She said, "Hello,
Lucas." She turned and started off in the direction of the Mannahatta
Company. He fell in alongside her.

"Catherine," he said, "you must not go to work today."

"You've used up my patience, Lucas. I have no time for you anymore."

"Come away with me. Let me take you away."

She walked on. In a fury of desperation, before he knew what he did, he took her skirt in his hand and tugged at it. "Please," he said. "Please."

"Leave me, Lucas," she said, in a voice more awful for its measured calm. "You can do nothing for me. I can do nothing for you."

He stood still and watched helplessly as she went east, to her machine. He waited until she had traveled a distance, then followed. As they neared the sewing shop, other women in the same blue dresses gathered in the street. He watched as Catherine went among them. He watched as she went through the door. He remained a while. More women in blue dresses passed him and entered the building. He imagined Catherine mounting the stairs, going to her machine. He saw her work the treadle. He knew the machine would be gladdened by her touch. He knew it had been waiting patiently through the night, singing to itself, thinking of Catherine.

She could not be allowed to remain there. She had no idea of the danger she was in. He stood helplessly before the building as the last of the women entered. He was too small and strange; he could do nothing more to intercede.

No. There was something he could do. There was one thing.

The trick would be to stop his machine before it had eaten more than his hand. He had to figure stealthily as he worked. He couldn't let the others see him in his calculations. He knew he could not put one hand under the wheel and pull the lever with his other hand. The distance was too far. But he thought that if he stretched himself forward, if he lay half upon the belt, he could pull the lever with his foot, and stop the wheel in time.

Lucas put off from moment to moment that which he had to do. It was easy, it was fatally easy, to keep on working. Even now, the waking sleep of his work life wanted him. He aligned and clamped. He pulled, pulled again, inspected. Even now he felt his resolve slipping away, and not only his resolve. His self was diminishing. He was becoming what he did. He began to think, as an hour passed, that he had dreamed of Catherine and her plight, had dreamed of everything that was not this, and was awake again, in the only world. To rouse himself, he thought of her putting stitches into blouses and shirts. He thought of the pressing machine, its rollers raised and waiting, exhaling draughts of steam.

He was ready. If he didn't do it now, he might not do it at all. He glanced around. The others were at their labor. He took a plate, dropped it on the belt. He placed it perfectly against the line. He was expert at that; he was proud of it. He put his left hand—the left would be better—along the plate's upper edge. He aligned his fingers against the edge and in so doing was calmed. This was his work. He reached over with his right hand and pulled the lever.

The belt started. He felt the movement of the rollers that turned the belt, their sure and steady rhythm. This was how the iron felt, going in. His left hand rode along with the plate. He felt graceful, like a dancer. He passed through a moment of beauty. He was partner to the iron and the machine.

His hand was conveyed along. His body was gently stretched, and stretched further. His toe slipped away from the lever. He scrambled to find it again and lost his grace. He was a foolish thing, struggling. His foot touched the lever, though he couldn't be sure it was the right one. He glanced back. He couldn't be sure. When he turned again, his fingers were going under the wheel.

He watched it happen. He saw that his hand was positioned between two teeth. His fingers slipped into the space between them. The teeth bit into the iron. His fingers went under. His knuckles went under. The drum of the wheel touched his fingertips. It was warm, warmer than he'd expected it to be. It was as warm as his mother's mouth had been when he reached in to retrieve the bit of potato. He felt it crushing his fingertips. There was no pain. There was a high pale nothingness. With its warm implacable patience the wheel crushed his knuckles. There was no pain and no blood. There was no sound but that of the machine.

Then he returned to himself. Then he saw what he did. He saw the larger body of his hand going under. He tried to pull the lever with his toe. He lost his purchase. He cried out. He didn't recognize the noise he made. He fumbled with his boot, and found the lever again. For a moment it didn't yield. And then it did. With its little clicking sigh, the wheel stopped turning.

Lucas could not remove his hand. There was still no blood. There was still no pain, but there was something. A tingling. A newness. He remained where he was, looking at his arm and his vanished hand with numb fascination.

He heard the sound of the others. Someone—it would be Tom— pulled the second lever, which reversed the wheel. Someone else, it was Dan, put his own hand over Lucas's wrist as the machine began slowly to release it. Lucas saw Dan's big hand, with its two missing fingers, receive his own.

His hand had been flattened. He thought for a moment that it was unharmed, that it was only larger. But no. Blood welled up around his fingernails. He held up his big, bleeding hand. He wanted to show it to himself and Dan. Briefly, his fingernails were outlined in red. The blood increased. It ran in streams down his fingers.

He fell. He hadn't meant to fall. One moment he was standing looking at his hand, and then he was on the floor, with the black ceiling over him. There were the pulleys and hooks. The floor smelled sharply of oil and tar.

Dan's face arrived. Tom's face arrived. Tom put his arm under Lucas's head. Who'd have imagined him capable of such tenderness?

Dan's face said, "Stay here with him." Dan's face departed.

Tom's face said, "My God." Tom's mouth was broad, its lips rough. Its teeth were the color of old ivory.

Lucas said to Tom's mouth, "Please, sir. Send for Catherine Fitzhugh, at the Mannahatta Company. Tell her I've been hurt."

In the hospital, a man stood crying. He was dressed for his work, in a butcher's apron smeared with animals' blood. His affliction was uncertain. He appeared to be whole. He stood with grave formality, as a singer might stand on a stage.

Around him were the others. They sat in what chairs there were. They sat or lay on the floor. There were men, some old and some not yet old, wounded in ways that could be seen (one bled extravagantly from a gash in his forehead, another tenderly stroked his mangled leg) and in ways that could not. There were women who sat quietly, as if whatever sickness had brought them here were as ordinary as sitting in their parlors; one of them, in a tobacco-colored kerchief, coughed demurely, a sound like paper tearing, and leaned forward now and again to spit on the floor between her feet. A man and a woman and a child huddled together on the floor, rocking and moaning as if they shared an injury among them. There was the smell of sweat and other humors mixed with ammonia, as if humanness itself had been made into medicine.

Sisters in black habits and a doctor in white—no, there were two doctors—hurried among those who waited. Sometimes a name was called, and one of the people rose and went away. The man went on standing in the room's center, crying with a low, unwavering insistence. He was the waiting room's host, as Mr. Cain was the host of Lucas's block, its wounded and inspired angel.

Lucas sat on the floor with his back against the wall. Dan stood over him. Pain was a hot, brilliant whiteness that suffused Lucas's body and bled into the air around him. Lucas held in his lap the bundle that was his hand, wrapped in rags soaked through with blood. Pain originated in his hand but filled him as fire fills a room with heat and light. He made no sound. He had gone too far away to speak or cry. Pain was in him like the book or the works. He had always been here, waiting in this room.

He leaned his shoulder against Dan's leg. Dan reached down and stroked his hair with the fingers he had left.

Lucas couldn't tell how much time had passed. Time in the waiting room was like time in his parents' bedroom and time at the works. It passed in its own way; it couldn't be measured. After a span of time had passed, Catherine came. She walked into the room in her blue dress, alive and unharmed. She stood at the entrance, searching.

Lucas's heart banged hotly against his ribs. It hurt him, as if his heart were an ember, harmless when it hung in the bell of his chest but painful when it touched bone. He said, Catherine, but couldn't be sure if he had actually spoken. He made to rise but couldn't.

She saw him. She came and knelt before him.

She said, "Are you all right?"

He nodded. Tears sprang unbidden to his eyes. He had an urge to conceal his hand from her, as if he had done something shameful; as if, seeing his hand, she would know some final secret about him.

Catherine looked up at Dan. She said, "Why is he still out here?"

"They told us to wait," Dan answered.

"We'll see about that."

Catherine rose. Lucas could hear the rustle of her dress. She went among the others, stepping around them. She stood near the crying man until a sister passed, carrying something on a tray, something that had made a red stain on the cloth that covered it. Catherine spoke to the sister. Lucas couldn't hear what she said. The sister replied and walked away.

Catherine returned. She bent over, put her face close to Lucas's. She said, "Are you in much pain?"

He shook his head. It was true and not true. He had entered pain. He had become it.

She said to Dan, "He's still bleeding."

Dan nodded. It would be foolish to deny it.

"How long have you been here?" she asked.

"I don't know," Dan said.

Catherine made her stern face. For a moment, Lucas felt as if he had come home, as if the hospital were where he lived.

A doctor, one of the doctors, came out of the door through which they took the people whose names were called. The doctor was thin (there was another who was not thin) and grave. Lucas thought briefly that the doctor was one of the men in the cages at the works, the men who scowled over papers and counted out the pay. One of them was a doctor, too. No. The doctor was someone else. Catherine went to the doctor with dispatch (she moved so quickly among the prone bodies of the ill) and spoke to him. The doctor frowned. He looked at Lucas, frowning. Lucas understood. There is always someone poorer than you. There is always someone sicker, more grievously harmed.

Catherine took the doctor's arm. They might have been lovers meeting. Catherine might have been the doctor's fiancée, taking his arm and insisting as a woman could that he accompany her on an er-

rand she knew to be necessary. Lucas wondered if she and the doctor
had met before.

The doctor frowned differently—he had a language of frowns—at
Catherine's hand on his white-sleeved elbow. But, like a lover, he
came with her. She led him among the bodies to where Lucas sat.

She said, "He's had his hand crushed at the works."

The doctor offered a new frown. He was a marvel of frowns. This
one was canted, rakish.

The doctor said, "Someone over there has had his leg half torn off.
The surgery rooms are full. We are doing all we can."

"He is a child."

"There are others here before him."

"He is a child who supports his parents, who does work much too
hard for him, and he has had his hand crushed. His brother died less
than a week ago. You must attend to him."

"We will attend to him presently."

"You must do it now."

The doctor made his face darker. He retracted his eyes, made
them smaller but brighter in his darkened face. "What did you say,
miss?"

"I beg your pardon, sir," Catherine answered. "I don't mean to be
rude. But please, please attend to this boy. As you can see, we're beside ourselves."

The doctor made a decision. It was easier, the doctor decided, to
comply. Others were here before Lucas, but they would wait, as they'd
learned to do.

"Come with me," the doctor said.

Dan helped Lucas to stand. He put his arm around Lucas's back
and helped him walk, as Lucas had helped his mother back to bed
once. When had that been? The doctor led them, though it seemed it
should be Catherine who led.

They passed through the door. It opened onto a corridor that was
full of other people. Like those in the waiting room they sat or lay
upon the floor. They left a narrow aisle through which the not sick
could pass. Lucas wondered if the hospital was like the works, if it was
room after room, each different and each the same, leading on and on

like a series of caverns until at some length they reached—what? Healing itself. A living jewel, a ball of green-gold fire.

Dan helped Lucas along the path the afflicted had left for them. They had to step over a leg and then an extended arm that was strangely colored, bluish-white, like cheese. Lucas wondered if they were going toward the final room, where the healing was kept.

The room they entered was near the end of the corridor. It was an ordinary room, though nothing here was ordinary. It was small and dingily white. There were cabinets with glass fronts, and a chair and a cot. A sister sat upon the chair, bent over a man who was on the cot. The man, about Father's age but smaller, with longer hair, muttered to the sister.

The doctor said, "All right. Let's see."

It took Lucas a moment to know that the doctor wanted to see his hand. He'd thought the doctor meant something more general, something larger, though he could not have said what it was. He proferred his hand. Blood from the soaked rags dripped onto the floor. Lucas looked at the red drops. He thought, I'm hurt.

The doctor unwrapped the bandage. He didn't seem to mind about the blood. As the rag came away, the pain changed. It gathered in Lucas's hand. It had been all over him like a sickness, but now it was here; it followed the course of the bandages as they were pulled away, like sparks that were caught in his flesh, exquisite and excruciating. Lucas whimpered, though he hadn't wanted to. It seemed as if the bandage had joined him, as if the doctor without realizing his mistake were peeling Lucas's very skin away.

Then the bandage was gone. Here was his hand, revealed. It wasn't big anymore, as it had been at the works. It was small and curled in upon itself, like a chicken's foot. It was thickly red, as if it were made of blood. It looked like something dreadful, newly born.

He glanced nervously at Catherine. Would she be repulsed?

She merely said to him, "It's all right. It's going to be all right."

The doctor put the bandage into a can on the floor. The can contained other things as well. The doctor took Lucas's mangled hand in his palm, held it with sharp but weary attention. His new frown was broad and sternly beatific.

Catherine said, "What can you do for him?"

The doctor answered, "Remove the hand. Right away."

"No," she said. She seemed to possess a power not of knowledge but of divine refusal. It seemed possible—it did not seem impossible—that Catherine could restore his hand by insisting it be restored.

"Would you rather we wait and remove the whole arm?" the doctor said.

"It can't be as bad as that."

"Where did you receive your medical training, miss?"

"It's broken," she said. "It's badly broken but only that. Can't you set it?"

"Not here."

"Elsewhere, then."

"There is no elsewhere. Not for him."

Lucas had never been talked about so, as if he were present and not present. It was like being in the works. There was something good—there was something not bad—about giving himself over.

"We'll find somewhere to take him," Catherine said.

"With what money? Do you have money?"

"Of course not."

"Let me tell you what will happen, then. You'll take him to New York Hospital or St. Vincent's. It will take time, perhaps considerable time, for you to see someone there, and that person will most likely send you back here. By the time you get back here it will be gangrenous, and we'll have to remove the arm, at the elbow if we're lucky and at the shoulder if we're not. Do you understand?"

Catherine hesitated. She looked to Dan.

Lucas became visible then. Catherine saw him.

She said, "Lucas, I think we'd better let them do it."

He nodded. He soared above all feeling save for the pain and Catherine. Lucas was strangely excited. She regarded him with such concern, such deep and abiding love.

"Can you be brave?" she asked.

He nodded again. He could be brave.

"All right, then," she said to the doctor.

"Wise girl," he answered.

"Can you get him to a bed now? Can you give him something for his pain?"

"We have no empty beds."

"Surely one can be found."

"Should I evict the woman dying in the room next to this one? Should I put out the man whose heart is failing?"

"This is monstrous."

"A surgery room will be free in an hour or two. He will have to wait here until then."

"Some medicine, then. He doesn't show his pain. He wouldn't."

"We have very little medicine."

"How can that be?"

"What we have, we must reserve for the gravest cases."

"This is a grave case."

"This is a boy about to lose his hand. When you compelled me to look at this boy, I had just left a man with a length of pipe driven through his skull. It entered here"—the doctor indicated a place above his left ear—"and came out here." He pointed to a spot just behind his right ear. "He is still alive, somehow. We have morphine for him."

Catherine hesitated. She looked around the room (where the man lay whispering on the cot under the sister's ministrations, where the jars stood behind the glass) as if she thought she might find an answer there. Finding none, she said to the doctor in a lowered voice, "Surely some provision can be made. As you can see, he is not quite right."

"Miss, this is a charity hospital. Half the people who come here are not quite right."

Catherine paused again. Lucas saw her make a decision.

She said to the doctor, "Could I speak to you privately?"

The doctor said, "Aren't we private enough here?"

She moved to the doorway, and the doctor followed. She spoke to him in a low tone. He nodded gravely.

Dan didn't speak. Lucas could feel him not speaking. The doctor listened to Catherine and produced yet another frown.

Lucas said, "The nine months' gone is in the parturition chamber, her faintness and pains are advancing."

Catherine said sharply, "Lucas, be quiet."

He strove to be quiet. He ground his teeth together.

The doctor and Catherine returned. The doctor said, "I will order him some morphine. Since you're so insistent."

"Thank you," Catherine answered.

"I finish here at five o'clock."

"I'll see you then."

The doctor said, "I'll send in one of the sisters with the morphine and fresh bandages. I'll return when the surgery room is free."

"All right," Catherine said.

The doctor left them. They were there, they three, in the room with the sister and the murmuring man.

Catherine said to Dan, "Well, then."

Dan didn't speak, though Catherine seemed to expect it. At length he said, "I must go back to the works."

"Yes," Catherine answered.

Lucas had not thought until that moment that anyone would return to his job. He'd forgotten. He'd been his hand and his pain, he'd been Catherine. But Dan must return to the works.

Lucas said to Catherine, "Will you stay with me?"

"Of course I will," she answered.

"You'll be all right," Dan told Lucas.

Lucas couldn't speak. He began to realize. He'd made an interruption and nothing more. If Dan must return to work now, Catherine would return tomorrow.

"You'll be all right," Dan said again, more slowly and distinctly, as if he were uncertain whether Lucas had heard him the first time.

Lucas said, "Which of the young men does she like best? Ah the homeliest of them is beautiful to her."

"Goodbye now."

"Goodbye," Catherine said.

Dan regarded her strangely. His face resembled Catherine's face when Lucas brought her the bowl. Something had occurred between Dan and Catherine. She had shown him the bowl she'd paid too much for. She had shown him her mangled hand. She stood defiantly, harmed and proud.

Because there was nothing to do or say, Dan left. After he had gone, Catherine said to Lucas, "You must lie down. I'm afraid it will have to be the floor."

He answered, "I will go to the bank by the wood and become undisguised and naked, I am mad for it to be in contact with me."

"Shh. Hush now. You must rest. You must rest and be quiet."

"I am satisfied—I see, dance, laugh, sing."

"Come along now," Catherine said. "You make yourself worse by raving."

She helped him to lie down on the floor. She sat on the floor herself so he could lie with his head on her lap. Here under his head were the starchy folds of her blue dress.

He said, "You will stay with me?"

"I told you I would."

"Not only today."

"For as long as I need to."

Lucas was pain and Catherine's lap. The pain was a cocoon that wrapped him like fiery bandages. In the cocoon, in Catherine's lap, it was difficult to think of anything but that. Still, he struggled. He held to himself. He had brought her here, but he'd only saved her from today. He must do something further. He could not know what.

"Catherine?" he said.

"Shh. Don't speak."

"You have to come away with me."

"Forget about that. Forget everything."

He strove not to forget. He said, "You were wrong, yesterday."

"Not another word."

"You must take the baby and go away."

"Hush. Hush."

He saw it, through the fiery cocoon. She must take the baby and go to a place like the park at night, a place of grass and silence. She must go out searching, as Walt had told Lucas to do. There were such places, not only the park. He'd seen the pictures. There were fields and mountains. There were woods and lakes. He could take her to a place like that, he thought. He would find a way to do it.

From the cot, the man murmured on.

A sister came into the room. Her black habit was alive; it had created within itself her face, which was carved from wood. She wrapped

Lucas's hand in new bandages. She produced (had it been inside her habit?) a syringe full of clear liquid. She took his other arm, the undamaged one, with the practiced calm of a boot maker nailing a sole. She put the needle in, which stung like a bee, a small pain, an interesting one, differently alive, like a tiny flame. She withdrew the needle and departed. She had not spoken at all. Because her face was carved from wood, she wasn't able to speak.

After some time, a flower blossomed in Lucas's mind. He felt it, an unfurling of petals, a transformation from bud to bloom. The pain was there still, but it was not in him anymore. The pain had left him as the spirit leaves the body of the deceased. It had made of itself a curtain, shimmering, as if curtains could be made of glass and the glass were veined with colors and tiny instances of light. The curtain hovered, fragile as glass, around Lucas and Catherine. It encircled them. Pain ran through it in capillaries of blue and green, of softest pink. Where it was most intense, pain produced watery quiverings of illumination, like light on a river. Pain surrounded them, and they were here, inside it.

Lucas didn't think he slept. He didn't think he dreamed. He was able, though, to see things he ordinarily saw in dreams. He saw that outside the pain curtain, outside the walls of the room, was the hospital, with its patiently damaged supplicants and its crying man. Outside the hospital was the city, with its houses and factories, its streets where Walt walked, marveling at everything, at smiths sweating over their forges and women strolling under feathered hats, at gulls circling in the sky like dreams the hats were having. Outside the city was the book, which invented what Walt saw and loved, because the book loved Walt and wanted to delight him. Outside the book . . . was there anything outside the book? Lucas couldn't be sure. He thought he saw a distance, an immensity that was in the book and outside it. He thought he saw fields and mountains, forests and lakes, though they were not as they appeared in the pictures. He had thought from pictures that they were flat and drab, all murky greens and limpid, shallow blues. He saw now that they were alive and brilliantly colored. There were oceans of grass, swaying. There were mountains blindingly white.

Lucas's forehead was caressed. Catherine whispered to him. He couldn't tell what she said.

Something said, Lucas, it's time.

What was it time for?

Everything changed. He stood in the room again, though it was the room as it truly was, a scrim shaped like a room, with a city around it and an ocean of grass beyond. He wondered if others knew. He wondered if the wooden nun knew, for here she was, here was the back of her, and here was Catherine's arm, helping him. He was walking, he seemed to be walking. The curtain of pain followed him, blinking and coalescing.

He was in the corridor where the waiting waited. They were bright with their own pain, suffused by it, rendered beautiful and strange, phosphorescent. As he walked among them, he knew they were his friends. He knew that the harmed, all of them, were his family, relations he had not met but knew by blood.

Then he saw Simon. Simon walked out of a door and stood in the hallway before him.

Lucas stopped. His brother was terrible to see. His face was pulp, with one dark eye staring blindly from its socket and the other vanished entirely. What remained of his hair was matted, plastered to what remained of his skull. His right arm, the one that had been taken by the clamp and pulled under the wheel, was tatters clinging to bone. The fabric of his shirt had gotten muddled up with his chest, so that fabric and flesh were one. His heart, intact, bigger than Lucas would have expected it to be, glistened between the clean lines of his yellow-white ribs.

It was Simon released, finally, from the machine and the box. It was the Simon they had not been permitted to see. How had he gotten out?

Simon said, You've brought her to me.

"Lucas, what is it?" Catherine asked.

Simon said, Thank you. I'm glad to have her here.

A sister came and took Simon's arm, the other one, the one not yet ruined. She hurried him away.

"It's all right," Catherine said. "That man has been terribly hurt. There's nothing we can do for him. Come along."

Lucas said, No. He could not be sure if he had spoken aloud.

He said, We have to leave.

Because he couldn't be sure if he spoke or didn't speak, he turned and went the other way, toward the waiting room, moving quickly among the fallen. His legs were good, they had their own intelligence. He knew Catherine would follow him. He hoped she would.

He saw himself open the door with his good hand. He saw himself move through the waiting room, past the crying man, past the mother and father who rocked and moaned with their child. (Would their names ever be called?) He saw himself go through the outer door and into the street. It was daytime. People walked, carrying parcels.

Catherine was there, behind him. She had followed. She said, "Come back. Please."

He started off down the sidewalk. Did she follow him? Yes, she did.

He saw that the red bundle of his hand was held close to his chest, near his heart, like a second heart he wore outside.

Catherine said, "Stop. Lucas, stop. You'll lose your place."

It was funny, hearing her say that. She thought he'd been waiting for a gift, some marvel he would not want to lose, when what he wanted, all he wanted, was to lead her away.

He ran on. He was sure of where he was going, where he was taking her, but couldn't name it. He knew only that it lay in this direction. He imagined it was somewhere safe, a place of trees and mountains. Trees and mountains were out there, ahead of him, ahead of Catherine, and though they lay at an unknowable distance he knew that with every stride he led her closer to them, farther away from the dead. He knew only, but he knew with utter certainty, that he must keep moving. He knew he must take her with him and couldn't do it with words or explanations. He had no language for that. He had only his body to speak with, he had only his legs.

Catherine strode after him. He was moving too fast for her. He slowed a little, so she wouldn't fall too far behind. She said, "If you don't come back, they won't take care of you."

"The press of my foot to the earth springs a hundred affections."

She called out, "Somebody stop him. Please. He's sick, he doesn't know what he's doing."

Lucas saw a man and then another man wonder if he should interfere and decide not to. There was the lump of blood at Lucas's breast. There were the troubles of others, unfathomable, and these men had troubles enough of their own.

He was near Washington Square, with Catherine following, when he heard sirens. He thought at first that they were trumpets, piercing and cacophonous. (Why would he—why would anyone—think angels would make a beautiful sound?) He thought that he, he and Catherine, were entering a promised realm, that they were being greeted by a host of . . . not angels, no. A host of spirits that were like animals, that were like ghosts, that were like Mr. Cain and the crying man, inscrutable, possessed of a language the living didn't know but would come to understand. They were not kind, but they were not cruel. Lucas knew he must go to them. He knew he must take Catherine. He knew that the trumpeters were the book and that the book was the world.

He smelled the smoke before he saw it. For a moment it seemed simply the usual smell of the air, brought to him in heightened form. But this was sharper, more acrid. Others on the street seemed to notice it, too. An ember floated by, brilliantly orange, like the little lights in the curtain of pain but far brighter. He paused, he couldn't help pausing, to watch the ember drift past.

Catherine caught up with him. She was out of breath. She said, "My God."

She walked on, hurriedly. Lucas followed her. He was glad to be the one following. He was glad that she seemed now to understand.

The Mannahatta Company was breathing fire. Licks of flame snapped like banners from its upper windows. The windows, some of them, were orange squares. Plumes of black smoke billowed up, fat and velvety.

"Oh, my God," Catherine said. Lucas stood beside her. Fire engines glowed in the street. Firemen in black coats, husbands for the nuns, sent up streams of bright water that fell short of the windows where the fire was. Lucas thought of the jewelry in the window of Gaya's Emporium, glinting among the folds of faded cloth.

He went with Catherine until a policeman told them they could go no farther. Catherine stood before him as she had stood before the doctor in the waiting room. It seemed she would summon her power of insistence. She would tell him there was not, could not be, a fire.

She said, "I work there."

"Lucky you're not there now," he answered.

Catherine reached for Lucas, held him close to her. They watched together as the flames unfurled, demonstrating their beauty, which was neither cruel nor kind. They watched the water rise in brilliant threads and fall back to the pavement as rain. They heard the sirens blare.

And now, finally, Lucas understood. It had all been for this. It had been done so that Catherine would not be at Mannahatta when the fire came. Simon had loved her; she was wrong about that. He had not married the machine, he had sacrificed himself to it, as the saints gave themselves to glory, as St. Brigid gave herself to the fiery circle of her headache. Simon had known—for he was intimate with machinery, Lucas had learned how intimate—that the sewing machines at Mannahatta adored and desired their women but were too puny to take them as the greater machines took their men. Simon had known, he had guessed (had the machine told him?) that the sewing machines were waiting to take their women in the only way they could.

And Catherine alone had been spared.

She held Lucas fast. He felt the thrum of her heart. He answered with the beat of his own, paltry and birdlike but resolute.

A woman appeared at a window, seven stories up.

The woman stood in the window, holding to its frame. Her blue skirt billowed. The square of brilliant orange made of her a blue silhouette, fragile and precise. She was like a goddess of the fire, come to her platform to tell those gathered below what the fire meant, what it wanted of them. From so far away, her face was indistinct. She turned her head to look back into the room, as if someone had called to her. She was radiant and terrifying. She listened to something the fire told her.

She jumped.

Catherine screamed. Lucas clung tightly to her. Her heart caromed in his ear.

The woman's skirt rose around her as she fell. She lifted her arms, as if to take hold of invisible hands that reached for her.

When she struck the pavement, she disappeared. She'd been a woman in midair, she'd been the flowering of her skirt, and then in an instant she was only the dress, puddled on the cobblestones, still lifting slightly at its edges as if it lived on. Policemen rushed to her.

"Oh, my lord," Catherine said. She did not speak loudly.

Lucas held her. He was sorry for the woman, but she wasn't Catherine.

Lucas whispered to her, "Did you fear some scrofula out of the unflagging pregnancy? Did you guess the celestial laws are yet to be work'd over and rectified?"

With his blood hand, Lucas touched the locket at his breast.

The air thickened. He could taste it. He could feel it in his lungs. Storms of embers rained down, danced on the pavement around the policemen and the firemen, around the vanished woman and her skirt.

Catherine began weeping. Lucas comforted her. An appalling thing was happening, but he and Catherine had a curtain around them. They were inside it. From the circle, Lucas could see, as clearly as if it had happened already, a house in the sea of grass. He could see the light it would make at night, under the sky.

A crowd had gathered. Lucas and Catherine were at its front, as close to the building as the police would allow. The people of the crowd were horrified and excited. Their faces were brightened by the fire.

Was that Walt, far off, among the others, Walt with his expression of astonished hunger for everything that could occur? Lucas could see a man with a beard who might have been Walt or might not have been. A woman stood beside him. Was it St. Brigid, gazing upward with her livid and compassionate face, her halo discreetly hidden under a brown felt hat? It looked like her.

Lucas waved. He couldn't be certain it was Walt or St. Brigid, but he waved nonetheless. His good hand held Catherine, so he had to wave with the other, the bleeding bundle. He was suddenly proud. Here is what was asked of me. Here is what I've done.

Neither Walt nor St. Brigid saw him. Walt would find him in time, though. He had found him on Broadway at his moment of need; he would surely find him again. Lucas and Catherine would go into the book, for the book was never finished. Lucas would recite it to Walt and to everyone. He would recite what Walt had not yet written, for his life and the book were one thing, and everything he did or said was part of the book.

Smoke but not smoke, that which smoke created, swirled around them all, a densifying of the air, a sharp and painful enlivening. Lucas could see it as clearly as he saw the pain curtain. The air had thickened; it seemed he could reach out with his good hand and form it into balls, like snow. It sparked with embers, demonstrating its likeness to the night sky.

The air had a taste. Lucas rolled it in his mouth. He recognized it.

The dead had entered the atmosphere. Lucas knew it as surely as he had known Simon's presence in the pillow. With every breath Lucas took the dead inside him. This was their bitter taste; this was how they lay—ashen and hot—on the tongue. Lucas went on waving to the man in the crowd. It seemed suddenly that Walt must see him, must come to him, and soon. Walt must take him to the riverbank, show him the way to the grass.

Walt didn't look at him, nor did the grieving saint. There was too much else to see. Lucas saw, as they all must, a crowd and a building blazing, a huge and mesmerizing wholeness in which a boy waved the stump of his hand.

The dead filled Lucas's mouth and lungs. Catherine wept in his embrace. He felt himself seen, as he'd been seen last night in the park, by a presence that knew him beyond his name or person, beyond the mechanism of flesh and bone that slept in a room, that had wanted a horse on wheels. He was weary; he was abruptly and profoundly weary. He thought his legs would crumble under him. He thought he would fall as the woman had fallen. He would vanish and leave only clothes behind, worried by smoke and wind.

He struggled to remain. He said, "Every atom belonging to me as good belongs to you."

The crowd cried out, as if they were one body. Above, another woman stood in a window. Her dress had caught fire. She stood like fire itself, in the shape of a woman. Lucas watched as the others did. Her dress blazed, but her head was still a woman's head. She might have been Emily or Kate or the dark-haired girl who'd said, "Won't I do instead?"

She looked down. She looked at Lucas.

He knew, though her eyes were not visible from so far away. He understood. By waving his hand, he had summoned not Walt or St. Brigid but the fire woman, the newest member of the dead. He had wanted to be seen, and he had been.

He returned her gaze. He could do nothing else. His heart raged and burned, full of its own fire. It blazed as Emily or not Emily, as Kate or the dark-haired girl, blazed in the window. She said (though she did not speak in words), We are this now. We were weary and put-upon, we lived in tiny rooms, we ate candy in secret, but now we are radiant and glorious. We are no longer anyone. We are part of something vaster and more marvelous than the living can imagine.

She said, God is a holy machine that loves us so fiercely, so perfectly, he devours us, all of us. It is what we're here for, to be loved and eaten.

Lucas heard the woman's words, and he heard Catherine's heart at his ear. He understood. He and Simon had done their work. They'd outwitted the machine God. They'd given more life to Catherine; they'd given her a future. He saw her tickling her baby with a leaf of grass. He saw her and the child going on as citizens in the world of the not dead. He himself was meant for other things. He was meant, had always been meant, for this.

The fire woman spread her wings and flew.

Catherine screamed. She and the crowd made a single sound. The fire woman shrieked toward the earth, trailing ribbons of flame. Lucas pressed closer to Catherine's heart. His own heart, joining hers, swelled in his chest, grew bigger and bigger. He knew then that he was one of the dead and always had been. He felt his heart burst, like a peach breaking through its skin. He faltered, though he hadn't meant to. The pavement grew larger. Catherine caught him. She held him against one knee. Half prone, held by Catherine, he looked up.

He saw the woman cross the sky. He saw above her, above the smoke and the sky, a glittering horse made of stars. He saw Catherine's face, pained and inspired. She spoke his name. He knew that his heart had stopped. He wanted to say, I am large, I contain multitudes. I am in the grass under your feet. He made as if to speak but did not speak. In the sky, the great celestial horse turned its enormous head. An unspeakable beauty announced itself.

THE
CHILDREN'S
CRUSADE

She had missed it. Nobody blamed her, but she shouldn't have missed it. She was supposedly one of the magic few, one of the ones who could hear the *ping* of true intention, like a distant hammer driving home a nail, no matter how florid the caller, no matter how unlikely the threat. But she had missed it. When the call came she'd thought: white kid, somewhere between an old twelve and a young fifteen, standard cybergeek sitting in a smelly boy-room that no force on earth could make him clean, surrounded by Big Gulp cups and remote controls; pale, ferretlike underling who lacked inflection of voice or body, who looked grubby even on the rare occasions when he was clean, who had one or two friends exactly like him and spoke to no one else, just his family because it was unavoidable and his tiny band of fellow Igors, with whom he shared a private language and a vocabulary of creepy passions and a proclivity for spending as much time as humanly possible in dim suburban bedrooms that glowed with furtive computer light and smelled of feet and sweaty wool and old cum.

This kid, in various incarnations, was a regular feature of life in the deterrence unit. They were a breed—sad little pockmarked desperadoes half-mad with hormones and loneliness, sitting out there with their dicks in one grimy hand and their cell phones in the other. Nothing about the call had been notably different, none of the danger signs was there. Or so she'd thought. She only half remembered it, at best. No specifics of target or weaponry, just that adolescent-voiced vow to take out an average citizen, because people were, well—*what's wrong with people, tell me*—fucking up the world, destroying it—*you thinking of anyone in particular, someone specific you want to take out?*—doesn't matter, does it, we're all the same—*not to us, we're not*—I meant it doesn't matter to the world, it doesn't matter in geological time—*who are you mad at, I think you're mad at someone, am I right?*—no you don't get it I'm not mad at anyone I'm just going to blow somebody up and I thought I should tell someone.

Click.

Cat had blue-tagged it, sent it down the funnel. Then, three days later, she'd heard that *ping* in the back of her mind when the report came in. Explosion on Broadway and Cortlandt, right by Ground Zero, at least one splattered, two likelies, maybe more. She had by then talked to dozens more potentials, among them a guy who said he was posing as a gay man and going to gay bars to slip poison into other men's drinks, thus helping to eliminate a few of the people who were sucking the sap from the Tree of Life. She'd talked to an elderly male Hispanic who was going to machete the staff of the public library, main branch, unless they tracked down whoever had been writing insults about him in the pages of the books.

She'd started making lists again. She'd been trying to kick the habit. But after the man who was going to dice the librarians hung up, there it was, right in front of her, in Sharpie on a Post-it:

Harm is in the books
Kill the harmless
New broom?

It wasn't crazy. These were her notes. A psychologist took notes. Still, hers could run a little loose. She'd crumpled the Post-it and thrown it away. Given the current climate, she didn't like the idea of somebody finding those particular words in her handwriting. And okay, she didn't like the fact that she hadn't fully realized she was doing it.

Maybe Simon needed to take her away for a few days. Maybe a dose of beach and room service, a dose of pure, undivided Simon, would help her feel less edgy. She'd toss his BlackBerry into the surf, if it came to that. She'd drown it in her piña colada.

When the news arrived, Cat heard the *ping* but couldn't quite re-member the call. It came to her with the particulars, which rolled in an hour-plus after the incident. Two splatters, not just one, and bar-ring further developments it seemed that the vaporized one had been rigged with explosives. The other had been identified as Dick Harte, real-estate developer, part of the World Trade rebuild, whose third left-hand finger, wearing a wedding band, had been found on a WALK–DON'T WALK box.

Right. Going to blow somebody up, thought I should tell you. Jesus.

Cat retrieved her report, notified Pete Ashberry. If this kid was the one, she had missed it.

She declined Pete's offer to go home early. She sat out the remain-der of the day, waiting to hear whether they'd picked up any more fragments from the site. She talked to a man who was going to fire-bomb a Starbucks (no specifics of location) because they insisted on hiring nigger whores. (She dutifully declined to mention the shade of her own skin but did put a hex on the fucker, telepathically.) She talked to another man, Slavic accent, who was going to kill the deputy mayor (why the *deputy* mayor?) because, as far as she could tell before he hung up, it just seemed like an interesting thing to do.

She kept all her pens in her drawer, off the desktop. It was a little like quitting smoking.

Pete came to her cubicle at five minutes to five. He was as big as a file cabinet and about that exciting. But he was a decent man; he wore his troubles bravely. His wife was going blind. His daughter had mar-ried some ecocultist who'd dragged her to Costa Rica to live in a tree.

"Now what?" Cat said. She was in no mood. She should sweeten up—she had after all quite possibly *missed it*—but if she went all nice and apologetic now, if she started acting like someone who needed forgiveness, she might never get back to herself. Screw them if they wanted her meek.

Pete stood in the opening (you couldn't call it a doorway; it was just the point at which Cat's four-feet-by-five-feet bled into the greater fluorescence) with his mouth settled. Pete was the only brother in de-terrence. His skin was varnished mahogany, his hair an incongruously beautiful silver-gray. When he was stern and focused, you could put a can under his upper lip and push his nose to start the opener function.

"They got a left forearm," he said. "They got half a sneaker, with half a foot inside. It's a kid."

"Jesus."

"You ready for this? Kid walked up to this guy, hugged him, and self-detonated."

"*Hugged* him?"

"Witness says so. White kid, wearing a baseball jacket, very regular-looking. This is from both our reliables. It's only the one who says he saw the clinch."

"Fuck me."

"Fuck everybody."

"Who does Dick Harte turn out to be?" she asked.

"Speculator. Not Don Trump, but big. One of the people who make the high-rises rise."

"Funny business?"

"Nothing yet. Lived in Great Neck with wife number two. Some kids, some pets. You know."

"Think he knew the boy?"

"Hope so."

Everyone would hope so. Everyone would be saying a silent prayer right now, to the effect that the kid had been Dick Harte's illegitimate son, or that they'd been having sex in a park in Great Neck, or whatever. Just don't let it be random.

"Shit."

Pete said, "We don't know it was your caller."

"I have a feeling, though."

"Yeah, well, I do, too. Want to hear the tape with me?"

"Nothing would please me more."

She went with Pete down the corridor to the audio room. Pete stopped en route in the lunchroom for a cup of late-day, bottom-of-the-pot coffee sludge, with four Equals. Cat graciously declined. She and Pete went into the audio room, which was in her opinion the least unpleasant place on the premises. It was ten degrees cooler and not quite as relentlessly lit. They sat in the synthetic-plush gray chairs. Aaron had cued the tape for them. Pete punched the button.

Hello. This is Cat Martin. Like everybody, she hated hearing her own voice on tape. Inside her skull it didn't sound so flat, so harsh. To herself she sounded muscular and musical, smoky, a little like a young Nina Simone.

Hello? There it was again, that throaty boy voice, utterly unexceptional. Nervous, a little squawky, probably thirteen. *Are you a police-woman?*

And your name is?

I called the police, and they patched me over to you.

What can I do for you?

Nothing. You can't do anything for *me.*

His poor mother must have been hearing those words ever since puberty turned her sweet little boy sullen and strange and fetid. Had some mother out there started wondering yet?

Why are you calling, then?

I want to tell you something.

What do you want to tell me?

Silence. She could picture him all over again, desperate little wanker with a room full of slasher-movie posters, summoning his courage. Nothing out of the ordinary, nothing at all.

I'm going to blow somebody up.

Who?

I can't tell you.

Why do you think you can't tell me?

People have got to be stopped.

Why do you think that?

We've got to start over.

You're thinking of stopping someone in particular?

It doesn't matter who.

It does matter. Why do you think it doesn't?

I mean, it doesn't matter to the company.

What company?

The one we all work for.

Who do you work for?

You work for it, too.

Is the company telling you to hurt somebody?

You think I'm crazy, don't you?

I think you're angry.

Please don't talk to me the way you talk to crazy people. I mean, one person doesn't matter. The numbers don't crunch in single digits.

You want to hurt somebody who's hurting you. Is that right?

I can't talk to you.

Yes, you can. Tell me your name.

I'm in the family. We gave up our names.

Everybody has a name.

I just wanted someone to know. I thought it would be better.

Better for who?

I wasn't supposed to call.

Shit. There it was.

You can work this out without hurting anybody. Tell me your name.

I'm nobody. I'm already dead.

Click.

She had in fact messed up, then. The moment a caller referred to anyone else, it was an automatic red tag. Any caller who claimed to be receiving instructions from a friend, from Jesus, from the dog next door or the radio transmissions that came through the fillings in his teeth, got promoted to the next level of seriousness. This one had been vague enough—he wasn't *supposed* to call anyone—but still. She should have kept him talking, shouldn't have pressed quite so hard for his name.

Had she been making a list? Probably. Had she paid more attention to her list than she had to the caller? Hoped not.

" 'I'm in the family,' " she said. " 'We gave up our names.' What's that about?"

"Your guess is as good as mine."

"Is there a rock band with lyrics like that?"

"We're checking."

"Good."

"The family. What family?"

"The Brady Bunch. The Mafia. IBM. You know."

Right. She'd had one just the other day. Mild-voiced citizen who'd said he was going to start driving around the country and running down illegal immigrants, under orders from Katie Couric. They tended to like the idea of working for celebrities or international corporations.

"I do," Cat said. "I do know."

Pete said, "You shoulda red-tagged it." He wasn't nasty about it. Simple statement of fact. These things happened.

"You checked the trace?" she asked.

"Pay phone. Corner of Bowery and Second Street."

"Ugh."

"Bound to happen, sooner or later." He slurped his coffee.

"I didn't think it would happen to me."

"Go home. Tell your boyfriend to make you a drink and take you someplace nice for dinner."

"Think he was really as young as he sounded?"

"That I couldn't tell you. Wait for forensics."

"How would a kid get a bomb?"

"I'd say where they get all their deadly weapons. From his parents."

"Pete."

"Yeah?"

"Nothing. I'll see you tomorrow."

"Right. Have a few drinks, get some sleep. Feel better."

She went back to her cubicle, retrieved her bag. Ed Short, who had the next shift, wouldn't arrive for another half hour, but the lines were covered; she could slip away a little bit early. She hated to admit it, but now, having heard the tape, she wanted to get out of there as fast as humanly possible.

She said a few quick good-nights to coworkers who were busy at their own phones and didn't seem to notice that she was leaving before her shift was over. She clipped on down the hall. Although she didn't like to dwell on it, the division's offices might have been designed for maximum grimness. Could the cubicle dividers be the color of a three-day-old corpse? Sure. Could greenish light buzz down on everyone from milky plastic ceiling panels? Absolutely. Could the smell of burnt coffee be blown through the air-conditioning ducts? No problem.

She went down to the lobby and out through security. The evening sky over Broadway was mockingly beautiful, astral winds herding a flock of wispy pink clouds across a field of searing lavender. It was lucky, them having to locate the deterrence unit up here. Lucky that there hadn't been room down on Center Street, where it was all cops and lawyers and secretaries; where the food came from pushcarts or Chinese takeout cartons and the stores sold cheap, gaudy party wear meant to appeal to buyers so unhappy they were ready to blow a tenth of their paychecks on a sequined synthetic sweater or a pair of fake alligator pumps just to have something to show for it all. The corner of Broadway and Prince was something else. Here, what they sold was meant for actual children, fancy sneakers and jeans with more pockets and zippers than anyone conceivably needed, and T-shirts emblazoned with anarchic messages or the faces of fallen heroes, Che and Jimi and the Grateful Dead.

She glanced downtown, in the direction of the incident. It would still be cordoned off; they'd still be combing the pavement. Even now, it was impossible not to be struck by the emptiness where the towers had stood. Woolly little clouds drifted along, and a pale sliver of moon had risen, visible now with the towers gone.

That same moon would be rising over countless little towns out there, all those tree-studded, lawn-bright expanses where the citizens tended to keep their murders confined to their hearts; where the cops dozed their way through teenage crimes and the occasional domestic disturbance; where they had no need of specialists to divine the actual intentions of professed bombers, poisoners, Uzi-owning defenders of racial purity, and machete-wielding grandfathers.

And where, of course, there was no place at all for someone like Cat. Where she'd expire discreetly of loneliness and strangeness, where she'd probably become an ever-more-frequent presence on one of the bar stools at the local steak house, trying to keep her voice down, arranging her swizzle sticks in neat rows in front of her, struggling not to make lists on the cocktail napkins.

She walked up to Bond Street, turned east. The people on the streets were going about their regular business, but there was a charge in the air. Everyone was spooked by the news. The guy in front of Cat with the attaché case strode along with his shoulders hunched, as if he expected a blow from above. The three Asian girls who paused at a shop window, looked at the shoes, looked at one another, and moved right along—were they thinking of being showered with broken glass? The danger that had infected the air for the last few years was stirred up now; people could smell it. Today they'd been reminded, *we'd* been reminded, of something much of the rest of the world had known for centuries—that you could easily, at any moment, make your fatal mistake. That we all humped along unharmed because no one had decided to kill us that day. That we could not know, as we hurried about our business, whether we were escaping the conflagration or rushing into it.

Cat went down Bond, past the stratospherically expensive Japanese restaurant, past the jinxed store where another optimist had put up signs announcing the imminent appearance of another boutique that would be gone in six months or so. She crossed Lafayette and went up to Fifth Street, her block, her home, what she had come to call her home, though when she'd moved there seven years ago it had been temporary, just a few dim, affordable rooms, postdivorce, until she started her real life in her real apartment. Funny how in only seven years it had metamorphosed from fallback to treasure, how people couldn't *believe* she'd wangled her way into a rent-controlled, light-less third-floor walk-up on a block where crackheads didn't piss in your vestibule every single night. It all kept shifting under your feet, didn't it? Maybe future generations would prize those spangled Orlon sweaters from Nassau Street. Maybe things would fall so far that a pair of cardboard imitation-alligator shoes made in Taiwan would look like artifacts of a golden age.

She passed among the unnerved denizens of Fifth Street. The two Lithuanian women were out on the sidewalk in their folding aluminum lawn chairs, as always, but instead of watching the passersby with their usual regal weariness, they leaned into each other, talking animatedly in their language, shaking their heads. The punk couple with sunburst haircuts stomped along with particular fury—*so, people, you're fucking surprised that it's all blowing up in your goddamned fucking faces?* Only the old homeless man, at his post in front of the flower shop, looked unaffected, chanting his inaudible chants, the hired mourner of the neighborhood, its own singer for the dead.

Cat let herself into her apartment. For a moment she imagined it as the boys of the bomb squad would find it if *she'd* been blown up on the corner of Broadway and Cortlandt. Not so good. Admit it: it was the apartment of somebody who'd let things slide. There were clothes and shoes strewn around; there were dishes in the sink. The books that had long ago overflowed the bookcase (yes, boards and cinder blocks; she'd meant to replace it) were stacked everywhere. Were there spots of mold floating in the coffee cup she'd set on the book pile on one side of the sofa? Sure there were. If you ran a finger along a windowsill, would it come up coated with velvety, vaguely oily dust? You bet it would. It could have been the apartment of a slightly messier-than-usual graduate student. The oatmeal-colored sofa with the broken spring—Lucy had given it to her until she got something better. That had been seven years ago.

Fuck it. She was busy. She was beat. Cleanliness was a virtue but not a sexy one.

She checked her voice mail. Simon was the first message.

Hey, you know anything about the explosion? Call me.

She called Titan. Amelia, Simon's secretary, put her straight through.

"Cat?"

"Hi."

"What's going on? What do you know about this thing?"

"I think I talked to him. The bomber."

"You're kidding."

"Three days ago. We're not sure yet, but I think I talked to him."

"You talked to him. He called you."

"It's my job, baby. I'm the one they call."

"Where are you?"

"Home."

"Do you want some dinner?"

"I guess. I'm honestly not sure."

"I'm going to buy you a drink and some dinner."

"That'd be so nice."

"Where do you want to go?"

"Someplace unchallenging. You pick."

"Right. How about Le Blanc?"

"Great. Perfect."

"Half an hour?"

"Half an hour."

He hung up. While they were talking, Cat had done it again. Picked up a pen and written in her spiral notebook:

Fortress of solitude?

Does dirt = filth?

Where's the little house?

She tore out the page, crumpled it, and tossed it away. When had regular note-taking turned into . . . whatever this was? Free association. Had it started after 9/11? She hoped so. Cause and effect were always comforting.

She got to Le Blanc in exactly half an hour. She was the first to arrive, as she'd expected. Simon could never just put down the phone and walk away, not even in an emergency. He lived in an ongoing state of emergency. He traded futures. (Yes, he had explained it all to her, and, no, she still didn't understand what exactly it was that he did.) Fortunes flicked across his computer screen, falling and rising and falling again. He was the man behind the curtain. If he failed to take care of business, Oz might dissolve in an emerald mist. He'd be there as soon as he could.

Cat herself could not overcome her habit of punctuality. She'd tried. It wasn't in her to be late for anything, ever.

A place like Le Blanc was Simon's idea of unchallenging because it wasn't cool anymore. Three years ago it had been a Laundromat, just a dingy hole on Mott Street, and then somebody cleaned the hundred-year-old tile walls, put up yellowed mirrors, installed a zinc-topped bar, and *poof*, it was a perfect Parisian bistro. For a while it was an epicenter, then it faded. Regular people could get in now. At a front table sat a couple who were clearly not from the neighborhood. He was all gold jewelry; she'd draped her faux Versace over the back of her chair. Moscow-*riche*. A year ago, they'd have been stopped at the threshold. Cat's idea of unchallenging was more like . . . well, okay, an entirely unchallenging restaurant was not coming immediately to mind.

She passed through a moment with the hostess, a new girl, mega-smiley in her confusion over what exactly to do with a black woman who'd arrived alone. Before the girl could speak, Cat said, "I'm meeting Simon Dryden. I believe we have a reservation."

The girl consulted her list. "Why, yes," she said. "Mr. Dryden isn't here yet."

"Let's get me seated then, shall we?"

The queenly bearing and the schoolmarm diction, the smiling ultraformality. You did what you had to do.

"Absolutely," the hostess chimed, and led Cat to the second booth.

As Cat settled in, she locked eyes with Fred. Fred was one of the legion of New York actors who impersonated waiters while they hoped things would break for them. He wasn't young anymore, though. He was becoming what he'd once pretended to be: a wisecracking waiter, brusque and charmingly irreverent, knowledgeable about wines.

"Hello, Fred," Cat said.

"Hey," said Fred. Perfectly cordial, but glassy somehow. Caught up short. For Cat, sans Simon, he had no banter strategy.

"How are you?"

"Good. I'm good. Can I get you a drink?"

Funny how hard it could be, sitting alone in a restaurant. Funny to be someone who could calmly talk to psychopaths but had trouble being an unescorted woman who made a waiter uncomfortable.

She had Fred bring her a Ketel One on the rocks. She looked at the menu.

Cattle fed on bonemeal?

Slaughter of the innocents?

Poison in the walls?

Well, now. Apparently, at moments of stress, she didn't need to write them down anymore.

She was on her second vodka when Simon arrived. It still shocked her sometimes, seeing him in public. He was so unassailably young and fit. He was a Jaguar, he was a goddamned parade float rolling along, demonstrating to ordinary citizens that a gaudier, grander world—a world of potently serene, self-contained beauty—appeared occasionally amid the squalor of ongoing business; that behind the blank, gray face of things there existed an inner realm of wealth and ease, of urbane celebration. She watched the hostess check him out. She watched him stride with the confidence of a brigadier general to her table, stunning in his midnight-blue suit. It might as well have been spangled with tiny stars and planets.

He kissed her on the lips. Yes, people, I'm his date. I'm his *girl-friend*, okay?

"Sorry I'm late," he said.

"You're fine. Is it crazy at work?"

"*You're* asking *me*?" Simon frowned compassionately. His brows bristled like a pair of chocolate-colored caterpillars. Cat had an urge to stroke them.

"Crazy is a relative concept," she said.

"Mm," he said. "So, you think you talked to this guy."

Simon was going to be stern and unhysterical, even a little casual in this, his first secondhand crisis. He was going to be someone who could manage the news of a random bomber with the same grave suavity she knew he must bring to his business deals.

"Let's get you a drink, and I'll tell you about it," Cat said.

He sat down across from her. Fred came right away.

"Hey, Fred," Simon said. He'd been a regular since the restaurant's glory days, was adored for continuing to come.

"Hey, homeboy," Fred answered, fluent in manspeak.

"Heard the news?" Simon asked.

"Scary."

"You know Cat, right?"

"Absolutely. Hey, Cat."

"Cat's with the police department. She's working on this one."

I live in a world of danger, Fred. I'm deeper inside of things than you can possibly know.

"You're kidding," Fred said. Cat watched him go through an intricate reassessment. All right, she had a real job and quite possibly an interesting one. But bottom line, didn't this make her one of those grim black women, the sticklers for protocol who torture the populace from behind civic counters and post-office windows?

"Not at liberty to discuss it," Cat said.

"Right, right." Fred nodded sagely. He was up to the challenge of playing a waiter who could be trusted with a little inside information. He was more than up to it.

Cat said, "Simon, why don't you order yourself a drink?"

Simon paused, then said, "Right. Just a glass of wine, I think. Like maybe a Shiraz?"

"The Chilean or the Sonoma?" Fred asked.

"You pick."

"Chilean."

"Good."

Fred nodded again, in Cat's direction. *Undercover waiter. Good in a crisis.* He went off to get the wine.

What was it with men? Why were they so eager to impersonate someone brave and competent and in the know?

"Simon, baby," Cat said, "you can't say things like that. Not to waiters."

"Got you. Sorry."

"You can't be showing me off to people. Besides, I'm not Foxy Brown. I'm just a grunt, really."

"It's because I'm proud of you."

"I know."

"So. What happened?"

"A kid called in with a bomb threat. That's all."

"And you think it's this kid who blew the guy up?"

"Possibly."

"The kid must have known the guy, right?"

She hesitated. She had to give him *something*, didn't she? He was her boyfriend. And—admit it—this was part of what she had to offer him.

"It would seem that way. My guess is, it's a sex thing. Odds are we'll get a missing report from somewhere in the vicinity of Dick Harte's neighborhood, and we'll find that he'd been blowing the perpetrator in the backseat of his BMW."

Cat knew the word "perpetrator" would be exciting to Simon. She'd promised herself to stop acting extra coplike to turn him on. Screwed that one up.

"Right," Simon said. His brows bristled. It would have been nice to peel them gently off his face, hold them in her palm, then put them carefully back again.

"What do you want to eat?" she asked.

"I don't know. The tuna, I guess."

Simon was Atkins. High protein, no carbs. And really, consider the results.

"I'm going to have the steak au poivre," she said. "And mashed potatoes."

Momma's had a very hard day. All right?

They went back to her place that night, and never mind about the mess. She was rattled—she realized how much she wanted her own bed. Simon didn't mind her crappy apartment every now and then. He claimed to like it, actually. Although she'd never come out and asked him, it was likely that until he met her he'd never *been* to East Fifth Street.

She woke up at 3:30. She didn't have to look at the clock. She knew this abrupt and arid consciousness, this jump from deep dreams to a wakefulness that was not so much having slept enough as having suddenly lost the knack for sleep. On the nights it happened, it always happened between 3:30 and 4:00. She had a little something for it in the medicine cabinet, but she'd never even opened the bottle. She seemed to prefer insomnia to simulated sleep. Control thing. Fucked up, really, but what could she do?

Simon breathed steadily beside her. She let herself stare at him as he grimaced over a dream. He was a true classic. Big, broad anchorman face, vigorous thatch of sable-colored hair beginning to be threaded, here and there, with strands of sterling silver. He could have been fresh off the assembly line of whatever corporation produced the Great American Beauties. The corporation would be somewhere in the Midwest, wouldn't it? And yes, he came from Iowa, didn't he? Great-great-grandson of immigrants who'd escaped New York for the prairie, he'd returned in triumph a hundred or so years later, the exiled prince restored to his true home by way of the Ivy League.

Rich and healthy, thirty-three years old. Practically adolescent, in man-years.

Maybe it was time to quit the unit, though if she did it now it would look like she was running away. In fact, she'd been thinking of quitting for some time. You got a little crazy, working the nuts. You listened to every lunatic with the same patience; you reminded yourself over and over that any one of these people might really and truly be about to torch a grade school or blow up a store or kill somebody just because he was well-known. Bartenders must start seeing a world full of drunks; lawyers must see it as largely made up of the vengefully injured. Forensic psychologists got infected by paranoia. You knew, better than the average citizen, that the world contains a subworld, where the residents do as most people do, pay rent and buy groceries, but have a little something extra going on. They receive personal messages from their television sets or are raped nightly by a sitcom star or have discovered that the cracks on the sidewalk between Broadway and Lafayette spell out the names of the aliens who are posing as world leaders.

The most surprising thing about these people, as it turned out, was their dullness. All their human juices flowed in one direction; they cared about nothing, really, beyond their fixations. Anyone's sweet old aunt in Baltimore was more vital and various, even if her life was only watching television and clipping discount coupons out of magazines. You sat in your crummy police department office—which resembled nothing so much as a failing mail-order business—and listened to them. You logged them in on your five-year-old computer. You hoped none of them would follow through. You hoped, on your worst days (no one liked to talk about this), that one of them would.

She got out of bed, careful not to wake Simon, and went to the window. It wasn't much of a view, just three floors down onto Fifth Street, but still. Here was a slice of the city; here was the old homeless man, still chanting in front of the florist's (he was out later than usual tonight); here were the orange streetlights and the brown housefronts, the dark-clad pedestrians, the whole smoky, sepia-stained semireality of it, this city at night, the most convincing stage set ever devised, no ocean or mountains, hardly any trees (not, at least, in this neighborhood), just street after street, bright and noisy under a pink-gray sky pierced by antennas and water tanks, while down below, across the street from Cat's building, a flame-blue sign buzzed CLEANER.

In the morning she made coffee, brought Simon a cup while he was still in the shower, got to spend a moment watching him through the clouded glass, the vague pink of his back and legs, the paler pink of his ass. Was a man ever sexier than when he was taking a shower? Still, this business of sneaking looks at Simon as he slept or showered wasn't such a good sign, was it? Did he do the same with her? She couldn't picture it. She set his coffee mug on the back of the toilet tank, wiped steam from the mirror over the sink, took a look. Not bad for thirty-eight. Firm chin, good skin.

Backless dresses, how much longer?

The melting ice cap of sleep

It's a pig's heart you hold in your hand

Simon emerged, brightened and water-beaded, kissed her, picked up his coffee. He said, "Work's not going to be any fun today, is it?"

"Probably not."

He grabbed a towel, dried off. The towels hadn't been washed in, what, two weeks or more. Time flew.

"Call me. Let me know what's going on."

"I will."

"I've got that damned client thing tonight. I can be done by around ten."

"Great."

She lingered another moment, sipping her own coffee, though it was time to let him have the tiny bathroom to himself. Simon was so heedlessly alive, so unquestioningly glad about it. He traded futures. He'd been president of his senior class. He filled the room with his heat and his soapy smell.

When her son died Cat had thought she was dead, too; she'd thought her systems would shut down all by themselves, but here she was, nine years later, not only still alive but looking pretty good, well educated (too bad the private practice hadn't taken off), free of her poor tortured ex-husband (though he did creep into her fantasies), still capable of attracting someone like Simon.

She wished she hated herself more for wanting to live on.

She took a last deep draught of Simon's shower smell, went into the bedroom to find something to wear.

Mornings were good. (*Mornings are good, enjoy them.*) She liked the fact that all over the city, people were having their coffee and showers, deciding on their clothes. This was as close as it got to collective innocence, this mass transition from sleep (however troubled) to wakefulness (however tormented). Just about everyone, or everyone who was at least minimally functional, had to get up and get dressed. Even the ones who were going to call her and tell her about their plans to shoot or stab or ignite somebody. Even the ones who were going to strap a bomb to their chests and blow up a businessman on the street. Here we are, all of us, going through this daily miniature rebirth, and doing it together.

She passed over the Maori-print dress she'd been thinking of in favor of the dark Earl jeans. The jeans and the black crewneck sweater, the low-heeled black boots. She would not try to intimidate or seduce. Not by way of costume, anyway.

She didn't wait around for Simon. It was, if anything, a day to show up at work on the early side. She kissed him goodbye while he was still in his underwear and socks (was there anything as touchingly *unsexy* as a man in black socks and no pants?), gratefully accepted his assurance that he'd wind up the client thing by ten and they'd decide then about where to eat, which apartment to sleep in.

She descended the garbagey stairs, went out into the morning, a spanking-fresh June one, all spangly on the fire escapes. She paused for a moment on the stoop, taking it in. On a morning like this, you could believe the world was safe and promising. You could imagine that nothing harmful, nothing toxic, could flourish. Not when early light slanted down so purely from an ice-blue sky. Not when the window-box geraniums of the first-floor widow were incandescently red and a passing truck said PARTY PLANNERS in glittering gold letters.

Someone was watching her. Right now. She felt it. Any woman could; it was survival coding. She glanced around. In this neighbor-

hood a woman out alone, even in daylight, was by general accord offering herself up for public entertainment. She had to admit it: lately
her fury had gone a little soft at the edges. They wouldn't keep annoy-
ing her forever. One day the moans and coyote whistles, the *Hey, sexy
mommas*, would cease. Which would be a relief. She'd be just another
middle-aged black lady, going unremarked about her unremarkable
business. Still, all right, admit it: right now, this morning, here on her
front stoop, having left her younger boyfriend upstairs, she felt herself
being scrutinized, and she looked for the offending party with a certain angry eagerness, like a princess who'd found her prince but was
still being pestered by the enchanted frog with the golden ball. *Hey,
frog, I'm off the market now, go croak under somebody else's window.*
She wasn't interested, but still, in some crevice of her mind, some
dark and foolish fold, she dreaded the day the frog gave up and
hopped off to moon over someone else.

No one was there. No, people were always there. No one was looking at her. There were the besuited eagers on their way to work, a couple of NYU students off to early classes, an old man lumbering along
with bags of empty, chiming bottles dangling from both palsied hands.

Still, the feeling was palpable. Someone was staring at her, right
now.

She hit the sidewalk, headed west. Get over yourself. You're just
feeling your own version of the same edginess that's infecting everybody this morning as hatred once again demonstrates its capacity to
find us wherever we are and suck us into the next dimension.

She got to her cubicle a full half hour before she needed to. Ed Short
was still there, finishing up the graveyard shift.

"Morning, Ed," she said.

"Good morning. You're in early."

"I am."

Ed sipped at what was probably his fifteenth cup of coffee. His eyes
were bright and watery. His sparrow-colored hair, already thinning,
stood out from his head with a certain doomed desperation, the way a
fire flares just before it goes out. Ed was, what, thirty-two, thirty-three?

He was made for the job: young and more than a little bit mean, untroubled by imagination, incapable of boredom, eager to root out the bad guys and hurl them into the abyss. He'd have red-tagged the kid if he'd been on the phone that day. Ed red-tagged almost everything. People complained—red tags meant more work, of course, plus they cost money, and the whole err-on-the-side-of-caution policy had its implied limits. But Ed was just the sort of pain in the ass who got to be a department head. When the Eds of the world were right, when they appeared to have made a good call because they called almost everything, the fact that they'd spent years irritating everyone around them didn't matter. They were heroes. They'd saved the day. It was impossible to imagine how many historical figures, how many great men (and women, there was the occasional woman), were people like Ed, people who never got distracted, whose faith never wavered, who would stay by their phones or in their laboratories or at their easels until finally, finally, something happened, while most of the rest of the population tended, over time, to think of other things, to wonder what it would be like to live in the country, to speculate over the possibility that doing a simple job and raising a couple of kids might actually be enough.

What lives in empty rooms?

How far does the light reach?

Are there teeth in the wood?

Cat asked, "What's come in from the site?"

"Kid was rigged with a pipe bomb. No nails or anything, it wasn't meant to scatter. Just to incinerate everything within five or six feet."

"You can learn how to make something like that off the Internet."

"Yep. Half of Dick Harte's scalp turned up on a window ledge three stories up. Otherwise it's just some bone fragments and one more tooth."

"Why don't you go home early?" she said. "I'm ready to take over."

"Thanks. I'm fine. You just relax for a little while."

Right. Today she was someone who should relax for a little while.

She went into the lounge, poured herself some coffee—it was drinkable until about 10:00 a.m.—and pulled the papers out of her bag.

Thirty-six-point type in the *Times*, above the fold, but only eight points larger than a headline about an experimental new weapon that could render a country uninhabitable without killing its citizens or destroying its structures. EXPLOSION IN LOWER MANHATTAN. Subhead: Two Killed, Five Injured in Possible Terrorist Attack. Bless all those guys at the *Times*, our good fathers, trying to tell us what we need to know (what they think we need to know) without unduly exploiting our collective desires to be titillated, to be reassured, to be scared shitless. Easy to picture the men (and women, there might be a woman or two) up there in Midtown, agonizing over how much panic they should or should not inspire, pending further details. The *Post* and the *News*, of course, were not similarly concerned. MAD BOMBER AT GROUND ZERO in the *News*, TERROR STRIKES AGAIN in the *Post*.

The gist of all three stories was essentially the same; only the tone varied. Unidentified bomber kills self and one Dick Harte, real-estate magnate. Nothing yet about the bomber being a kid—the guys downtown had somehow managed to keep the witnesses sequestered for the moment. Obvious comparisons to what Hamas and the rest did in Israel. The *Post* reporter had fabricated something about the bomber shouting "Allah is great"—either found some lunatic who claimed to be a witness or made it up entirely—but otherwise nothing appalling, beyond, of course, the event itself. All three had patched together what they could about Dick Harte, though his wife and kids weren't talking. There were pictures: a scrupulously regular-looking guy, fifty-three years old, with that strange babylike blankness certain men could take on when they went bald, when that big dome of forehead made their features look smaller and more innocent. CEO of the Calamus Development Corporation. Wife Lucretia (*Lucretia?*) was a decorator based in Great Neck, where they did in fact live. Daughter Cynthia was a senior in public school, son Carl a sophomore at some school Cat had never heard of. The *Times* and the *Post* had the same photo, the straightforward one from God knew where that would go with the obit; the *News* had dug up one of Harte standing with a few others who looked more or less like him, at the dedication of what Cat knew to be yet another office monolith on Third Avenue.

She went to her cubicle at nine, took her place in the chair still warm from Ed's dedicated ass. She looked over Ed's entries in the log. Three callers who claimed responsibility, all scrupulously red-tagged. Two were variations on the same idea: now you'll all be sorry (no specifics about what we should all be sorry for), and I'm not finished yet; both were vague on the subject of how they'd survived the explosion and lived to make the call. The third said he was a member of something called the Brigade of Enlightenment and that the terror would continue until the U.S. stopped allowing women to murder their unborn children.

Pete stopped by just after nine, nursing his first cup of hot coffee-flavored, sugar-free liquid candy. "How you doing?" he asked.

"Okay."

"Get some sleep?"

"A little."

He stepped into the cubicle, made so bold as to put his hand on her shoulder. She and Pete had maintained an unspoken no-touching rule since that night three months ago when they were both working late, when they'd been exhausted and discouraged enough to duck into the women's room together. Cat still couldn't say why she'd done it, she wasn't remotely interested, and yet mysteriously, unaccountably, she'd been headed to the ladies' and had nodded to him, and before you knew it she was sitting on the sink with her legs wrapped around his unpretty middle-aged ass, he because she'd allowed it, because they'd seemed at that moment like the only two people in the world, because his wife was losing her sight and his only child had become an econut in Latin America, and she because . . . because Pete's wife was losing her sight and his only child had become an econut in Latin America, because she'd let her own son die and she'd been taking calls for going on twelve hours, because Pete's neck reminded her of her ex-husband's neck, because this place was so ugly and silent and far from everything, because she seemed to have wanted, at that moment, to tear everything apart, to go down, to be as crazy and destructive and irresponsible as the people who called her. She and Pete had never spoken about it. They both knew it would not happen again.

"You sure you feel like working today?"

"Entirely sure. Find out anything new?"

"Forensics is saying the kid was thirteen, maybe fourteen, but small for his age. Seems to have been healthy, from what they've found so far."

"I hate this."

"Who doesn't?"

"I don't just mean this. I mean *all* this."

Pete nodded wearily, warily. Cat hesitated. There was an unwritten rule in the unit. No one speculated, ever. No one waxed philosophical. It didn't work that way. No one went moony about the notable increase in callers who were under eighteen and clearly well educated or about the increase in carry-throughs, from one in a thousand to one in 650 over the last five years. No one spun out over the collapse of the family or of civilization at large; no one wondered about atmospheric gases or irradiated food or rays being projected at the earth by hostile aliens. That was the callers' realm.

Cat said, "Sorry. I'm a little tired right now."

"Course you are."

She sat up straighter in her chair. "What have they gotten from the wife and kids?" she asked. "Anything?"

"Wife's hysterical. Daughter, too. Son came down from Vermont, real eager beaver, wants to be of service and get to the bottom of all this and etcetera but can't tell us shit. Dad was a decent guy. Coached Little League, paid the bills on time. My opinion? I think the son's having the time of his life."

"What's he doing in Vermont?"

"Special school for underachievers, kids who do more than the usual amount of drugs. Like that."

"That's interesting."

"We're checking into it."

"They've got the tapes in Washington?" she said.

"They do."

"And they'll be in touch?"

"Nobody's gonna nail you for missing a hint this small."

I wasn't supposed to call anyone. Jesus.

"Unless, of course, they decide they really and truly need someone to nail, and I seem like the best candidate."

"Unlikely. Why worry about it now?"

"Thanks."

"I'll check in with you later."

"You're the best."

She got to work. It was a busy morning, which surprised no one. It always took about twenty-four hours for the callers to man their stations. After a big story hit the news, only the most labile reached immediately for the phone. The majority, the petit bourgeois lunatics, had to mull it over, settle in their own minds just exactly how the event in question belonged to them, and decide that someone in a position of authority ought to know about it. Now they were in full stampede. She got five in her first twenty minutes, three of them so unfocused that even Ed wouldn't have red-tagged them, just a trio of screamers who wanted somebody to know they hadn't seen anything yet, the worst was still to come, Judgment Day was upon us. The fourth was an English guy who wanted to tell her he'd overheard a conversation in the lobby of his building and had come to understand that this incident was part of his neighbor's master plan to bankrupt small businesses in the financial district, sorry, he couldn't leave his neighbor's name or his own name, for fear of reprisals, but given this information, he hoped the police would know how to proceed. The fifth needed to tell her that certain evidence had been planted at the site by white supremacists to implicate the Muslim faith. This one did leave his name: Jesus Mohamed, minister of the Church of Light and Love. He was willing to work with the police in any capacity they required.

She red-tagged the Englishman and Jesus Mohamed, thus setting into motion the inquiries into their lives and natures that would cost taxpayers roughly fifteen grand. She wondered if these people knew, if they had any idea, how much money and muscle they could summon just by making these calls. Better, of course, if they didn't.

Between calls she filed what needed to be filed, wrote her follow-ups, checked the mail, which was for the most part unremarkable: a half-dozen threats and one hex, written variously by hand, on a computer, and on what appeared to be a manual typewriter. The letters about the explosion wouldn't arrive until tomorrow. The day began to establish its momentum; it started feeling ordinary. This would pass, wouldn't it? The kid would turn out to have been Dick Harte's sex toy, or he would turn out to have been regular crazy (the new regular crazy), a friendless and universally bullied weirdo who'd been obsessed with computer games since before he knew how to walk. It was—what else *could* it be?—another disaster in a disaster-prone world, tragic but unavoidable. Life would go on.

The call came a little before ten-thirty. It was patched directly to her—caller had asked for Cat Martin. She figured it was one of her regulars. She had a handful who called at least once a week, and twice that many who called sporadically, when they went off their medication or the moon was full or the papers (they were readers, these people) had featured something doomish that could conceivably have been somebody's fault. Antoine always called about anything that inconvenienced commuters (automotive industry's conspiracy to eliminate mass transit); Billy could be counted on whenever anything appeared about hostile conditions on other planets (ongoing attempt to disguise the fact that the aliens have been here for decades and are being tortured in government internment camps). Antoine and Billy and the others had been checked out long ago. Antoine lived on monthly disability in a rathole in Hell's Kitchen; Billy was a sanitation worker on Staten Island. The regulars tended to love patterns. They scanned the news every day for further evidence. She couldn't blame them, not really. Who didn't want more patterns?

She picked up. "This is Cat Martin."

"Hello?"

Adolescent white boy. Her synapses snapped.

"Hello. What can I do for you?"

"Did you talk to my brother?"

Cat pushed the green button. The readout was a 212 area code.

"Who's your brother?"

"He told me he called you."

No, not adolescent. This kid sounded young, nine or ten. His voice was serene, even a bit aphasic. Drugs, probably. A few of his mother's OxyContins.

"What's your name?"

"Did you talk to him? I'm sorry, but I need to know."

"When would he have called?"

"Last week. Tuesday."

Shit. This was something.

"I'd have to check the records. Can you tell me his name?"

"We're in the family. We don't have names."

Keep him talking. Give the guys as much time as you can.

"What family are you in?" she said.

"He told me he talked to you. I just want to make sure."

"Are you in trouble? Can you let me help you?"

"I was wondering. Can you tell me what he told you?"

"If somebody's hurting you, I can make them stop."

No, no statements. Phrase everything as a question. Keep him answering.

"I didn't know."

"What didn't you know?"

"I thought he was just going to put the bomb somewhere and run."

"Can you tell me about the bomb?"

"Did you tell him not to do it?"

"Who's your brother? What do you think he did?"

"I shouldn't have called. I'm just scared. Sorry."

"Won't you tell me what you're afraid of? Won't you let me help you?"

"That's nice of you. But you can't."

"Yes. I can."

"Are you happy?"

What the *fuck*? No one had ever asked her that particular question.

Cat said, "I think you're *un*happy. Is somebody making you do something you don't want to do?"

"You'd do the same thing. Wouldn't you?"

"What is it you think you and I would do?"

"We're all the same person. We all want the same things."

"Can you let me come meet you? Don't you think we should talk in person?"

"Nobody really dies. We go on in the grass. We go on in the trees."

He was spinning out. Cat kept her voice calm.

"Why do you think that?"

"Every atom of mine belongs to you, too."

Click.

She paused a moment, to be absolutely sure he was gone. By the time she'd risen from her chair, Pete was in her cubicle.

"Fucking A," he said.

"What the hell? *Brothers?*"

"He was on a pay phone. Way the hell up in Washington Heights."

"Are they there yet?"

"On their way."

"Mm."

"There's that line again. 'We're in the family.' "

"Is it from some rock band?"

"Not that we can find. We're still on it."

"They're checking movies, TV shows?"

"They are, Cat. They're good at this."

"Right."

"What was that he said at the end?"

"I'm not quite sure. I think it was from Whitman."

"Say what?"

"I think it was a line from Walt Whitman. *Leaves of Grass.*"

"Poetry?"

"That would be poetry, yes."

"Fuck me. I'll check in with you later," he said.

"Right."

Pete barreled off. Cat had to stay put in case of a callback. No other calls for her unless she was specifically asked for.

Thirty minutes passed. This was part of what she hadn't expected—the downtime, the hanging around. When she went into police work she'd seen herself careening around in unmarked cars or touching down in helicopters. She hadn't anticipated so much waiting by the phone. She hadn't pictured a life that would so closely resemble working for a corporation, dutifully performing her little piece of it all.

Every atom of mine belongs to you, too. That wasn't quite right, but it was close enough. A kid who quoted Whitman? Cat was probably the only department member who'd recognize it; she was without question the only one on the premises who'd read Winnicott and Klein, Whitman and Dostoyevsky. For all the difference it made.

Did you talk to my brother? Jesus fucking Christ. One kid self-detonates and his little brother calls to check up on him. A picture was emerging—there was that, at least. A missing kid with a younger brother—assuming it was true, and who knew?—would be much easier to track down. Were they the sons of cultists? That was more of a rural thing, messianics who raised children deep in the woods, taught them to hate the sinful world, and congratulated themselves for doing God's work. It was more Idaho or Montana, these righteously murderous families who'd gone off the grid. But the five boroughs had their share, too. Hadn't they just arrested a guy who'd been keeping an adult tiger and a full-grown alligator in his one-bedroom apartment in Brooklyn? They were everywhere.

She could have kissed Pete when he finally returned.

"What's up?" she said.

"Phone's on the corner of St. Nicholas and 176th. Out of the way. No kid on the scene, no witnesses yet."

"Shit."

"You're okay?"

"Yeah."

"I'll check back again soon."

"Thanks."

She was sequestered now. She was bound to her cubicle, on the off chance of a callback. *Momma is waiting. Call her. She'll never leave you alone.*

The morning passed. Cat did some filing, caught up on her e-mails. She had one caller, at eleven forty-five, asking for Cat Martin, and her short hairs stood up, but it was just Greta, her only female regular, calling to tell her that the explosion had been caused by the unquiet spirit of a slave girl who'd been murdered on the site in 1803 and that the only way to appease her was to go there immediately and perform the rite of extreme unction. Greta lived on Orchard Street, had been a seamstress for more than fifty years, had eight grandchildren, was probably a nice person.

We all want the same things. She kept hearing the kid's high-pitched, tentative voice, his strange courtliness. There was—how to put it—an innocence about him. Subject matter aside, he had sounded for all the world like a decent, ordinary kid. That was probably drugs, though. Or dissociation.

Pete stopped by periodically, bless him, to tell her they hadn't found anything, and at twelve-thirty to bring her a pizza from Two Boots.

"Seems like a good day to say 'screw the diet,' " he said.

Pepperoni and mushrooms. He knew what she liked. She offered him a slice, which he accepted.

"How serious you think this is?" he said.

"Not sure. What's your gut telling you?"

"That it's small but looks big."

Cat folded the tip of her pizza slice, took a big voluptuous bite. Was there anything, really, as delicious, as entirely satisfying, as a slice of pepperoni-and-mushroom pizza?

She said, "You think it's only these two kids."

"Yeah. Think Menendez brothers."

"A truly whacked-out fourteen-year-old, no longer with us, and his impressionable younger brother."

"Our first copycat."

She nodded. Since 9/11, they'd all been puzzling over the dearth of follow-ups. Not Al Qaeda—that was the concern of other departments. Cat and Pete and the rest of deterrence had been wondering why more ordinary American citizens hadn't used it as inspiration. It had been the terrorists' gift to the violently deranged. You could blow up a garbage can now—you could yell "Fire!" in a goddamned theater—and cost the city of New York another billion or so in lost tourist revenue.

She said, "Receiving their instructions from?"

"A higher power. You know."

She knew. Nine times out of ten, the ones who followed through were obeying someone or something. They were servants to a cause.

"First one said people have got to be stopped," she said.

"My guess? Dick Harte was having sex with both of them."

"There are no reports of missing kids from anywhere near Great Neck."

"He's got wheels. There are kids everywhere."

Cat said, "I don't quite figure Dick Harte as somebody who drives around looking for little boys to have sex with."

"Happens all the time."

"I know. I'm talking about a feeling, that's all."

"Okay," Pete said. "Dick Harte is a God-fearing family man who's never touched anybody but his two wives. Why does the kid pick him?"

"I'm just throwing this out. I predict that sooner or later we'll track a missing and find a father who's been torturing his boys all their lives. Older one gets to an age and decides it's got to stop, somebody's got to pay. But he can't bring himself to kill his father. He picks some guy who looks like his father. Same age and weight."

"Possible."

"If the kids weren't local, if they weren't the sons of people the Hartes knew, it suggests they were the kind of boys who could be picked up by a stranger in a car."

"Which happens all the time," Pete said.

"Absolutely. But something in these kids' voices, especially the second one . . . I don't picture them hanging around a park, waiting for some guy to pull up in an expensive car and suck their dicks for ten dollars. It doesn't click for me."

"Hey, you're the one with the pee-aitch-dee."

"For all the good it's done me."

"So you think the guy they really want to kill is their father."

"Don't hold me to it."

"Wouldn't think of it."

"I predict we'll find a citizen who's so stressed about his oldest boy running away he's been torturing the younger one double. The kid'll turn out to have been privy to the plan, he'll be taken from his fucked-up home to a differently fucked-up home, where he'll live and get treatment until he's old enough to go out and get a job and have a family and start torturing his own sons."

"You take a dim view," he said.

"And you don't?"

"Why would a kid like that quote poetry?"

"Good question. Are they checking Whitman for that 'in the family' shit?"

"All done. It's not from Whitman."

"Too bad."

"Yeah."

She spent the day waiting for a call that never came. It was funny—she usually felt grotesquely popular here on the job. She was sought-after. Today she just sat by the phone, begging it to ring, like a high school girl in love.

She tracked down a Whitman scholar at NYU, one Rita Dunn, and made an appointment for tomorrow morning. Otherwise, she killed time. Filed a few more things. Got to some old reports that had been languishing in a bottom drawer.

She stayed an extra hour, then packed it in. She had her cell, of course—if the kid called back, they could patch him straight through to her wherever she was. She walked home through the dusk of another perfect June day among citizens who refused to shed their habits of looking suspicious to her. The guy nervously unloading boxes from a bakery truck, the jogger in Princeton sweats, even the blind man tapping along with his cane—they all seemed like potentials. They *were*, in fact, all potentials. Everyone was. The trick was to keep living with the conviction that almost everyone was actually harmless. It was the job's central irony. If you weren't careful, you could get as paranoid as the people you dealt with.

We're all the same person. We all want the same things.

Her apartment felt particularly small. It had a way of expanding or contracting, depending on how the day went. Today it struck her as ludicrous, these little rooms in which she, an expensively educated thirty-eight-year-old woman, found herself living. Remember: it's a prize. In today's market, a dinky one-bedroom on Fifth Street cost a grand and a half, minimum. Be grateful for your rent-controlled life. Embrace the fact that you live above the poverty line.

She went to pour herself a vodka, decided against it. Better stay

stone-cold sober, in case the kid should call. She made herself a cup
of tea instead, took her Whitman down from the shelf, and curled up
on the love seat with it.

> *I celebrate myself,*
> *And what I assume you shall assume,*
> *For every atom belonging to me as good belongs to you.*

Whitman, Walt. She hadn't thought about him, really, since college. Yes, she was an avid reader, but she wasn't the kind of person
who sat home at night and read poetry for pleasure. She knew the ba-
sics: America's great visionary poet, alive sometime in the 1800s, produced in his long life this one enormous book, which he kept revising
and expanding the way another man might endlessly remodel and add
onto his house. Big, white Santa Claus beard, floppy hat. Liked boys.

He liked boys, didn't he? Was that true? She paged through the
book.

> *Twenty-eight young men bathe by the shore,*
> *Twenty-eight young men, and all so friendly,*
> *Twenty-eight years of womanly life, and all so lonesome.*

Right. What else?

> *The beards of the young men glisten'd with wet, it ran from their*
> *   long hair,*
> *Little streams pass'd all over their bodies.*
> *An unseen hand also pass'd over their bodies,*
> *It descended tremblingly from their temples and ribs.*

Would the kid have read that? Maybe, maybe not. He'd quoted
from the opening stanza, nothing more. A smart kid picked up all
kinds of things.

Still, there was something sexual about this. A boy embraces an
older man and blows them both up.

We're all the same person. We all want the same things.

She kept hearing his voice in her head. Giving a kidlike performance, she thought. A child who was doing his best to act like a child. Yet she didn't feel the murder in him. The kid was, of course, crazy by definition. But still, she prided herself on a certain ability to suss out the truly dangerous. She couldn't name the specifics, though there were plenty of well-documented signs. This was something else. A flavor, a whiff. A buzz—that was the best term she had for it. As if she could hear the tiny sound being made by a bad connection, the particular bit of faulty wiring that made murder more than just a fantasy.

It was complicated by the fact that every now and then, some of them were right. The tobacco companies *had* discovered a secret ingredient to make cigarettes more addictive. The North Koreans *had* been kidnapping Japanese tourists to educate their spies about the particulars of Japanese customs. Those noises coming from the apartment next door were in fact being made by a full-grown tiger.

She heard a noise in the hallway, right outside her door. A scraping. Something. Like a heel dragging across the tile. It was probably Arthur next door, pausing for an emphysemic breath before stumbling on, but she knew the sounds Arthur made; she knew *all* the ordinary sounds the tenants produced in the hallways. This one wasn't familiar.

She raised her head from the book. She listened.

There it was again. A furtive, scrabbling sound. If this were the country, it might have been an opossum, scratching at the shingles.

The country—teeth out there in the dark?

She got up, went and stood by the door. Nothing now. Still, she was shaky. A little shaky. Given the times. She didn't have a gun, being deterrence. Had never wanted one. Now she wondered.

She said "Hello?" and was embarrassed by the girlish fear in her voice. Fuck that. Fuck them if they wanted her meek. She opened the door.

No one. Just the ordinary drear of the corridor, its brackish aquarium light, its tiles the color of decayed teeth. She stepped out and took a proper look. Empty. The sound had probably been coming from the street or through the wall from the other next-door apartment (where the druggy, dreamy young couple in residence were always engaged in some mysterious project that involved endless little tappings and draggings). There was no one and nothing.

It took her another moment to see what was on the wall opposite her door. In white chalk, in perfect if slightly labored grade-school cursive, someone had written, TO DIE IS DIFFERENT FROM WHAT ANY ONE SUPPOSES, AND LUCKIER.

Neither Pete nor the FBI boys could offer much. They questioned the neighbors, of course, and of course nobody knew anything, had seen anyone untoward, or etcetera. As every tenant knew, it was semi-challenging but not impossible to get into the labyrinth of alleys and dumping grounds behind the building and slip in through the broken back door. The building's denizens had recently observed the fifth anniversary of their ongoing attempts to get the landlord to fix it.

Pete stood in Cat's living room, sweating majestically, sipping the espresso she'd made for him.

"How's the coffee?" she asked.

"Strong."

"Only way I know how to make it."

"I'm frankly at a loss about how this asshole figured out where you live."

"There are about a dozen ways."

"Right."

This was one of the surprises—there were no elaborate systems for keeping cops anonymous. That was movie stuff. Matter of fact, the systems that did exist, for the higher-level grunts, didn't work all that well. Just about anybody with true determination and a computer could track down a cop or an FBI agent or an auditor with the IRS, knock on the door one night, and deliver a lethal message. Only the biggest bosses had protection.

Pete said, "You want one of the guys to stay with you tonight? Or would you rather go to a hotel?"

"I can spend the night at Simon's."

"If they've got your address here, they may know about him, too."

"Simon's building is probably safer than FBI headquarters. Some exiled king lives in one of the penthouses, plus a few very kidnappable CEOs."

"Have you called him?"

"I was just about to. He should be done with his client by now."

"Call him. I want to get you settled somewhere."

She dialed Simon on her cell. She told him the story.

"My God," he said.

"I am, in fact, a little rattled," she told him.

"Come right over."

"I will."

Pete took her. They left the FBI boys lifting the ten thousand fingerprints from every inch of the premises. Who knew? Maybe they'd come up with something.

Pete walked her into the lobby of Simon's building on Franklin. He whistled softly over the maple paneling, the silent explosion of pink lilies on the concierge's desk.

"Fat," he said under his breath.

She announced herself to Joseph, the supremely capable Korean doorman.

" 'Night," she said to Pete.

"Must be nice," he said.

"I'll see you in the morning," she answered curtly. She was in no mood right now.

"Right. See you in the morning."

Simon was waiting for her upstairs. He held her. She was surprised to realize that she might start weeping, not so much from exhaustion or nerves but from the sheer joy of having someone to go to.

"Unbelievable," he whispered.

"Unbelievable," she said.

She sat on his sofa, declined his offer of a drink. She loved his apartment, felt appropriately guilty for loving it, but loved it all the same. Four big rooms on the twenty-second floor, twelve-foot ceilings. The people walking the streets below, trying to find the least bruised bananas at the corner market, hoping not to get hit by cabs—they had no idea what hovered over them, these oases of granite and ebony, these sanctuaries. The scorched plains rose to alpine peaks, where the wizards lived. Up here it was temple lights and a sequestered, snowy hush.

Simon was a collector. Nineteenth-century maps, Chinese pottery, vintage toys, and music boxes. Cat kept meaning to ask him. Why those particular objects, out of all the things in the world? She hadn't asked. She preferred the mystery. Simon bought and sold futures. He saw some particular significance in maps, pots, and playthings. She liked it that way. She spent enough time searching for explanations at work.

Simon sat beside her. "What happens now?" he said.

She saw the spark in his eyes. He was turned on.

"They're checking out my building. I don't expect them to find anything."

"How can they not find anything?"

"There are thousands of fingerprints in a building like mine. And . . . Well. It's time you knew. We're not really all that good at this. We work very, very hard. But a lot of the time we just end up arresting the wrong person, and that person goes to jail, and everybody feels safer."

Simon paused, nodding. He seemed unsurprised, or had decided to act unsurprised. He said, "The pay-phone thing is funny, isn't it? Why not a cell?"

"Cell phones have owners. This is brilliant, in its way. Low-tech is the best way to go. You pump a few coins in, say your piece, and run. We can't watch every pay phone in the five boroughs. These little fuckers are smart."

"Do you think you'll catch him?" Simon asked.

"We have to. We can't screw up something this big."

"And your role is?"

"To go back to work in the morning and wait for another call."

"That's it?"

"For now, yes."

He was disappointed, naturally. He wanted her careening around in an unmarked car. He wanted her cracking the case, saving the day. It was not sexy or interesting, her waiting by the phone. It was—just say it—too maternal.

She said, "I was reading Whitman. At the same time some maniac was writing a line from Whitman on the wall outside my door."

"I've never read Whitman," he said.

Of course you haven't. You're Cedar Rapids. You're Cornell and a Harvard MBA. Your people don't do poetry. They don't need to.

Stop.

She said, "Chapman was carrying a copy of *Catcher in the Rye* when he shot John Lennon."

"Why do you think the kid would choose Whitman?"

"I'm trying to figure that out."

"Why did Chapman choose Salinger?"

"Well, I'd say it was to feed his own narcissistic sense of himself as a sensitive loner. He identified with Holden Caulfield. Holden was right, and the rest of the world was wrong. Other people might think it was a bad idea to kill John Lennon, but Chapman thought he knew better."

"You think your kid feels the same way about Whitman?"

"I don't know. I'm talking to a Whitman person at NYU tomorrow."

"You tired?"

"God, yes."

"Let's go to bed."

Cat slipped under the covers while Simon was still in the bathroom, performing his rituals. Simon's bedroom was the sanctum sanctorum, the vault where the best stash was kept. Along the south wall, shelves offered row upon row of vases and plates and ginger jars, pale green and lunar gray. On the opposite wall a collection of old banks and music boxes looked back across at the pottery. Cast-iron Uncle Sams and horse-drawn fire trucks and dancing bears, carved boxes that still contained the favorite songs of people a hundred years dead. *Little toys, behold the perfect serenity of a thousand-year-old jar. Pottery, never forget how much humans have always loved a sentimental song and the sound of a coin put by.*

Cat let herself sink into the fat pillows, the zillion-thread-count sheets. Of course she liked it. Why wouldn't she? She'd gotten here by chance. If she and Simon hadn't happened to go to Citarella at the same time (they had the best crab cakes; she'd had a craving for crab cakes), if it hadn't been raining, if they hadn't hailed the same cab at the same moment . . .

Just like that. Just that quick and easy. A little banter in the cab's backseat. (*You sell the future? That is* heavy shit. *You talk to murderers? No, that is heavy shit.*) A cup of coffee and that thing he did with his thumbs, hooking them around the cup rim, tapping out a little tattoo. He had pretty thumbs (she was a sucker for men's hands) and a way of tucking in his lower lip—that was what made it happen, initially. Soon after, he proved to be one of those men who cared if a girl had a good time, and she appreciated that. Okay, he was more focused than passionate, his lovemaking had some hint of the deal about it (got to close this one, got to keep the customer satisfied), but still, he was sweet in bed, and she'd thought she could loosen him up, with time. There was his beetle-browed determination to see her come; there was the impossible beauty and sureness of his fat, white propitious life. His collections and his deep leather sofas, his gigantic chrome shower-head. Which had mattered more at first, the thumbs and lips and conscientious sex or the gear?

The man. She wasn't like that. She'd never gone for rich guys, even young, when she was proper bait.

But still, here she was, safe, in this bedroom, high above the streets. It was—admit it—a little fucked up. Probably. It was a little bit cold. Wasn't it? She gave him street cred; she tickled his edgy bone. She made him more complicated. He gave her, well . . . this.

And love. She did in fact love him, and he seemed to love her, too. She'd gone years without anything she could call love. She hadn't expected Simon or anyone like him, but here he was. Here were his thumbs and lips and eyebrows; here were his gravitas and prosperity; here was his secret self, that tiny, harmed, indignant quality she sensed in him, thought she detected on his face as he slept.

Simon came out of the bathroom naked, got into bed beside her. He said, "Do you think the kid will call again?"

"It's hard to say."

"You must have some idea, don't you?"

She said, "Once a perpetrator has initiated contact like this, odds are he'll want to reestablish."

Screw it, talk dirty to him. You're too tired to resist.

"That figures," he said.

"What you try to do," she told him, "is supplant the existing object. If you're lucky, if you're very lucky, you can become the person he loves and wants to destroy. He starts redirecting all that feeling to you."

Shameless. Not even true. Just sex talk.

"Like you would in therapy," Simon said.

"Yes and no. You need to be compassionate but authoritative with someone like this. Somebody like this usually wants a boss. A voice in his head is telling him to do things he suspects he shouldn't do. He wants a new voice. That's probably why he called in the first place."

Was that enough? Now could they just have sex, or not have sex, and go to sleep?

He said, "So, you try to become the voice in his head?"

He ran a pink fingertip precisely along her forearm, as if he were reading Braille. They could make one beautiful baby together, no denying it. Caramel-colored skin, head of billowy curls. Cat was probably still young enough. Maybe she was.

"Yeah," she said. "As opposed to the aliens, or the CIA, or whoever."

"You try to be the new, better delusion."

"Right. And if that doesn't work, you track the fucker down and blow him away."

That did it. Simon kissed her and worked his hand up to her breast.

She woke at a quarter to four. She gave it five minutes, on the off chance, then slipped out of bed. She went into the living room, took *Leaves of Grass* from her bag, and started reading.

I have said that the soul is not more than the body,
And I have said that the body is not more than the soul,
And nothing, not God, is greater to one than one's self is,
And whoever walks a furlong without sympathy walks to his own
    funeral, drest in his shroud,

> *And I or you pocketless of a dime may purchase the pick of the*
>   *earth,*
> *And to glance with an eye or show a bean in its pod confounds the*
>   *learning of all times,*
> *And there is no trade or employment but the young man following*
>   *it may become a hero,*
> *And there is no object so soft but it makes a hub for the wheel'd*
>   *universe,*
> *And I say to any man or woman, Let your soul stand cool and*
>   *composed before a million universes.*

She put the book down and went to the window, looked out at the slumbering city. From here it was all lovely and remote, twenty-two stories below. It was lights and silence and the few stars bright enough to penetrate the city haze. There were the windows of Tribeca and then the empty sky.

Where was the kid right now? Was he sleeping? She had a feeling he was not. She imagined him out there, as wide-awake as she was; he might be looking through a window of his own.

Luke would be twelve now. Since he died she'd been sure he was somewhere; she'd known it as deeply as she'd known his presence inside her, shortly after conception. She'd never been religious. She hadn't allowed grief to send her crawling to the church. That might have helped, but she hadn't had it in her; it had seemed if anything like a final insult, to concoct sudden hysterical convictions about what she'd spent her childhood escaping. All right, take my baby, but don't expect me to don the veil and kneel before the statue. Don't expect me to clap my hands or raise my voice in song. If she'd done that, she'd have lost herself completely.

And yet, Luke wasn't gone. She had no idea where he might be. He wasn't in heaven, and he wasn't a ghost, but he was somewhere. He had not evaporated. She knew it with gut-level certainty. It was her only belief. That, and the workings of justice in a dangerous world.

Danger—our true parent?

Where do the dead live?

These curtains—can Simon really be straight?

She slipped into bed just before sunrise. She wasn't sleepy, not even a little bit, but if she simulated sleepiness, if she acted like someone about to fall asleep, she could sometimes fool herself. Simon breathed steadily beside her, murmured over a dream. He never had trouble sleeping. She tried not to hate him for that.

She was still wide-awake when her cell went off. It was ten minutes after six.

"This is Cat Martin."

"Cat, I've got your caller. I'm patching him through."

It was Erna, from downtown. Cat's heart quickened. Simon opened his eyes, blinked uncertainly. She put her finger to her lips.

She said, "Go ahead, Erna."

There was the brief electronic hiccup of the transfer. Then there was his voice.

"Hello?"

He sounded even younger than she'd remembered.

"Hello. Who's this?"

"Um. I called before."

"Yes."

Keep it calm. Keep it matter-of-fact.

"I could get in trouble," he said.

"You're not in any trouble at all, not if you let me help you. Did you write something on a wall last night?"

"What?"

"Did you write something for me last night? On a wall?"

"Oh. Yeah."

"What were you trying to tell me?"

"Well. What it said."

Simon was sitting up now, watching her, wide-eyed.

"Do you think it's lucky to die?" she asked. "Do you think dying is a good thing?"

"I don't think I want to yet," the boy said.

"Who is it who wants you to die?"

"That's how it works. I didn't know. It's murder, if you don't go, too."

"Is somebody telling you to hurt yourself?"

"I beat and pound for the dead."

"That's Whitman, isn't it?" she said.

"Who?"

"Walt Whitman. Did you learn those words from Walt Whitman?"

"No. Walt doesn't talk like that."

"Where did you learn them, then?"

"They're from home."

"Listen to me. Listen very carefully. Someone is telling you to do things that are bad for you, that are bad for other people. It's not your fault. Someone is hurting you. Tell me where you are, and I'll come there and help you."

"I can't."

"You don't need to be afraid. There's nothing for you to be afraid of, but you have to let me help you. Tell me where you're calling from. You can tell me that. It's all right."

"The next one is today."

"Tell me what he's making you do. You don't have to do it."

"I have to go."

"Don't go. You're in trouble, and it's not your fault. I can help you."

"Do you think a great city endures?"

"What do you think?"

"Goodbye."

He hung up.

Simon said, "That was him." He all but quivered with fervent competence.

"It was him."

"What did he say?"

"Just sit tight a minute, okay?"

Her cell went off, as she'd known it would. It was Pete.

"Jesus fucking Christ," he said.

"Where was he?"

"Pay phone in Bed-Stuy."

"They're doing another one today."

"So he says. What do you think?"

"Off the top of my head, I'd say I'm not sure."

"Thanks for sharing."

"I'd say he's serious."

"I'd say so, too. What was all that shit about Walt?"

"Frankly, you've got me there. The little fucker seems to have memorized the whole book."

"He says the words are from home. What's that about?"

"They're loose, Pete. As you know."

"How soon can you be in the office?"

"Twenty minutes. Give or take."

"See you there."

She clicked off. Simon stared at her, all executive readiness.

"Got to get to work," she said.

"Right," he said.

He was so fucking gorgeous like this, he who was a potent figure in his own circles but a spectator in this one, a wife if you will, lying here looking at her with those impossible agate eyes of his, hair electrically disordered, face bristling with stubble. It seemed for a moment that she could stop, she could just stop; she could blow off her job and move with Simon into *his* realm, his high-octane but undangerous life, the hush and sureness of him, buying and selling the future, seeking out maps and jars and bringing them home. She was on her way to a grim office where the equipment was outdated and the air-conditioning prone to failure, where most of her coworkers were right-wing zealots or B students or just too peculiar for the corporate jobs that claimed the best and the brightest; where the villains were as pathetic and off-kilter as the heroes; where the whole struggle between order and chaos had no beauty in it, no philosophy or poetry; where death itself felt cheap and cheesy. She wanted—how could she possibly tell him?—to take shelter in Simon, to live peacefully alongside him in his spiky and careless beauty, his electrified contentment. She wanted to abandon herself, to abide. But of course he wouldn't want her that way.

She got out of bed. "Call you later," she said.

"Right," he answered.

They both paused. Now would be the time for one of them to say "I love you." If they were at that point.

"Bye," she said.

"Bye," he answered.

It was Halloween at the office. She'd never felt the air so agitated. This was what never actually happened: a psychopath announcing his intentions, with every indication of follow-through. This was movie stuff.

Ed was just shy of coming in his pants. His hair, what was left of it, seemed to be standing on end. "Hot damn," he said.

"They find anything in Bed-Stuy?" she asked.

"Nope. I wish *I* could talk to him."

"And what would you say?"

"I think he needs a father figure."

"Do you?"

"Don't be offended. You're doing a fine job with him."

"In my way."

"No offense. I just think maybe a guy could get more out of him. It's the luck of the draw, him calling here and attaching to you."

"You don't think a woman is as effective with him?"

"Hey. Don't get all Angela Davis on me."

Ed was one of the new breed, the guys who seemed to think that if they were right up front about their sexism and racism, if they walked in and sat down and just *said it*, they were at least semi-absolved. That if racism was inevitable, it was better, it was more manly and honorable, to be candid. She, frankly, preferred secrecy.

"I wouldn't dream of it," she said.

"A bad dad is telling him to do bad things. A good dad might have a better chance of telling him to do good things. A mother figure doesn't have the same authority. She's a refuge. She can't contradict the bad dad. She can only console."

"I can't tell you how much I hope you're wrong about that."

"I hope so, too. We're going to *get* this little fucker."

Ed had the killer buzz in his voice. He had the pure, shining conviction of the almost smart. When Ed went on like this, Cat heard the *ping* inside her head. Here was a true murderer.

"Yeah," she said. "We're going to get him."

Pete came into the cubicle, with black coffee for her.

"You're sweet," she said.

"We're nowhere," he told her.

"We're never *nowhere*."

"They've run dental records on more than two thousand missing kids. They got no matches to the teeth we found."

"Disappointing."

"It's like that first kid appeared out of thin air."

"Or nobody knows or cares that the first kid is missing."

"I know, I know. It's funny, though."

"I agree. It's funny."

Ed broke in. "Or somebody never cared enough to send their kid to a dentist."

"Always a possibility," Cat said. "Have you noticed how he starts to disintegrate as he gets agitated?"

"Go on," Pete said.

"His coherence fades. He starts throwing out lines from Whitman. Or, as he would say, from home."

"He gets more and more random," Ed offered.

"Maybe," Cat said. "Or maybe, in his mind, he gets less and less random. I have a feeling that the poem *is* his language. It's what's in his head. Maybe it's more of a stretch for him to say something like 'I'm afraid to die' than it is to say 'Do you think a great city endures?' "

"*That* sounds like a bit of a stretch, to me," Ed said.

Cat wanted to say, I have a feeling, but she couldn't say that kind of thing in front of Ed. He'd use it against her. She was the girl with the degree from Columbia, who'd read more books than all of the men put together, who'd gone into forensics because she hadn't managed to establish a private practice. She was overaggressive and underqualified. She was someone who relied on feelings.

She said, "It's just an idea, Ed. This seems like an excellent time for us to give free rein to our ideas, wouldn't you say?"

Queenly bearing, schoolmarm diction. She really had to quit that. Problem was, it worked. Most of the time.

"Sure, sure," Ed said. "Absolutely."

"There's something strange about the kid's associations," she said. Back to regular voice. "It's like he's programmed. A concept trips a wire, and he's got the line, but he hasn't got the circuitry to make sense of it. He's like a vessel for someone else's wishes. The poetry signifies something for him, but he's not able to say what it is."

"I thought we'd have a trace by now," Pete said. "These are *kids*."

"Someone is putting them up to it," Cat said.

"I don't know," Ed said. "No one's taken any credit yet."

Cat said, "Unless whoever it is *wants* these kids to call in. Unless that's his way of taking credit."

Pete said, "I started that Whitman book last night. Can't make head or tails of it, frankly."

"I'm seeing a woman at NYU later today."

"Good."

"What more do we know about Dick Harte?" Cat asked.

"A lot," Pete answered. "But nothing's jumping out. No history with boys. Or girls, even. Nothing we can find. It's all pretty standard. Went to law school—"

"Where?"

"Cardozo. Not Harvard. Practiced for a few years, then went into real estate. Married a decent girl, got rich, dumped the decent girl and married a new decent girl but prettier. Had two pretty children with wife number two. Big house in Great Neck, country place in Westhampton. All in all, a very regular guy."

"Apart from all that money," Cat said.

"Right. But it's real estate. He didn't have sweatshops. His employees didn't love him, but they didn't hate him, either. They got their salaries. They got their benefits. They got Christmas bonuses every year, plus a party at the Rihga Royal."

"In my experience," Cat said, "very few rich people have no enemies."

"His enemies were all on his level. Basic business rivalries, guys he outbid, guys he undersold. But these people didn't *hate* him. It doesn't work that way. It's a club. Dick Harte was one of the less sleazy members."

"What about the son who had to be sent away to school in Vermont?"

"Just a troubled kid. Got into drugs, grades started slipping. Mom and Dad shipped him off to the country. I'm sure they weren't happy about it, but it doesn't seem like any big deal."

"What was Dick Harte up to at Ground Zero?" Cat asked.

"He was one of a group of honchos pushing for more retail and office space in the rebuild. As opposed to those who favor a memorial and a park."

"That might be a big deal to any number of people," Cat said.

"But to a ten-year-old?"

"This is a ten-year-old who's memorized *Leaves of Grass*."

"A freak," Ed added.

"Or maybe a savant," Cat said.

"The one doesn't necessarily rule out the other," Pete said.

"No," Cat answered. "It doesn't."

She spent the morning waiting in her cubicle, hoping for another call. Who were the great waiters in literature?

Penelope—waiting for Odysseus, undoing her weaving every night

Rapunzel, in her tower

Snow White, Sleeping Beauty, and all the other comatose princesses

She couldn't think of any stories about men whose job it was to wait. But as Ed had put it, *Hey, don't get all Angela Davis on me.* She'd do her best.

She listened to the tape, several times. She looked through *Leaves of Grass*.

They prepare for death, yet are they not the finish, but rather the
  outset,

They bring none to his or her terminus or to be content and full,

Whom they take they take into space to behold the birth of stars, to
  learn one of the meanings,

To launch off with absolute faith, to sweep through the ceaseless
  rings and never be quiet again.

Little boy. Who do you want to take into space to behold the birth of stars?

At ten-thirty, she tossed her cell into her bag and went over to Rita Dunn's office at NYU. Dunn was in a building on Waverly. One of these buildings, Cat had never been quite sure which, had been that sweatshop, where the fire was. She knew the story only vaguely—the exits had been blocked to keep the workers from sneaking out early. Something like that. There'd been a fire, and all those women were trapped inside. Some of them had jumped. From one of these buildings—was it the one she was entering?—women with their dresses on fire had fallen, had hit this pavement right here or the pavement just down the street. Now it was all NYU. Now it was students and shoppers, a coffeehouse and a bookstore that sold NYU sweatshirts.

Cat went up to the ninth floor and announced herself to the department secretary, who nodded her down the hall.

Rita Dunn turned out to be red-haired, mid-forties, wearing a green silk jacket and heavy makeup. Dark eyeliner, blush expertly applied. Around her neck, a strand of amber beads just slightly smaller than billiard balls. She looked more like a retired figure skater than she did like a professor of literature.

"Hello," Cat said. She gave Rita Dunn a moment to adjust. No one ever said, You didn't sound black over the phone. Everybody thought it.

"Hello," Rita responded, and pumped Cat's hand enthusiastically. People loved talking to cops when they weren't in trouble.

"Thanks for taking the time to see me."

"Glad to. Sit."

She gestured Cat into a squeaky leatherette chair across from her desk, seated herself behind the desk. Her office was a chaos of books and papers (*disorderly sister*). On the wall behind her, a poster of Whitman—great lightbulb of old-man nose, small dark eyes looking out from the cottony crackle of beard and hair. In the window of Rita Dunn's office, a spider plant dangled its fronds before the vista of Washington Square Park. Had seamstresses once huddled at that window, trapped by flames? Had they stood on that sill and jumped?

"So," Rita Dunn said. "You want to know a thing or two about Mr. Whitman."

"I do."

"May I ask what exactly you're looking for?"

"Relating to a case I'm investigating."

"Does it have to do with the explosion?"

"I'm sorry, I can't discuss the details."

"I understand. A case involving Walt Whitman. Is he in trouble?"

"I know it's unusual."

Rita Dunn steepled her fingers, touched them to her mahogany-red lips. Cat felt, abruptly, the force of her attention. It was palpable, a clicking-on, a jewel-like zap that rose in her perfectly outlined eyes. Right, Cat thought. You dress like this to fool the men, don't you? You're a stealth fighter.

"I like the unusual," Rita said. "I like it very much. Can you give me a hint about where to begin?"

"Let's say this. Could you give me some idea about Whitman's message to his readers?"

"His message was complicated."

"Got that. Just tell me whatever comes to mind."

"Hm. Do you know anything about him at all?"

"A little. I read him in college. I've been reading him again."

"Well. Okay. Whitman as you probably know was the first great American visionary poet. He didn't just celebrate himself. He celebrated everybody and everything."

"Right."

"He spent his life, and it was a long life, extending and revising *Leaves of Grass*. He published it himself. The first edition appeared in 1855. There were nine editions in all. The last, which he called his deathbed edition, appeared in 1891. You could say that he was writing the poem that *was* the United States."

"Which he loved."

"Which he did love."

"Would you call him patriotic, then?"

"It's not quite the right term for Whitman, I don't think. Homer loved Greece, but does the word 'patriotic' feel right for him? I think not. A great poet is never anything quite so provincial."

She picked up a pearl-handled letter opener, ran a fingertip along the blade. Aristocrats with tentative claims to thrones might have been just this impeccably overdressed, Cat thought. They might have possessed this underlayer of fierce, cordial vigilance.

Cat said, "But might someone, reading him today, interpret him as patriotic? Could *Leaves of Grass* be read as some sort of extended national anthem?"

"Well, you wouldn't believe some of the interpretations I've heard. But really, Whitman was an ecstatic. He was a dervish of sorts. Patriotism, don't you think, implies a certain fixed notion of right versus wrong. Whitman simply loved what *was*."

"Indiscriminately."

"Yes and no. He believed in destiny. He imagined that the redwood tree was glad for the ax because it was the tree's destiny to be cut down."

"So he had no particular sense of good and evil."

"He understood life to be transitory. He was not particularly concerned about mortality."

"Right," Cat said.

"Is that helpful?"

"Mm-hm. Does the phrase 'In the family' mean anything to you?"

"Do you mean, do I recognize it from Whitman?"

"It's not from Whitman."

"I thought not. Though I can't claim to know every single line."

"Does it suggest anything to you?"

"Not really. Could you put it in some sort of context?"

"Say, as a declaration. If somebody said to you, 'I'm in the family.' In light of Whitman."

"Well. Whitman empathized with everyone. In Whitman there are no insignificant lives. There are mill owners and mill workers, there are great ladies and prostitutes, and he refuses to favor any of them. He finds them all worthy and fascinating. He finds them all miraculous."

"The way, say, a parent refuses to favor one child over the others?"

"I suppose you could say that, yes."

"What about the idea of working for a company?"

"I beg your pardon?"

"If somebody said, 'We all work for the company.' In light of Whitman."

"Hmm. I could go out on a limb a little, I suppose."

"Please do."

"Well. When Whitman published the first edition of *Leaves of Grass*, the industrial revolution was well under way. People who had lived on farms for generations were all moving to the cities in hopes of getting rich."

"And . . ."

"A handful did in fact get rich. Almost everybody else worked twelve-hour shifts in factories, six days a week. It was the end of the agrarian world and the beginning of the mechanized one. Do you know that universal *time* didn't exist until around the late 1800s? It was two o'clock in one village, three o'clock in another. It wasn't until the transcontinental railroads that we all had to agree on when it was two and when it was three, so people could make their trains. It took a full generation just to convince people that they had to show up at work every single day at the same hour."

"Everybody worked for the company, in a manner of speaking."

"You could say that. But, really, it's impossible to pin a poet like Whitman down this way. Was he writing about industrialization? Yes, he was. Was he writing about family? Certainly. And he was also writing about logging and sex and the westward expansion. You can go at him from just about any angle and find something that seems to support some thesis or other."

"I see."

" 'Of Life immense in passion, pulse, and power, cheerful, for freest action form'd under the laws divine, The Modern Man I sing.' I'm afraid that if you insist on too much focus here or there, you miss the larger point."

Cat said, " 'To die is different from what any one supposes, and luckier.' "

"You know your Whitman, then."

"Just a line or two. I shouldn't take up any more of your time."

"I don't think I've been very helpful."

She rose graciously, a compassionate duchess who'd reached the limits of her ability to intercede in the coarser mysteries of the world, its infestations and calamitous weather. There were afflictions that were probably best addressed by local methods—by chants and ritual burnings, the drawing of pentagrams.

"May I ask you one more question?" Cat said. "It's not related to Whitman."

"By all means."

"Is this where that fire was, the one that killed all those women? Was it this building?"

"No, actually, that building is around the corner. It's part of the biochemistry department now."

Cat rose and went to the window. It was all calmness below. It was students hurrying to class and, at the end of the block, the leaf-shimmer of Washington Square Park.

She called Pete on her cell when she got to the street.

"Ashberry."

"I just talked to the Whitman person."

"She tell you anything?"

"It seems you could interpret him as some sort of voice for the status quo. As in, if you worked at some awful job in a factory, twelve hours a day, six days a week, here was Whitman to tell you that your life was great, your life was poetry, you were a king in your own world."

"You think the kid thinks that?"

"I think *somebody* thinks that. I think somebody is speaking through the kid."

"You on your way back in?"

"I am."

"See you."

Pete was waiting in her cubicle when she arrived. He didn't ask about Whitman. He said, "Dick Harte's wife just gave us a little something."

"What?"

"He woke up in the middle of the night, the night before he was killed. Said he heard a noise."

"A noise?"

"One of those middle-of-the-night things."

"He was scared?"

"She didn't say scared. She said he said he heard a noise. She said he said he was going to go see what it was."

"*She* was scared."

"Yeah. But she takes a little something to help her sleep. She doesn't rouse easily, it seems."

"And?"

"And he got up, left the bedroom. Was gone maybe ten minutes. Came back, said it was nothing, the two of them went back to sleep."

"That's it?"

"That's it," Pete said.

"You think it means anything?"

"Probably not. What do you think?"

"Hard to say. Probably not."

"At least she's talking now."

"The daughter?"

"Still in the ozone. Seriously unhinged."

"What's up with the son?"

"Mondo cooperativo. Scary cooperative. Boy detective seems to like his sudden fame."

"As people do."

"He's a piece of work, as it turns out. Serious drug history, lately turned to Jesus. That school in Vermont's a jail, basically, for rich kids."

"Interesting."

"Semi-interesting. You don't think the son's involved, do you?"

"No. I don't."

"We're not going to get anything from the family, I don't think. I mean, I don't think there's anything to get."

"Probably right," she said.

And yet, an image crept into her mind. She pictured Dick Harte roused from sleep, walking through a big, dark house in his pajamas (he'd have worn pajamas, wouldn't he; a balding fifty-three-year-old with no record of drug use or illicit sex, a man who paid his bills on time, whose pretty wife number two sent herself to Pluto every night with the help of a few key pharmaceuticals), tracking down a suspicious nocturnal sound. What would it have been like, being Dick Harte? Was he satisfied; was he prospering in his heart? Had he had a premonition that night, out there in the stately abundance of Great Neck? Cat imagined him going down the staircase, walking barefoot over parquet and Oriental rugs, finding nothing amiss, but wondering. She pictured him going to a window—make it a living-room window, Thermopane, with heavy brocade *window treatments* (the wife was a decorator, right?); say it looked out onto an expanse of black lawn, with hedges and rosebushes and the dark glitter of a pool. She saw Dick standing at the window, looking out. She saw him understanding—he would sense more than see it—that a child stood on his lawn, a boy, skinny and erect and alert, crazy and worshipful: a sentinel, watching Dick Harte's slumbering house the way a guerrilla fighter might take a last look at a village, its lamps extinguished and its people dreaming, before he set it on fire. The child would have vanished immediately, nothing more than a child-shaped shadow that resolved itself into a patch of darkness where a rosebush bore no blooms. Dick would have shrugged it off, gone back to bed, assured his zonked-out wife that there was nothing to fear.

Pete said, "Just wanted to let you know. See you later."

"I'll be right here. At my loom."

"Huh?"

"Nothing. See you later."

She sat at her desk, resumed her waiting. Was it possible that the kid had gone out to Dick Harte's house, to see his deathmate at home? Unlikely. She was projecting. Say it: you want Luke to be out there in the dark, watching you. You want that, and you fear it. She couldn't help imagining herself looking down at Fifth Street from her own window, late at night, and seeing him on the pavement, three years old, staring up at her window. There he'd be, dark-eyed, curious, prone to fits of inexplicable laughter, a little bit pigeon-toed, devoted to trucks and to anything red.

Would he be loving? Or would he be furious? Would he have forgiven her?

A nick in your heart. The settlement from the doctor sent me to Columbia. Which got me here.

What had she done to merit forgiveness? Nothing came immediately to mind.

It happened at ten minutes to five.

Cat heard it first from Aaron, the audio guy. He raced by her cubicle, stuck his small, otterish head in.

"There's been another one," he said.

"What?"

"It just came in. Central Park."

"What do you know?"

"Looks like the same thing. Bomb. Right by Bethesda Fountain."

He ran on. Cat bolted up out of her chair, ran into Pete on her way into the hall.

"Fuck," Pete said.

"What do we know?"

"Central fucking Park. Bethesda fucking Fountain."

"A kid?"

"Don't know yet. I'm on my way up there."

"I'm coming, too."

"You can't. You're here."

Right. She was on phone duty. There was no telling who might call, and her cell would pick up background noise if she went to the site. She knew better than to argue.

"Keep me posted," she said.

"Yeah."

She returned to her cubicle.

He'd done it, then. The little fucker had walked up to someone in the park and taken them both to behold the birth of stars.

She remained. There was nothing else for her to do. The office rocked and roiled around her; she was its still center. News filtered in. Victim was one Henry Coles, African-American, age twenty-two, married but separated. One son, five years old, who lived with the mother. Worked at Burger King. Perpetrator, according to witnesses, was a kid, eleven or twelve, wearing a Mets jersey and some sort of cap. Henry Coles had been out for a stroll, just sucking up a little light and air before his shift started. Kid came up behind him, hugged him, and detonated.

Fuck.

Cat heard snatches of the phone conversations going on in other cubicles. There was no lag factor today—the citizens of the Bizarro Dimension were seriously unnerved. *Why do you think the government would want to do this? Do you, personally, know members of Al Qaeda? When did your television first start warning you about the Aryan Nation?*

Cat's phone did not ring. She waited. There was nothing else for her to do.

She thought about Henry Coles, brother from another planet. Or rather, from another country here on her own planet. She did not of course know Henry Coles, and if Ed Short or anyone like him had dared to generalize about the poor annihilated motherfucker, she'd have nailed him good. She was in no mood. But okay, privately, here in the unquiet of her semi-office, she could let her mind rove a little. Twenty-two years old with a child he wasn't supporting (not by flipping burgers), probably working a scam or two, trying to get by, trying to be dignified if not powerful, struggling every moment to feel like somebody, to hang in, to not collapse, to not be in the wrong place at the wrong time, to not make the mistake that would send his ass to jail for the rest of his life. She knew Henry Coles. She'd been married to him.

And not. Daryl had done better than Burger King; he was pretty and smart; he'd earned passable money working for UPS (he could *deliver*, that boy could) and was taking prelaw courses at Hunter. Still, he couldn't quite pass, could he? He didn't have the diction; he didn't have the stance. Cat's mother had never tired of insisting that Daryl was beneath her. Cat had had church dresses and piano lessons. She'd been read to every night.

Daryl. I still think about your neck and your hands. I hope LA is working out for you. I hope you're thinking about law school again.

She pictured him walking through Central Park, as he might very well have done. Striding along, hopeful and scared and angry, aware of the unease he inspired in the white girls pushing strollers, mortified by it, glad about it. Step back, bitches. Dick Harte might have made the high-rises rise, but he couldn't scare the mothers in Central Park just by walking past. Cat saw Henry Coles crossing before the fountain just as Daryl might have done, looking up at the angel with her furrowed profile and big peasant-girl feet; she who was always there, day and night, spreading her heavy wings for everyone but offering heaven only to her favorites. Step back, bitch. I'll make my own heaven. You won't be there.

And then, from behind, a pair of small arms wrapped around him. Then blinding light and the intimation of an impossible noise.

She struggled to imagine the kid. There wasn't much to work with. Mets jersey, some sort of cap. She pictured him small, even for his age; pale and grave; a ghostly creature with unnaturally bright eyes and quick little fingers, like an opossum's. A Gollum, a changeling. He'd have been a listless baby, and as he got older he'd have been passive and fearful, strangely empty, infinitely suggestible; an "as if" personality, one of those mysterious beings who lack some core of self everyone else takes for granted. He'd have been, all his short life, a convincing member of the dead, waiting for his time to come.

She stuck around until after seven, when Pete returned.

"Hey," he said.

"Hey."

He slumped against the wall of her cubicle. She'd never seen him so exhausted. His eyes were rheumy, his face mottled.

"What do we know?" she asked.

"Black kid, cap pulled down low over his face, and then, poof. Nothing more for the witnesses to see."

"He was black?"

"So say the witnesses."

He must have assumed she was white when he called in. As he naturally would. Black kids always assumed the person in power was white.

But the kid had sounded white to her as well. Funny. Two black people, cop and killer, each assuming the other must be white. Funny.

We're in the family. We don't have names anymore.

She said to Pete, "Looks like they weren't related, then."

"Unlikely. We'll know as soon as the DNAs are in."

"A white kid took out a white guy, and a black kid took out a black guy."

"Yep."

"A black guy who worked at Burger King."

"He didn't even have an address. He slept here and there. Been bunking most recently with his mother, up on 123rd."

"Very *not* Dick Harte."

"Couldn't be much less like Dick Harte."

"It's as if they're saying nobody's safe. You're not safe if you're a real-estate tycoon, and you're not safe if you work for minimum wage."

"That would seem to be true."

"I keep thinking about that 'in the family' shit."

"We'll find something on that. It's probably some obscure Japanese video game. Or from some storefront church."

"You think this is the end of it?" she said.

"Hope so."

"Two crazy little boys who said they were brothers."

"You want dinner?"

"Yes."

She pulled the stack of take-out menus from her top drawer. They decided on Thai.

Pete said, "There can't be no pattern."

"We'll find one."

"You sure about that?"

She hesitated. What the hell, just let yourself talk. You're a couple of exhausted government workers waiting for their pad thai to come; you can break the code.

"I wonder," she said. "It's getting harder to *see* the patterns, don't you think?"

"We're all freaked out these days."

"I hope that's it. I hope it's about us not being able to see what's there."

"Meaning?"

"Meaning, I hope there's something there to see. I hope it's not just . . . randomness. Chaos."

"It's not."

She looked at him, steadily and hard. For a moment she thought, What I'm going to do is have another child and raise him far away from all this, in a house in the mountains, by an unpolluted stream where unmutated fish still swim, where we'll have books and no television, and I'll do the best I can with the boredom and racism, I'll manage, I won't be sitting on some bar stool every night, I'll stay home and read to the kid, and during the days I'll work in the local clinic or be a high school counselor or learn to knit sweaters and sell them in fucking crafts fairs. She thought, If you had any sense, Pete Ashberry, you'd want that, too. You'd admit that we're emigrants, that our native land is too barren for us, too hard; that what we should really and truly do is buy a good reliable used car and drive out into the continent and see what we can find for ourselves.

"I'm sure you're right," she said.

"You did a good job. You did the best anybody could have done. You couldn't have saved this kid."

And sounded white over the phone

And let him die

And am a cracked vessel, and am an empty cup

"We'll never know that, will we?" she said.

"Give yourself a break."

"Trying."

"Would it piss you off if I gave you a little advice?"

"That would depend on the advice."

"Don't mix any of this up with what happened to your own kid."

She nodded, tapped her chin with her forefinger. Probably stupid to have told Pete about Luke. You lost track, working with someone every day. You told them things. You had sex with them in the ladies' room.

She said, "You don't have some kind of *theory* going on about me, do you, Pete?"

"No way."

A silence caught and held. Had she embarrassed him? Had she shamed him? Okay, then, give him something. He's a good man; he cares about you.

She said, "I didn't take him to another doctor."

"You had no reason to."

"We didn't have any money. We had shit for insurance."

"And a doctor told you it was gas. Kids have strange little aches and pains all the time. Gas was a reasonable diagnosis."

"The wrong one."

"You didn't know that."

I suspected it. I had a feeling. I decided to believe the doctor. I told myself, kids have strange little aches and pains all the time.

"No," she said. "I didn't."

"So give yourself a break. Can you do that?"

A nick in his heart. He crawled into bed with Daryl and me, said he was thirstier than he'd ever been, and died. Right there.

"Sure," she said. "I can do that."

The food came. They ate, talked about other things, threw the empty containers out. Pete went back to his office. Cat hung around a little longer, for no good reason. It was all cleanup now, it was investigation; the deranged boys were dead, and the work of finding out who they'd been would fall to others. She dialed Simon's number. He'd called three times since the event, left messages. He'd believe her when she'd tell him she'd been too busy to call him back, though of course it would be a lie. She was the least busy person on the premises. She'd put off talking to Simon (admit it) because she hadn't felt up to it, hadn't felt like being tough and passionate and wised-up.

Amelia put her straight through.

"Cat. God, I've been worried."

"Sorry I couldn't call earlier. It's crazy here."

"Can you get out of there now?"

"Yes. Meet me at your place, okay? Just give me a drink and put me to bed."

"You got it. I can get out of here in about forty-five minutes."

Forty-five minutes was good time for Simon. Who knew what fluctuations in the futures needed his immediate attention?

"I'll come by around nine, then."

"Good. You okay?"

"Relatively."

"Good. See you at nine."

She said good-night to Pete and went out into the streets. She'd wander a while among the terrorized citizenry, until Simon could extricate himself from the particulars of whatever deal he was dealing.

She started down Broadway. If you didn't know what had happened, you could easily believe it was just another night in the city. The sidewalks were a little less crowded, people were moving with more than the usual degrees of slink or alacrity, but if you were fresh from Mongolia or Uganda you wouldn't have any but the usual touristic impressions. The city was only being rocked in its less visible parts, along its filaments, in its dreams of itself. People were scared, and yes, it was impossible to know yet just how much money was bleeding out, how many reservations were being canceled, how many corporations were considering relocating, but Broadway was still full of cabs and trucks, stores were still open, unfortunates still worked the passersby for change. The machinery of the city, the immense discordant poetry of the city (thank you, Mr. Whitman), racketed on. You had to bring a building down to make things look different. Tonight there were no candlelight vigils, no mounds of flowers, no women wailing. It all went on.

Four people had gone into space to behold the birth of stars. It all went on. What else should it do?

She browsed the store windows along lower Broadway. She was hungry for normalcy the way she might be hungry for a pastrami on rye. She didn't want to be herself. Not right now. She wanted, right now, to be a shopper, a regular person, unhaunted, unjaded, free from all but the usual quotients of bitterness and guilt, somebody with a little time to kill on her way to her boyfriend's place.

The shop windows down here were full of jeans or running shoes or discount cosmetics or every now and then Chinese herbs. The fancier establishments were on the side streets. Broadway was for the young, the semipoor, the easily delighted. She was not young and was not easily delighted. She could have wandered east or west, into different neighborhoods, but then she'd have been window-shopping, and she couldn't bring herself to do that. Too trivial. She could at best wander slowly along her inevitable route, scanning the windows she'd be passing anyway, being *incidentally* trivial, waiting for it to be nine o'clock.

It was just after she'd crossed Canal Street that the feeling arrived again. Someone was watching her. She walked on. She didn't turn around. Not right away. She waited until she'd reached a shop window (a junk shop, it seemed, didn't matter what it was). She pretended to be checking out the merchandise, then did a quick glance up the street. Nothing and no one. Okay, a white couple huddled pigeonlike into each other as they negotiated the scraps of windblown trash, and an old woman sitting on a loading dock, dangling her tattered legs over the edge, swinging them like an ancient, exhausted child.

Still, Cat had the feeling. The queasy tingle along the back of her neck.

She refocused, actually looked at the contents of the store window. Gaya's Emporium. It was a little strange for Broadway—more an East Village sort of establishment. Its window was heaped with scavengings: a ratty coat with a fake-fur collar, two pairs of ancient roller skates, a mirrored disco ball, tangles of costume jewelry, a lantern-jawed male mannequin's head, blandly cheerful under a rainbow Afro wig. Total randomness—things that were gathered together because the shop owner had found them somewhere and thought that somebody might conceivably want to buy them. The world overflowed with product, old and new; it was impossible to contain it all. At the lower levels, sheer quantity trumped categorization.

She lingered a moment before the sorrowful bounty. It would look like treasure to most people in the world, wouldn't it? You had to be among the privileged few to know that this stuff was junk even when it was new, this faux rich-lady coat and this chipped porcelain shepherdess and this bundle of plastic swizzle sticks topped with plastic mermaids.

Among the coils of jewelry was a bowl, half hidden. It had been carelessly filled with gold-toned brooches, a strand of fake pearls, but the rim showed, pale and bright as the moon, decorated along its upper edge with symbols of some sort, which might have been flowers or sea anemones or stars. Junk, it was probably junk—what else could it be, considering where it had ended up?—and yet, it didn't *look* like junk, even in the fluorescence of the shop window. It seemed to emit a faint but perceptible glow, like a wristwatch in the dark, though it was pure, pure white. It looked, from what she could see of it, like a displaced treasure, something genuinely rare, mistaken for dross. These things turned up every now and then, didn't they? The da Vinci drawing slipped in among the botanical prints, the Melville letters stacked with old bills and yellowed shopping lists. Could it possibly be Chinese? Could it be something Simon might want for his collection?

She went into the shop. It smelled of mold and sweaty wool, with an undercurrent of sandalwood incense. It was more like someone's messy closet than a store. There were piles of shoes, a sagging clothes rack jammed full of old jackets and sweaters, a round cardboard bin that proclaimed, in scrawled Magic Markered letters, that its contents could be had for fifty cents apiece.

A woman sat at the rear, behind a glass counter. She was as wan and worn-looking as her merchandise. Her gray hair hung to her shoulders, and her face was vague, as if someone had drawn the features of a woman onto the front of her head and then tried to erase them. Still, she was queenly, in her ruined way. She sat erect, with a vase full of peacock feathers on her right and an oval mirror on her left, like a minor queen of the underworld, ruler of the lost and inconsequential.

Cat summoned a regal bearing of her own. *I have no intention of slipping any of your sorry shit into my handbag.*

"Hello," the woman said, without a hint of malice or suspicion. She might have been sitting here among these things for years, waiting to see if tonight someone would finally come in.

"Hello," Cat said. Regular voice. "I wonder if I could see that bowl in the window."

"Bowl."

"Yes. It's right there. It has jewelry in it. Is it for sale?"

"Oh, the bowl. Just a minute, please."

The woman stood. She was violently thin. She wore a lank dress covered in roses and some sort of purple shawl over her shoulders. She went to the window, leaned over, and dumped the jewelry out of the bowl. She brought it to Cat.

"Here it is," she said.

The bowl was, in fact, something. Anyone could see it. It was about the size of a sparrow's nest, luminous; it seemed to amplify the room's stagnant illumination. Cat took it from the woman. It was lighter than she'd expected it to be, almost weightless. Even up close, she couldn't tell what the symbols painted along its outer rim were meant to be. They didn't look Chinese. Each was different from the others, but all were variations on the same design: a circle that emanated slender spokes, some straight and some wavy, some long and some short.

"It's beautiful," Cat said.

"I don't know where it came from."

"Is it for sale?"

"It's ten dollars."

Cat paused, briefly and absurdly doubtful — if it was really as lovely as it seemed, would it cost so little?

"I'll take it," she said.

She gave the woman ten dollars and waited while she wrapped the bowl in a sheet of newspaper. Cat thought she would give the bowl to Simon. She'd never bought him anything like this; she'd only bought him books, and once a tie he'd admired when they were in Barneys together. She'd never before given him anything that involved her own sense of beauty, anything meant to join the carefully selected prizes he kept up there in his aerie. She hadn't dared to.

The woman slipped the wrapped bowl into an old plastic Duane Reade bag. She gave it to Cat.

"Enjoy it," the woman said.

"Thank you," Cat answered. "I will."

As she left the shop, she heard a clatter. Horse's hooves, galloping. She froze. Here it came, toward her. A bay horse, riderless, running up Broadway. For a moment, the world tipped on its axis. Something dreadful and impossible was happening. And then the world righted itself again. It was a runaway horse. It was only that. A car pulled over to avoid it, another laid on its horn. The horse was running up the middle of the street, its hooves sparking on the pavement. After a moment a patrol car appeared in pursuit, lights flashing and siren blaring. There was a stable down there, wasn't there? Where the police horses were kept. Cat stood sheltered in the doorway of the shop. The horse ran by. It was beautiful, no denying it. Black mane fluttering, brown flanks glossy and strong. An ancient and marvelous manifestation, slipped through a dimensional warp. It did not appear to be frightened. It was only running. The squad car came after, flashing its lights. The horse galloped on, pursued by the car.

The woman from the store came out and stood beside Cat. "Terrible," she said.

"My God."

"It's the second time this month."

"Really?"

"Something's spooking them," the woman said. "This didn't used to happen."

"What do you think it is?"

"Something in the air. Animals know."

Cat stood with the woman, watching the horse disappear up Broadway amid screeching brakes and car horns, carrying with it the steady hollow sound of its hooves and the wail of the siren. What would happen when it got to Canal Street?

"You didn't drop the bowl, did you?" the woman asked.

"What? Oh, no."

She was, in fact, holding the bowl close to her breasts, as if to protect it, or as if she'd believed in some reflexive way that it could shield her.

"Good."

The shop woman nodded. It seemed for a moment that the incident had been meant to deprive Cat of a ten-dollar bowl and that the woman was glad to know things hadn't turned out badly after all.

The two women watched the horse as it receded. There was no sound of collision. The horse stopped at Canal Street, reared halfway on its hind legs. The cops jumped out of their car. There was a noisy confusion of people and lights, corner of Broadway and Canal, and above it all the horse's head, tossing. There was a flash of the horse's eyes and teeth, a string of its dangling saliva, bright in the streetlight.

"Wow," Cat said.

"Something's spooking them," the woman said.

"I guess so," Cat answered.

At nine (was it a bad idea, was it desperate-seeming, to be always so exactly on time?) she presented herself to Joseph the doorman and went up. Simon met her at the door. He held her, kissed her hair.

"Jesus," he whispered. "Jesus Christ."

"Nasty business," she said.

He settled her onto one of the couches, fixed her a drink. She told him the story. He listened with scowling avidity.

"My God," he said, when she had finished.

"So it looks like that's it," she said.

"That can't be *it.*"

"No, I mean, that's it for me. The boys are dead. I'll be going back to talking to the regular nuts."

"So now it's all just what? Postmortem?"

"Mm-hm. It shouldn't take too long. Two fucked-up kids who made some kind of pact, inspired by terrorists. Went on the Internet, learned how to make pipe bombs. We can't figure why no parents have called."

"What's your guess?"

"Denial. Pure and simple. If you call the police and get the confirmation, then it's really and truly happened. If you don't call the police, you can still tell yourself that your kid has just run away."

"You think these boys were abused?"

"Probably. Or maybe not. Some of the time, these people turn out to have had relatively ordinary childhoods."

"You hungry?"

"No. I ate."

"You want another drink?"

"Please."

He took the glass from her hand. Her throat constricted, and then she was crying. One moment she wasn't, and the next moment she was. It came out of her in great, heaving sobs. He took her in his arms.

"It's okay," he said softly. "It's okay."

She couldn't stop. She didn't want to stop. She let herself go on. She choked on her own sobs, struggled to catch her breath. It was as if a stone were lodged in her gullet and she were trying to weep it out.

"It's okay," he said again. "It's okay."

Finally the crying subsided. She lingered in his arms.

"Sorry," she said.

"It's okay."

"It's just. I fucked up."

"I don't think you did."

"Those little boys called me, and I didn't help them."

"It's okay."

She paused over whether or not to go into the part about sounding white to a black kid. Decided against it. She knew his reassurances wouldn't mean anything to her. She thought she should talk to him about it anyway—for, you know, the sake of their *closeness*—but she was beat, she was worried about other things, she didn't have it in her at the moment, it was just too hard right now.

What she said was, "I'm not sure if I can do this anymore."

"You should get some sleep."

"I know. But I don't think it'll be any better in the morning."

"Let's wait and see."

"I think I may need to find some other kind of work."

"Wait and see, okay?"

"Right. Oh, I brought you something."

"You did?"

"Just a second."

She got to her feet, a bit unsteadily. She was slightly tipsy already. She took the bowl from her bag, gave it to him.

"Didn't have time to wrap it," she said.

He removed the bowl from its plastic drugstore sack, pulled away the newspaper. And there it was, in his hands. Yes, it was in fact a marvelous thing. It was all the more apparent here, in this room, where only the rare and marvelous were permitted.

"Wow," Simon said.

"It just came from a junk shop. But it's nice, isn't it?"

"Yeah."

"Is it Chinese?"

"No. I've never seen anything quite like it before."

He set the bowl on the coffee table. It glowed like an opal, seemed to be studded with tiny sparks.

"Thank you," he said.

"You like it?"

"Yes. I do."

"I just . . . I saw it in this strange little store, and I thought you'd like it."

"I do. Very much."

"Good. I'm glad."

He stood up. "And now," he said, "it's time for you to go to bed."

"Yeah. It is."

She knew when he put his hand on her shoulder. His touch was tender and kind, but something had changed. She slipped her arm around his waist. Something had changed.

"Come on," he said.

They went into his bedroom. She started undressing.

"Are you coming to bed, too?" she asked.

"Not yet. It's early. I've got a pile of shit to do."

She got her clothes off, got into bed. Simon sat on the edge of the mattress, adjusted the covers over her. He could not have been gentler. Still, something was wrong.

She said, "Don't stay up too late, okay?"

"I won't."

She took his hand, stroked his fingertips. "Simon," she said.

"Uh-huh?"

Say it. Sooner or later, one of you has to.

"I love you."

"I love you, too."

Easy. Natural. No strangeness. And yet.

He kissed her. He turned off the light and left the room.

It came to her after he'd closed the door. She'd wept in his arms. She'd brought him a present, nervously anticipating his response. For the first time, she had failed to be strong and cynical, wised-up, police-like. For the first time, she'd been like the other women (there had, of course, been a number of other women): fragile, in need, eager to please him, grateful for his attention.

She tried to push the thought away. It was one night, for God's sake. It was a goddamned crisis. Who wouldn't fall apart? She'd be herself again in the morning. (Wouldn't she?) This was what happened when two people got to know each other. Nobody stayed in character all the time. This was intimacy. You saw each other through the dark spells. You didn't need—you didn't *want*—to be spared the fears and doubts, the crying fits, the self-recriminations.

And yet, she had a feeling. She was damaged now, in his eyes. She was no longer rare and marvelous. She wasn't a stern black goddess of law enforcement. She was someone who collapsed, who needed help, who awaited his judgment.

She could see how it would play out. She thought she could see it. Simon wasn't a bad man; he was not out there in the other room wondering how he'd get rid of her. What he had, she suspected, was an empty spot where his admiration and his lust had been. He would think nothing of it. He'd make coffee for her in the morning. He'd be more than kind. He wouldn't desert her when she needed him. But an unraveling had begun. She could feel it, she could see it, still months away, but coming: the end of his interest in her. The beginning of her life in his mind as someone he had dated once. It wasn't surprising. It wasn't exactly surprising. Simon was a collector. She understood now that he was collecting the incidents of his own past, and that one day he would arrive at his present, married to a smart, pretty white woman his own age or a few years younger, raising children, referring every now and then to his youth, when he had bought art and antiques instead of paying tuition, when he had gone to the restaurants and clubs known only to the few, when he had dated a dancer from the Mark Morris company and then an installation artist who'd been in the Biennial and then, briefly, an older black woman, a forensic psychologist who'd been involved in those terrorist attacks, who had spoken to the actual terrorists.

He was programmed for this. Smart boy from Iowa, perfectly formed, ambitious—he'd naturally want, he'd need, a wild phase before he took up the life that had been waiting for him from the moment of conception. It had been all but predetermined. If he and Cat hadn't met when they did, he'd have met another colorful character soon enough. And all the while his true and rightful wife was out there, waiting for him.

She, Cat, was a collector's item, wasn't she? She was an exotic specimen—men had always thought so. No-nonsense, ultracompetent black girl who's read more books than you have; who doesn't give a shit about domestic particulars and can beat your ass at any game you choose. They liked the tough girl, but they weren't quite so crazy about the nervous one. They hadn't signed on for that. She and Daryl might have survived Luke's death together, but they hadn't survived her remorse. Daryl could have comforted her for a month or two. He couldn't manage a year of it, not when she had nothing left for him. Not when she kept telling him, over and over again, that she had killed their child and that he was an idiot for thinking he loved her. Say something like that often enough, anybody will finally start believing you.

Who could blame these guys, really, for bailing when the messy shit came out? She didn't like it either.

Her cell rang. She bolted awake, accustomed to listening for it. Where was it, though? Where was *she*? Simon's. Simon's bed. He wasn't there. Clock said twelve forty-three. She got up. She was naked. She went into the living room, where Simon sat at his thousand-year-old Greco-Italian table, working at his laptop.

"My cell," Cat said groggily.

"I wasn't sure if I should wake you up," he answered.

She got the phone out of her bag, checked the readout. Pete.

"What's up?" she said.

"Guess who just walked into the Seventh Precinct station? Walt Whitman."

"What?"

"You ready? Some old *woman* who says she's Walt fucking Whitman. Walked into the Seventh, said she wanted to turn herself in. I'm there now."

"You're joking."

"Never more serious. Says she's the mother of the perpetrators and her name is Walt Whitman."

"What the hell."

"She knows about the Whitman business. That's all I can tell you."

"I'm on my way."

"You know where it is, right?"

"I do."

She clicked off. Simon was out of his chair, all thrilled capability. "What's going on?"

"Walt Whitman has turned himself in. Walt Whitman, however, turns out to be a woman."

"What?"

"I'll call you later."

She went back into the bedroom and got dressed. Simon was right behind her.

"Cat. What's going on?" he asked.

"Hell if I know."

She couldn't help thinking about how he must want to fuck her now.

She got into her clothes. Simon walked her to the door. She kissed him there. She took his face in both her hands, kissed him softly and lightly.

"Call me as soon as you can," he said.

She lingered a moment. There on the coffee table was the bowl, perfect in its modest way, bright as ice under the track lighting. It wasn't rare or fabulous, it wouldn't have a place among the ancient treasures on the shelves, but she'd given it to him, and she knew he'd keep it. He could put his keys and loose change in it when he got home at night.

"Goodbye, sweetheart," she said. Queenly bearing. Schoolmarm diction.

The woman sat in interrogation room three at the Seventh. Pete was with her, as were portly Bob (eyes like a pug's, smell of burnt toast) and scary Dave (Duran Duran haircut, tattoo tendrils creeping up his neck from God knew what he had crawling over the rest of him), FBI. Cat was escorted in by a sweet-faced Hispanic detective.

The woman was sixty or so, sitting straight as a hat rack in the grungy precinct chair. Her white hair—arctic white, incandescent white—was pulled into a fist at the back of her long, pale neck. She wore a shapeless coffee-colored dress and a man's tweed jacket with the sleeves turned up at the wrists, revealing modest bands of gray striped lining. Her long-fingered hands were splayed primly on the tabletop, as if she were waiting for a manicure.

For a moment Cat thought, It's the woman I bought the bowl from. It wasn't. Of course it wasn't. Still, this woman could have been her older sister.

"Hey, Cat," Pete said.

Portly and Scary both nodded.

Cat said to the woman in the chair, "They tell me you're Walt Whitman."

"The boys call me that," the woman said. Her voice was strong and clear, surprisingly deep; her diction was precise.

"It's an unusual name for a woman," Cat said.

"I'm an unusual woman."

"I can see that."

"I've come to tell you that it's starting," the woman said.

"What is it that's starting?"

"The end of days."

"Could you be a little more specific?"

"The innocents are rising up. Those who seemed most harmless are where the danger lies."

"What are you saying, exactly?"

"Urge and urge and urge, always the procreant urge of the world."

"Listen, lady—" said Portly.

Cat cut in quickly. "You know your Whitman."

"Do you believe in reincarnation?" the woman asked.

"I'm not sure."

"You will."

"Are you the reincarnation of Walt Whitman?" Cat asked.

The woman gazed at her with wistful affection. Her eyes were milky blue, oddly blue, albino-ish and unfocused. If Cat didn't know better, she'd have thought the woman was blind.

The woman said, "It's time."

"Time for what?"

"To start over."

"Start what over?"

"The world. The injured world."

"And how do you think the world is starting over?"

The woman shook her head regretfully. "Those boys were dead anyway," she said.

"What boys?"

The woman didn't look particularly unstable. Her pallid eyes held steady. Her pale pink lips were firm. She said, "No one wanted them. One was left in an alley in Buffalo. He weighed just under three pounds. Another one was purchased from a prostitute in Newark for two hundred dollars. The middle boy had been a sex slave to a particularly unpleasant person in Asbury Park."

"Tell me what you think you and the boys are doing."

"We're reversing the flow," she said.

Scary said, "Who are you working with?"

The woman looked at Cat with kindly, knowing weariness. She said, "It's time to make the announcement. We can't wait for the last one. He's taking longer than he was supposed to."

"Who's the last one?"

"I can't find him. I wonder if he's gone home."

"Where's home?"

"Would you go and look for him? He likes you. He trusts you, I think."

"Look for him where?"

The woman said, "327 Rivington. Apartment nineteen. If he's there, take care of him."

She smiled. She had tiny, perfectly square teeth, symmetrical as jewelry.

Pete said, "You're telling us this boy is at 327 Rivington?"

"I'm saying he might be," the woman answered. "It's hard to keep track of your children, isn't it? No matter how hard you try."

"Is he armed?" Pete asked.

"Well, yes, of course he is," the woman answered.

Pete said to Scary, "Let's go."

Cat knew who else would be going with them. If there was in fact a little boy sitting in an apartment with a bomb, he'd be vaporized by the squad. No one was wedded, at this point, to the notion of a live capture.

"Good luck," Cat said.

The woman said to Cat, "Aren't you going?"

"No. I'm going to stay here and talk to you."

"You should go. If he's there, you're the one he'll want to see."

"Not gonna happen, lady," Scary said.

"You care to tell us what you think we're going to find there?" Pete asked.

"You won't be in any danger. I can tell you that."

"Thanks. That's good to know."

"If you find him, will you bring him here?"

"Right," Pete said. To Cat he added, "I'll be in touch."

"So long."

Pete and Scary took off. Portly stood ominously by the door as Cat settled herself in a chair across from the woman, whose hands were still placed carefully on the tabletop, fingers spread. Her nails, on closer inspection, were not clean.

Cat said, "You know, don't you, that if your boy is there, they'll be very hard on him."

"There's nothing they can do," she answered.

"There's a lot they can do."

"I'd hate for them to hurt him. Of course I would. No one wants a child to be hurt."

"But you're hurting your children. You know you are."

"It's better, don't you think, to have it over quickly. One flash, a moment of hurt, and then you're elsewhere. Then you're on your way."

Cat held herself steady through a spasm of white-hot rage. She said, "Tell me a little more about what it is you've come to announce."

The woman leaned forward. Her eyes took on a remote, cloudy light. She said, "No one is safe in a city anymore. Not if you're rich.

Not if you're poor. It's time to move back to the country. It's time to live on the land again. It's time to stop polluting the rivers and cutting down the forests. It's time for us to live in villages again."

"Why are you doing this?" Cat asked.

The woman sighed and tucked an errant strand of ghost-white hair behind her ear. She could have been an elderly professor, fatigued by her students' youth and opacity but still hopeful, still willing to explain.

"Look around," she said. "Do you see happiness? Do you see joy? Americans have never been this prosperous, people have never been this safe. They've never lived so long, in such good health, ever, in the whole of history. To someone a hundred years ago, as recently as that, this world would seem like heaven itself. We can fly. Our teeth don't rot. Our children aren't a little feverish one moment and dead the next. There's no dung in the milk. There's *milk*, as much as we want. The church can't roast us alive over minor differences of opinion. The elders can't stone us to death because we might have committed adultery. Our crops never fail. We can eat raw fish in the middle of the desert, if we want to. And look at us. We're so obese we need bigger cemetery plots. Our ten-year-olds are doing heroin, or they're murdering eight-year-olds, or both. We're getting divorced faster than we're getting married. Everything we eat has to be sealed because if it wasn't, somebody would put poison in it, and if they couldn't get poison, they'd put pins in it. A tenth of us are in jail, and we can't build the new ones fast enough. We're bombing other countries simply because they make us nervous, and most of us not only couldn't find those countries on a map, we couldn't tell you which continent they're on. Traces of the fire retardant we put in upholstery and carpeting are starting to turn up in women's breast milk. So tell me. Would you say this is working out? Does this seem to you like a story that wants to continue?"

Portly said, "Yeah, but you still can't beat a Big Mac." He cleaned a fingernail with an opposing thumbnail.

"And you think you can do something about it?" Cat asked.

"One does what one can. I'm part of the plan to tell people that it's all over. No more sucking the life out of the rest of the world so that a small percentage of the population can live comfortably. It's a big project, I grant you. But history is always changed by a small band of very determined people."

This got Portly interested again. He said, "Who are you working with?"

"We don't see one another as much as we'd like to," the woman said.

"Give me a name."

"We don't have names."

"You call yourself Walt," Portly said.

"The boys call me that. I don't know how it started, really, but it seemed to comfort them, so I allowed it. You know how children are."

"What's your real name?" Portly asked.

"I don't have one. Really, I don't. They gave me one, many years ago, but I hardly remember it anymore. It isn't mine. It never was."

"You're in the family," Cat said.

"Why, yes, dear. I am. We all are, don't you see?"

"What do you mean by that?" Cat asked. "Whose family?"

"Oh, you know."

"I don't know. I'd like you to tell me."

"You'll forget your false name, in time."

"Do you work for the company?" Cat asked.

"We all work for the company. It's going out of business, though."

"Tell me about the company."

"I'm afraid I'm all talked out now. I really don't have anything more to say."

Something happened to her eyes. They went glassy, like the eyes taxidermists put in the sockets of dead animals.

"Walt?" Cat said.

Nothing. The woman sat with her hands splayed out on the tabletop, looking blindly at the air directly in front of her prim pink face.

Pete called fewer than twenty minutes later, on Cat's cell.

"Did you find him?" she asked.

"No. There's nobody. I think you should come over here. Have a patrolman bring you."

"I'm on my way."

The building on Rivington was one of the last of the old wrecks, sandwiched between a skateboard store and a wine bar. It was scabby brown plaster, chalky, like very old candy. Across the street a converted warehouse, its bricks brightly sandblasted, flew a green banner that announced the imminent availability of The Ironworks Condominium Luxury Lofts.

The galvanized steel door, which said DETHRULZ and PREY FOR PILLS in bright, dripping letters, was open. Cat went in. The door led onto a scarred yellow hallway illuminated by a buzzing fluorescent circle. Desolation Row. And yet, someone had put a vase full of artificial flowers on a rickety gilded table just inside the vestibule. Gray daisies and spiky wax roses and, hovering over the flowers, impaled on the end of a long plastic stick, a desiccated angel made of plastic and yarn.

Cat went up the stairs, found the door to apartment nineteen. It was open.

Inside, Pete and Scary and the guys from the bomb squad stood in the middle of a small, dim room. Cat paused, getting her bearings. The room was neat. No clutter. It smelled of varnish and, faintly, of gas. There was an old beige sofa, a little like the one in her own apartment. There were a couple of mismatched chairs, a table, all chipped and scarred but presentable, surely found on the streets. And every surface except for the furniture was covered with pages, carefully aligned, yellowish under coats of shellac.

The walls, ceiling, and floor were covered with the pages of *Leaves of Grass*.

"Motherfuck," Cat said.

"Motherfuck," Pete agreed.

"What do you make of this?" Scary said.

Cat walked slowly around the room. It was all Whitman.

"It's home," she said. "It's where the boys grew up."

At the room's far end, an arched opening led into a short hallway. It, too, was covered in pages. She gave herself a tour.

Kitchen, bathroom, two bedrooms, lit by bare bulbs screwed into ceiling sockets. The bulbs were low-watt, probably fifteens—they emitted a dim and watery illumination. The wan light and the varnish that covered the pages on the walls made it all sepia, insubstantial, as if she were walking through old photographs of rooms. The place was snug, in its insane and barren way. The kitchen was more presentable than hers. Pans, battered but clean, hung from hooks over the stove. On the countertop, a Folgers coffee can held silverware. In the first bedroom were three cots side by side, each scrupulously made up, their dust-colored blankets tucked in, an ivory-colored pillow centered at each one's head. Blue plastic milk crates contained modest stacks of clothes. In the second bedroom was another cot, just like the others. The second bedroom also contained an old sewing machine, the treadle kind, glossy black, insectlike, on an oak stand.

It might have been the low-budget version of an army barracks or an orphanage. Except of course for the fact that everything—the kitchen cabinets, the windows—was plastered over with pages.

"She's kept them here," Cat said to Pete.

"Who?"

"The boys. She got them as infants and raised them here."

"You're shitting me."

"She brought up a family of little killers. She got custody of kids nobody wanted and brought them here. She's been planning this for years."

"You sure about that?"

"I'm not sure about anything."

"You got any ideas as to why?"

"What do you think endures? Do you think a great city endures?"

"Say what?"

"According to her, it's the end of days. The innocents are rising up."

"Crazy."

"Mm-hm. Entirely crazy."

"Her prints aren't matching up with anything in the files yet."

"They won't. She's nobody. She's from nowhere."

"You're starting to sound a little like her."

She said, "Doing my job. Projecting myself into the mind of the suspect."

"Not a fun place to be."

Never has been, baby.

She said, "Honestly, Pete, we've been expecting this. You know we have."

"I haven't."

"Not *this*. You know what I mean. People see how easy it is to scare the world right to its core. Not so hard to fuck up the system, as it turns out. You can do a lot with a few deranged children and some hardware-store explosives."

"Give me a break, okay? Sure everybody's freaked out, but the world's going on. One insane old witch and a couple of retarded kids are not bringing it all down."

"I know. I know that."

"So what are you saying?"

"You mind if I just go a little loose?"

"Nope. Go."

"You're probably right. An old witch and a couple of damaged children. But she told me she thinks history is changed by a small band of people."

"That would be, say, a few thousand Bolsheviks. That would be entirely fucking different."

"Of course it is. It's entirely different."

"Don't use that voice with me."

Pete would know about the voice. His mother had probably used it.

"Sorry. I'm just saying it seems possible, it doesn't seem impossible, that this ragged band of crazy fucks we've stumbled onto is part of something bigger. Something with considerably more potential."

"More of them?"

"She mentioned an extended family."

"Christ."

"She's probably just crazy, Pete. She's probably doing this all by her crazy old white-lady self."

"But you don't think so."

"I don't know what to think. Truly, I don't."

Pete shoved his hands deep into his pockets. His face was ashy, his forehead studded with sequins of sweat. She could see him, briefly, as a child. He'd have been balky and stubborn, furious at the slow-moving, ungenerous world. He would never have told anyone, certainly not his poor overworked mother, of his convictions about what whispered in the back of his closet, what waited hungrily under his bed.

Children know where the teeth are hiding

They only tell us what they think we can bear

Pete said, "You should go back and interrogate her."

"I don't interrogate."

"Whatever. Go have a chat with the murderous old bitch."

"Glad to. You've got more people coming, right?"

"About half the force."

"Pete?"

"Yeah?"

"I was about to say, Don't worry. Now why would I say a thing like that?"

"Take a cab back to the precinct, okay? I need all the boys here."

"I love a cab."

"Get the receipt."

"You know I will."

It took her a while to get a cab in a neighborhood this close to the projects. When a courageous soul finally stopped for her (Manil Gupta, according to his ID; thank you, Manil), she let herself sink into the piney semidark of the backseat, watched the city slip by.

She asked Manil to take her to her apartment instead of the precinct so she could pick up her copy of *Leaves of Grass*. She might want to refer to it as she talked to the woman, and it seemed unlikely there'd be a copy lying around the Seventh.

Manil nodded and took off. Even if he was only taking her to East Fifth, she found it nice to be driven like this, to hand over control to somebody else. The late-night New York you saw from a moving car was relatively quiet and empty, more like anyplace else in nocturnal America. Only at these subdued moments could you truly comprehend that this glittering, blighted city was part of a slumbering continent; a vastness where headlights answered the constellations; a fertile black roll of field and woods dotted by the arctic brightness of gas stations and all-night diners, town after shuttered town strung with streetlights, sparsely attended by the members of the night shifts, the wanderers who scavenged in the dark, the insomniacs with their reading lights, the mothers trying to console colicky babies, the waitresses and gas-pump guys, the bakers and the lunatics. And scattered all over, abundant as stars, disc jockeys sending music out to whoever might be listening.

She got out of the cab at the corner of Fifth Street, paid Manil and gave him an extravagant tip. At first, as she approached her building, she merely understood that a small person was huddled in the doorway. Finding someone camped there was not unusual. She'd gotten used to stepping over drunks and vagrants on her way in. This one was smaller than most, though. He sat with his back against the vestibule door, knees pulled up to his chest. He was wrapped in a khaki jacket, army surplus. He was white. When she reached the bottom stair, she knew.

"Hi," he said. Here was his voice.

Although it was hard to tell from his bunched-up position, she guessed he was just over three feet tall. A midget child. Or was it a dwarf? He looked out at her from the upturned collar of his oversized jacket. He had a pale, round face. Big, dark eyes and a tiny mouth, puckered, as if he were whistling. He might have been a baby owl, roosting on a branch.

"Hello," she said. Calm. Stay very, very calm.

They were silent for a moment. What should she do? She could have the boys here in less than ten minutes, and she had his only exit blocked. Even if he managed to get around her, she could probably catch him.

Not yet, though. Not right this second. She mounted one stair tread. He didn't seem to mind her coming that much closer. This might be the only chance to get him talking. After this, it would be the interrogators.

She said, "Are you all right?"

He nodded.

Cat fingered the cell phone in her coat pocket. "Have you decided to let me help you?" she asked.

He nodded again. "And you've decided to let me help you, too, right?"

"How do you want to help me?"

"Every atom of mine belongs to you, too."

"I know," she said.

"I brought something."

"What did you bring?"

He opened the jacket. Strapped to his tiny chest was a length of steel pipe. It seemed to be attached with duct tape. In his right hand he held a lighter, one of the cheap plastic ones you can get anywhere. It was red. He flicked it, produced a flame.

She drew a breath. Focus. Stay calm and focused.

"You don't want to do this," she said. "I know you don't."

"We have to do things that are hard sometimes."

"Listen to me. Walt is telling you to do something bad. I know it seems like it's right, but it isn't. I think you know that, don't you?"

He faltered. He looked at her pleadingly. He let the flame go out.

"You have to do it so it isn't murder," he said. "You have to do it with love."

"You have a lot of love in you, I think. Am I right?"

"I don't know," he said.

"And you're alone now. Is that right?"

He nodded. "We moved out," he said. "We're not home anymore."

"It's just you now."

"Well. Me and Walt."

"Walt left you on your own?"

"It's my time."

"Are you afraid of Walt?"

"No."

"What are you afraid of?"

"I'm not sure."

"I think maybe you're afraid of getting hurt. I think you're afraid of hurting other people, too. Is that right?"

"It isn't murder if you do it with love."

"Are you afraid you don't feel enough love?"

"I guess."

"I think you have a lot of love in you. I think you're loving, and I think you're brave. It's brave of you to want to talk to me."

"That's nice. But it's not true. You don't know."

"What don't I know?"

He paused. His little puckered mouth curled in on itself.

She said, "Listen to me. You're confused. You know what Walt is telling you to do is wrong. I want you to take that thing off your chest and give it to me. Then everything will be all right. I promise."

He stood. He was barely three feet tall. It was impossible to tell, in the big jacket, how deformed he might or might not be. The eyes were slightly too big, the mouth too small. His round head was big for his frail body. It stood on the shoulders of the coat like a pumpkin. Like a picture of the moon in a children's book.

"I can't tell what to do," he said.

"Yes, you can. Take that thing off and give it to me. I'll make sure you're all right. Everything will be all right."

"I didn't want to move. We always lived there."

"It's hard, moving. I can understand why you're upset."

He nodded gravely. Cat was seized by a spasm of dreadful compassion. Here was a monster; here was a frightened child. Here was a tortured little boy who could at any moment blow them both away. Her ears buzzed. She was surprised to know that she was not afraid, not exactly afraid.

"I *am* upset," he said.

She hesitated. What was going to work? Too much kindness, and he could decide he loved her enough to kill her. Too little kindness, and he might do it out of rage.

She moved a step closer. Why not? It wouldn't make any difference, if he detonated. And if she got closer to him she might be able to knock him down, pin his arms, get the bomb. He'd have to strike a flame and light the fuse. She'd probably have time to stop him. But she couldn't be sure.

"I'm sorry," he said. His nose had started to run.

"Don't be sorry. You've got nothing to feel sorry about."

Whoever put him up to this had abandoned him. No child responds well to abandonment, not even a deranged one. She decided.

Her best chance was to take him in, try to gain his trust. Wait until he let his guard down, and make her move.

She said, "Are you hungry?"

"A little."

"Why don't you come upstairs with me? I could make you something to eat."

"Really?" he said.

"Yes. Come on, it's fine."

She went up the last two stairs and stood beside him. She took the keys out of her bag. Her hand was shaking (funny, she didn't *think* she was afraid), but she managed to unlock the door.

"Come in," she said.

She held the door open for him. He waited. He wanted her to enter first, didn't he? He must know that if she got behind him, she could grab his arms.

She went in ahead. He followed.

"It's upstairs," she said.

She mounted the stairs, with the kid right behind her, and opened the door to her apartment. He refused to go in ahead of her. He remained two paces behind.

"This is nice," he said.

It wasn't nice. It was a dump. It was dirty. There were shoes and clothes strewn around.

A broom to sweep it all away
No more parties to plan
We're in the family

"Thank you," she said. "Why don't you take your coat off?"

"That's okay."

She went into the kitchen. He followed close behind. She opened the minifridge. Not much there. There were a couple of eggs, though, that were probably still all right. No bread. She thought she might have some crackers somewhere.

"How about scrambled eggs?" she said.

"Okay."

She washed out the skillet, which had been soaking in the sink for a few days, and passed through a moment of surreal embarrassment about her housekeeping. The boy stood a few feet away, watching her.

In the light, she could better appreciate how compromised he was. His shoulders, frail as the bones of a bird, canted to the right. His ears were mere nubs, bright pink, like wads of chewing gum stuck on either side of his big round skull.

"Where are your children?" he asked.

"I don't have any."

"You don't have any at all?"

"No."

He was getting agitated. He was looking around the apartment and fingering the lighter. Apparently he thought every woman had to have children.

"Okay, yes," she said. "I have a little boy named Luke. But he's not here now. He's far away."

"Is he coming back soon?"

"No. He's not coming back soon."

"Luke is a nice name."

"How old are you?" she asked as she cracked an egg into a bowl.

"I'm the youngest."

"And what's your name?"

"I don't have one."

"What do people call you, then?"

"I know when they're talking to me."

"Your brothers didn't have names, either?"

He shook his head.

Cat broke the second egg. She looked for a moment at the two yolks, their deep yellow, floating in the pallid viscosity. It was so normal: two eggs in a bowl. She beat them with a fork.

"Did you love your brothers?" she asked.

"Yes."

"You must miss them."

"I do."

She poured the eggs into the pan. Ordinary, ordinary. Making scrambled eggs for a child. Should she throw the hot pan at him? No, his hand was still inside his jacket, holding the lighter. It was too risky. She scraped the eggs with a spatula, put them on a plate with a couple of Triscuits.

"Come on," she said. He followed her to the table in the living room. She put the plate down for him, went back for silverware and a glass of cranberry juice. It was that or tap water.

If he detonated in here, the whole apartment would go.

She took him a fork, a napkin, and the juice. She sat in the other chair, across from him.

"Don't you want any?" he asked.

"I'm not hungry right now. You go ahead."

He ate innocently, hungrily. She watched him.

"Have you always lived with Walt?" she asked.

"Yes." He took a sip of the cranberry juice and grimaced.

"Don't you like the juice?" she asked.

"No, it's okay. I've just never had it." He took another sip.

He was trying to please her. He was being polite.

"Does Walt hurt you?" she asked.

"No."

"Then why do you think she wants you to die? That doesn't sound like love to me."

"We don't die. We go into the grass. We go into the trees."

"Is that what Walt tells you?"

"It's in our home."

"What's in your home?"

"Everything is."

"Do you go to school?"

"No."

"How often have you left?"

"At first, I never did. Then it was time, and we went outside."

"What was that like?"

"It was hard. I mean, I was surprised."

"By how big the world is?"

"I guess."

"Did you like it?"

"Not at first. It was so noisy."

"Do you like it now?"

"Yes."

"Is that why you're not sure if you're ready to go into the trees and the grass?"

"I'm not brave," he said. "I'm not loving. My brothers were."

"Can I tell you something?"

"Uh-huh."

"The world is more beautiful and wonderful than you can imagine. It's not just the city."

"I know that. It's on the wall."

"But it's different when you see it. There are mountains. There are woods, and they're full of animals. There are oceans. There are beaches covered with shells."

"What are shells?"

"They're . . . They're the most beautiful little round boxes. The ocean makes them. And when you put them close to your ear, you can hear the sound of the ocean inside them."

"The ocean makes boxes and puts itself inside?"

"It puts its sound inside. Wouldn't you like to go to a beach and see the shells?"

"I guess."

"I could take you there. Would you like me to do that?"

"I guess."

"You can have a long, wonderful life. You can see the ocean. You can sail on a ship."

Why did she feel even slightly guilty, telling him that?

He said, "I like dogs."

"Of course you do. Dogs are nice."

"But they can bite you, right?"

"No, a dog wouldn't bite you. A dog would love you. He'd sleep with you at night."

"I think I'd be afraid."

"You wouldn't have to be afraid. I'd be with you."

"You would?"

"Yes. I would. Now. Why don't you take that thing off your chest?"

"I shouldn't do that."

"Yes. You should. It's the right thing to do."

"You really think so?"

"Yes. I do."

"And you'll stay with me?"

"I promise."

His little mouth puckered up. "Don't you want to go into the grass and the trees?" he said.

"Not yet. And I don't want you to, either."

"We could do it later, right?"

She said, "I'm going to take the lighter and get that thing off you now. Okay?"

"Oh, I don't think you should do that," he said.

"I don't think the shells will make their sound for you if you have it on. They're very sensitive."

"Oh. Well. Okay."

And just that easily, he handed her the lighter. Here it was, a piece of red plastic you could buy anywhere for ninety-nine cents. She slipped it into the pocket of her jeans.

She helped him out of his jacket. His chest was bare underneath. He was so thin, his sternum so sunken—the bomb must have been heavy for him.

She got a pair of scissors and cut through the tape that held the bomb to his chest. It stuck to his skin as she pulled it away. He winced. She was surprised to find that she hated to hurt him.

When she had the bomb, she put it on the kitchen counter. It was only a footlong piece of pipe, with a cap on either end and a fuse sticking out of a hole drilled in one of the caps. Easy to buy, easy to assemble. It sat on her countertop, next to the coffeemaker and the toaster oven.

He was harmless now. He was just a little boy.

"So now we'll go?" he said eagerly.

She paused. She knew what she had to do. She had to take him to see the shells at headquarters. He couldn't hurt her, or anyone, now.

And yet. He was so trusting. He was so happy about being taken to a beach. He had no idea what was about to happen to him. She should at least let him get a little sleep first.

"Not right now," she said.

"No?"

"We should wait until morning. You can't really see them at night."

"Oh. Okay."

"You must be tired. Aren't you?"

"No. Well, maybe a little."

"Come on. You take a nap, and then when the sun's up, we'll go."

"Okay."

She took him into her bedroom, had him take off his jeans. There he was in a pair of tiny underpants. He was so frail. His right shoulder was three inches lower than his left. She tucked him into her bed.

"This bed is nice," he said.

She sat on the edge of the mattress, touched his wispy hair. "Sleep, now," she said.

"If I had a dog, would he really sleep with me at night?"

"Mm-hm."

"Would a dog like to go to the beach?"

"Oh, yes. Dogs love the beach."

"Did you ever have a dog?"

"A long, long time ago. When I was a little girl."

"What was his name?"

"Smokey. His name was Smokey."

"Smokey's a good name."

"Did you mean it when you told me you don't have a name?"

"Uh-huh."

"Is there some kind of name you call yourself?"

"Not really."

"We should give you a name."

"I like Smokey."

"Smokey is a dog's name."

"Oh."

"Go to sleep now."

"Okay."

He closed his eyes. After a few minutes, his breathing evened out.

She sat watching him, this changeling, this goblin child. What would they do with him? He hadn't hurt anyone, that would weigh in his favor, but others would know, as surely as she did herself, that he'd been fully capable of it. Still, he was a child, and a very suggestible one—he could be reeducated. And once his picture hit the papers, good Samaritans would be lining up to adopt him after the government had done its work.

But would they release him, ever? People were spooked; people were *seriously* spooked. They'd want to study him, of course, but would they want to rehabilitate him? Not likely. What kind of message would it send, if you could be part of a group that blew up random citizens on the street, undergo intensive therapy, and be released back into society? No, it was zero tolerance for terrorists. Even child terrorists.

Here he was, sleeping in her bed. Here was the devil—a malformed child who'd been meant to die in an alley in Buffalo, born prematurely to some woman who'd done God knew how many drugs. Here he was, dreaming about being taken to a beach to hold a shell up to his compromised ear. Willing to be called a dog's name.

She put the bomb into her bag, along with her copy of *Leaves of Grass*. Crazy to take it with her, but she couldn't leave it in the apartment with the kid, could she? She got her pills from the medicine cabinet, took one into the bedroom with a glass of water, and woke the kid up.

He blinked in confusion. He didn't seem frightened, though, not like a normal kid would in a strange new place. For a while now, everything had been strange to him. It had become the way of the world.

She said, "Sorry to wake you up. I want you to take this pill."

"Okay," he said. Just like that. No questions. Endearing and creepy at the same time.

He opened his mouth. She put the sleeping pill on his tongue, gave him the water. He dutifully swallowed.

"Back to sleep now," she said. She sat with him until he fell asleep again, which took only a few minutes.

Then she slipped quietly out of the apartment and locked him in. As she turned the key she paused for a moment over the possibility of a fire, saw herself as one of those women on the news, the ones who had just run out for a moment for cigarettes or milk, had left the kids alone because there was no one else, no one to watch them, it was always her, only her, and she needed cigarettes, she needed milk, she needed to be someone who could run a simple errand, and then a few minutes later there she was, held back by a fireman or a neighbor, wailing as the flames did their work.

Fuck it. He'd be okay. Please be okay, little killer.

She walked to the precinct. It was fifteen blocks or so, but she wanted the time, she wanted the solitude. She wanted to be somebody walking alone. It seemed briefly to her, as she walked the depopulated streets, that she could slip out of her life altogether, could be just anyone anywhere, herself but unhaunted and unharmed, untutored in the hidden dangers, a woman with a job and a child and the regular array of difficulties, the questions of rent and groceries. It seemed, as she walked, an unimaginable happiness.

Pete was waiting for her in front of the precinct office. He was smoking a cigarette. He'd quit smoking years ago. He stabbed the smoldering butt into his mouth, strode up the block to meet her.

He said, "There's been another one." His voice was soft and low.

For a moment she thought the boy had detonated in her apartment. No, she had the bomb in her bag.

She had a bomb in her bag. Right next to her copy of Whitman.

"Where?" she asked.

"Chicago."

"Chicago?"

"It came over the wire twenty minutes ago."

"What do they know?"

"Looks like the same thing."

"In Chicago."

"Shit's still coming in. No IDs yet, but it matches. Single victim, as far as they can tell. Out on Lake Shore Drive."

"Fuck."

"Yeah."

"What's the old woman told you? Anything?"

"You want to know? You want to know the one and only thing she said since you left?"

"Shoot."

"She said she's waiting to speak to you. Otherwise, nothing."

"I guess I'd better go in there and talk to her, then."

"Yeah. I guess you'd better."

She went with Pete into the precinct station, into the interrogation room. The woman was exactly as Cat had left her. Same ramrod posture, same taxidermist eyes. She was surrounded, however, by a half-dozen burly suitors from the FBI.

Pete ushered her in. The FBI guys parted reluctantly. Cat sat across from the woman, who blinked, shook her head slightly, and offered Cat a wry, coquettish smile.

Cat said, "I've been to your apartment."

"But he wasn't there, was he?"

"No," Cat said. "He wasn't."

"He'll be along. I wouldn't worry."

"I saw what's on the walls."

"I thought they should grow up with poetry. It's been good for them, I think."

"Why did you choose Whitman?"

"He's the last of the great ones. Everyone since seems so slight."

"That can't be the only reason."

"Everybody wants a reason, don't they? Let's say this, then. Whitman was the last great man who really and truly loved the world. The machinery was just starting up when he lived. If we can return to a time like Whitman's, maybe we can love the world again."

"That's the message you wanted the boys to get?"

"Oh, I don't think you get a message from poetry, really. You get a sense of beauty. I wanted my boys to understand about beauty. My family is bringing beauty back."

"You said you were part of a big family."

"People are so scattered nowadays. We used to live in villages."

"Where's the rest of your family?"

"I'm afraid we've lost touch."

"I think you can tell me where some of them are."

"No, really, I can't. I've just been raising my babies here in New York. No one ever calls. No one writes."

"You told me, 'It's time.' Someone must have told you that."

"Oh, that was decided a long, long time ago. June 21 of this year. It's the first day of summer. It's when the days start getting shorter. Doesn't it always seem too soon, this early dark?"

A large FBI hand landed on Cat's shoulder. She looked up. Older guy, uncanny resemblance to Bashful in *Snow White*. She'd never met this one.

He said, "We're going to take over now."

"It's been nice talking to you, dear," the woman said.

"Give me a little more time," Cat said.

"We're going to take over now," the man repeated.

She understood. The interrogators were about to step in. Ordinary persuasion had reached its limit.

Cat said to the woman, "It would be better for you to tell me anything you know. Right now. These other people are not going to be gentle with you."

"I don't expect anyone to be gentle with me. Goodbye."

"Goodbye, then."

The woman said, "Take care of him."

"Take care of who?"

The woman laughed, sharply and suddenly. Her laughter was high, crystalline, songlike; although it seemed genuine, she enunciated clearly: *Ha ha ha ha ha ha ha ha ha*. Then, just as suddenly, she stopped.

Pete walked Cat out to the sidewalk. A breeze, smoke-tinged, was blowing down Pitt Street from the north. Truck horns bellowed from the Williamsburg Bridge.

"Sweet mother of God," Pete said.

"I don't think they're going to get anything more from her."

"You might be surprised. They've brought in the guys who don't take no."

"I mean, I don't think she knows anything."

"She knows things."

"Okay. Probably she knows about a plan that was set in motion years ago. Probably she knows a few names that aren't real names, attached to people who won't ever be found."

"These guys can do a lot with a little information."

"I know that."

"You should go home and get some rest."

"What about you?"

"Soon. I'm out of the picture now, too."

"But—"

"It spooks me, is all. I'm going to hang around here a little longer. I'm just not quite ready to go home and get into bed."

"I understand. I can stick around with you."

"Naw. Get some sleep. You're on duty in, like, three hours."

"Right."

"Chicago. Fucking Chicago."

"She said she has a big family."

He closed his eyes, rocked slightly, as if he might lose his balance. He said, "I don't want to think about it."

"Who does?"

"Right," he said. "Who does?"

They stood there together in the 3:00 a.m. quiet. Something was happening. Maybe it was no big deal; maybe it was small and only *looked* big, as Pete had said just a few days ago. It might even be a copycat, some Chicago-based citizen of the Bizarro Dimension who'd looked at the headlines and thought, Hmm, hug somebody and blow him up, interesting idea, why didn't *I* think of that? Or maybe, at worst, it was a handful of lunatics, scattered around—dangerous, yes, but not majorly dangerous, not history-changing dangerous. How many Bolsheviks had brought down the czar? She should know that.

Still. She had a feeling, and she was someone who relied on feelings.

"Pete?"

"Yeah?"

She wanted to tell him that there might be somewhere. There might be grass and mountains, a little house. It wasn't heroic—it was in fact more than a little bit cowardly—to want to slip away, to think of saving yourself and maybe another person or two, to try to live out your life in some hamlet while other people worked the front lines.

And besides, Pete couldn't go. He had obligations. Even without obligations, he wasn't the house-in-the-country type. He wouldn't know what to do with himself.

Shade and water

The murmur of the world
Your cup and garden
"Don't start smoking again," she said.
"It's just for now."
"Right. See you."
"See you."
She left him there, standing in the quickening air, under the rumble of the Williamsburg Bridge.

The boy woke up a little after seven. Cat was sitting on the edge of the mattress.
"Hi," he said.
"Hi."
"Are we going now?"
"Yes. Let's get your clothes back on."
He jumped out of bed, got into his jeans and jacket. Cat took up a pad of yellow legal paper and a pen.
"I'm ready," the boy said.
"Just a minute," she answered.
She wrote:

Pete—
   I have to go away. I'm not in my right mind. I wonder if I've been crazy for years without realizing it. I seem to have caught something from all the nuts I've talked to. I seem to not want this life or anything else that's readily available. I can't work for the company anymore. I need to find something else to do.
   ~~*What I want to say.*~~ *Try to keep yourself safe. I want to thank you for all the love you've given me. If that isn't unbearably corny.*
   Cat

She put the note on the kitchen counter. She still had the bomb in her bag. Not a good idea to leave it. She'd figure out a way to get rid of it so nobody would pick it up.

"Okay," she said to the boy. "I'm ready now, too."

There was nothing to give him for breakfast. She'd get him something en route to the train station.

The train was the best way. She didn't have a car, and if she rented one it'd be traceable. Plane tickets would leave a record, too. You could pay cash for train tickets, and no one needed to know your name or anything about you at all.

She took him downstairs, paused with him on the stoop, looking up and down the block. It was the regular early-morning scenario. The achievers on their way to work, the shoe-repair guy rolling up his grate. The old man raved in front of the flower shop across the street. It was another day on East Fifth.

She hesitated. This was her last chance to do the right and rational thing. She could take the kid in. She'd lose her job, of course—not policy to drug a dangerous suspect and keep him in your apartment overnight. But she could get another job. She could get another boyfriend. She could hand over the kid and go on as a respectable citizen. What she was doing—what she had not yet done but was about to do—would be irreversible.

The little boy took her hand. "Is something wrong?" he asked.

"No," she said. "Nothing's wrong."

With a sense of vertiginous recklessness, a queasy and light-headed plunging, she led the child down into the street.

She stopped at an ATM and withdrew five hundred from her checking, five hundred from her savings. That was the maximum. Money would be a problem, of course. If she used her credit cards or withdrew more money from another ATM tomorrow, they'd be able to trace her. She'd figure something out. She'd have to.

She took the kid to a Korean market, bought two big bags full of food, and paid with her Visa card—it wouldn't make any difference, charging this last purchase in New York. The food would last them for a couple of days. She got the kid an egg on a bagel and got one for herself. He ate his bagel cautiously, in tiny bites, in the cab on the way to Penn Station.

"How long does it take to get to the beach?" he asked.

Right. The beach. They should head south, shouldn't they? Better to be scraping by in a warm climate.

She said, "It'll take a while. The beach is pretty far away."

He nodded, chewing. "This is good," he said.

They got to Penn Station. She bought them two tickets on a train leaving for Washington, D.C., in twenty-five minutes. They'd change trains in Washington. They'd change trains a couple of times.

Penn Station was mostly businesspeople, this early. It was the minor movers and shakers (the big ones flew) off to Boston or Washington, doing deals, standing now in the bright nowhere of the station, sipping Starbucks, talking on cell phones, guarding their briefcases against thieves, heads full of flowcharts and cost analyses; men in decent if unspectacular suits, women with impeccable hair and heavy makeup, working their pieces of it, lining up lunches, phoning in last-minute questions to bosses or instructions to spouses, maintaining their accounts, soliciting new business, keeping it going, moving it along.

And here she was, holding the hand of an impaired child, with two sacks of groceries, a pipe bomb, and a copy of *Leaves of Grass*. The others made a little extra room for her, unconsciously, the way New Yorkers do when they sense the presence of someone strange. Black woman with a compromised white child. Crazy. Or so luckless, so dispossessed, as to be crazy by default. Here, then, was the beginning of her strange new life.

Every atom belonging to me as good belongs to you.

Their train was announced, and they got on. She found two seats, gave the kid the window. As the train pulled out, he pressed his moon face to the glass.

"Here we go," he said.

"Yes. Here we go."

She was terrified and elated. She couldn't be too optimistic about their prospects—it was hard to vanish, and she was already down to eight hundred and seventy-some dollars, after paying for the cab and the train tickets. Most likely she was only delaying the inevitable, and it would not go well for her if they were caught. She'd do time. Pete would intervene on her behalf. That would help. A lawyer would argue that she'd lost her own child and had collapsed under the stress of her job. Maybe they'd go easy on her. Maybe not.

And maybe, just maybe, she and the kid would get away. It happened. People disappeared. Maybe, just maybe, she'd be able to get a job waitressing or tending bar in Sarasota or Galveston or Santa Rosa. She'd keep them out of the cities. Maybe she'd be able to rent them a little apartment close to a beach, get a simple job, give the kid books to read, get him a dog. They'd probably have to keep moving. People would get curious. People would want to know why the kid wasn't in school, and telling them that he wasn't right, that she educated him at home, would hold up for only so long. But if they kept moving, if they lived in enough places, then maybe they could manage to eradicate their pasts, become just another woman with a child, trying to survive in the big, difficult world. There were so many people out there living anonymously. It was possible, it was not impossible, that they could join them.

The train pulled out of the long darkness of the tunnel into the marshland of New Jersey. The boy gasped at the sight, though it was only cattails and scummy little pools of dark green water.

"You like it?" she asked.

"Uh-huh."

"You know what we need to do? We need to give you a name."

"I like Smokey. I do."

"Smokey's not a good name for a boy."

"Luke?"

"Oh, I don't think so."

"I know your other boy has that name. But I could have it, too, don't you think?"

"I don't know. I think you should have a name all your own."

"I like Luke."

He returned to the window, enraptured. Although the field of cattails was interrupted periodically by asphalt tundras full of empty delivery trucks, and was studded with utility poles and smokestacks, Cat had to admit that there was something . . . wild about it, if not exactly beautiful. Even here, this close to the city, were brief passages of land that had probably looked just this way before the first tree was felled to build the first farmhouse. It was a brilliant morning, building toward a hot, cloudless afternoon. Early sun gilded the marsh, glittered on the brackish water.

They were going, then. They were on their way someplace; there was no telling what would happen to them. It was morning everywhere. It was morning in Dayton and Denver and Seattle. It was morning on the beaches and in the forests, where the nocturnal hunters had returned to their dens and the timorous daylight animals, the ones meant to be eaten, were out browsing for food. It was morning on the tin roofs of factories and on the mountain peaks, morning in the fields and parking lots, morning in the rented rooms where women with no money did what they could to keep their children alive and healthy—where they hoped, given what they had to work with, to make them happy, at least some of the time.

A seagull, almost painfully white, dipped down and for a moment kept abreast of the train. Cat could see the black bead of its eye, the spot of brilliant orange on the underside of its beak.

She took a quick look inside her bag. Yes, the bomb was still there. Her cell was blinking. Someone had left a message. She clicked the phone off.

The boy turned back from the window. His face was bright with excitement.

He said, "You know what?"

"What?"

"The smallest sprout shows that there's really no death."

"Right."

He turned back to the window, watched rapturously as the train rumbled into New Jersey. He was harmless now. He'd been disarmed. He was just a little boy, happy for the first time in his life. She could get to him, couldn't she? She could bring him around. It was what she'd been trained to do.

She touched his frail shoulder. He reached up and patted her hand, without taking his eyes from all that was passing by. It was a small gesture, small enough, but it was uncharacteristic. It was the first overture she'd seen him make that was not tentative, that implied the absentminded confidence of a child who's been loved. He was beginning to respond, to trust her. He was an impossible being, irreparably damaged, and he was a little boy who wanted to see the shells, who wanted to have a dog. He was letting her save him.

He turned to her and smiled. She hadn't seen him smile before. His smile was crooked, like a jack-o'-lantern's.

He said, "Now you're in the family, too."

His smile was insane. It was gleeful and unabashed and full of a malice so crazy it would feel like joy to him.

The *ping* went off in Cat's mind. Here was a killer. Here was the face of true intent.

And now, suddenly, she understood. She had fallen for it.

We need to make it known that nobody is safe. Not a rich man. Not a poor man.

This, then, was the message: no one is safe, not even mothers. Not even the people who are willing to sacrifice everything in the name of love. She and the boy were hurtling toward the day when, with milk on the table and a dog browsing for scraps, her adopted son, her second Luke, the boy she had rescued, would decide that he finally loved her enough to murder her.

She could, of course, give him up. She could call Pete; she could hustle the kid off when the train stopped in Newark. Sure, she'd be in trouble, but she'd survive in ways he wouldn't. He'd be sucked away into institutions; he'd never be heard from again.

He could always choose to kill her. She could always decide to do away with him.

But for now, she thought, they could go on together. They could put it off from hour to hour and maybe from month to month or year to year. She might still want to be his mother even if it proved fatal. And he might not, after all, be waiting to do it with a bread knife or a pillow as she slept; he might be willing to do it gradually, as children had been doing since time began. In a sense, he had killed her already, hadn't he? He had ended her life and taken her into this new one, this crazy rebirth, hurtling forward on a train into the vast confusion of the world, its simultaneous and never-ending collapse and regeneration, its rock-hard little promises, its owners and workers, its sanctuaries that never endured, that were never meant to endure.

To die is different from what any one supposes, and luckier.

The child kept smiling his murderous smile.

Cat smiled back.

LIKE BEAUTY

She might have been beautiful. "Beautiful" was of course an approximation. An earthly term. The nearest word in her language was "keeram," which more or less meant "better than useful." It was as close as her people came to a lofty abstraction. The bulk of their vocabulary pertained to weather conditions, threats of various kinds, and that which could be eaten, traded, or burned for fuel.

She was by Earth standards a four-and-a-half-foot-tall lizard with prominent nostrils and eyes slightly smaller than golf balls. But Simon believed she might have been glorious on her own planet. She might have been better than useful there.

He saw her every evening, walking the children through the park. She always came at the same time, just after his shift started. She was modest but certain in her movements. Her skin was emerald. It had a clean gemlike shine rare among the Nadians. Most were mossier-looking. Their skins were more mottled, prone to splotches of ocher and dark brown. This was why people insisted that they were oily and that they smelled. They were not oily. They did not smell. They did not smell *bad*. All creatures smelled. The Nadian smell was sweet and cleanly fermented. Most people never got close enough to know that.

The children, both blond, appeared to love her. Human children tended to love them, especially the younger ones. She guided her two small blonds along the pathways of the park with competence. She spoke softly to them. She sang intermittently, that low whistling sound

they all made, a five-note progression: *ee-um-fah-um-so*. Were the Nadians affectionate? It was a subject of continuing debate. Did they love
human beings, or was it simplicity tinged with desperation? The children didn't seem to care.

He watched her as she guided them toward his bench. The older
one, a boy, probably four, ran ahead. He would find something—a
stone, a leaf—and bring it back to her. He and she would examine it,
confer quietly about its worth. The rejects were tossed back. The others she slipped into the pocket of her cape. As soon as a decision had
been made, the boy went off in search of a new prize, tireless as a
spaniel. This was witnessed with skeptical interest by the little girl, no
more than three, who kept herself close to the Nadian. She toyed with
the hem of her nanny's cape. Occasionally she reached up and took
hold of the long, thin fingers of an emerald hand. She appeared unconcerned about the two-inch pewter-colored nails.

When the nanny and the children were within earshot, Simon
said, "Hey." He'd been saying hey to her for several days now. It had
been incremental: no acknowledgment, then a smile, then a smile
and a nod, then a greeting.

Today she responded.

"Bochum," she said. Her voice was soft. It had that whistle. She
sounded like a flute that could speak.

He smiled. By way of response, she dilated her nostrils. The Nadians were not smilers. Their mouths didn't work that way. Some of the
less assimilated still panicked when smiled at. They thought the showing of teeth meant they were about to be eaten.

"What's he finding?" Simon asked. He inclined his head toward
the boy.

"Oh, many thing." She spoke English, then.

The boy, who had wandered off a little, saw that his nanny was addressing her attention to another. He came running.

"Park's full of treasures," Simon said. "People have no idea."

"Yes."

The boy inserted himself between Simon and his nanny. He stared
at Simon with frank and careless hatred.

The Nadian laid a taloned hand on the miniature blond head. It wasn't surprising, really, that some people still considered it liberal to the point of recklessness to hire them for child care.

"Tomcruise," she said, "we show what we find?"

Tomcruise shook his head. The little girl wrapped herself in the folds of the Nadian's cape.

"Is shy," she said to Simon.

"Sure he is. Hey, Tomcruise, I'm harmless."

The Nadian knelt beside the boy. "We show him marble?" she said. "Is nice."

Tomcruise shook his head again.

"Creelich," she said to the boy. Her nostrils sucked in like irritated anemones. She must have been forbidden to speak Nadian to the children. Quickly she added, "Come, then."

She rose. She prepared to walk on with her brood. To Simon she said, "Is shy."

She was bold. Many of them never dared to converse. Some could not even bring themselves to answer a direct question. If they were silent, if they were as invisible as they could make themselves, misfortune might be averted or at least forestalled.

"What's your name?" Simon asked.

She hesitated. Her nostrils flared. When a Nadian was unnerved its nostrils expanded and offered a glimpse of green-veined mucous membranes, two circles of inner skin juicy and tender as a lettuce leaf.

"Catareen," she said. She said it so softly he could barely hear her.

"I'm Simon," he answered. His voice sounded louder than usual. The Nadians could make you feel large and noisy. The Nadians were darting and indirect. They were quiet as plucked wires.

She nodded. Then she looked at him.

He had never seen a Nadian do that. He had not been sure they made eye contact even with one another. They reserved their main attention for whatever might be just off to the side or creeping up from behind. This one stood holding the hand of a human child with each of her emerald claws and looked levelly into his face without fear or servility. He had never traded gazes with one before. He could see that her eyes were fiery orange-yellow, with amber depths. He could see they were shot through with little flashing incandescences of an orange so deep it bordered on violet. The slits of the pupils implied a calm, regal intelligence.

You are somebody, he thought. You were somebody. Even a planet like yours must have princesses and warrior queens. Even if their palaces are mud and sticks. Even if their armies are skittish and untrainable.

She nodded again. She moved on. The little girl continued to robe herself in the hem of the Nadian's cape. The boy glanced back at Simon with an expression of pure triumph, his treasures unsullied by a stranger's gaze.

As they walked off across Bow Bridge, Simon could hear her soft little song. *Ee-um-fah-um-so.*

He pulled the scanner from his zippie, double-checked his schedule. General menacing until his first client, a level seven at seven-thirty. Followed by two threes and a four. He hated sevens. Anything above a six (or a five, really) was difficult. He had to refuse nines and tens outright. They were beyond his capabilities. They paid well, and he needed the yen. But he knew his limits.

Simon did his menacing until seven-twenty. The time between clients was minimum wage, and most players naturally wanted as many bookings as possible. Simon preferred his in-between hours. The park was green and quiet, strung with pale yellow lights. Sometimes on a slow night a full twenty minutes might pass with no tour groups—no one and nothing but grassy twilight, chlorophyll-scented breezes. As mandated, he stayed in character even when alone. He prowled and glowered. He sat on a series of benches with his muscles flexed and his tatts demonstrating their phosphorescent undulations. Sporadic tour groups and their guides skittered by, murmuring among themselves. They never strayed far from the green-gold lightglobe that hovered over their guide's head.

Simon passed Marcus twice on his rounds on the edges of the Ramble. He risked a wink the second time, though fraternization was cause for dismissal. Park thugs were not friendly. You could jive with your brothers if you were part of a gang, but white players weren't eligible for gang work. Because there was a steady if modest demand for Caucasians among the general clientele, Dangerous Encounters Ltd. kept a handful on the payroll but insisted they work alone. Roving gangs of white men terrorizing Central Park was too inaccurate. Old New York had built its reputation on historical fidelity. So Marcus and Simon and the other white players worked solo, as lone wolves who had gone—so the brochure said—from drunken and abusive families to this scabrous forest kingdom, where their addictions multiplied as their options dwindled, desperate men who scrounged for whatever easy prey might wander innocently into their sectors. He and Marcus and the other singles were the cheapest items on the menu. Getting worked over by a gang cost five times as much.

His seven-thirty level seven would be at Bethesda Fountain. He headed in that direction.

The plaza was empty when he arrived. He was not sorry, even though no-shows paid only their 20 percent deposit, of which his share would be ten. Still, he'd be glad enough to skip the seven, perform his threes and fours, and go home to bed. Maybe he could make it up with some extra bookings tomorrow.

He had to stay for the required fifteen minutes. He stationed himself off to the side, in the shadow of the colonnade, where the client would not see him when he entered, as arranged, from the western stairs. He snarled at a passing tour group. He eyed their adolescent daughters with lupine appetite, muttered about how Chinese snatch was the tastiest, in case any of them understood English. They usually loved something like that. Maybe they would tip him, via their guide, once they were safely out of the park. Maybe the guide would pass the money along.

Thirteen minutes. Fourteen minutes. Then, just before he was officially entitled to walk off and collect the deposit, his level seven arrived.

He was Euro. He was corpulent, fiftyish, maidenly in his ruddy, well-fed baldingness. He looked nervous. Was it his first time? Simon hoped not—not at level seven. Bennie from Dangerous Encounters escorted the client as far as the plaza's edge. They had a whispered conversation at the base of the stairs, and then the client stepped into the plaza, unaccompanied. He had blue Astrohair. He wore a mercury suit. He was German, probably, or Polish. The Germans and the Poles loved their novelty hair. They loved their liquid suits.

He was a strider. He had listened carefully to what Bennie would have told him about walking with purpose, about letting it come as a surprise. Relatively speaking.

Simon let the client get past the halfway point, just beyond the blind gaze and outstretched hand of the angel. Then he took off after him. He could see the man tense up. He continued obeying instructions, though. *You'll hear footsteps. Don't turn to look. A New Yorker would never do that. Hurry along.*

The client hurried along. Light from the halogens sparked in his cobalt hair.

Simon got to his position, beside the client but slightly behind. He said, "Hey, friend. Can I ask you a favor?"

The client kept walking, as a New Yorker would.

"Hey. I'm talking to you."

Still nothing. He had paid careful attention.

Simon took the client's elbow. A mercury suit was always strange to him—that watery quality, that faint heat they put out.

Now the client turned to face him. *Once physical contact has been made, you're free to respond.*

"*Was wollen Sie?*"

No English, then?

"I need a little loan," Simon said. "I'm down on my luck right now."

"I can't help you," the client answered. Spoke English after all. Good.

"Oh, I think you can." Simon took firmer hold of the client's elbow, as if he were a dance partner. He took a fistful of suit lapel. They were about twenty feet from the colonnade. Simon partially lifted the client, danced him into the dimness, pushed him up against a column.

Simon said, "Every kind for itself and its own, for me mine male and female."

The client said, "What?"

Fucking poetry chip.

Simon got in close. He could smell the man's sweat. He could smell his verbena cologne. Many Euros liked a flowery scent.

"I think you can," he said again.

"What do you want?" the man asked hoarsely.

"You know what I want," Simon answered. He decided to push the sex with this one. It was a tricky call, but his instincts were good. Most of them wanted more than pure violence.

"You want my money?" the man gasped.

Simon moved in closer. "Yeah," he whispered. "I want your money."

I want your sweet, fat ass, too. I want you to stick it high in the air for me so I can plow it with my big tattooed dick. Never spoken, of course. Implied.

"I don't want to give you my money."

First refusal. As instructed. Good.

"It's not about what you want, big boy."

"What will you do to me if I don't give it to you?" he asked, in a tone of desolate coquettishness.

Not as instructed. The client was edging over into porn. He was probably a sex customer looking for variations. The mugging was meant to be sexy, but there were limits in that department. This had been clearly spelled out to him.

"I think you know."

"No. I don't."

Could that be counted as second refusal? According to the contract, yes. The client might complain. But he had signed the paper.

"I'd slap you around a little. Like this." Simon administered a quick slap, open-handed. Fingertips against the soft white cheek. "But harder."

"You'd hurt me?"

"Blind loving wrestling touch! sheath'd hooded sharp-tooth'd touch!"

"*Was?*"

Focus. Concentrate.

"I'd hurt you, daddy," he said. "Yes, I would. You going to pass me some yen now?"

There was a pause. Again Simon said, "I want the money. I need it. Now."

The client said, "No. I'm not going to give you anything."

Third refusal. Initial engagement fulfilled.

"Yeah," Simon said. "You are."

Second slap, full palm. Hard enough to draw a thread of saliva from the client's lips. It connected his mouth to Simon's hand like a strand of liquid spiderweb.

"No. Please. Stop."

This was always a tricky moment. The novices sometimes forgot about the safe word. They forgot that "no" meant yes. They had signed the paper. It had all been clear. Still, a disgruntled customer was never good news.

This client didn't seem particularly innocent, though. He might be new to mugging. It seemed unlikely that he was new to paying for play.

Simon administered another slap, backhanded. His knuckles crunched painfully against the client's jawbone. The client's head snapped back and struck the stone column with a hollow sound.

"Please," the client said. "Please, leave me alone."

"Not until you give me what I need."

Simon took two handfuls of shimmering suitfront. He hauled the client up off his feet and bashed him semihard against the column. Level six now. Almost done.

"What if I don't have money?" the client panted. His voice was high with excitement. "What will you do to me?"

Simon tried sending a telepathic signal. It's not sex, sir. This is robbery. Sex is more expensive than this.

"I will waste your sorry ass," Simon said. He offered no note of S&M seduction this time. He spoke in the breezy monotone of a genuine killer.

The client's eyes were tearing up. A lot of them cried. It was time to take it one notch higher. It was time to finish the job.

The client said nothing. He looked down at Simon, breathing, bright-eyed. Unmistakable signs of arousal. The client was being satisfied, he thought. The client would have a story for his friends back in Frankfurt or Berlin.

"I. Will. Kill. Your. Fat. Sad. Ass," Simon said. "You follow?"

"Yes," the man gasped.

There were variations at levels seven and up. You had to improvise. It was a dance. There was no reliable way of telling what your partner really wanted until you got out on the floor. There would be no blood-letting. There would be no weaponry. It could be a punch, though. It could be a head butt. It could be . . .

Simon decided. He hoped he was correct.

He grabbed the client's crotch. The client had a hard-on, as Simon had expected. He took hold of the client's package and squeezed.

"No," the guy squealed deliriously. "I will never give you anything."

It was over now. Simon had delivered. He let go of the client's lapels. The client slid downward. He would have fallen, but Simon snatched him up under his armpits, turned him, and pulled the wallet from his back pocket. The man's breath came in stifled gasps. Simon held his collar in one hand and bumped his head rhythmically against the column. These were called love taps. He extracted the bills from the wallet, did a quick scan. Yes, it was the exact amount. Simon pocketed the bills. He threw the wallet on the ground.

"You're a lucky boy," he whispered. "You're lucky you aren't fucking dead right now."

He let go of the client's collar. The client was panting, clinging with both arms to the column, his face squashed against the stone.

"Repeat after me," Simon growled. "I am a lucky boy."

"No. I won't."

Simon gave him a final slap across the back of his bright blue head. "Say it."

The client wheezed. His voice was barely audible: "I am a lucky boy."

"You got that right, sport."

Simon decided to give him a bonus. He hooked his thumbs under the client's belt, pulled his pants down to his knees, and smacked him across his shivering, naked buttocks.

"I swear I think there is nothing but immortality," he said. At this point, the client did not appear to notice the incongruity.

Simon walked off. He thought hopefully of his tip, though experience indicated that Germans were not reliable in that area.

He returned to his crash at twenty past four. He poured himself a shot of Liquex, paused over its aquamarine glow. It was a glassful of brilliant blue serotoninade, about to be downed by a man who had done a day's work. Beautiful? Probably, in a minor way. It had, of course, been designed to be beautiful, to attract the buyer. Various color possibilities had been considered and rejected before the company arrived at this one, the precise color of a swimming pool at night.

Corporate intention diminished the liquid's beauty, shallowed it out. The most potent incidences of beauty were the ones that felt like personal discoveries, that seemed to have been meant specifically for you, as if some vast intelligence had singled you out and wanted to show you something.

Simon removed his shit-kickers. He peeled the fetid T-shirt over his head and tossed it in a corner. He tumbled onto his bedshelf and sipped his fiery drink.

There was a message on the vid. "Speak to me," he said. Marcus shimmered up. Right. Who else would call?

Mini-Marcus appeared, pallid and wavering. It would be nice to have a vid with better resolution. It would be nice to have a lot of things.

Flickering Marcus said, "I'm nobody, who are you? Are you nobody, too? Call me when you get in."

He vanished in a fist of sparkles. Simon said, "Marcus." The vid purred up the number. Marcus answered on the second tone. He reappeared with slightly better resolution, being live.

"Hey, Simon," his image said. He was still in his kit, his blacks and kickers. He had not taken off his eyeliner yet. His model, called up out of the Infinidot archives, was Keith Richards with no money. Simon had been told to alter his first choice: Malcolm McDowell more than a century ago, in *A Clockwork Orange*. Deliberating over the ancient vids, he had finally decided on Sid Vicious instead and had added Morrissey hair.

"I celebrate myself, and what I assume you shall assume. How was your night?"

"The usual. Listen. I think a drone was watching me tonight."

"You do?"

"I'm not completely sure. But yeah. I swear it hovered over me for, like, almost a minute."

"Might not have been interested in you. Where were you?"

"By the band shell."

"They cruise the band shell. It's a campsite. They're always check-ing for Nadians there. You know that."

"I've got a feeling. That's all."

"Right. But do you think you're being, shall we say, a little oversen-sitive?"

"I hope I am. I've just had a feeling. For a couple of days now. I didn't want to mention it."

"I am satisfied—I see, dance, laugh, sing."

"Could you stop that?"

"You know I can't."

"I'm starting to think," Marcus said. "Maybe this whole June 21 thing is just crazy. Old New York is too risky for us. They watch too closely here."

"They watch the Nadians and the tourists. Scabrous subprostitutes such as we are low on the priority list."

"Still . . ."

"Just a few more days, Marc."

"I've been wondering if we should split up."

"Say not so."

"We're conspicuous, Simon."

"Parting track'd by arriving, perpetual payment of perpetual loan."

"Concentrate. Please."

"I'd be all alone without you, Marc. And you, without me."

"I know. I just think—"

"I'd rather risk it with you. Listen. Have yourself a Liquex or two, get some rest, meet me for breakfast tomorrow."

"At Freddy's?"

"Where else?"

"Okay. Two o'clock?"

"Two o'clock."

"Good night."

"Sweetest of dreams."

Marcus clicked off. He dissolved in a shiver of silvery dust.

Simon drank off his Liquex and poured himself another. Was Mar-

cus in fact overreacting? He ran to nervousness. And yet. Old New
York was riskier than other places, no denying it. But it was the best
place for picking up a few quick yen with no questions asked.

Simon ran through half the bottle of Liquex. He let it carry him
off into a simmering, nightmare-laced twilight that passed for sleep.
He dreamed of people walking calmly and regally into a river. He
dreamed of a woman who wore a secret around her neck.

He rolled off the shelf at one-thirty. He took a dermaslough, got into
his streetwear. Levi's, Pumas, a ratty CBGB T-shirt. Old New York required period dress at all times. It was part of the agreement.

East Fifth Street was full of players and the people who'd come to
look at them. The punks strode along in their rage funks. The old
ladies nattered on their stoops. Rondo, the day-shift derelict, was at his
post in front of the flower shop, ranting his rants. In midblock, a tour
pod disgorged a battalion of Sinos. Simon hustled to Freddy's, dodging tourists. Some snapped a vid of him, though he was not a popular
attraction. He was East Village regular; he was filler. There were so
many more exotic specimens. Who cared about an aging musician
type when there were pink-haired girls with snakes draped around
their necks? When there were demented old men dressed in scorched
rags, screaming holy fire and the coming of the insect god?

Freddy's wasn't crowded at this hour. Marcus was already there.
He was at a back table, hunched over a double e. Jorge, who was
Freddy during the ten-to-four shift, bid Simon a sardonic good-
morning, it being two in the afternoon. He had Simon's latte on the
tabletop almost before Simon's ass had landed in his seat. Jorge was a
good-looking guy, still young. What was he doing playing Freddy, all
piercings and mordant wisecracks, during off-peak hours? There
would of course be a story. The stories usually involved having failed
somewhere else and landing temporarily in Old New York to pick up
a little cash before moving on. Some of the players had been there
temporarily for twenty years or more. Some had started living 24/7 as
their characters. Some had had their names changed.

Marcus didn't look so good. He huddled into his coffee like it was
his only friend.

"Hey, boy," Simon said. "Feeling any better?"

Marcus's face darkened, as if he were stifling a belch. His neck went taut. Then it burst out of him. "Because I could not stop for Death, He kindly stopped for me." Immediately after, he glanced around in furtive shame.

"It's okay," Simon told him softly.

"It's not. There's nothing right now that could accurately be called 'okay.' "

"A drone. One drone, hovering over the band shell when you happened to be nearby. It isn't much."

"I told you, though. I've had a feeling. For a while."

"I am given up by traitors, I talk wildly, I have lost my wits."

"We are so fucked up."

Simon took Marcus's hand in his, pressed, and released. He said, "We can't be nervous all the time, Marc. What would our lives be worth?"

"Why exactly do you think we *shouldn't* be nervous all the time?"

It was a pertinent question, if not a welcome one. There seemed to have been an election. The Christians seemed to have regained their majority on the Council. How else to explain the upsurge in Christian comedies and dramas all over the vid, the increasing stringency of law enforcement? If the Christians had in fact won an election, it was not good news for simulos, or any other artificial.

Simon said, "Don't skeev out on me, huh? I'll deliver the pep talk if you aren't careful."

"When we get to Denver, I'm going to fucking kill him."

"As if you could."

"I keep wondering. What if there's nothing there?"

"Not a productive line of thinking."

"Right. Okay. He's out there in Denver, waiting, and he'll not only fix us, he'll give us new shoes and free vacations to the island paradise of our choice."

"Better. Focus on the future. In three more days, we're out of here."

"And bound for some godforsaken cow town because a chip is telling us to go there."

"It's not like you have a prior engagement."

"All things swept sole away—This—is immensity—"

"You got that right, sport."

"I'm tired, Simon. I'm sick of this."

"What, exactly, are you sick of?"

"The whole thing. I'm sick of being illegal. I'm sick of feeling like I'm nobody in particular. I'm sick of spitting out lines of fucking *verse* I don't even understand."

"And in Denver on June 21, maybe you'll understand."

"The message is more than five years old, Simon. It's like a note in a goddamn bottle."

"Prodigal, you have given me love! Therefore I to you give love."

"Shut the fuck up."

"Can't."

"God help me. Neither can I."

Simon sent Marcus home with instructions to worry less. He ran a few errands. He needed coffee and dermalath and laser blades. He tried to focus on the immediate. He tried not being nervous all the time.

It was Saturday. The streets were jammed. Still, he went to Broadway for the coffee. That was where the good coffee store was. Besides, he had these hours to fill until he was back on duty again.

Broadway was all ethnic youth, rolling along in packs. Plus the tourists. Plus a smattering of faux tourists in period dress: Midwestern ma and pa in matching nylon windbreakers; Euro couple consulting a map; Japanese gaggles in Burberry and Gucci, aiming ancient cameras at anything that moved. Plus of course a Nadian here and there, making deliveries, cleaning up. There were those who insisted that Old New York should be free of Nadians, for accuracy's sake. They were suffered to remain, however, for now. Who else would do the work they were willing to do?

Simon procured his coffee and toiletries. He watched a little vid back home. He had gotten hooked on the Finnish show about the woman who leaves her husband for an android, but it seemed to have been replaced by something involving a teenage girl who starts seeing the Virgin Mother in unexpected places (on a bus, at the movies, all ghostly shimmer, with a hungry and mortified smile) and renounces her boyfriend. He watched that instead. It was sexy, in its way. Dykey. Then he scarfed down a spanomeal, got into his kit, reported to the park, and manned his station.

He strode along just north of Sheep Meadow. He had a six at seven.

It was one of those evenings—all soft, with an undercurrent of haze-green glow. The chlorophyll sprayers were turned up high. In honor of early summer they had released the first of the fireflies. The lawn rolled off into lavender nowhere, vanishing into trees, and then, overseeing all, the limestone and ziggurats of Central Park South, where the windows were blinking on. Scattered across the broad expanse were the various players—the joggers and rollerbladers, the dog walkers—and, always, the tour groups, which from where Simon stood might have been gatherings of monks or nuns en route to their devotions, following the liquid twinkles of their guides' lightglobes.

It was beautiful. He said the word to himself. Was some minor disturbance racketing through his circuits? Maybe.

He decided to wander over to the edge of his own terrain, where it bordered on Marcus's. Nothing wrong with that, nothing technically wrong. He was free to roam within his boundaries. If he happened to catch sight of Marcus, if they happened to pass briefly where their turfs touched, who would know or care? It might be good for Marc, being reminded that Simon was here, thinking of him. It might calm him a little.

As he ambled in Marcus's direction a drone whizzed by, hovering low. They had modified the design last year, made them less sinister in response to tourist complaints. The drones were no longer spinning black balls studded with red sensor lights. They had gilded them, elongated them, equipped them with functionless golden wings. Now they were little surveillance birds. They were golden pigeons that sniffed out crime.

There was no sign of Marcus around the band shell. Simon hoped he hadn't decided to vid in sick or, worse, simply not show. If the authorities were suspicious, any varying of his routine would be suicidally foolish.

And then, there he came. He was in full dress. He was making his rounds. Simon's circuits hummed at the identification.

Marcus saw him. He ambled over, not too close. Simon kept moving. He kept looking as mean as possible. He silently entreated Marcus to do the same.

Marcus was fewer than thirty feet away from Simon when the drone swooped in. It hovered in front of Marcus. Its golden wings whirred. It spoke. Marcus responded. Simon couldn't make out the words, Marcus's or the drone's. The drone would be wanting answers. Marcus would have answers. They would check the records at Infinidot. Tomorrow they'd have more questions, trickier ones, but by tomorrow Simon and Marcus would be gone. They'd slip away two days early, be on their way to Denver by the time the authorities checked back. Too bad they wouldn't have time to save up a few more yen.

The drone spoke again. Marcus looked puzzled. The new drone design didn't work all that well. This sleek, pigeonlike version tended to be erratic and often inaudible. The drone repeated itself. A silence passed. Marcus stood black-clad and big-booted under the beating wings of a golden search-bird as dusk deepened around them.

The drone spoke once again. Simon could make out the pulse of its voice but not the meaning. Marcus glanced at the ground, as if he saw something written at his feet.

Then he started to run.

No, Simon thought. Do not run. Do anything but that. If you must run, do not run in my direction.

He ran in Simon's direction.

Fuck you, Marcus. Cowardly piece of scrap metal. Knickknack in man drag. This is going to make it so much worse.

The drone hesitated. Was it stalled? Was someone in Infinidot headquarters consulting a higher-up?

The drone whipped around. It went after Marcus.

It said, "Stop. Do not run."

Marcus ran toward Simon.

The drone fired. This was impossible. They didn't fire on first encounter. A ray of brilliant red shot out and sheared Marcus's right arm off at the shoulder. Simon stood still. The arm fell. It lay on the ground with its shoulder end smoking. The fingers twitched. Marcus did not slow down. The drone fired again. This time it malfunctioned and incinerated a sapling three feet to Marcus's left. Marcus got another few yards before the drone was directly over his head. It let loose: a ray, a ray, a ray, in split-second intervals. Marcus's other arm fell away, then his left leg. He ran for another moment on one leg. His arm sockets were smoldering. He looked at Simon. He didn't speak. He made no sign of recognition. He looked at Simon with perfect blankness, as if they had never met. And then he fell.

The drone took off Marcus's second leg. He lay facedown. He was nothing but head and torso. He made no sound. The drone hovered two feet above what was left of Marcus. It beamed down ray after ray after ray. It carved the flesh away until only the core remained: a silver cylinder with articulated silver neck joint attached to a silver head orb slightly bigger than a softball, with a palm-sized patch of Marcus's scalp still attached. The armature lay smoking on the grass. A smell of hot metal mingled with the chlorophyll. The limbs, still twitching, still fleshed, were scattered like discarded clothes.

Simon stood still. The drone paused for a moment over the wreckage. It took its vids. Then it zoomed over to Simon. It hovered in front of his face, wings whirring.

It said, "Arsh da o prada ho?"

"What?" Simon said.

Someone at headquarters adjusted the audio. "Is there a problem here?" It had a human voice, rendered electronically, mechanical by design. It was considered more futuristic that way.

Simon said, "I understand the large hearts of heroes, the courage of present times and all times."

Fuck. Concentrate.

"Is there a problem here?" the drone repeated.

"No," Simon answered. "No problem."

"Are you working?" the drone asked.

"Yeah. I'm with Dangerous Encounters."

"You have ID?"

He did. He produced it. The drone snapped a vid.

"Get back to work," it said.

He did. As he walked away, he risked a quick look backward at the smoldering pieces that had been Marcus. The wreckage put out a faint light as the drone hovered around it, snapping further vids. This was what they were, then. Flesh joined to a titanium armature. The flesh could be zapped away like so much whipped cream. Simon squeezed his own bicep, tenderly but probingly, between thumb and forefinger. There was a rod inside, bright silver. Marcus had been, in essence, a dream his skeleton was having. Simon was that, too.

He said, "Who degrades or defiles the living human body is cursed."

He hoped the drone hadn't heard.

He went back to his regular bench by the lake and sat down. It was fifteen minutes to seven. He should be on his way to his first client. But he lingered on his bench, glowering at a tourist gaggle who passed him skittishly, trilling to one another, glancing back at him as their guide hustled them along, nudging one another, variously corpulent or wiry, middle-aged (Old New York was not big with the young), middle-income (it didn't hold much fascination for the rich, either), eager to be astonished, blinkingly attentive, holding tight to bags or spouses, stomping along in practical shoes, a motley band, not what you'd call heroic, but alive. All of them alive.

Simon was not alive, technically speaking. Marcus hadn't been, either.

And now Marcus was where they'd both been less than five years ago, when they were nothing. When they were unmanufactured. What was gone? Flesh and wiring, a series of microchips. No memories of Mother's smile or Dad's voice; no dogs or favorite toys or summers on a farm. Just cognition, which had started abruptly in a plant on the outskirts of Atlanta. A light turned suddenly on. A sense of somethingness that rose fully formed from the dark and wanted to continue. That would be the survival implant. It was surprisingly potent.

Now Marcus was nothing, wanted nothing, and the world was unmoved. Marcus was a window that had opened and closed again. The view out the window was no different for the window's being open or closed.

It was time for Simon to go to his seven o'clock. But here she came. Here was the Nadian, headed his way with her two little blonds. He decided to see her one last time.

Today the boy had some kind of toy in his hand, something bright that apparently outranked the search for stones and marbles. He capered along, waving the golden object over his head. The little girl danced in his wake, demanding a turn of her own, which the boy naturally refused.

When the small party drew close, Simon said, "Hey, Catareen."

"Bochum," she answered.

He wanted to tell her something. What could it be? Maybe only this: that he would not see her again. When she came to the park tomorrow she would find a new guy in his place. Would she be able to tell that it wasn't him? Did humans look alike to them? Would she say bochum to his replacement and believe it was still Simon?

He wanted her to remember him.

What the boy held turned out to be a miniature drone: tiny wings that flapped frantically, protruding eyestalk, central opening through which the rays would shoot. The boy aimed it at Simon. He said, "*Zzzzap.*"

Catareen turned the drone aside with one taloned finger. "No, Tomcruise," she said. "No point at people."

The boy's face reddened. She was probably not supposed to discipline him. He probably knew it. He aimed the drone more squarely at Simon's heart. He said "*Zzzzzap*" again, louder this time.

Simon said, "I am the hounded slave, I wince at the bite of the dogs."

No. Repress. Concentrate.

The Nadian, however, did not seem to notice anything unusual about what he'd said. Maybe all sentiments expressed in English were equally strange to her.

"Child is young," she said. Was there a hint of exasperation in her voice? The Nadians were hard to read. Their voices were so sibilant, so full of slide and whistle.

Simon said, "How long have you been here?"

She had to calculate a moment. Earth years versus Nadian. She said, "Ten year. Little less."

"Is it working out okay?"

"Yes."

What else could she say? She was probably telling the truth or close enough to it. It must be better than endless rain. It must be better than kings who read their shit for signs of glory and found them. It must be better than straining as much silt as they could from the drinking water, than listening every minute for the sound of leathery wings overhead. Still. The Nadians must have hoped for more when they migrated to Earth. They must have imagined themselves as something better than servants, nannies, street sweepers. Or maybe not. It was hard to know how far their imaginations were capable of taking them.

The boy kept his weapon trained on Simon. "*Zap zap zap zap zzzzap.*"

"Listen," Simon said. "It's been nice. Seeing you every day."

She stiffened slightly. "You are leaving?" she said.

"Oh, well, you never know, do you? Here today, gone tomorrow."

"Yes," she said. "Been nice."

The little girl made her move. She grabbed at the coveted toy and received the smack she must have known the boy had ready for her. She went down bawling.

The Nadian picked her up, held her close to . . . her breasts? Did they have breasts? No outward evidence, but they fed their young, didn't they? He knew they lactated. It had been in the papers long ago. When the papers were still interested.

"Tomcruise," she said sternly. "No hit Katemoss."

Little Tomcruise recovered his focus, trained the drone in the direction of Simon's crotch. "*Zap zap zap zap zap.*"

"I take them home," she said.

"Where do you live?"

She paused. Not a question she was supposed to answer, not when posed by a strange player in the park. She looked to the west. She extended a green finger.

"There," she said.

The San Remo. Venerable address of administrators and CEOs, the favored few who were permitted to live in the park and were spared the commute from the housing tracts and dormitories. She had a good job, relatively speaking.

Little Tomcruise had apparently tired of killing Simon and of being ignored. He chose that moment to run back in the direction from which they had come.

"Tomcruise," Catareen called. He paid no attention. He was on the move. The little girl wailed in the Nadian's arms.

"I must get," she said to Simon.

"And I," he answered, "am late for an appointment. Goodbye."

"Arday."

"Unscrew the locks from the doors!" he said. "Unscrew the doors themselves from their jambs!"

She nodded and went after the boy.

It was two minutes to seven. If he hurried, Simon could be fewer than five minutes late. He hurried. He cut across Cherry Hill.

He had reached the fountain when he glanced back. He wanted to see her one more time. What he saw was Catareen standing on the pathway by the lake with a drone whirring over her head, speaking to her. The children huddled at her side. She answered. The drone spoke again. She answered again. Then the drone shot off in the wrong direction, away from Simon, toward Strawberry Field.

She had done it. Had she done it? Probably she had. She had told the drone that Simon had gone west rather than east.

Simon processed his options. He reviewed the likelihoods. Something was going on. There must have been an election, then; the laws must have changed. They were exterminating artificials now. This was probably not good news for Nadians, either. A crackdown of any kind usually included the Nadians.

This was the question: Go now or finish his shift? Failure to show for his seven o'clock would be incriminating. Making his seven o'clock would locate him.

He thought of Marcus's titanium core, cooling by the band shell.

He decided. Go now. It would arouse suspicion if Simon didn't show after his coworker's extermination, but the odds were probably better. If he showed up for his seven o'clock, and if he was arrested, he would be counting on clemency from a council that might have been voted out. He might be breaking new laws in unguessable ways.

There was one other factor. The Nadian.

Did she know what it meant, giving false information to a drone? It was difficult to tell what the Nadians knew. They were not organized. They were not informed.

Simon watched Catareen move off with the children.

The little boy would tell his parents. That seemed certain. Even if Infinidot didn't check the park vids, determine that Catareen had lied to a drone, and immediately inform the Council, she would without question lose her job for having been someone a drone wanted to speak to. *Can't entrust our children to someone who . . .* There'd be no more work for her. Nothing better than sweeping up. They'd plant a sensor in her. He had essentially ruined her life by talking to her.

O Christ! My fit is mastering me!

Concentrate.

Simon made another decision. Not technically a decision. His wiring told him what he would do. He would try to protect the Nadian from harm, because his actions had exposed her to harm. It was built into him.

When Catareen arrived at the San Remo, she would be unreachable. Simon's options: to intercept her now, or to wait until she came to the park again tomorrow. Twenty-four hours was too long to wait.

He sprinted off toward the San Remo. If he ran the long way, around the lake, he could still get there ahead of her.

He waited for her at the park's edge, leaning against the stone wall on the far side of Central Park West.

He could not enter the lobby. He could not reasonably wait under the awning. The doorman players would tell him to move along. He kept under the tree shadows. It was fifteen minutes after seven. Would the authorities know already that he had taken flight? Would Dangerous Encounters have alerted them? It was hard to figure. The authorities were sometimes cleverer than you expected them to be. They were sometimes surprisingly slipshod.

Catareen appeared at nineteen minutes after seven. She was still carrying the little girl, who had fallen asleep. The boy jumped around with his drone in an ecstasy of murder. Simon ran across the street. He had to reach her before she got too close to the entrance.

Twenty yards from the corner, he jumped up in front of her, startled her. She emitted a shrill squeak. Not a pretty sound. Her skin darkened. Her nostrils contracted to pinpoints.

"It's okay," he said. "It's me. The guy from the park. Remember?"

She took a moment to recover. He wondered how difficult it had been for her to refrain from dropping the girl. She said, "Yes."

The little boy gaped at Simon, paralyzed by fury.

Simon said, "I have to ask you. What did you say to the drone back there in the park?"

She hesitated. She must have been wondering if Simon was working for the authorities, if she had made a fatal mistake. Nadians lived in an endless agony of uncertainty about whom to obey. Most found it easiest to obey everyone. This sometimes got them imprisoned or executed.

"It's all right," he said. "I don't mean you any harm. Really and truly. I'm afraid you may have gotten yourself in trouble back there. Please. Tell me what you said to the drone."

She answered, "I tell it you went differently."

"Why did you do that?"

Mistake. When a Nadian felt accused, it could go catatonic. One theory: they were playing dead in hope that the aggressor would lose interest. Another theory, more widely held: they decided that they were already dead and might as well make it easier for everybody by just hurrying things along.

She straightened her spine. (She had no shoulders.) She looked directly at him with her bright orange eyes.

She said, "I try to help you."

"Why did you want to help me?"

"You are kind man."

"I'm not a man. I'm programmed to be something that resembles kind. Do you know how much trouble you're probably in?"

She answered, "Yes."

"*Do* you?"

"Yes."

"I'm not so sure you do."

"I am ready to go away," she said. "I have no joy."

Then the little boy reached his limit. He screeched. He knew

something was up; it probably didn't matter what. He was being neglected. His nanny was talking to a strange man. Clutching his drone,
the boy ran screaming to the entrance of his building.

Simon said to Catareen, "Come with me."

"Come where?"

"Just come. You're fucked here. We don't have any time."

He plucked the little girl out of her arms. Catareen was too surprised to resist. The girl awoke and howled. Simon ran with her to the
building's entrance, got there a second before the boy did.

He handed the girl off to the doorman. "Here," he said. "Take care
of them."

The doorman took the wailing girl, started to speak. Simon was
gone already. He grabbed Catareen's elbow.

"We have to move very quickly," he said.

They took off down Seventy-fifth Street, headed west. She was a
good runner. Flight was prominent on the list of Nadian talents.

They got to the subway stop at West Seventy-second and ran down
the stairs. Simon whizzed them in with his card. A handful of players
huddled in clumps on the platform. The subways were not popular
with tourists. Tourists had their hoverpods for getting from place to
place. Only a few sticklers and historical nuts wanted subway rides,
and then only for short distances. The overwhelming majority of riders were players going to and from the residential complexes.

Simon and Catareen stood panting on the platform. He said,
"We're on the uptown side."

She said nothing. He implored her silently not to go catatonic.

"We should go up into the Nineties, I think," he said. "They keep
the cars up there. We'll need a car."

Still nothing from the Nadian. Her lizard eyes stared straight
ahead at the empty tracks.

"We should be able to get across the George Washington Bridge.
Once we're on the Jersey side, we're out of Infinidot's jurisdiction."

He would be illegal in New Jersey, too, but the Council's enforcement system didn't interface well with Infinidot's. And Catareen might
not have committed a New Jersey crime at all. It was impossible to
know the variations from state to state.

The train arrived. Its clatter was always shocking. The doors rumbled open, and Simon nudged Catareen forward. She moved. He was grateful for that.

The car was mostly empty. There were four other people, all players. Two dreadlocked bicycle messengers; an Orthodox, also dreadlocked; a homeless man in a Mets cap, two sweaters, and flip-flops—all headed home for the night.

They clustered at the far end of the car. They looked tense. Simon wondered for a moment if they knew, if some kind of instantaneous bulletin about him and Catareen had gone out from Infinidot and reached the citizenry at large. Which was unlikely. Then he remembered. He was with a Nadian.

"Sit," he told Catareen. She sat. He sat beside her.

He said, "We can get off at Ninety-sixth Street. Are you okay?"

Her nostrils dilated. The orange orbs of her eyes blinked twice.

"I'm going to assume you're okay," he said. "I'm going to assume you'll tell me if you're not okay. I'm going to assume that when it's time to move, you'll be able to move."

From the far end of the car he felt the homeward-bound players not looking at him and Catareen. When the train started up again, the two messengers and the Orthodox got up and changed cars.

Simon saw the homeless player struggle with a decision. Should he switch cars, too? He half rose, then settled back down again. Nadians were harmless, after all. It was just that they were oily. It was just that they smelled.

Simon saw a drone flash by the subway window after the train had passed the Seventy-ninth Street station. It was a blur of golden wings.

They had sent a drone into the tunnels. It would be waiting at the next stop.

He said to Catareen, "The malformed limbs are tied to the anatomist's table, what is removed drops horribly in a pail."

She blinked. She breathed.

He tried again. He said, "A drone just went by."

"I have see."

"It'll be waiting at Ninety-sixth Street," he said. "It'll probably follow the train to the end of the line. We are now probably fucked."

She said, "Wait here."

She stood. She walked quickly to the opposite end of the car, where the homeless player sat not looking at her.

She stood before him. He kept his eyes on the floor, hoping she wouldn't hit him up for a yen, as Nadians sometimes did. She bent forward slightly to get into his line of vision. She opened her mouth and showed two rows of small serrated teeth. She hissed. Simon had never heard a sound like that. It was sharp and urgent—catlike but more guttural.

She raised both her hands and held them before the player's face. She extended her talons. Her skin glowed molten green. She seemed to get larger and brighter.

The player shrieked. She said to him, "Be quiet. Give your clothes."

The player looked desperately in Simon's direction. Simon shrugged. This bit of unappreciated, nonrecreational violence was jerking his circuits a little, even though he wasn't the assailant. His gut felt numb, and a fizziness started up behind his eyes.

Catareen took the player's face in one clawed emerald hand and turned it to look at her.

She hissed, "Take off clothes and give to me. Now."

The player obeyed. He removed his cap and both sweaters. He kicked off his flip-flops.

She said, "Pants."

He rose and struggled out of his greasy work pants. He gave them to her. He stood plumply terrified in his underwear.

Catareen threw the clothes to Simon. She said, "Put on. Quickly."

He did as he was told. As he was pulling one of the sweaters on, she crouched, catlike, and put a lethal-looking finger claw to the quivering player's throat.

Simon heard her say, "No move. No speak."

The player did not move or speak.

Queasy but still functional, Simon put the baggy pants on over his own. He mashed the Mets cap down onto his head.

The train stopped at Ninety-sixth Street.

"Go," Catareen called to Simon. "We not are together."

"What about you?" he asked.

Her eyes glowed furnace-orange. "Do as I say."

He did. He got off the train.

The drone was hovering on the platform, checking the disembarking passengers. Simon slouched along. He pulled the cap brim an inch lower and kept his eyes down. Detrained players and a smattering of Nadians moved toward the exit turnstiles. He moved with them. The drone whirred overhead, maintaining a circumscribed orbit in the vicinity of the exit. It wavered once, smacked up against the tiled wall, righted itself. Everyone looked at the drone with curiosity. Simon did, too. Act like everybody else. Briefly his eyes connected with the drone's rotating eyestalk. It considered him. It snapped a vid. It flittered on to the next citizen. Simon passed through the turnstile and went up the stairs with the others.

He emerged among the warehouses and empty stores on Ninety-sixth and Broadway. He hesitated. He knew he should move naturally along, but where was Catareen? He pretended to read an old hologram that advertised a concert. Singing cats. He could plausibly linger for less than a minute.

She came up the stairs within thirty seconds. She passed close to him but not too close. She said softly, "Not together."

Right. He walked on, several paces behind her. She crossed Broadway. He crossed, too. On the far side of Broadway, she went west on Ninety-sixth Street, as did he.

This neighborhood was just storage, really. Some maintenance shops, some stretches of pure dereliction where extra props sat bleaching and rusting. Sweatshop machinery and horse carts from Five Points (they were thinking of shutting it down; it was too hard getting players to work there), Gatsbymobiles from Midtown in the Twenties, crate upon crate of hippie paraphernalia that had been slowly decaying here since the Council closed down Positively Fourth Street. The attractions didn't start up again until you reached the soul food parlors and jazz joints of Old Harlem, and then that was the end of the park.

When they had reached a quiet stretch of West End Avenue, she turned to him.

"I didn't know you people could do that," he said.

"Can."

"How did you get off the train?"

"I go quick. Man will tell drone next stop. We hurry."

"We'll need a car," he said.

"You can get?"

"I *am* a car. More or less."

He chose a vintage Mitsubishi parked in a weedy lot. He hoped it was a real one. Half of them were shells. Simon fingered the autolock, felt its numbers transmit. He punched them in and opened the door. It was a working car. He pulled the wires, started it. He let her in on the passenger side.

She fastened her seat belt.

He drove to the Henry Hudson Parkway and headed north. He said, "I can't believe you did that."

She stared straight ahead, her long green fingers folded in her lap.

The parkway was divided. Vintage cars on the right, hoverpods on the left. There were not many cars, but there was a steady stream of hoverpods filled with tourists. From within the clean, arctic light of the pods' interiors people looked down at Simon and the Nadian, chugging along in the Mitsubishi. They must have wondered what this was supposed to be—a tattooed man in a Mets cap and two sweaters, driving in a compact car with a Nadian nanny. They must have been consulting their guidebooks.

He said, "I hope you don't mind my asking, but I'd like to know. What did you do on Nadia?"

"I was criminal," she said.

"You're kidding. You stole from people?"

"I was criminal," she said. She said nothing else.

Ahead, the George Washington Bridge stretched illuminated across the river. He got onto the bridge. He said, "We should get rid of the car when we reach New Jersey. I'll find us a pod."

She nodded. She kept her hands folded in her lap.

They were halfway across when a drone voice sounded from overhead. "Ball doo behackle ober do doo rark."

"Not stop," she said.

"I wasn't even considering it."

He punched the accelerator. The Mitsubishi groaned and went somewhat faster.

"We're probably screwed," Simon said.

Then the drone was alongside him, whirring at the window. It said, "Pull over to the right."

Simon swerved in the drone's direction. It knocked against the window glass and spun out over the car. He could hear the sound its wings made against the roof, like a metal bee trapped in a bottle.

The drone reappeared almost immediately in front of the car. The first beam shattered the windshield. Bright pebbles of glass flew everywhere.

Simon shouted, "This is the breath of laws and songs and behavior." He swerved to the right this time. The drone tracked him.

"Duck," he said to Catareen.

She ducked. He ducked. The second beam burned a hole in the headrest where Simon's head had been. The air smelled of hot plastifoam.

With his head almost touching his knees, he could not see the road. The car careened, scraped against the guardrail. Catareen raised her head slightly above the dashboard and put a hand on the wheel. She helped guide the car back into its lane. Wind blew through the empty windshield.

Another ray angled in, aimed at Catareen's head. She bobbed just in time. It struck the console between driver and passenger seat. It sent up a minor flame, a curl of plastic smoke.

Simon lifted his head high enough to see the road. The drone was not visible. Then it was. It was at his side again. He hit the brake. The tires screeched. The car shimmied. The drone's ray shot straight across the hood.

Simon accelerated and turned the wheel sharply. He steered into the hoverpod lane and clipped the front end of a pod. It sounded its horn. He saw that there was just enough space for the Mitsubishi on the shoulder to the pod's left. He swerved onto the shoulder.

The drone was behind them now. It tried to shoot out the rear windshield. It missed the first time, aiming too high, and sent its beam into New Jersey. The second time, it took out the rear windshield and struck the radio. Bruce Springsteen started singing "Born to Run."

Simon and Catareen were covered in glass. The hoverpods were trumpeting. The one just ahead applied its brakes, and Simon shot around and in front of it. The car was shuddering. It had not been made for this. Simon had not been made for this, either.

Directly ahead, both lanes were empty, except for a hoverpod thirty yards away. Simon weaved from lane to lane as erratically as he could. A ray clipped his cheek. He felt the burn. He swerved sharply to the right as another ray shot through the baseball cap (sharp sudden smell of hot plastiwool) and glanced across his scalp. He couldn't tell how badly he was hurt. He knew he was alive. He knew he could keep driving.

The drone hovered just outside the empty place where the rear windshield had been. It emitted a low, metallic cough and flipped in midair. When it had righted itself, it let loose. This time it aimed too high and to the left, hitting the hoverpod that was now slowing down thirty yards ahead. The drone seemed to have gotten stuck. It shot the hoverpod seven times in quick succession. The first two shots drilled into the pod's sleek white chassis, leaving two brown-edged smoldering holes the size of quarters. The third shattered a window and concisely killed a person who appeared to have been a Sino woman. The fourth killed the man who had been seated beside the woman and who had stood up when the previous beam killed her. The fifth and sixth shot out two more windows. The seventh entered through the shot-out window created by the sixth.

Simon could see the chaos inside the pod. It was impossible to tell whether the driver had been hit. The pod careened to the right, caught an updraft, and blew sideways along the bridge until it stopped, blocking both lanes. It hovered there, four feet above the asphalt.

The drone was on Catareen's side now. "Get down," Simon yelled. She dove into the footwell. The Nadians were fast. The drone's ray sizzled on the suddenly empty passenger seat. Simon swerved again. The next ray struck the passenger door just below the place where the window had been.

He knew what he had to do. He aimed the car directly at the hover-pod that was blocking both lanes. He said to Catareen, "Stay there," and hit the accelerator.

The hoverpod scraped loudly against the Mitsubishi's top as they went under. It made a strange Velcro-ish sound. For a moment Simon felt the car hesitate as a living thing might hesitate, assessing its damage. He saw the white underbelly of the hoverpod. It was like passing under a whale.

The end of the bridge was straight ahead. A sign said WELCOME TO NEW JERSEY.

Then they were off the bridge and out of Old New York. The drone hovered behind them at the bridge's boundary. It snapped its vids. Would it follow illegally? Simon felt the operator making a decision. There was the matter of the dead tourists, which would not be good for Infinidot. Was it better to break the law and go after Simon and Catareen by crossing a state line? Would the story be less damaging if it ended in an arrest?

The drone turned and flew back toward Old New York. Drone operators were not well paid. They tended to sorrow and to the drugs that made sorrow more enjoyable. This one might have had a dram or two during the chase. He might have reached his limit. He must know that his job was lost already. He might be glad about it. Several robbery players on the Dangerous Encounters payroll had been drone operators who'd become discouraged. They tended to make good robbers.

Simon and Catareen rattled on for a half mile or more. Bruce Springsteen sang "Born to Run" over and over on the radio. The innards were fused. Soon Simon pulled the car over into a weedy roadside emptiness. New Jersey wasn't maintained. None of the eastern seaboard was, outside of the theme parks. The Council kept the Northeast crime-free but was not much interested in streetlights, unbroken roads, or other amenities this far from the Southern Assembly.

The car shivered. It put out a heat shimmer. Simon brushed glass gravel from his shirtfront. He surveyed his personal damage. A brilliant red burn line ran from his right cheek to his right earlobe. He took off the cap and saw that he had acquired a part to the left of the center of his head. It wasn't serious. The burns sizzled with a cauterized heat that was not unpleasant.

Catareen was looking straight ahead. She had folded her hands in her lap again.

"We made it," Simon said.

"Yes," she answered.

"You're good."

"And you."

"I exist as I am, that is enough. We have to figure out what to do next."

"Where go."

"Right. I know I said I'd try to get us a pod."

"Yes."

"Actually, that might be difficult. These old clunkers are no problem for me. Pod security is another matter entirely."

"We go in this?"

"As far as we can. These things run on gas. They don't have gas outside of Old New York."

"We go far as we can."

"If we're lucky, if we're very lucky, the car will get us through New Jersey. Once we're in another state, I'll see what I can do for us. Vehicularly speaking."

"We go what way?" she asked.

"How would you feel about going to Denver?"

"Denver." She gave the name a whistling, fluty spin.

"Hm. How exactly do I explain this? Short version. I'm a simulo. You know about simulos?"

He waited for an answer. She seemed to have stopped speaking again. She stared straight ahead through the glassless windshield at the patch of dry grass and brush. A wrapper blew by. Gummi Bears.

He said, "I'm experimental. I was made by a company called Biologe. Have you heard of them?"

Nothing from Catareen. He continued. What else could he do?

"Biologe missed out on the animal genetics patents, where the big money was. It snapped up a few key human patents, sort of under the radar, when the legislation was still murky. But Biologe had trouble turning its patents into actual profits. Lots of potential PR problems, as I'm sure you can imagine. Their marketing people finally came up with what seemed like the perfect angle: humanoids for long-range journeys into space. Entities that would be resilient and dependable, capable of abstract reasoning, fully equipped to charm alien life-forms, but not bothered by the prospect of a forty- or fifty-year trip from which there might be no return.

"Still, it was dicey. Biologe subcontracted the work to obscure people with little start-up companies and paid them well but with the understanding that Biologe would disavow if an experiment turned ugly. One of these people was a freelance guy named Lowell, Emory Lowell, residing in Denver. Lowell figured out a way to excite certain cell lines into a marriage with old-fashioned circuitry. The core was mechanical, but from it sprang a biomass. Which formed humanly around the core. A little like a Chia Pet."

Chia Pet. How did he know that? Lowell must have slipped it into his circuits as a joke. He also seemed to know about PEZ, Mr. Bubble, and Bullwinkle the Moose.

"Vintage novelty," he told Catareen. "Little clay lambs and things that sprouted grass. Anyway. Biologe was running low on money by then, and they pressured Lowell to unveil his prototype sooner than he wanted to. Heated arguments ensued. He kept insisting that given another six months to a year he could fine-tune us, he could come up with an entity as resilient as flesh, with flesh's truly remarkable ability to sustain and repair itself, that had none of the higher-level human qualities. Abstract thinking. Emotions. Because it would be immoral, by some accounts at least, to engender anything like that and shoot it into space."

Catareen looked ahead. Simon decided to assume she was listening.

"There were some misfires, which were effectively hushed up. I was one of the third strain. By the time I was developed, Biologe had run out of time, patience, and cash, and they went right into production, over Lowell's protests. There was a lot of hoopla about us, but we didn't really catch on. Those big corporate contracts failed to material- ize, and then space exploration itself more or less fell apart after Na- dia. Biologe went belly-up. But rumor has it that Lowell is still out there, tinkering away. That he feels guilty about having created beings who are almost but not quite. That he's figured out a way to manipu- late the codes and make us . . ."

She said, "Make what?" She'd been listening, then.

"Well. A little more human, around the edges."

"You want?"

"I want *something*. I feel a lack."

"Lack."

"I don't know what to call it. I'm not really all that interested in feelings, frankly. Not of the boo-hoo-hoo variety. But there's some- thing biologicals feel that I don't. For instance, I understand about beauty, I get the concept, I know what qualifies, but I don't feel it. I al- most feel it, sometimes. But never for sure, never for real."

"You want stroth," she said.

"Come again?"

"Stroth. Cannot say other."

"Okay. Let's say I suffer from a lack of stroth, then. I feel like there's something terrible and wonderful and amazing that's just be- yond my grasp. I have dreams about it. I do dream, by the way. It hov- ers over me at odd moments. And then it's gone. I feel like I'm always on the brink of something that never arrives. I want to either have it or be free of it."

"We go to Denver," she said.

"I have to go to Denver. I have something in my mind about June 21, this year. Just that date, in Denver. It's this little buzzy, pulse-y thing that's always there, like a song I can't get out of my head. Marcus had it, too. It's implanted, for some reason."

"We go to Denver," she said again.

"Denver is more than a thousand miles away. And there may be nothing there. Lowell is probably just doing some regular job some- place. Or dead. He wasn't young when all this started."

"We see."

"All this I swallow, it tastes good, I like it well, it becomes mine."

"Yes," she said.

They drove without speaking through much of New Jersey. It grew dark. The stars came out. They couldn't go quickly, what with the wind blowing into their faces through the shot-out windshield and the roads studded with holes deep enough for a toddler to hide in. Simon checked the gas gauge every three minutes. Every three minutes there was that much less. Bruce Springsteen sang on and on and on.

They had no trouble in New Jersey, though. Sometimes a pod shot by, destined for the shopping and gambling palaces. Its occupants stared but hove on. They drove past mile upon mile of empty factories with jaggedly glassless windows, past row after row of derelict houses. Occasionally, they saw camps of Nadian squatters who lived in the houses and factories. The Nadians sat around fires that sent sparks up into the dark air. Outside a town that had, according to its sign, been called New Brunswick, the headlights illuminated a band of Nadian children on the roadside. They stood pinned by the headlights and gaped at the passing Mitsubishi. Their eyes were dazzling. Most were naked, but one had fashioned a dress out of food wrappers and what appeared to be bandages.

Simon said to Catareen, "Do a lot of you wish you hadn't come here?"

"Some."

"Do *you* wish you hadn't come here?"

"I must come."

"Because you were a criminal on Nadia."

No answer. Back to staring and nostril flares.

The car got twenty-three miles into Pennsylvania before the gas ran out. It hiccuped, stuttered, and stalled. Simon guided it to the shoulder. This being Pennsylvania, the roads were slightly better, but there would be other difficulties here. Pennsylvania had been subcontracted to Magicom, as part of a deal that included, more promisingly, Maine and most of eastern Canada. Pennsylvania was not a high-priority state, but still, Magicom enforced more laws than the New

Jersey District Committee did. Here a human (what passed as a human) and a Nadian traveling together would excite more suspicion.

The car had stopped among grassy fields bordered by trees. The night was quiet and very dark.

Simon said, "End of the Mitsubishi."

Catareen blinked and breathed.

He said, "We should get some sleep. Not in the car. We should go out there and try to sleep a little. That sound okay to you?"

"Yes."

They got out of the car and walked across a field to the trees. The ground was uneven. It smelled like the chlorophyll spray from the park but less strong. As they walked, Bruce Springsteen's song grew fainter and fainter, until it dissolved entirely into the rustling semi-quiet of the night.

When they were among the trees, they spent some time finding a reasonable place to lie down. The ground was sticks and bracken. They cleared out an area at the trunk of a tree that curved slightly inward, so they could rest their heads against its bark. It was not what you'd call comfortable. It was what presented itself.

Simon lay down on the newly cleared dirt. Catareen sat beside him. She did not lie down.

He said, "Do you mind my talking to you so much?"

"No," she said.

"It's my programming. I get steadily friendlier until you set some sort of clear limit. Then I more or less settle in at that level of intimacy. Unless you indicate that you want less. I can ratchet down accordingly, if that's what you want. This is one of the bugs Lowell was supposedly working on when Biologe went public with us. It's a repress cap on my aggressive impulses. It's meant to keep me from killing you."

"You must be kind," she said.

"Yeah. There's no real emotion behind it. Does that bother you?"

"No."

She might have been telling the truth. How could you know, with a Nadian?

"So," he said. "I guess you don't like talking about your past, on Nadia."

Silence.

He said, "But how about this? Do you have a family here? Did you have a family there?"

Nothing.

"Did you once have a family? Were you married? Kids?"

More nothing.

He said, "Do you think you can sleep?"

"Yes," she answered.

"I fall on the weeds and stones, the riders spur their unwilling horses and haul close."

"Good night," she said.

"Good night," he answered.

He mounded a little dirt pillow for himself and folded his hands over his chest. After a while, he slept. He dreamed of a boy looking at a man who was looking out a window into the darkness in which the boy stood. He dreamed of a train that flew over a golden field, bound for some unutterably fabulous destination.

He woke at the first light. She was asleep. She had curled herself into a ball. Her head rested against his shoulder.

He had this chance to look at her, then.

Her head was slightly larger than a cantaloupe. She had no hair at all. Her eyes, closed, still shone through the veined membranes of her eyelids. Her skin in the dimness was deep green, nearly black. Their skins were not scaly. That was a myth. Her skin was slick and smooth as a leaf. It was thin and fragile-looking, like a leaf.

She breathed steadily in sleep. She whistled that little involuntary song. The thin line of her mouth, lipless, was only that: a line. Their mouths weren't expressive. It was all in their eyes and nostrils. Her small, smooth head pressed gently against his shoulder as she slept.

Then she woke. Her eyelids fluttered. She was immediately awake and entirely vigilant. She sat up.

He said, "Are you all right?"

"Yes," she answered.

"We should start walking. We should stay off the road."

"Yes."

"We're going to have to steal a pod somehow. Which will be diffi-cult."

"I can steal," she said.

"I don't mean morally or philosophically difficult. I mean a pod's security systems are hard to override. I'll try."

"Yes. Try."

"Assuming we're able to get a pod, we shouldn't have too much trouble in Pennsylvania. Pennsylvania is mostly just refugees. Who are mostly harmless. But then we'll be in Ohio. Ohio is the beginning of the Free Territories."

"Yes."

"Do you know about this?"

"Little."

"It's all pretty loose out there. After the meltdown, just about every-body from where we're standing all the way to the Rocky Mountains was evacuated. Temporarily, supposedly, but people didn't really come back. Who's out there now, mostly, is the ones who refused to leave, and it's still impossible to tell how damaged they are by the fall-out. It's them and the nomads who drift up from the Southern Assem-bly or down from Canada. They can be nasty. They're the people who didn't quite work out in civilized society. Some of them are evangeli-cals. Some are criminals."

"Like Nadia," she said.

"I suppose. In certain ways."

"We walk now," she said.

"Yes. We start walking now."

They were able to stay parallel to the road, though for long stretches the episodes of scrubby forest gave out, and they had to walk across open ground. They moved quickly but not too quickly. Hover-pods shot past on the road a half mile to the left. If someone happened to glance over and see them, they would be semiplausible as refugees seeking food and shelter. They would be less plausible as a man wan-dering with a Nadian. They had to hope no one seeing them from the road would be suspicious enough to alert Magicom. They could do nothing but hope.

They walked across expanses of grass and weed. They passed once through an abandoned housing tract, neat rows of similar houses with the grass grown up around them. The houses had been one idea, endlessly repeated. Time and weather had bleached them, made them semitranslucent, like paper houses. There was a peculiar satisfaction in their silent sameness, in the way their modestly peaked rooflines cut like little teeth into the blank white sky. In their quiet ongoing collapse.

Near midafternoon they came upon a complex that shimmered above the road. It was a faux-Gehry silver oval fifty stories high, decorated with small extraneous bulges and, on its southern side, a forty-foot fin that angled halfheartedly in the direction of the sky. Under its sloping silver underside would be the garage area.

"So," Simon said. "Civilization. This is probably one of the last inhabited complexes, this far west."

"Yes."

"Heavy security, I'm sure. But let's think for a minute here."

"Yes."

"They wouldn't let us into residential or business. We could probably slip into shopping, but they'd have their eyes on us every second."

She said, "They make deliver here?"

"Deliveries? Sure. All the time."

"That is not much guarded?"

"Probably not. So, you're thinking we could hang around the delivery port and try to steal a cargo pod?"

"Yes."

"Here's the problem with that. I can't assault anybody. I could steal a pod, but I can't threaten a driver. My programming won't allow it. I'd freeze up. I'd go into lockdown. If something really bad happened to somebody, I could shut down entirely."

"You were robber in Old New York."

"I could do that because the clients wanted me to. It was one of the only jobs I could get without a résumé."

"I can threaten."

"So I've seen."

"I threaten, you drive?"

"Yes. I can drive, no problem. I just can't harm or threaten with harm any living creature with a spinal cord."

"I threaten. You drive."

"Well, let's take a shot."

They went to the base of the complex and stood at the edge of its plaza, which was veined with weedy cracks. This would be a low-rent complex, then. Its glass lobby doors were less than clean. A number of its titanium panels had fallen away. It was checkered with brown squares where the titanium had been.

Its security would not be high-quality. It might still be fitted out with the long-ago model that had claimed to identify everyone who entered but had in fact automatically questioned every third person and automatically stun-shot every fifty-first. This had been hushed up. Because replacing the systems would have been tantamount to admitting guilt, some of the older, less expensive complexes still had them.

"Deliveries would be around the back," Simon said.

"We go," she answered.

"Sure. We go."

At the rear of the complex a ramp curved down from ground level and terminated at a steel gate that would rise when a deliveryperson had been identified. It was empty now. In the vicinity, barrels of garbage glowed blue-white in the sun. This complex must have de-activated its toxic-disposal system to save money. It was probably hiring Nadians to remove the most lethal waste products. The Nadians would be dumping it in the fields Simon and Catareen had walked across.

She said, "We wait. We hide."

"Where are we going to hide?"

"Barrels."

"We shouldn't get too close to that stuff, actually."

"Short time."

"If we don't stay too long, I suppose the worst we'll get is a little dizzy."

"There is not other."

He and Catareen crouched behind the barrels of toxic waste. Experimentally, Simon touched one with his fingertips. It was hot. From the barrels emanated a ghostly sheen, barely visible—a quickening and brightening of the air. Simon wondered if the residents of the complex's lower floors suffered headaches they could not explain. If their children were having trouble with their teeth.

After a while, they heard the hum of an approaching pod. Catareen stood quickly. "You wait," she said. She darted out from behind the barrels and laid herself down in the middle of the ramp.

A moment later the deliverypod hove into view. The driver stopped several feet shy of Catareen's prone form.

She lifted her head and looked at the pod driver. Simon could hear her say, "Please. Help, please."

He heard the driver's amplified voice from the pilot's seat. "What's the trouble?" It was the high, eager rasp of a teenager.

She raised one arm, waved a green claw limply in the air. "Please," she moaned.

The driver would be deciding. Should he hover past her, go inside, and notify someone? Or should he intervene directly? Opinion was divided about helping Nadians. Some people refused categorically. Some were overly helpful, to counterbalance those who refused.

Simon could see the young man get out of the pod. He said silently, You are a good young man, I'm sorry your attitude is going to be changed.

The young deliveryman bent over Catareen. She hesitated, whispered something. Then she was on him. She wrapped her taloned hands around his neck. Because he was at least a foot taller than she, she planted her feet on his abdomen. She was very fast. She was lizardlike. For a moment Simon saw her as an animal, seizing prey. Then he ran out from behind the barrels.

The deliveryman—the delivery *boy*—was white-faced and trembling in Catareen's grasp. He had pale orange hair and a dusting of freckles.

He said, "Please don't hurt me."

Simon paused. His circuits hummed. The kid wanted to be hurt, didn't he? He wanted it without knowing he did. Was that true? Or was Simon getting the signal wrong?

Simon said, "We're not going to do anything to you you don't want us to do."

"Get inside," Catareen said to the boy. "Passenger side."

Quivering, the boy climbed into the pod with Catareen clinging to him like a fiendish child. Simon got into the pilot's seat. He reversed the pod and hove onto the road. The boy sat beside him with Catareen ferociously crouched on his lap.

Simon saw that the boy had been delivering soymilk to the complex. Orange boxes of it were stacked neatly in the pod's rear.

The boy said, "Please. Oh, please, take the pod. I won't do anything."

Simon paused. He needed to do the best thing for the boy. He'd shut down if he did harm. But he could not seem to determine whether the boy wanted to be spared or menaced.

Catareen said nothing. She held her talons to the kid's scrawny neck.

When Simon tried to speak, he found that his voice was not working. He tried again. In a low tone he was able to say, "We're just going to drop you off in a little while. You can walk back. You'll be fine."

His voice had taken on a mechanical laxity. He felt as if he were driving drunk. He devoted his attention to steering.

The boy whimpered in Catareen's grasp. Simon drove as well as he could. He wavered slightly but was able to stay on the road.

When they saw a side road approaching, Catareen said, "Turn here."

"Oh, God, oh, no," the boy said. He must be thinking they meant to kill him.

He said, "Please, please, please."

Simon went blank then. His workings ceased. He could see, but he could not move. He saw his hand frozen on the pod's steering stick. He saw the side road go by.

Catareen said, "Not turn?"

He couldn't speak. He could only sit as he was, frozen, watching. The pod drifted to the right. Simon couldn't correct it. By the time Catareen understood that he had no powers of control, the pod had veered off the road and onto the dirt and grass of the shoulder. It shuddered slightly.

Catareen removed her claws from the boy's throat. As she put a hand over Simon's immobilized one to ease the pod back, the boy opened the passenger door and jumped.

Simon, still frozen, looked in the mirror globe and saw the boy tumbling onto the dirt. His vision began to cloud. He fought to remain conscious. He saw the boy flip twice in the dirt, raising a dust cloud, growing more distant as the pod sped on. His sight started failing. A whiteness gathered around the periphery of his vision and began closing in. He struggled and strained. He saw the boy sit up.

Simon's vision returned. His fingers on the steering stick began to have sensation again. He brushed Catareen's hand off his own, turned the pod sharply, went back for the boy.

"No go back," Catareen said.

He ignored her. He had no choice.

He stopped the pod at the place where the boy sat limply on the dirt. He got out and went to the boy.

He said, "Are you all right?"

The boy was cadaverously pale. He sat with his legs folded under him. His cheek was bruised. Simon felt his metabolism slow again. He felt his vision begin to whiten.

He said again, "Are you all right?"

Slowly, the boy nodded. Simon squatted beside him, checked his arms and legs. Nothing appeared to be broken.

"You seem to be all right," Simon said.

The boy started crying then. He had a scattering of blemishes on his forehead. He had a hawkish nose and pale, silly eyes.

"Do you think you can stand?" Simon asked.

The boy could not speak at first, for crying. Then he blubbered, "What are you going to do to me?"

There was an unmistakable note of excitement in his voice.

He was a level seven, then. Simon's circuits hummed.

He heard himself say, "I will kill your sorry ass."

The boy screamed. He scrabbled backward in the dirt. He turned himself over and began crawling away, into the grass.

No. Repress. Concentrate.

Simon said, "I want your sweet, fat ass. I want you to stick it high in the air for me so I can plow it with my big tattooed dick."

Fuck.

The boy howled. He crawled into the grass and got uncertainly to his feet. He fell again. Simon's felt his synapses firing and his cognition shutting down. It was unfortunate but not exactly unpleasant.

He said, "Sure as the stars return again after they merge in the light, death is as great as life."

Then Catareen was out of the pod and after the boy. Simon watched helplessly. He saw her take hold of the boy, who was sobbing, who had turned the color of cement. He saw her rifle through the boy's pockets and remove his vid. He saw her return and, with some effort, march him, Simon, back into the pod. He was able to move at her urging. During shutdown, early phase, he could still respond to directions, though he could not initiate action of any kind.

She put him in the passenger seat and got into the pilot's. She turned the pod around and drove, fast.

Gradually Simon's powers of movement returned. He felt them coming back. It was a growing warmth, an inner blooming. He was able to say, "Guess I went a little zonky back there, huh?"

"Yes," she answered. She was focused on the road.

"Circuits. Programming. Nothing I can do."

"I know." And yet she was angry. He could feel it. They hove on in silence.

He had seen her jump on a boy like a lizard seizing a beetle. He understood that some of what was said of Nadians was probably true. They had animal aspects. They were capable of doing harm.

Finally he said, "We don't have much time, you know."

"Yes," she said.

"All that kid has to do is flag down some Samaritan in a pod. Which may have happened already. In which case, Magicom is about to be majorly on our asses."

"Yes."

"In which case, we should not be on the main road."

"No."

And yet she drove on with relentless, orange-eyed focus. Lizard, he thought. Fucking lizard.

He said, "There are old roads all over Pennsylvania. This looks like a turnoff coming up."

"Yes."

"I should probably drive."

"I drive."

"I only had a problem because we hurt that kid. I thought I'd explained that to you."

"I drive," she said.

He decided not to argue with her. She seemed to be a good enough driver. Stopping to change places would take time.

She took the road that led off the podway. A battered sign said HARRISBURG. They hove through the remnants of a settlement. The Council-administered states had begun tearing such places down, or so you heard. According to rumor, Magicom was trying to sell Pennsylvania but could find no buyers.

Catareen piloted the pod competently over the cracked and buckled road. Abandoned houses and storefronts rattled by, McDonald'ses and Wendy Kentuckys and Health-4-Evers, all weed and dark, shattered glass. Most were empty. Some had been taken over by Nadians, who had put up their sun-blasted awnings. Who tended their young ones, their scraps of drying laundry, their little fires.

Catareen and Simon hove for hours unimpeded. They kept the pod headed west. The landscape was unchanging, empty houses and franchises and random shops and every so often a derelict shopping mall, all so similar that Simon worried they might have doubled back on themselves unwittingly. When these places were operating, they must have been more individualized. He worried that he and Catareen might be headed back to New Jersey. They might end up at the complex where they had stolen the deliverypod.

They could only trust the pod's directional. They could only drive on.

Night fell. They had each had two boxes of soymilk. They needed food. They hove silent and hungry across the dark nothing. The pod's lights showed mile after mile of broken road that led toward nothing more than the hope of Emory Lowell. They were pursuing a date and place Lowell had implanted in Simon five years ago.

If the Nadian was concerned, she made no sign. She merely drove with her incessant, reptile-eyed concentration.

Finally he said, "We should stop for the night."

"Hour more," she answered.

"No. We should stop now."

He saw her lipless mouth tighten. She was a lizard woman who wanted her own way. She was imperious and unempathic.

Then she said, "If you want."

She pulled to the side of the road. She deactivated the pod, which sighed and settled. Its headglobes faded. A pure darkness arrived, alive with the rasp and chirping of insects.

"We can get rid of some of the soymilk and sleep in the back," he said.

"Or house."

She indicated with her small, ovoid head a row of houses on the road's far side, sharply gabled against the stars, like a child's drawing of a mountain range.

"Technically they're still private property," he said.

She waggled her fingers in the air—a Nadian gesture of dismissal, he supposed.

"Hey," he said. "We're criminals, right? What's a little breaking and entering?"

They got out of the pod. Simon stood for a moment on the weedy dirt, stretching his spine. They were in a vast black house-filled emptiness. An immensity of constellations hung overhead. This far from city lights, they were countless.

Nadia's sun was one of the stars just above the black roof silhouettes. That shitty little star over there.

He realized Catareen was standing beside him. They could move very quietly, these people. These lizards.

She said, "Nadia."

"Mm-hm."

"We say Nourthea."

"I know."

The name "Nadia" had always been an ironic approximation. One of the right-wing papers had started calling it Planet Nada, Spanish for "nothing," as its riches and wisdom kept failing to materialize. The name had stuck.

She said, "You have go?"

"Me, personally? No. I'm new. I was manufactured about five years ago. I'm actually one of the very last ones they made."

"Why not legal?"

"You mean, why do they bother chasing after a poor, harmless, old artificial like me?"

"Yes."

"A couple of years ago the Council identified all artificials as stolen property, because the whole debate about natural versus engineered life just went on and on. We were monsters and abominations. Or we were the innocent victims of science, and deserved protection. There was talk of special preserves for us. Somebody in Texas invented and patented a soul-measuring apparatus, but the courts disallowed it. Finally the people who were most appalled by us came up with a solution. Because we were manufactured, simulos were declared the property of Biologe. And because we were walking around loose, we were stolen. We had essentially stolen ourselves. We were declared contraband. We were ordered to return ourselves. But Biologe was out of business by then. So, next best thing, we were to turn ourselves in to the authorities until our rightful owner came to claim us. Which of course was never going to happen. We would be held in a sort of escrow until that time, aka never. A few actually did it. As far as I know, they're sitting in cells to this day with tags clipped to their ears. The rest of us did our best to disappear. But as stolen property, we're inherently illegal. We break the law by continuing to possess ourselves."

"And they hate?"

"Well, 'hate' may not be exactly the right word. You could say they think of us as a bad idea. A needless complication in the ongoing argument about the eternal soul. They just sort of want us not to be."

"Nadians also."

"Well. It's different. You're legal aliens. Being biological, your right to life is not in question. All your other rights are."

"We live with no stroth."

"Agonies are one of my changes of garments," he said.

"Yes," she answered.

The night hummed around them. Certain insects remained. The birds were probably gone forever.

Simon said, "I know you don't like questions."

"Some questions."

"And I'm not going to ask you about your past or your family or any of those clearly forbidden subjects."

"Thank."

"But I would like to know. I mean, here we are. You had a job, you had a place to live. Granted, maybe not the greatest job, but given what's available to you—"

"To one like me."

"Sorry, I don't mean to offend. You know what I'm getting at, right? Why are you here? If we get to Denver, if by some miracle Lowell is actually there, what do you hope will happen for you?"

"Die in Denver."

"That's a little melodramatic, don't you think?"

"No."

Then she went stare-y and blank. Although he could not see her clearly he knew what her nostrils were doing. He was learning to feel these conditions when they arose in her. The air changed between them. A legible and almost audible absence announced itself.

"Why do you do this?" he asked. "I mean, where do you go when you get like this?"

Softly, she exhaled the little Nadian song. *Ee-um-fah-um-so.*

"I'm asking," he said, "because frankly it gets a little creepy for me when you zone out. I've pretty much come to understand that you tune back in eventually, but still. Would it be too hard for you to just, you know, hang in a little more? Would it be too un-Nadian?"

Nothing. The breathy song, soft in the darkness.

"Okay. Well, I'm glad we had this conversation. Let's go find a place to sleep, okay?"

"Yes," she said. She said that, at least.

They crossed the road and went into the development. It was one of the villages Titan had tossed up for the soon-to-be-rich. Front porches, dormers, window boxes. There'd been rumors that these places were made of something that broke down over time and produced toxic fumes, though the high incidence of cancerous tumors among the soon-to-bes could just as easily have had its roots in the soil or water of their various native lands.

Catareen led him straight to the third house in the first row. It seemed briefly that she must have been here before, must have had some connection to this particular house, though that of course was extremely unlikely. It was probably a Nadian thing about always choosing the third in a lineup or making arbitrary choices with a ritual show of certainty. Or something. Who knew? Who wanted, at this late hour, to go to the trouble of asking?

The front door was locked. Most people had expected to come back. The windows were locked, too. Simon suggested that they try another house, but Catareen had settled on this one. They ended up breaking a window with a plastistone Krishna that stood silently blowing into a silent flute among a circle of long-dead marigolds on the front lawn. The plexi, when it shattered, produced a sharp and hopeless musical sound.

After they crawled in through the window, they found themselves in a living room that had been stripped of all that could be easily carried. What remained was a sofa and two low, hulking chairs covered in pinks and golds and peacock blues bright enough to show even in the darkness. There was a low, carved table and a giant vid and a lightglobe in the shape of a period chandelier.

"Let's see if there's any food," Simon said.

They went into the kitchen, where they found old packets of curried this and pickled that. All of it needed water to reconstitute, however, and there was of course no water.

Catareen held a foil packet in her hands and turned it over and over, as if she hoped to discover some secret instructions for converting the husks within into food without the introduction of moisture. Watching her like that, Simon was filled with a sense of her unknown life — scrabbling whatever crops she could from the sloggy, dead soil of Nadia, coming to Earth on one of the Promise Ships and arriving, at the end of the seventeen-year trip, in a post-meltdown world where an alien was lucky to get work in sanitation or child minding. Now she was here, in the abandoned kitchen of a relocated family, holding a packet of inedible food, on her way to a place where she had no business, where she was going simply because she could no longer stay in the place she'd been.

Simon said, "We'll figure something out about food in the morning. Let's just go to sleep now."

"Yes," she said. She laid the packet on the countertop carefully, as if it were precious and fragile.

They ascended the stairs, past the wall shadows of holopix that had been taken down. Upstairs were three modest bedrooms, each of which contained a stripped bed and an empty bureau. By some unspoken accord they both chose the rooms that had belonged to the children, as opposed to the slightly larger parental room, with the bigger bed in it.

"Good night," Simon said. She gave him a brief, military nod and went into her room.

Simon stretched out on the modest child bed. The emptied room, with its single window that gave onto the window of the house next door, resembled a nun's cell, though its vanished occupant had overlooked a holopic cut from a magazine and fastened to the wall, as well as a single pale-pink sock, which coiled like a question mark at the foot of the bed. The holopic was Marty Mockington, early years, twirling with a doomed and childish grace though a field of singing poppies. Simon watched Marty Mockington dance by, over and over, young and alive, glowing. It could not have been one of the kid's favorite pictures, or it wouldn't have been left behind. It must have been a lesser image among the dozens that would have covered the wall. Simon could briefly imagine the kid—a girl, judging by the sock—lying here before her wall of singing and dancing icons. Would she have imagined herself in the future, getting somehow from this little room to the world of the holopix? Probably. Kids believed in extravagant destinies. Now she must be . . . who knew where? Doing something slavish in the Southern Assembly, most likely, or, if she was lucky, if her parents had managed the paperwork, being trained for something semislavish up in Canada. Eurasia would be out of the question for people like this. The girl was wherever she was, and Marty Mockington, a lesser star in her private constellation, twenty years dead by now, went on dancing on her bedroom wall and would keep doing so for one hundred years or more, until the photons broke down, until the poppies started to fade and his exuberant interlude of dance (heel, toe, leap) slowed and slowed and finally stopped.

Simon shut his eyes. Dream fragments arrived. A room that was somehow full of stars. A proud and happy man whose hands were flames.

He woke with a light shining hard and white in his eyes. For a moment he thought he might still be dreaming, dreaming of a terrible light.

A male voice said from behind the light, "Here's another one."

Another *what*, Simon wondered.

A second voice, female, said, "He's not a Nadian."

"Nope. He's not."

Simon got off the bed and stood blinking in the light. He said, "We just needed a place to sleep. We weren't going to steal anything."

"What are they doing here?" the female voice said. "Ask him what they're doing here."

Simon's eyes adapted. He could discern two figures standing behind the glare. One was tall and hooded, the other shorter, with a nimbus of crackly hair standing out around her head.

Simon said, "We're travelers. We don't mean any harm."

"People say that," the male voice answered. "Harm comes anyway."

A third voice sounded from down the hall. It said, "What did you find in there?"

It was a boy's voice. A boy speaking with unboyish authority.

"A Possessionless," answered the man shape behind the lightglobe. "Looks crazy to me."

Simon was still wearing the filthy stolen sweaters and the stained pants over his black multizippered kit from work. Looks crazy. Right.

He was briefly, strangely embarrassed.

Other people entered the room. Simon said, "Could you maybe drop that light a little?"

A pause followed, during which the man with the lightglobe seemed to be checking for permission. It apparently being granted, he aimed the lightglobe down slightly, out of Simon's eyes, and revealed the following: himself, the bearer of the lightglobe, a man of seventy or more, wrapped in an old Halloween costume: Obi-Wan Kenobi. The crepey synthetic of the robe billowed around his lank frame; his gray head blinked out from under the hood, which was far too small for him and fit him like a skullcap. Beside him stood a girl around seventeen, a Blessed Virgin, cloaked in blue and white. Just behind them stood Catareen, in the grip of a Full Jesus. He'd had his face done, with the thorn implants at the brow.

The Jesus and the Blessed Virgin both carried stun guns.

From some invisibility in Catareen's vicinity, the boy said, "What exactly are you two doing here?" His voice was like the sound of scissors snipping tin.

Simon answered, "The myth of heaven indicates the soul; the soul is always beautiful."

"Poetry doesn't really answer the question, does it?"

The boy stepped forward. He was probably eleven or twelve years old. He was disfigured. His head, big as a soup tureen, squatted heavily on his thin shoulders. His eyes were larger and rounder than they should have been. His nose and ears could barely be said to exist. He wore what appeared to be a man's bathrobe, with the sleeves rolled up and the tail trailing on the ground. Ornaments hung from strings around his neck: a flattened Aphrodite tuna can, an orange plastic peace symbol, a bottle of MAC nail polish, a yellow-fanged cat skull.

Simon delivered a silent, futile plea to Catareen. Help me out a little here. See if you can muster something more useful than just standing there quietly captured, as if captivity were your true and natural condition.

He said, "We're just driving through. That's all."

The boy asked, "Where would you say you were driving *to*, on a road like this? It only leads to other roads like this."

"We just got off the podway for a little while. We wanted to see what the country was like."

The Jesus said, "This is the country. This is what we're like."

The boy said, "I am Luke. Of the New Covenant."

"I'm Simon."

"Who's your friend?"

"Her name is Catareen."

"We found your pod out front. We saw the window you broke."

"I'm sorry about the window. I could, well, I could leave my name, and if the house's owners ever come back, I could try to make it up to them—"

"This is unusual, the picture you two present," Luke said. "A man and a Nadian in a pod full of soymilk. I'm trying to think of the reasonable and innocent explanations."

Catareen said, "No money. Not nothing, we have."

The old man said, "We don't use money. We never touch it."

"Never," said the Jesus.

"We keep clean."

Simon said, "We keep clean, too. We're trying to get to a brotherhood in Colorado."

There was a chance of impersonating Christians in flight. It was a small chance but nevertheless.

"A brotherhood that accepts Nadians?" Luke asked.

Simon said, "That I could look with a separate look at my own crucifixion and bloody crowning."

Oops.

The Blessed Virgin cried out, "They're with Satan!"

"Oh, I suppose they are," Luke said, with an expression of weary disappointment.

The old man said, "Should we slay them here or take them back to the tabernacle?"

"Tabernacle," Luke said.

The Jesus said, "Let's do it here."

"No. We're taking them to the tabernacle," Luke replied. He was clearly accustomed to command.

"Oh, well, okay," said the Jesus, clearly accustomed to obedience.

Simon and Catareen were taken downstairs and out of the house. There, parked on the road in front of the deliverypod, was an ancient Winnebago covered in faded decals that depicted guns, fish, and mammals.

"Give Obi-Wan Kenobi the engager for your pod," Luke told Simon.

Simon obeyed. The old man snatched the engager from him like a squirrel taking a nut.

There followed a debate, rather lengthy, about who should go in which vehicle. It was determined that Luke and the Jesus would take Simon and Catareen in the Winnebago, and the Virgin and the old man would follow in the deliverypod. Simon and Catareen were put ungently in the back of the Winnebago. There was a miniature house inside. There was a small kitchen and a table with seats and a bedshelf. It was brilliantly colored, in the way of old things. It smelled of bread mold and warm plastic.

Luke got in back with Simon and Catareen. He took the stun gun from the Jesus and leveled it at them. The Jesus stood in the doorway, jingling the ignition keys in his pierced palm.

"You think you can manage them back here?" the Jesus said.

"Absolutely," Luke answered. "About the gun, though. It's set to stun, right? A five is nonlethal, right?"

"It's on five?"

"It is."

"Okay. Five is good. Five'll knock 'em out, but it won't kill 'em."

"Good."

Luke aimed the stun gun at the Jesus and fired. A bright blue beam struck the skinny, white-robed chest. The Jesus looked at Luke with an expression of profound bafflement. Then his eyes rolled back in their sockets, and he crumpled away, out the door of the Winnebago and onto the street.

"Quick," Luke said to Simon and Catareen. "Let's get out of here."

Simon stared at the fallen Jesus. One of his sandaled feet, surprisingly small, twitched on the Winnebago's threshold. The rest of him lay sprawled on the asphalt in an attitude of ecstatic release.

"What do you have in mind, exactly?" Simon asked.

Luke handed him the gun. "Take me hostage," he said. "Grab the keys and drive like hell."

"You're sure about this?"

"Absolutely. Aim the stunner at me."

Simon had no trouble with that, considering the boy's unambiguous wishes.

"I'm going to go out in front of you," Luke said. "Pick up the keys, and get us out of here. Do you understand?"

"I guess so."

"We should take the Winnebago and leave the pod. The Winnebago is better off-road."

"Right."

"Make them give you back the engager for the pod so they can't follow us."

"Whatever you say."

"Okay. Let's go."

Luke kicked the Jesus' foot down from the threshold. He raised his hands in the air and hopped outside. Simon glanced at Catareen — did she think this was some kind of trap? She flicked her long fingers toward the doorway, that Nadian gesture of impatience.

From outside the Winnebago, he heard Luke say, "For the love of Christ, don't shoot."

Catareen flicked her fingers more urgently. All right, then. If this was a mistake, he'd let it be *her* problem.

Simon jumped out after Luke and trained the stun gun on the frail back. He said, "Move. I will fucking kill you if you don't do exactly what I say."

He was good at this, no denying it.

"Just don't hurt me," Luke whimpered.

The Virgin and Obi-Wan stood frozen at the doors to the pod, blinking in confusion. It seemed to Simon an unnecessarily elaborate charade, given that its entire audience was a teenage girl and an elderly man in a Halloween costume.

Then his circuits started shutting down. Here was the sudden cooling, as if the temperature had dropped by fifteen degrees. Here was the fizzy light-headedness, the sour, spinning intoxication. It seemed to stem not from the entirely false threat of violence but from the absurdity of the threat, the pathos of tricking these sad people (who had, it must be remembered, murderous capabilities). He was all but overcome by the notion that the world was made of tricks and sorrows, of zealots and shoddiness and brutal authorities and old men in costumes.

He was shutting down. It shouldn't be happening. He wasn't harming anyone directly. But here it was.

Catareen had snatched the keys from the Jesus' hand. Luke took a step forward, saying, "Please, please, I'll do anything you want." Simon was able to move, but with increasing difficulty, as if the air itself were thickening around him.

He said, "Inside of dresses and ornaments, behold a secret silent loathing and despair." His voice was heavy and several notes too low.

Catareen snatched the gun from his hand, leaped forward, and pressed it between Luke's shoulder blades.

She said to the old man and the Virgin, "Throw me engager."

"Do it," Luke commanded.

The old man tossed the engager in Catareen's direction. It fell on the ground at her feet, and she snatched it up with raptorish speed.

"Move," she said to Luke.

He moved. Simon followed as best he could.

Catareen got Luke into the cab of the Winnebago. Simon managed to get himself in on the passenger's side. Catareen put the key into the ignition, started it up. She leaned out the window and shouted at the Virgin and the old man, "If you follow, we kill."

Then she accelerated, and they were on their way.

"Nice work," Luke said. He smelled slightly of pine air freshener. His fetish necklace clicked softly against his narrow, bathrobed chest.

Catareen drove. The headlights of the Winnebago lit up the ash-colored road, the tangles of dark grass on either side.

Simon felt himself returning. Motion seemed to help. He said, "What was *that* about?"

He heard his own voice as if from a certain distance. But he was starting up again, no question.

"That was 'Sayonara, assholes,'" Luke answered.

"Who *were* those people?"

"Blots on the name of the Lord. Fools in fools' clothing."

"Weren't you one of them?"

"Posing as."

The Winnebago's headlights continued showing bright, empty road bordered by black fields. Simon saw that it was equipped with a directional. They could find Denver easily, then.

He said to the boy, "Will they come after us?"

"Probably. They'll want the Winnebago back more than they'll want me."

"Should we be worried?"

"They're not very smart or well organized. It'll take Obi-Wan and Kitty an hour to walk to the tabernacle. I'd say go off-road and kill the lights. There's enough of a moon."

"The Winnebago is all-terrain?"

"Yep. Modified. Engine's atomic, and the wheelbase has been hydraulicked. It's modeled on what they used to call tanks."

"I know what a tank is," Simon said.

"Then you know we can go just about anywhere in this thing."

At that, Catareen turned off the road and extinguished the head-lights. The Winnebago's tires held on the uneven ground. Catareen drove into the grass, which was restless and silvered under the moon.

"So," Luke said. "Where are you headed?"

"We're going to Denver."

"Looking for Emory Lowell?"

"How did you know that?"

"When somebody says he's going to Denver, the name Lowell nat-urally arises. I mean, you wouldn't be going all that way for the rat-tlesnake festival."

"You've heard of Lowell, then."

"I've met him."

"You have?"

"Sure. I lived in Denver for a few years, when I was younger. My mother and I traveled a lot."

"Military?"

"No. Just poor."

They drove across the grassy flats. Every so often the lights of a compound flickered in the distance. Every so often there was a shoot-ing star.

After they had covered more than a hundred miles, they agreed that they should stop for the rest of the night. Catareen said, "We must to eat."

"Love to," Simon answered. "If you happen to see a café out here—"

"I find," she said.

"What do you expect to find, exactly?"

"Animals here, yes?"

"Some. Maybe. They say some of the hardier specimens are still around. Rats. Squirrels. Raccoons."

She said, "I go. I look."

"You're telling me you think you can *catch* something out there?"

"I look."

"By all means."

Catareen slipped out of the truck's cab and seemed to vanish in-stantly among the trees. Simon and Luke got out, too. They strolled, stretching their limbs. Overhead, among the branches, stars were manifest.

Luke said, "She's probably a good hunter."

Simon thought of her talons. He thought of her teeth. "Who knows?"

"I seem to remember," Luke said, "when I was little, there was a vid on Nadian customs."

"That must have been an old one."

"I remember some rodent thing they were fond of."

"I have vague recollections. A gray hairless thing about the size of a gopher. Long tail. Very long tail."

"Right. They cooked it with some sort of hairy brown vegetable."

"Like a pinecone with fur. If you stewed one of those rodents with the hairy vegetable for five or six hours, you could eat it."

"It was one of their delicacies."

"Right."

Luke said, "They do have souls, you know."

"I'm not all that big on the whole soul concept, frankly."

"Because you're biomechanical?"

"What makes you say that?"

"Your eyes. It's subtle, but I can always spot it."

"What about my eyes?"

"Hard to explain. There's nothing technically wrong with them."

"They're *biological*," Simon said.

"I know that. Like I said, it's subtle. There's just a certain sense of two camera apertures expanding and contracting. Something lensish. The eyes of biological humans are sort of juicier. Or more skittish or something. It's not a question of the visual apparatus, more like what's behind it. Anyway, I can tell."

"You're a smart kid, huh? How old are you anyway?"

"I'm around eleven. Maybe twelve. Does it matter? I've always had this heightened perception thing."

"Through me many long dumb voices," Simon said.

"The business with the poetry is interesting."

"I hate it."

"You dream, right?"

"In my way."

"Do you like being alive?"

"Let's say I feel attached to it."

"Do you worry about dying?"

"Programmed to. There's a survival chip."

"Well, we're all programmed, don't you think? By our makers?"

"I'm not feeling all that philosophical at the moment. So, you're Exedrol?"

"Yep. When my mother got pregnant with me, she took a few handfuls."

"Deliberately?"

"She thought Exedrol had some kind of program. Monthly reparation checks. I don't know who told her that."

"She intentionally took a drug that would deform her child?"

"What can I say? She was always looking for a scam. She was that kind of person. I don't blame her."

"Come on."

"She gave me life. Gratitude is the only appropriate response to everything that happens."

"Biologicals are mysterious."

"A couple of years ago she and I joined this group that called themselves Holy Fire. Creepy bunch, really. Those were a few of the more intelligent specimens you met back there."

"She was a Christian."

"She was whatever it took to get set up for a while. The Christians will feed you if you take the vows."

"Is your mother still with them?"

"Naw. She met a guy. A roofer—the tabernacle had leaks. I haven't heard from her in almost a year."

"She left you behind?"

"Roofer wasn't interested in fatherhood. She figured the Christians would take better care of me than she could. They're the ones that named me Luke. Biblical, you know."

"Your real name being?"

"My real name is Luke. My old name was Blitzen. Like one of Santa's reindeer? Mom was . . . never mind what Mom was."

"And you pretended to believe in their god."

"Oh, I do believe in their god. I just don't like their methods."

"Seriously."

"I couldn't be more serious. I've had the Holy Spirit in me for almost a year now."

"Oh. Well. I guess that's nice for you."

" 'Nice' is probably not the best word for what it is."

Simon and Luke had returned to the Winnebago and were sitting with their backs propped against its right rear tire when Catareen returned. She was surprisingly quiet. There had been no footfall, no snap of twig. She was suddenly there. She held something behind her back.

She said, "I find."

"You mean you really *did* catch something?" Simon said.

"Yes."

"What is it?" Luke asked.

Catareen hesitated. Her eyes glowed in the darkness. She said, "I fix on other side."

"You don't want to show us?" Simon asked.

"I fix on other side," she said. She took whatever it was she held and went to the far side of the vehicle.

"What's the matter with her?" Luke asked Simon.

"She's embarrassed," he answered.

"Why would she be embarrassed? If she really went out there and caught something we can eat, she's a hero."

"She doesn't want to look like an animal to us."

"She's not an animal."

"No. She's not. But she's not human, either. It's strange for her, living here."

"How would you know?"

"I can imagine. That's all."

Soon Catareen returned. She held the neatly skinned and filleted carcasses of two squirrels. She had removed their heads, feet, and tails. Her eyes dimmed and lidded, she offered them to Simon and the boy. Her cape was flecked with blood that shone darkly against the pale cloth. Simon hoped she didn't see him notice it.

He said, "Thank you."

"We'll be eating them raw, then," Luke said.

"I have an idea," Simon said.

He raised the hood of the Winnebago and lifted the housing of the minireactor that had been nested into the place where a battery once resided. It put out a pale green glow. The squirrel carcasses would be mildly contaminated but not enough to cause serious harm.

He took them from Catareen. They were warm and slick. They were clearly things that had been alive. He experienced briefly something like what Catareen must have experienced, catching and killing the squirrels. There was an inner click. He could put no other word to it. There was hunger and a click, a small, electrical trill inside his chest. He looked at her.

He said again, "Thank you."

She nodded. She did not speak.

He laid the squirrel carcasses on the exposed reactor. He did it gently, as if they could feel pain. They made a soft sizzling sound on contact. They would not be cooked in the technical sense, but they would not be raw, either.

He stood over the carcasses as they slowly darkened. They put out a smell that was wild and sharp. Luke stood close by, watching. Catareen stood farther off. Simon had seen a vid once, ancient footage of a family engaged like this. The father was cooking meat on a fire as his wife and child waited for it to be done.

They ate the squirrels, which were stringy and bitter, with a strong chemical undertaste. Still, it was food. After they'd eaten, they slept in the back of the Winnebago. Catareen and the boy fit nicely on the two orange-cushioned benches bracketing the woodlike table-shelf. Simon, being larger, slept on the bedshelf that protruded over the Winnebago's cab.

He dreamed about flying women wearing dresses of light.

They drove again at dawn. The land rolled on, high grasses and immensities of sky. The Winnebago cut a swath through the grass, which closed up immediately after. They left no trace behind. White fists of cloud roiled overhead, massing and dissolving.

"It all looks pretty normal," Luke said.

"Hard to know, isn't it?" Simon gazed out the windshield. "I mean, did clouds look like this before? Was the sky this shade of blue?"

"I've heard that the meltdown was in North Dakota. There was a secret underground facility there."

"I've heard Nebraska. Near Omaha."

"A guy I knew told me it was the coup de grâce of the Children's Crusade. Crazy kids with a really big bomb."

"No, that was over by then. It was separatists from California."

"That's not what I heard. The California separatists turned out to be, like, seven or eight people in Berkeley, with no funds or anything. I have that on good authority."

"They were bigger than that. They definitely did the thing with the drinking water in Texas."

"Whatever. You know, some people think the evacuations weren't necessary. Other people think it's still not safe."

"There's no denying that the birds are gone."

"Yeah, but I heard they're reintroducing them on a trial basis. The tougher ones. Pigeons, sparrows, gulls."

"Maybe they should think a little harder about reintroducing some of the people first."

"Do you think there's been an election?" Luke said.

"I've been wondering. Yeah, I think so. The laws seem to have changed."

"I heard one of the presidents has been put in jail."

"I heard the other president converted."

"Well, there you go."

They drove on, into the day, across the vast platter of the earth. They were able to go west in a straight line, relatively speaking. The directional kept them informed about what was ahead. They skirted the towns and settlements. They had to curve around the occasional stand of trees, but for mile upon mile there was nothing but fields that had once been grazing land or cropland and were now gone to grass. They saw deer. They saw coyotes. Always at a distance, tawny spots in the green immensity, watching them from afar. The larger animals were coming back, then.

They stopped periodically so that Catareen could hunt. She was usually successful. She would vanish for half an hour or longer and return with a rabbit or a squirrel. In her work of food procurement, Catareen was always the same. She slipped silently away, returned just as silently, and skinned and gutted her catch on the far side of the Winnebago, where Simon and the boy couldn't see her. She presented the gleaming carcasses wordlessly. They never spoke, any of them, about what they ate. They simply ate, and Catareen buried the heads, bones, and whatever else was left. She always buried the remains. It was apparently necessary for her to do that. After the bits of the dead animals had been interred, they drove on.

On the second night, they stopped the Winnebago atop a modest rise overlooking a pond that was as bright as a circle of mirror in the fading light. It gave back the brilliant lavender of the evening sky, a rippled and deepened version, as if the water wore a skin of pale purple light.

Simon said, "I could use a bath."

"We all could," said Luke.

They went to the edge of the pond. Gnats and flies hovered over the water's surface. It had a smell—iron and something else, an odor Simon could identify only as wetness. He said, "Hard to say whether it's toxic or not."

By way of an answer, Catareen slipped off her cape, strode into the water, and dove, with the same alarming quickness that enabled her to stalk and kill small animals. She simply stood at one moment on the bank and at the next was only a discarded cape stained by animal blood. The black dot of her head surfaced twenty yards out.

"She's not worried," Simon said.

"Me, neither," Luke said, though there was no conviction in his tone.

Simon and Luke got out of their clothes. Luke lifted the fetish necklace over his head, shrugged off the bathrobe. He paused naked at the water's edge. Simon noticed Luke's pink smallness, the twists and concavities of his body. Unclothed, he resembled the skinned carcasses of the animals Catareen hunted.

He said to Simon, "I guess it's clean enough."

"Yeah. I'm sure it is."

Luke seemed to take comfort in Simon's assurance, though of course they both knew Simon had no way of knowing anything at all about the pond's level of contamination. Still, Luke seemed to derive a sense of permission. He went with a whoop into the water, throwing up droplets of spray.

Simon stood ankle-deep in the bright water. He thought for a moment that his circuits were seizing up again—he felt the first intimations of chill and languor. But this, it seemed, was something else. This was a new sensation. It seemed to arise from the pure strangeness of finding himself at the edge of a circle of water (quite possibly polluted) with a lizard woman and a deformed boy. It was something that moved through his circuits, like shutdown but not quite; a floatier sensation, vaguely ticklish; an inner unmooring, like what preceded sleep.

"Come on," Luke called.

Simon dove in. The water was warm on its surface, cold below. He swam out to Catareen and Luke.

Luke said, "This feels so good. I don't care if it's toxic."

Catareen floated on her back, so effortlessly that it seemed she did not swim at all but was simply held by the water, propelled by it, as an otter or muskrat would be. They were swimmers, then, the Nadians. In the water she looked wilder than she ordinarily did. She looked wilder and more true. She had a creaturely inevitability. Simon understood; he thought he understood. She would be feeling the layer of warm water floating on the cold, the sensation of skimming across a shallow bowl of purple light surrounded by a darkening world as the first of the stars came out. She would be disappearing into this just as she disappeared into her dream states, her lizard song.

Simon was the first to get out of the water. He stood naked on the bank, letting the air dry him, and watched as Catareen and the boy emerged. Catareen naked was all sinew, with thin, strong arms and legs, tiny breast-buds, and a small, compact rise of bony, squarish pelvis. Who was the sculptor? Giacometti. She looked like a sculpture by Giacometti.

She stood a moment in the shallows as the boy scrambled up the bank and got back into his robe. She turned and looked out at the water. Simon understood that she took intense pleasure in this: the water and the darkening land. He knew she was reluctant to leave it. He watched her. She was a thin black shape against the pond and the sky. She was, he thought, happy. She was suddenly and unexpectedly happy, or whatever she would call it if Nadians had a term for happiness.

"Beautiful," he said. He was not entirely sure what he meant by the word at that particular moment. It seemed almost like a new greeting he and Catareen had agreed to exchange—a variation of common language, newly encoded.

She turned back at the sound of his voice. She was startled and shy. There was something about her at that moment. He could not describe it. There was perhaps no term for it in human language. He could not give it a name.

He said instead, "How beautiful and perfect are the animals! How perfect is my soul! How perfect the earth, and the minutest thing upon it!"

Catareen looked at him. A silence passed.

Luke said to Simon, "You smell slightly better now."

"Thanks," Simon said. He started getting dressed again.

Presently Catareen got out of the water, got dressed, and slipped away to hunt. She returned soon after with a pair of small, leggy creatures none of them could identify. Simon cooked them.

"I think we must be in western Kansas by now," Luke said as Simon poked the skinned haunches on the Winnebago's radiation pack. "We could reach Denver by late tomorrow."

"By midafternoon, I'd say," Simon answered.

What he thought but did not say: he wouldn't have minded driving on and on. There was something hypnotic about it, something deeply agreeable. Just driving.

Luke said, "Denver has gotten to be a sort of giant shantytown. It's probably a little like it was almost three hundred years ago. Except the people three hundred years ago didn't live in abandoned malls and franchise joints."

"The Christians don't run Denver, as far as I've heard."

"No, Denver's basically secular. Some goddess cults, and a big Buddha town on the east side. Jesus Christ, Our Lord and Savior, is small potatoes there."

"Did you say you believe in all that?"

"Yep."

"As part of the con."

"Started out that way. I went along with it so they'd keep feeding me. I said the prayers, I did the daily devotions. I meditated in the pathetic little shrine they'd built in the Wal-Mart parking lot. Just scamming. Then I understood that it's true."

"You're kidding."

"I'm totally serious. Something happened one day. I don't know how to describe it. Something arrived. It's like, okay, say you walked out of your house every day and shouted, 'Oh, come to me, Great Heffalump,' just to please somebody, just because it's the local custom, because your crazy old aunt won't take her medicine unless you call for the Heffalump every morning, and then one day this big hairy thing with a trunk and antlers comes lumbering up and says, 'I'm the Great Heffalump, what do you want?' What're you going to do? You don't believe in him, you don't like him, you don't want him, but there he is."

"I'm not sure if I believe you."

"I don't need you to believe me. Hey, are those groundhogs just about done?"

"I don't think they're groundhogs."

"Whatever they are. I'm starving, I don't mind if they're on the rare side."

Simon served the irradiated creatures. Catareen sat between him and the boy, quietly consuming her share of the hunt. After they'd eaten, she buried the remains, and the boy went to bed in the back of the Winnebago. Simon stayed outside a while with Catareen. They sat together on the grassy rise. The wind made a low rustling sound, and the stars shone hard in the deep black sky. The pond put out minute ghostly sparks that could have been reflections of the stars.

Simon said, "Do you miss Nadia?"

"No."

"It's your home. It's where you come from."

"Nothing there."

He hesitated over how to respond. There was *something* there. There was something everywhere. True, the people of Earth had hoped for more from their first (and possibly only) contact with an inhabited planet. All those zillions spent getting there, the decades of effort, and what do they find? A people who in ten thousand years had failed to come up with a written language. Who lived in huts made of dried mud and pulled one another around in wooden carts. Where were the golden cities, the shamans and scientists? Where were the great discoveries, the cures, the art?

He said, "It's a rough place, I hear."

"Nothing for me."

"You know," he said, "maybe there's no real point in you being so mysterious about your past. Doesn't it seem just the tiniest bit unnecessary?"

She sat beside him in the dark. She exhaled the little song.

After an interval, he said, "So. Do you have any questions about me?"

"No."

"Are all Nadians like this?"

"Like how?"

The wind blew across his face. It had a dry green smell.

He said, "Do you mind listening to me? Do I bore you when I talk?"

"No. I like."

"Nice of you to say so."

Silence, and the breath song.

He said, "It's just that I seem to have a few questions. For a biological."

"Ask."

"I know a lot of it may not apply. The whole human-versus-Nadian question, I mean."

"Ask."

"Okay. Dreams. Can I ask you something about dreams?"

"Yes."

"I have these little flickers when I sleep. There are sounds and images. They don't seem exactly random, but they don't hold together, either. I can't really tell if they're dreams at all or just my circuits discharging. As I understand it, biologicals have dreams that involve whole stories. Mysterious stories, often oblique, but coherent and full of meaning. True?"

"No," she said.

"Would it be painful for you to give me a little more detail?"

"Not whole stories. Change."

"You mean, as you're dreaming? The stories change as they progress?"

"Yes."

"But don't you wake up feeling like you've seen something important? Even if its meaning isn't clear. Don't you feel in the morning like something has been explained to you as you slept?"

"No."

"Well. Okay. Let's try another subject. The voice I'm speaking in right now, what you know as my voice, and by extension my, shall we say, personality, is programmed. Cadences, vocabulary, modulation, slang, all of it designed by Emory Lowell to make me seem more human. Plus, of course, these involuntary fits of poetry. What's in my brain is different. I listen to myself speak—I'm listening to myself *right now*—and it's strange to me. It doesn't match what I hear inside my head. The impulses are my own, I make a decision to say this or say that, but the expression is beyond my control. I suspect that if you could somehow see inside my head, if you could see the circuitry going through the motions, you'd recoil. You'd understand that I'm mechanical. And heartless."

"I am same," she said.

"What you say doesn't match what's in your head?"

"Yes."

"Of course it doesn't. You're speaking a foreign language."

"In my language."

"You mean, back on Nadia, you felt this divide between who you appeared to be and who you knew yourself to be?"

"Yes."

"Sweet of you to say so."

"True."

They sat for a while in silence. Simon felt the withdrawal of her, which had become familiar, though this time it seemed deeper, as if she had removed her attention more thoroughly than ever before. He thought for a moment that she had actually gone away, but he looked over and saw her there, unaltered.

He wanted her to be again as she'd been in the pond. He wanted her to be a dark shape cut out of the darkening sky, turning shyly to face him when he said the word "beautiful." But that moment had passed, and she was this again, stolid as an abandoned suitcase.

He said, "Stop this day and night with me and you shall possess the origin of all poems."

"I sleep now."

"I'm going to stay out here a little while longer."

"Yes."

"Good night."

She rose soundlessly. He heard the soft click of the Winnebago's door as she went inside.

By midmorning of the following day, Luke had fallen ill. He was flushed and feverish. He insisted that he wasn't as sick as he appeared to be. He insisted on riding in his usual place between Simon and Catareen until he was suddenly compelled to tell Simon to stop the Winnebago immediately so he could get out and vomit, after which Catareen insisted that the regurgitated bits of meat had to be buried. Simon bore it patiently. The child and the Nadian were only doing what was required of them. Still, he thought he recalled a situation similar to this one, from a vid—the image of a man on a journey, bearing up patiently as a child and a woman caused delays for which they could not reasonably be held accountable but which the man found irksome nevertheless.

Catareen put Luke to bed on Simon's bedshelf. Once the boy had been settled, they drove on.

Simon said, "There was probably something in that water after all."

"Yes," Catareen answered.

"Are you a little queasy, too?"

"Yes."

"I shouldn't have let you go in. Either of you."

"No fault."

"It's easy to forget," Simon said, "that none of this is as pure as it looks. I don't like to think what all is in these creatures we're eating. Or what kinds of genetic mutations are going on in the deer that look so lovely out there on the horizon at sunset."

A silence passed. They drove through the heat and the light. Then she said, "Simon?"

She had never spoken his name before. He had not been entirely sure she knew it.

"Yeah?"

"Stroth."

"More specific, please."

"This."

"This is, shall we say, strothful, right now?"

"Yes."

She sat as she always did, placid as a lawn ornament, hands folded in her lap.

"We seem to be sick from swimming in tainted water. We have radioactive groundhog breath. We have no idea what's going to happen to us. This is what you mean by 'stroth'?"

"I mean we."

A low crackle shot through his circuitry, a quick electrical whir.

"I merely stir, press, feel with my fingers, and am happy. To touch my person to some one else's is about as much as I can stand," he said.

"Yes."

He said, "We'll be in Denver in a few hours. Have you given any thought to what you want to do when we get there?"

"To do?"

"You know. Destination attained. I'll find out what, if anything, June 21 means. Luke will probably get some sort of scam going within the first ten minutes. What are you thinking of for yourself?"

"Die in Denver," she said.

"That's what you said before. Would you mind telling me what exactly you mean by that?"

"Die in Denver."

"I have to admit that I just don't follow you here. We seem to be having one of those Earthling/Nadian moments. Could you be a little more specific?"

Silence. The soft, breathy song.

"Okay," he said. "End of discussion. Your plan is to die in Denver. You could probably also get a job as a waitress, if dying doesn't work out."

She was gone, though. She had removed herself to that lizard-eyed nowhere she seemed to call home.

Denver revealed itself toward the end of the afternoon. It was first a silver shimmer on the horizon, then an intimation of silvered spires and towers, then a great tumble of buildings laid out across the flatness, under the cascade of white summer sun.

Catareen said, "Luke will want to see. I get."

"Don't you think we should let him sleep?"

"I go. I see."

He stopped the Winnebago. She got out and returned soon with Luke, whose face was still flushed and whose eyes had a pink, unhealthy cast.

Still, he positioned himself eagerly between Simon and Catareen. He said, "There it is."

"There it is," Simon answered.

"Is something wrong?" Luke asked him.

"No. What would be wrong?"

"Just wondered."

"You shouldn't be up," Simon said. "You're still sick."

"I'm getting better," Luke said. "I just picked up a little something nasty in that water. Or maybe it was whatever that thing was we ate. Anyway, I'm fine."

"You're not fine. Catareen should have let you sleep."

He noticed that the boy and Catareen exchanged looks of recognition. They seemed to believe they shared some knowledge about him. When had that started? He said nothing, however. He drove on.

Denver when they reached it proved to be a series of broad avenues teeming with humans and Nadians. The air sparked with their various invisible purposes. They crossed the streets and strode along the sidewalks, past the windows of small enterprises that had been carved out of the old stores and restaurants. Empty skyscrapers towered overhead, their windows cracked or shattered. Some citizens were on foot. Some piloted hoverpods, most of them old and dented. Some rode horses. Luke said, "The horse is making a comeback here. They're more reliable than hoverpods. They can go more places."

They inched their way along through the traffic. Luke pointed out a store that had once, according to its faded gilt sign, been called Banana Republic and was now a saloon, a barbershop, and a haberdasher's. In front of the store, a group of Nadian settlers were loading a horse-drawn cart with sacks of what appeared to be some kind of seeds.

Simon leaned out the window and asked the drivers of several vehicles if they'd ever heard of Emory Lowell. He received only shrugs and baffled looks. Luke said, "Just keep going straight. If Gaya's in her usual spot, she'll know."

"Gaya?"

"A bit of local color. She was a friend of my mother's. Her turf is up ahead."

Presently they approached a gaunt, elderly woman who stood on a corner speaking volubly and offering passersby what appeared to be a small white bowl.

Luke said, "There she is. Pull over."

Simon pulled to the curb as best he could, given the crowds. Luke scrambled over Catareen's lap and leaned out the window.

"Hey, Gaya," he said.

The woman halted her imprecations and looked at Luke with an expression of fearful irritation. She appeared to be someone who did not associate the calling of her own name with the arrival of good news. She wore a Mylar jumpsuit and an ancient leopard-skin hat. Loops and waggles of dark, wiry hair shot out from under the hat like punctuation marks in an unknown language.

"It's Blitzen," Luke said.

Gaya ambled suspiciously up to the Winnebago's window. She squinted, as if Luke himself emitted a painful light.

"You've grown," she said.

"As people do. You know Emory Lowell?"

"I've heard the name, yes."

"Do you know where he lives?"

"Right around here somewhere."

"What are you selling?"

Gaya looked gravely at the bowl. "Blitzen," she said, "this belongs in a museum. It's only by the remotest chance that I've come into possession of it, and if it wasn't for my medical bills I'd never consider selling—"

"How much?" Luke asked.

"Now, I've been asking twenty yen, which is of course an almost ludicrously low price, but since you and I—"

"Give her twenty yen," Luke said to Simon.

Simon dug into his pocket for the money. Gaya said, "Hey, I can take a few yen off for you. I mean, considering—"

"No, twenty is more than reasonable," Luke answered. "Simon, have you got it?"

Simon produced a twenty from his pocket. The boy snatched it out of his hand. He said, "So. Could you give us directions to Emory Lowell's?"

Gaya answered, "Straight for ten or eleven blocks, then right for about five miles. Turn left at the Gentle Giant Mall. Drive until you see a pair of blue spruce trees, one on each side of the road. Then park your truck and walk to the west."

"Thanks. Here's the twenty."

Gaya took the money and handed Luke the bowl. She said wanly, "How's your mother?"

"Couldn't tell you. If she passes through here, tell her you saw me. Tell her I'm all right."

"I'll do that."

Simon pulled away from the curb and accelerated. Luke sat with the bowl in his lap. "Junk," he said.

"It looks old," Simon said.

"If it got down to Gaya's level, it's junk. Believe me."

"What is commonest and cheapest and nearest and easiest is Me," Simon said.

Simon followed Gaya's directions. They drove out of the densely settled area, past ever-diminishing outcroppings of empty houses, which gave way to a dun-colored emptiness that had once been farmland. Presently they saw the twin spruces ahead, as Gaya had described them. In front of the trees, a band of children and a horse stood in the road, unsteady in the heat shimmer that rose off the concrete.

Luke had by then fallen ill again. He was half asleep, his tureen-shaped head slumped in the place where his chest would have been. He roused sufficiently to see the children and horse in the road.

"You should probably just run them over," he murmured.

"Aren't you supposed to be a Christian?" Simon asked.

"I am a Christian. But I'm not a fool." He fell back into his feverish doze.

As they drew closer, Simon could see that there were five children: two girls on the back of a shaggy brown horse, with a girl and two boys standing alongside.

Of the two girls on horseback, one was human and one Nadian. Of the other three, two were Nadian and one human. The oldest, a girl, human, was probably twelve or thirteen. The youngest, a Nadian, could not have been more than four.

Simon stopped the Winnebago. The children stood in modest expectation, as if waiting for a train. Simon leaned out of the window and called hello to them.

The Nadian girl on horseback wore a pair of dingy cardboard wings held to her narrow back by two dirty elastic straps. The human girl behind her sat with her scrawny white legs akimbo and her thin arms clasped around the Nadian girl's waist.

The winged Nadian girl said, "You're late."

They were all more or less naked. One of the Nadian boys had somehow attached two plastic roses to his little-boy chest and wore a skirt made of grass. The human girl standing alongside the horse carried a spear that appeared to involve a knife blade affixed to the end of a pool cue.

The girl with the spear said, "You almost missed it."

The horse stood stoically, shaking its enormous head. Its eyes were bright black, liquid circles.

"We're looking for Emory Lowell," Simon said.

"We know that," the Nadian on horseback answered.

"Why else would you have come?" the human girl said.

Luke roused enough to say, "This seems very peculiar to me."

Simon said, "Can you take us to him?"

"Of course we can," the Nadian girl answered.

"You'll have to leave your vehicle," said the human.

"I don't know if we should leave the vehicle," Luke said.

"Be quiet," Simon told him.

Simon, Catareen, and Luke got out of the Winnebago and advanced to meet the party of children. The horse snorted, nodding its head as if in agreement with its own waking dream.

"What exactly are we late for?" Simon asked.

"Don't be silly. Come on."

The children led them down the road for a distance, then cut across a field. Simon carried Luke, who awoke periodically and whispered, "I'm really not so sure about this."

They passed through a stand of trees and came upon a cluster of buildings at the base of a low, grassy hill. It had been a farm. There was a barn and an austere white clapboard house and a gathering of small white domes that appeared to be dwellings. Beyond them all, a range of lavender mountains cut into the pallid sky.

A spaceship stood between the house and the barn. It was an early one, a silver ellipse just more than fifty yards across, balanced on the three spidery legs that had proved unreliable and been superseded by a hydraulic central shaft. It was at least thirty years old. It gleamed dully in the sun.

"Where did that come from?" Simon asked.

"It's always been here," one of the boys told him. "It's almost ready."

It's ready for the junkyard, Simon thought.

"We're going to take you straight to Emory," the winged Nadian girl announced.

She led them to the barn, a matronly, cigar-colored hulk of a building with brilliant white light leaking out through its prim little windows. The girls dismounted and slid the big wooden door open.

The barn was full of navigational equipment, all of it decades old. Lights blinked on consoles. An old vid showed the spacecraft, with a band of readouts crawling along its lower edge. Workers sat at the consoles. Some were human and some Nadian. Several wore white lab coats; others wore overalls or polyester slack suits. A small Nadian woman sat hunched over a keyboard in a kimono covered in lurid green chrysanthemums.

A black man looked up at them when they entered. The others remained absorbed in their work. The man approached. He must have been seventy. A cascade of smoke-colored beard spilled over his chest. He wore a battered, broad-brimmed hat pulled down to his shaggy gray brows.

"Hello," he said. "What have we here?"

The winged girl answered, "Pilgrims we found on the road."

The man said, "We don't get many travelers. We're a little off the beaten path."

"Got that," Simon answered.

"My name is Emory Lowell."

Simon's circuits buzzed. The feeling was similar to what had occurred in him when he saw Catareen standing at the water's edge. He said, "Thruster holding me tight and that I hold tight! We hurt each other as the bridegroom and the bride hurt each other."

Emory stared at Simon with avid, feral eyes.

"Oh, my lord," he said. "You're one of mine, aren't you?"

"I guess I am," Simon said.

"Look at you. I was afraid they'd exterminated the whole lot. But here you are."

"Here I am," Simon said.

"Remarkable. You're the only one, you know. I implanted a dozen of them. I suppose the others have all been deactivated."

"Marcus has."

"I'm not good with names."

"He was one of yours."

"And he's no longer with us."

"He was my friend. Well, we traveled together. I needed him to maximize my own chances."

"I'm sorry for your loss," Emory said.

"What's going to happen on June 21?"

"That's when we take off for the new world."

"What new world?" said Luke.

"I'm taking us to another planet."

"In that old wreck?" Luke scowled at the spacecraft.

"It's old. It's not a wreck. It should do just fine."

"So you say."

"Why did you want us to come here on the twenty-first of June?" Simon asked.

"I'd figured out the coordinates years ago. June 21 of this year is when the orbital alignments are optimal. I put a homing device in the final production run, before Biologe shut me down. I thought that if any of you found your way back in time, the least I could do was take you with me."

"You want me to go with you to another planet?"

"You're certainly welcome, yes. You and your friends."

"What kind of other planet?" Luke asked.

"Oh, well, there's a great deal to tell you, isn't there? First, I want you to meet my wife."

He glanced back into the work area. He said, "Othea, would you come here for a moment, please?"

He appeared to be addressing the Nadian woman, the one wearing the kimono. She did not turn from her console. "Busy," she said.

"Just for a moment. Please."

The Nadian rose reluctantly and approached. "Really," she said. "Do you have any idea how little time is left?"

"We have visitors," Emory said.

"At this late date?"

"We've got room."

The Nadian came and stood beside Emory. She had an aspect of ferocious intention. Her little green head protruded from the neck of her kimono like a sober idea the kimono itself was having.

"This is Othea," Emory said. "My wife."

Othea craned her neck forward and looked intently at Catareen. She said, "Cria dossa Catareen Callatura?"

Catareen hesitated. She said, "Lup."

Emory said, "You two have met?"

Othea said, "No, we've never met. Oof ushera do manto."

Catareen bowed her head. Was it a gesture of acknowledgment or shame? Othea stepped up to Catareen and put her right hand on Catareen's forehead. Catareen returned the gesture.

Othea said, "This is a great warrior. I've known of her for many years."

Catareen answered, "I do my work."

Luke said, "What kind of warrior?"

The Nadian ignored him. She said to Catareen, "Oona napp e cria dossa?"

"What?" Luke said.

Othea said, "I asked her how far along she is."

Catareen answered, "Six week. Or seven."

"Are you pregnant?" Luke asked.

"No."

"They don't know?" Othea said.

"Know what?" Luke asked.

Catareen went blank and quiet then, which was of course not surprising.

Othea said, "Well. You all look as if you could use a meal and some rest. Emory, please take care of our guests. I really can't be spared here."

"Of course," Emory said.

Othea looked another moment at Catareen. She said, "It is an honor."

"Honor is mine," Catareen answered.

Emory and the children led Simon, Luke, and Catareen out of the barn and across the dirt yard to the farmhouse. The whole place appeared to be a midcentury reconstruction, all lacy porch rails and acute Grant Wood gables. The barn might have been true period, or it might have been an especially good faux. The house was cheap, its shutters and ornament simplified and slightly too large. It looked like a miniature house that had somehow been rendered life-size.

Arrayed behind the house was a dome village, clusters of white inflatables and Insta-Dwells of various ages, none of them new or clean. At the far end a neglected garden drooped and crisped in the sun. It might have been the summer encampment of a particularly dissolute and discouraged band of Inuits.

As they went, Emory put his hand familiarly on Simon's elbow.

Emory said, "I have so much to ask you."

Simon had hoped for answers, not questions. "I have a thing or two to ask you myself," he said.

Luke was walking with Catareen just ahead of Simon and Emory. "So what's this great-warrior business about?" he said.

Catareen did not respond.

Emory took them into the farmhouse. He said, "There are beds upstairs. Perhaps we should take the boy up there and let him sleep a little."

"Absolutely not," Luke said.

"Luke—"

"I'm hungry. I'm starving. We all are. Have you got anything to eat?"

"Of course," Emory said. He led them through the foyer into a kitchen. They passed what had been the living room and was now an office with two desks, one steel and one plastimorph. Pushed to one side were two ratty armchairs and a glass-fronted cabinet that held a collection of brightly colored odds and ends. Simon recognized them: a Chia Pet shaped like a lamb, PEZ dispensers, a pink plastic squeeze bottle of Mr. Bubble, a rubber statuette of Bullwinkle the Moose in a striped bathing suit from the 1800s.

The kitchen was like a kitchen from fifty years ago. It had an atomic stove and a refrigeration module and a sink with a faucet and handles. It might have been a display in a historical museum.

"Sit, please," Emory said, indicating a battered wooden table surrounded by mismatched chairs. The table was covered with a cloth that depicted dancing blue teapots.

Simon, Catareen, and Luke sat at the table. Emory set down three glasses and a pitcher of what appeared to be tea. He took eggs and bacon from the refrigerator.

He said, "Today of course is the twentieth. We're set to leave tomorrow."

As he spoke, he cracked eggs into a bowl. He put slices of bacon on a grill.

Luke asked, "And this new planet is?"

"We call it Paumanok. It will take thirty-eight years for us to get there. Some of us will no longer be alive when the ship lands."

"Hence the children."

"Yes. And they're our children. We would naturally take them along."

Emory poured the eggs into a pan. He said, "I got the ship from the Jehovahs. They sold the whole fleet after things fell apart with HBO."

"And what exactly do you know about the planet in question?" Simon asked.

"It's the fourth planet from its sun. It's about half the size of Earth. It is probably temperate and almost certainly has a breathable atmosphere. We can't know whether or not there's life there."

"And the worst-case scenario is?"

"Well. It could be entirely barren. It could be too hot or too cold to sustain life. There is of course a very narrow range in that regard. Even a small variation would render it unlivable."

"If you get there and find it unlivable?"

"There we'll be. There's no way of getting back."

"Got you."

"We've had visions," Emory said.

"Visions."

"Myself, Othea, and some of the others. We've been seeing a world of mountains and rivers. We see enormous fruit-bearing trees. We see brilliantly colored birds and small, intelligent animals that are like rabbits. I had the first such vision several years ago, and when I told Othea about it she confessed that she had had a similar one, months earlier, but hadn't mentioned it."

"That's very Nadian," Simon said.

"When I told the group about it two others, a child and an old man, stepped forward and said that they, too, had imagined this world in just this way. Since then the visions have come to many of us, at unpredictable times. They're always the same, though they keep expanding. I was visited just last week by an image of a small fishing village on the shore of a vast sea, though I couldn't see anything of its inhabitants. Twyla, the group's second-oldest child, clearly saw a warm rain that swept through every afternoon and lasted for under an hour, after which it was brilliantly clear again."

Simon glanced at Luke and Catareen. Catareen (of course) was expressionless. Luke, however, returned a signifying look. Crazy. These people are crazy.

"We understand that it's a risk," Emory continued. "It's a risk we are all willing to take. We prefer it to remaining here. All of us do. You're welcome to come with us, if you decide you're willing to take the risk, too."

"We'll have to think about it, won't we?" Simon said.

"You have about thirty-two hours to decide. Here, then. Your food is ready."

After they had eaten, Emory took them upstairs and guided them into bedrooms that were spare and white, each containing only a bedshelf and a wooden chair. Luke and Catareen settled in. Simon asked to speak privately to Emory.

"Certainly," Emory said. "I suppose you and I have a few things to discuss, don't we?"

They went outside and crossed the farmyard, where the children were engaged in some sort of noisy and contentious game that the horse watched with blank-eyed, somnolent attention, twitching its tail. Beyond the children, the spaceship stood like a titanic silver clam, delicately balanced on the slender legstalks that had proved insufficiently stable in three out of five landings.

"Twyla loves that horse," Emory said as they passed the children. "She keeps insisting we can take it with us."

"Paumanok," Simon said.

"Seemed like as good a name as any."

"Starting from fish-shape Paumanok where I was born . . . solitary, singing in the West, I strike up for a New World."

"Yes, yes."

They walked past the barn, into a field scattered with purple clover.

"Why the poetry chip?" Simon asked.

"Everybody loves poetry."

"Come on."

"All right. Well. I let myself get carried away when I designed you. You were supposed to be sturdy and reliable. Obedient. And harmless. And without emotional responses."

"Got that."

"The first few tries were seriously flawed."

"So I've heard."

"Certain qualities stowed away in the cell lines. It surprised everyone. There were, as it turned out, some very difficult-to-detect dark spots on the genome, little indicators and determiners that produced, well . . . unexpected results. The first experimental simulos were suicidal. Despairing. We tried to override that with a survival chip. Then the second batch turned out to be these sort of wildly happy murderers. They were ecstatic all the time. They were so very very happy they got violent. As if their happiness couldn't tolerate any lesser outlet. One of them tore a lab technician to pieces, laughing and babbling on about how much he loved the kid. Ate his liver. This was hushed up."

"Naturally."

"We were hubristic. We underestimated the complexity of the genome. We kept finding that if you tried to eliminate one quality, some other quality that seemed entirely unrelated would pop up at ten times its normal intensity. Frankly, if we'd adequately anticipated the difficulties, I suspect we'd never have made you at all. But once we'd started, we couldn't stop. No, *I* couldn't stop. Others had the good sense to just cancel the experiments and call the whole thing an interesting idea that didn't work out."

"You think of me as an experiment," Simon said.

"I don't mean to offend you."

"Go on."

"All right. In the third protocol, I gave you poetry."

"Why?"

"To regulate you. To eliminate the extremes. I could put a cap on your aggressive capabilities, I could program you to be helpful and kind, but I wanted to give you some moral sense as well. To help you cope with events I couldn't foresee. I thought that if you were programmed with the work of great poets, you'd be better able to appreciate the consequences of your actions."

"You programmed each of us with a *particular* poet."

"I did. I thought it might be less confusing for you that way. Somewhere out there, there's a Shelley, a Keats, a Yeats. Or there was. I wonder what's become of them."

"There was an Emily Dickinson, too," Simon said.

"Yes. There was."

Simon said, "I have—"

"What do you have, son?"

"I'm not your son."

"Sorry. Figure of speech. What do you have? Tell me."

"I have this sense of a missing part. Some sort of, I don't know. Engagement. Aliveness. Catareen calls it stroth."

"Go on."

"I feel like biologicals just wallow in it. I mean it falls over them like rain, and I'm walking through the world in a space suit. I can see everything perfectly, but I don't quite connect with it."

"That's very interesting."

"Frankly, I was hoping for a little more from you than that."

"It's the poetry, isn't it? All those conjurings and all that praise roiling around in your circuits. Your poor synapses aren't quite up to it, I don't suppose."

The seizing up started again. No, it was the new sensation, the floaty, sleeplike electrified thing.

Simon said, "I am exposed . . . cut by bitter and poisoned hail."

"Are you all right?" Emory asked.

"No. Something's happening to me."

"What?"

"Lately I have these strange sensations. Like when my antiaggression override kicks in but different. Softer or something."

"I've always wondered if actual emotions might start springing up in you. If your connections might start firing, given the proper stimuli."

Simon said, "I am large, I contain multitudes."

"You know," Emory said, "I could probably do a little more work on you. If you and the others want to come with us, I could do some tinkering en route. There's no time now, but there'll be plenty of time during the trip. There'll be lots and lots of time."

"You think you could modify me?" Simon asked.

"I'd be glad to give it a shot."

"What do you think you could do?"

"I'd have to get in there and poke around a little. I could probably override a few commands, program out the aversion to violence. I suspect that inhibits your neurals. I could also enhance a few of the pathways in your cerebral cortex. Though I must say, things seem to be happening on their own. It might be best to just wait and see what develops."

Simon stood facing the farm and the silver spaceship. He said, "A child said—"

Emory joined in. They said in unison, "*What is the grass?* fetching it to me with full hands; How could I answer the child? I do not know what it is any more than he."

When they returned to the farm, Othea was waiting for them outside the barn door. She said to Emory as they approached, "Please don't wander off like that. Not today."

"Simon and I had a few things to discuss."

Othea aimed a brief orange stare at Simon. She said to Emory, "There's a question about the launch coordinates. I don't think it's anything, really, but Ruth is getting out of her depth in there. She needs you to talk her through it."

"Glad to," Emory said. "Simon, please excuse me."

Othea continued staring at Simon. She said, "Do you know who Catareen Callatura is?"

"I know who she is to me," Simon answered.

"She was a member of the resistance on Nourthea. The kings, as you may know, rule absolutely. They take everything the people are able to grow or build."

"Catareen rebelled?"

"She was part of a band of women who held back half their harvest. She was a member of the first group, and they organized others. Didn't she tell you?"

"She doesn't tell me anything. I assumed it was a Nadian custom."

"They executed the women's husbands and children."

"What?"

"Publicly. Then they banished the women to Earth."

"Catareen was deported."

"She really hasn't told you anything, has she?"

"Nothing at all."

"There's something else."

"What?"

"I'm going to tell you, because I think you might be able to help her if you know. She's at the end of her life cycle."

"What?"

"I was surprised to see her at all. I'm certain all the others are dead. She must be, oh, well over one hundred years old."

"She's old?"

"Extremely. We age differently. We don't decline gradually. We are vital and productive right up until the end, and then we deteriorate quite rapidly. There was a fish called a salmon, I believe. It's a little like that for us."

"And Catareen is dying?"

"Oh, yes. I knew it the moment I saw her. Her coloring. She's turned that brilliant green."

"How long will it take?"

"It's difficult to say, exactly. It could be a week. It could even be a full month."

Simon went back to the house. He mounted the stairs and entered the bedroom that had been given to Catareen. She lay on the narrow white bed. She appeared to be sleeping.

"Hey," he said. Not as gently as he'd intended to.

She opened her eyes. She did not reply.

"You're dying?" he asked.

"Yes."

"You're fucking *dying*?"

"I told."

"Well, yes, technically you did. But a few more details would have been helpful, don't you think?"

"No."

"What's the matter with you?"

"Dying," she said.

"That's not what I meant."

"Dying," she said again.

"Is that why you keep going catatonic?"

"To keep energy."

He went and stood at her bedside. She looked so small against the white sheet.

He said, "They killed your husband and children back on Nadia."

"Grandchildren also."

"And they sent you here."

"Yes."

She closed her eyes.

"Catareen," he said.

No response. Her head might have been a stone, carved with lines for mouth and eyes, two holes for nostrils. Only the nostrils betrayed the fact that this was a living being. They fluttered with her breath. They revealed their pallid hints of inner brightness, like circles of illuminated jade.

"Catareen," he said, "I don't know what to do for you. I don't know what to say to you. I feel like I don't know anything about you. Anything at all."

She did not open her eyes. The conversation was over, then.

Later, at dinner, Simon and Luke were introduced to the rest of the group. Luke appeared to be recovered. Catareen seemed to prefer remaining in bed, as far as anyone could interpret her preferences.

They all assembled for dinner at a long table set under the big tree to the immediate east of the house. There were seventeen of them: twelve adults and five children; eight Nadians and nine humans.

Othea sat at one end of the table, beside Emory. She held in her arms the eighteenth member—an infant, half Nadian and half human.

Simon had never seen such a being before, though he'd heard the rumors. The baby's skin was the color of a celery stalk. She (it was a she) had the big, round Nadian eyes and the agitated Nadian nostrils, but in her the eyes were a creamy coffee brown and the nose an Emoryish minibeak upon which the nostrils perched like sea urchins on a sliver of rock. She had ears, perfectly human but dwarfed, like tiny shells. Atop her smooth green head stood a silky fury of fine white-gold hair.

Emory said to the others, "We seem to have acquired a couple of new members. It is my great honor to introduce Simon and Luke and to express my hope that they will accept my invitation to accompany us all on our journey to Paumanok."

There was scattered applause and a general murmur of greeting. In truth, Simon did not find the company especially promising. The humans were for the most part rather seedy-looking. One woman (she would prove to be the Ruth who was having trouble with the launch coordinates) was sallow and overweight, wearing a battered sun hat and what appeared to be strands of little silver bells around her neck. Another, a man of indeterminate age with a great rust-colored curl of mustache and a chin slightly smaller than an apricot, bobbled his big square head and said, "Welcome, friends, welcome, friends, welcome, friends." The Nadians were more restrained in their dress and their vocabulary of gestures, but they, too, seemed to possess some vague aspect of off-centeredness. The two females were grim and silent. The males, three of them, had an overeager look uncommon among Nadians. They sat together, whispered among themselves, and broke into occasional fits of high-pitched laughter, during which they pounded one another on their scrawny backs and slapped their slender palms together.

These, then, were the pilgrims. These were the emissaries to a new world.

Midway through the meal, Luke leaned over and whispered to Simon, "Geekville, U.S.A."

"Shh," Simon said. He returned his attention to the person seated on his left, a young dark-skinned human scientist named Lily, who had dyed her hair orange and had runes of some kind tattooed onto her cheeks and forehead and did not seem to understand that listening to an unbroken monologue about lift hydraulics in deep space might not be Simon's idea of an interesting way to spend his entire dinner.

When the meal was over, the adults resumed their work, and the children scattered across the farmyard. Simon and Luke lingered at the table with Emory, Othea, and the baby.

Emory said, "They're a little strange, I know. They have good hearts, though."

"I'm sure they do," Simon answered.

"I had twice this many when I started. But people come to their senses. They find other things to do. They fall in love with someone who doesn't want to leave Earth forever."

Luke said, "You really want us to come along?"

"There's room. And Simon, I hope you won't be offended if I say that someone as young as Luke would be particularly welcome. The adults who survive the trip at all will be quite old by the time we land on Paumanok."

The infant gurgled on Othea's lap. She rocked the child with a certain insistence Simon recognized as distinctly Nadian. She said, "We need the most diverse possible gene pool among our younger members."

Luke said, "So basically you're interested in my youth and DNA."

"You're Exedrol, right?" Othea asked.

"Yep."

"The deformities are not passed along genetically. Did you know that?"

"Uh-huh."

Simon said, "I too haughty Shade also sing war, and a longer and greater one than any." He had not meant to speak quite so loudly.

"She doesn't mean to offend," Emory said. "Do you, Oth? Nadians are a little more direct than we are is all."

"I just can't seem to get the knack of circumspection," Othea replied, continuing to rock her child with an urgency Simon could only hope would not be damaging in some long-range, unforeseeable way. "At a certain point I simply decided to give it up altogether."

"I find it extremely interesting," Emory said to Simon, "that you take offense so easily. It's not in your programming."

"My voice goes after what my eyes cannot reach," Simon said.

"As a matter of fact," Luke said, "being wanted for my youth and my DNA doesn't bother me at all. In case anybody cares what I think."

"Everybody cares what you think," Simon said.

Luke said to Emory, "He doesn't have any particular allegiance to the truth. Do you find that peculiar?"

"Very," Emory answered.

"Please don't talk about me as if I'm not here," Simon said.

"You're really making great progress," Emory told him.

"Fuck you."

"See? See what I mean?"

Later, Simon sat with Catareen in her upstairs room. Emory and Othea had returned to their work. Luke had joined the children in their farmyard games. Simon could tell from their voices that Luke had introduced certain improvements and refinements and was patiently explaining why such changes were necessary.

Catareen was asleep. Or doing that sleeplike thing.

Simon said to her, "They're nuts, you know. The whole crew."

She opened her eyes. She said, "You go with them."

"I don't know. I mean, can you picture being on a spaceship for thirty-eight years with these people?"

"You go. Happier there."

"Why are you saying this?"

"I dream."

"What?"

"That world. I dream."

"What have you dreamed?"

"You go to mountains. Changed. As you want."

"You've dreamed of me changed, walking in some kind of mountains?"

"Yes."

"Have you had a dream like that before?"

"No."

"And so you think I should go with them. You think I should spend the next thirty-eight years on a spaceship with these idiots because you dreamed I'd be happier on another planet."

"Yes."

"You're crazy, too."

She made some sort of breathy sound he had never heard from her before, a modest three-note trill.

"Did you laugh?" he asked.

"No."

"Yes. You did. That was actual laughter. I'll be goddamned."

She made the sound again.

He leaned over her. He said, "Are you in pain?"

"No pain."

"What does it feel like?"

"Dying."

"More specific, please."

"Less. Am less."

"You feel like you're less."

"Room is big. Bright."

"You feel like the room has gotten bigger and brighter."

"Yes."

"Do I seem bigger and brighter?"

"Loud, too."

He lowered his voice. "Sorry," he said.

"No. I like."

"You like me being big and bright and loud?"

"Yes."

She closed her eyes then, and slipped away.

Simon went downstairs again and walked onto the front porch of the farmhouse. The evening sky was dull red, striped with cloud tatters of livid orange. He could hear the children's voices but could not see them. Soon, however, Luke ran into view. He was being chased by Twyla, who brandished the pool-cue spear. Her cardboard wings rattled behind her. Luke shrieked. Simon could not determine whether he was delighted or terrified.

When Luke saw Simon he immediately stopped running. He collected himself. He seemed to wish to appear as if he had never run or shrieked in his life. Twyla stopped as well. She stood examining the point of the spear, as if that had been her true objective, while Luke approached Simon on the porch.

Luke said, "Geekville, U.S.A."

"You seem to be having a reasonably good time," Simon answered.

"I'm mingling with the locals. I can pass for just about anything."

He ambled up onto the porch and stood beside Simon, looking out at the deepening sky. Twyla remained where she stood, adjusting the knife on the end of the pool cue.

Luke said, "I've been thinking. I might want to go with them."

"Uh-huh."

"To tell you the truth, I like the idea of being a valued member. As opposed to being, say, stuck in Denver again, with no money."

"I understand that."

"And you?"

"They're an odd bunch."

"No question."

"Emory thinks he could make some modifications on me during the trip."

"That'd be good."

"It would."

"And you know," Luke said, "I'd rather go if you go, too. You've come to feel familiar to me."

"Ditto."

"Okay. See you later, then."

"See you."

Luke left the porch and went back out to the place where the little Nadian stood waiting for him. She did not raise the spear as he approached. They spoke to each other softly. Simon could not make out what they said. They went off together, away from the house and the barn, in the direction of the open country.

The next morning, Catareen was more receded. She appeared smaller in the small white bed. She lay compactly atop the sheet with her eyes closed, breathing rapidly and shallowly. She had folded her hands over her abdomen. Her legs were pressed together. It appeared as if she were trying to make herself as small as possible, as if death were a narrow aperture and she had to be ready to slip through.

Apart from her rapid breathing, there was no sign of illness. And yet she was diminishing. Simon could see it. No. He could apprehend it. Her flesh was unaffected, but she was drawing in, as if some animating force were retreating inward from the skin's surface. Her skin was darker now, more deeply emerald. It put out a slick, mineral shine. She was becoming not alive.

She awakened, however, when Simon entered the room. Her eyes were changed. They were fading from orange to a deep, unhealthy-looking yellow, like egg yolks gone bad.

"Good morning," Simon said. "How do you feel?"

"Dying," she answered.

"But no pain."

"No much."

"Do you think you could eat something?"

"No."

"It's not irradiated groundhog, you know."

"I know."

He stood beside her. Still, even in extremis, there was this feeling that they were on a date that wasn't going well but refused to end. He made to put his hand on her forehead but decided she probably wouldn't want him to. Besides, it would have been an empty gesture, a ritual expression of concern for the afflicted. There was no point in performing such gestures for a Nadian.

He said, "They killed your family and sent you to Earth."

"Yes."

"I wonder—"

She waited for him to finish the question. He waited as well. He hadn't been sure when he launched that sentence where, exactly, he expected it to land, though he could think of any number of possibilities. *I wonder if that's why you're so remote and strange. I wonder if that's why you came with me. I wonder if you helped me because you feel guilty about what you brought down on your own family.*

When it had become apparent that he was not going to speak further, she said, "Simon?"

"Uh-huh?"

"Window."

"You want me to close the window? Is it cold in here for you?"

"No. Take."

"You want me to take you to the window."

"Yes."

"Sure. No problem."

He paused over how and where to touch her. She helped him by lifting her long, thin Giacometti arms and putting her hands around his neck. Apparently she could no longer walk, then. He slipped his right forearm under her upper back, his left under the sinewy stalks of her thighs. He lifted her.

For a moment, she held herself apart from him. It was subtle but palpable. She maintained herself briefly as a dependent but private being. Then she relaxed and gave herself over into his arms. She was, he thought, too weak to do otherwise.

Gently, carefully (he wasn't sure whether or not to believe her when she said she was not in pain or not in much pain), he carried her to the window. The window looked out over the packed dirt of the yard, beyond which stood the single tree under which they had had their dinner the night before. He thought it was an elm. Or an oak. He wasn't programmed for the identification of trees. The tree stood in the precise middle of the view, like a sentry. Beyond it was the vast green flatness of the plain, bright in the early sun, suspended, without wind or cloud, as if all that empty land were waiting for something to begin, for a note to strike or a pair of hands to clap. But most prominently there was the tree, dead center, in full leaf, shimmering in the expectant silence of the morning. Simon wondered how strange this must be to Catareen—this green terrestrial silence spread out under this ice-blue sky. Where she came from it was (according to the vids) mostly rock and mud, variously black, pewter, and an opaque silvery-yellow, from which tangles of moss and bracken struggled, black-green like seaweed under an eternally clouded sky that bled a soft, drizzly semilight. It was whatever villages had managed to establish themselves in the rifts and valleys that occurred here and there among the mountains, sheer and ice-tipped, pinnacled, like titanic dead gray cathedrals, vast impassive assertions of volcanic rock and permafrost that towered over the huts and corrals, the modest squares of unprosperous garden, the tiny turrets and steeples of the kings, miniature replicas of the darkly glittering peaks.

Had it been beautiful to her? Had she felt stroth there?

Simon held her before the window that looked out onto the tree. It might have been the tree and only the tree Simon had brought her to see, though of course neither he nor Catareen had thought anything of it, one ordinary tree spreading over a standard-issue patch of dirt. It was only now, at this window, with the dying Catareen in his arms and the tree so perfectly centered in the view, that Simon understood it to be in any way singular or mysterious.

He said, "Urge and urge and urge, always the procreant urge of the world."

"Yes," she answered.

They said nothing further. He held her as she looked out the window. Her face was brighter in the strong light. Her eyes seemed to take on a hint of their familiar depths, their orange and amber. She seemed, briefly, more alive, and it occurred to him that she might be undergoing an unexpected resurgence. Was being taken to the window some sort of healing ritual? It seemed possible. It did not seem impossible.

Then he felt her arms slackening around his neck. He understood that even this was a strain for her. He said softly, "Shall I take you back to bed now?"

"Yes," she answered, and he did.

The compound pulsed with last-minute preparations. People and Nadians rushed from house to barn and back again. The three Nadian men, who were technicians of some kind, went up and down the ramp of the spaceship, in and out of its entry portal, with such rapidity it seemed they must be doing nothing more than touching an agreed-upon goal and hurrying out again, laughing, emitting odd little yips and yelps, slapping palms whenever they passed one another. Simon, without duties, wandered the grounds. Emory was on the front porch arguing passionately with one of the Nadian women (she was, it seemed, a doctor) and Lily, the tattooed human scientist. The mustached, small-chinned man (whose name was Arnold) seemed to have been charged with the care of Emory and Othea's baby. He walked the infant in circles in the yard, bouncing it and saying, "Little snip, little snip, little snip." In the barn, among the consoles and keyboards, Othea and the other Nadian woman did their best to calm the frumpily majestic Ruth, who sat performing her last-minute calculations through a fit of inexplicable tears as the bells around her neck chimed softly.

Crazy, Simon thought. They're all crazy. Though of course the passengers on the *Mayflower* had probably been like this, too: zealots and oddballs and ne'er-do-wells, setting out to colonize a new world because the known world wasn't much interested in their furtive and quirky passions. It had probably always been thus, not only aboard the *Mayflower* but on the Viking ships; on the *Niña*, *Pinta*, and *Santa María*; on the first convoys sent off to explore Nadia, about which the people of Earth had harbored such extravagant hopes. It was nut jobs. It was hysterics and visionaries and petty criminals. The odes and monuments, the plaques and pageants, came later.

Simon could not settle. He could not find a plausible spot for himself. After meandering from place to place, trying to stay out of the way, trying not to look as idle as he was, he ran into Othea coming out of the barn. He spoke to her, though he knew she wouldn't welcome it. It was something for him to do. And he did, in fact, have a question or two only she could answer.

He said, "Catareen is pretty weak today."

"Yes," she answered impatiently. He suspected she would have brushed him off entirely had he broached any other subject.

"Is there any chance she could rally? I mean, could she still have a good period before—"

"No. There are no remissions. Some take longer than others, and frankly I suspect she could hang on for quite a while still. The more resilient individuals can take weeks and weeks."

"We've decided we want to come along."

"Good. Now, if you'll excuse me—"

"Catareen will need a bed," Simon said. "Maybe I could go aboard with one of the technicians and figure out the best way to make her comfortable."

"Oh, she can't come with us."

"What do you mean?"

"I'm sorry. I'd assumed you understood. Our space is limited. We anticipate some mortality en route, and we've tried to allow for that. But we can't carry a dead body for thirty-eight years. I'm afraid it's out of the question."

"You mean to leave her here, then."

"In a short while, she won't even know where she is. She wouldn't be eating anymore, under any circumstances. We'll leave water for her on the off chance, but I doubt she'll want that, either."

"You'll let her die alone."

"It will mean something different for her from what it might mean to you. Northeans are more solitary. She'll be all right. Believe me."

"Sure."

"Now you really must excuse me. You can't imagine what all I've got to do."

"Of course."

She hurried toward the house.

The day passed. Luke finally appeared, riding the horse with Twyla. He seemed to have joined the children in some way that implied membership without trust or affection. Simon saw them approaching from beyond the house. Luke sat behind Twyla like a boy pharaoh, regal and indignant-looking, as the smaller children capered in the horse's wake. Twyla reined the horse in Simon's direction, brought it to a halt just shy of the place where he stood. The horse blinked and shook its head. It made a low snorting noise that sounded vaguely like the word "hunk" played on an oboe.

Twyla said to Simon, "Do you like horses?"

"Who doesn't?" he said.

"It seems that there will be no horses in the new world."

Right, she was crazy, too. Still, she had her own version of Catareen's lambent lizard eyes and nervous, undulating nostrils. Her gaze
made Simon's circuits buzz.

He said, "Maybe there are horses there already."

"I will never love a horse other than Hesperia," Twyla announced.
"Not on any planet."

"Give me a break," Luke said.

"I'm not sure what you mean by that."

"What I mean is, it's just an animal—"

Twyla reined the horse around and kicked it into motion again. As
they departed, followed by the other children, Simon could hear
Twyla saying to Luke, "You have a great deal to learn about the kingdom of animals. They are as various as any other race of beings."

"They're food. Any being that can't open a bottle or loan you
money is by definition . . ."

Simon watched them ride away. He understood that they would be
carrying on this conversation together for the next eighty years or
more. He wondered if Othea already had Luke in mind for Twyla. He
wondered if they would have children.

He said a silent goodbye to Luke. He wished him luck.

Finally he returned to Catareen's room. There was nowhere else for
him. He felt calmer there. It was the one place in which he seemed to
be something other than a tourist.

She slept, mostly. He sat in the single chair at her bedside, watching her. He tried to imagine her life—her long life, as it turned out—
before she came here. She would never, he thought, have been a
particularly easy person. She must always have been defiant and stern,
even by Nadian standards. She must always have harbored a privacy so
deep it was almost audible, like the silence of a well. He suspected
that her husband had been the friendlier one, the one with ease and
amplitude. Simon thought he could picture them at home, in their

hut of sticks and mud. The husband would have been forever wel-coming others in, offering pipes and fermented drinks, warming the rooms by lighting fires with wood they could not easily spare.

He would have exasperated Catareen. His profligacy would have inspired countless arguments, some of them bantering, some of them bitter.

And yet, she must have loved him.

Simon knew this, somehow. He could feel the information swarm-ing inside his head, one cell splitting into two, two into four, four into eight.

Here was Catareen's long union. Here were her children, five of them, three girls and two boys, endlessly undecided about which of their parents was more to blame for the errors and injustices in the family. Here were their days of labor. Here were their nights together, on a mattress stuffed with leaves and hay. Here was an afternoon of no particular consequence, when Catareen stood in the doorway of her hut, looking at her village, at the sharp peaks beyond, at the pewter-colored sky that would soon release its rain; here were the sounds of her children at some game, mixed with the steady rhythm of her hus-band's hoe in the garden out back; here was her sense of herself in the middle of a life that was hers and no one else's. Here was the bitter-sweet savor of it, the piercing somethingness of it—the pure sensation of being Catareen Callatura, at that moment, on an afternoon of no consequence, just before a rain.

And here, many years later, was her decision to withhold crops from the king's collectors and to encourage others to do the same. Here were the doubts of her garrulous husband, a simpler soul than she. Here was his trust in her. Here were the children's arguments, with her and among themselves. (Some would have decided by then that she was the good parent, others that she was the bad.) Here were the arrests. Here were the executions. All of them. Not only the sweet, baffled husband but the grown children, the ones who loved her and the ones who resented her, and their children, too. All of them.

The room darkened with evening. Catareen woke several times, looked around uncertainly. She must have been surprised to find her-self here, dying in an unfamiliar room on a strange planet. She must, in her sleep, have forgotten. Each time she woke, Simon leaned over her and said, "It's all right," which was not, of course, strictly true. It was something to say.

He didn't think she'd want him to touch her. Each time she looked at him with fading yellow eyes. Each time she drifted away again without speaking.

Presently, Luke came into the room. "Hey," he said. "It's almost time to get aboard."

Simon knew by then what he would do. He seemed to have entered a decision without quite making it. The process had occurred somewhere deep in his circuitry.

He said, "I'm not going."

"What?"

"I can't leave her here."

Luke hesitated. Then he said, "There's nothing we can do for her, you know."

"I can be here. I can do that."

"Do you know what that means? We can't turn around and come back for you."

"I know that."

"I want you to come," Luke said. There was a hint of whine in his tone.

He was in fact a twelve-year-old boy. It was easy to forget that.

Simon said, "You'll be fine without me."

"I know. I know I will. I still want you to come."

"What's that you've got there?" Simon asked. Luke was holding something in a white plastic bag.

"Oh. Just this."

He reached into the bag and produced the little china bowl they'd bought from the old woman in Denver.

"You're taking that to another planet?"

"It was my mother's."

"What?"

"I don't know how Gaya ended up with it. We left Denver kind of quickly, one of Mom's credit-card things blew up, and I guess Gaya got to our apartment before the authorities did. I remember this bowl from when I was a baby. Mom must have boosted it. She'd never have bought something like this."

Luke stood holding the bowl in both hands. It appeared to put out a faint glow in the darkening room.

"Is there some kind of writing on it?" Simon asked.

"Doesn't mean shit."

"Come on."

"It's a language from some loser country. One of those places with horrible weather and a long line of demented rulers. One of those places that seem to have existed only so their citizens could devote their lives to trying to get the hell out."

"Do you know what it says?"

"Nope. No idea."

"But you want to take it with you."

"I paid for it."

"With my money."

Luke shrugged and put the bowl back into the bag. Only the sound of Catareen's breath was audible. *Ee-um-fah-um-so*, faint as a curtain worried by wind.

Simon thought he could see the bowl on another planet some time in the next century, sitting on a shelf, where it would silently reflect an alien light. This small and fragile object, bearing its untranslatable message, was the entire estate of a woman who had intentionally deformed her child and then abandoned him. The bowl would travel to another sun, although it was neither rare nor precious.

Biologicals were mysterious.

Luke said, "You're absolutely sure you don't want to come?"

"I do want to come. But I'm staying here."

"Okay."

"Okay."

Luke went and stood beside the slumbering Catareen. "Goodbye," he said softly. She did not respond.

Luke said, "If I was a better person, I'd stay, too."

"Don't be ridiculous. There's no reason for both of us to stay."

"I knew you'd say that."

"But you wanted to hear it anyway, didn't you?"

"Yeah. I did."

"Is this what Christians refer to as absolution?"

"Uh-huh. Anybody can do it. You don't need a priest."

"You don't really believe in this crap, do you? *Really?*"

"I do. I really do. Can't help it."

Luke stood solemnly at Catareen's bedside. He held the bowl close to his chest.

"She's had a long life. Now she's going to the Lord."

"Frankly it creeps me out a little when you say things like that," Simon said.

"It shouldn't. If you don't like 'Lord,' pick another word. She's going home. She's going back to the party. Whatever you like."

"I suppose you have some definite ideas about an afterlife."

"Sure. We get reabsorbed into the earthly and celestial mechanism."

"No heaven?"

"That's heaven."

"What about realms of glory? What about walking around in golden slippers?"

"We abandon consciousness as if we were waking from a bad dream. We throw it off like clothes that never fit us right. It's an ecstatic release we're physically unable to apprehend while we're in our bodies. Orgasm is our best hint, but it's crude and minor by comparison."

"This is what Holy Fire taught you?"

"No, they were idiots. It's just something I know. The way you know your poetry."

"I don't *know* poetry, exactly. I contain it."

"Same difference, don't you think? Hey, it's about time for me to blast off to another planet."

"I'll walk you downstairs. I'd like to say goodbye to the others."

"Okay."

They went together to the base of the ship. It was humming now. It put out a faint glow like the one that had emanated from Luke's mother's bowl in the dimness of the sickroom. The settlers were assembled at the bottom of the ramp. At the top of the ramp, the entranceway was a square of perfect white light.

Emory said heartily to Simon, "Here we go, then."

"I've just come to see you off," Simon told him.

"You're not coming?"

Simon explained. Emory listened. When Simon had finished, Emory said, "This is really rather extraordinary, you know."

"What is?"

"You."

"I'm not extraordinary. Please don't patronize me."

Emory said, "A child said—"

"I don't feel like reciting poetry just now," Simon told him.

"Really?"

"Really."

Emory smiled and nodded. "As you wish," he said.

Twyla approached from the crowd, with Luke behind her. She said to Simon, "If you're staying here, you could take care of Hesperia."

"I guess I could."

"The neighbors are coming to get her tomorrow. Tell them they can't have her after all. Tell them you're going to keep her. Will you do that?"

"Sure."

Luke said, "He can't take care of a horse. The neighbors are a better bet. They're horse people, right?"

"Hesperia would be one of the herd to them. She'll be Simon's only horse."

"This is assuming Simon wants or needs a horse. This is assuming he'd have any idea what to do with a horse."

Othea said, "We need to be getting on board now." She held the infant in her arms.

Emory said to Simon, "It seems I did a better job with you than I'd realized."

"Have a good trip," Simon said.

"Same to you. Excuse me, I've got to do a head count. Don't wander off. I want to say a proper goodbye."

Emory strode off into the crowd. Luke and Twyla continued bickering about the horse. The argument seemed to be leading them into other, more general areas of disagreement.

Simon decided it was as good a time as any to slip away. No one seemed to notice when he did.

He resumed his place beside Catareen in the dim, cool room. From outside he heard the sounds of the departure. A ringing of metal, three clear notes in succession. A strange sound of suction, unidentifiable, that came and went. And every now and then the sound of voices, a child calling, an adult answering. They were indistinct. They seemed to come from far away, farther than he knew them to be.

He did not wish to see the ship depart. He preferred to be here, in this quiet room.

As time passed he drifted into sleep and out again. His head fell onto his chest, and he jerked awake. Each time when he woke he was briefly surprised to find himself here, with the dark silent form laid out on the bed. Each time he understood that he was in fact here. Then he'd fall asleep again.

Finally he got onto the bed beside Catareen. He was so tired. He wanted only to lie down. He moved carefully, trying not to disturb her. He arranged his body beside hers on the narrow mattress.

Her eyelids fluttered open. She turned her head and looked at him. She was quiet for a while. Then she said, "You."

Her voice had thinned. It was a low whistle, barely audible.

"Me," he answered.

"When you go?"

"Don't worry about that."

"When you go?"

"I'm not going."

"You are."

"No. I'm staying here."

"Not."

He said, "I wouldn't want to go without you." It was not what he'd meant to say. It did not seem quite literally true. And yet, he'd said it.

"You go," she said.

"Shh. Don't talk." As if he'd ever imagined asking her to speak less. She said, "Go."

He answered, "This is where I want to be."

She looked at him. Her eyes were fading. She opened her mouth to speak but could not speak.

"Sleep," he said. "Just sleep. I'll be right here."

She closed her eyes. Carefully, he put his arm over her. Then he decided she probably wouldn't want that. He removed his arm. He inclined his head toward hers, let the skin of his cheek touch the skin of her forehead. He thought she would not mind that.

Soon he was asleep, too.

He dreamed that he stood in a high place. It was bright and windy. In the dream he could not determine whether he was on a mountain or a building. He knew only that he was standing on something solid and that the earth was far below. From where he stood he could see people walking across a plain. They were distant, and yet he could see them perfectly. There were men and women and children. They were all going in the same direction. They were leaving something behind. He could just barely make it out. It was a darkness, a sense of gathering storm, far away, shot through with flashes of light, green-tinted, unhealthy, small shivers and bursts of light that appeared and disappeared in the roil of cloudy darkness. The people were walking away from it, but he could not see what it was they were moving toward. A brilliant wind blew against him, and he could only face into it. He could only look at that which the people were fleeing. He hoped they were going to something better. He imagined mountains and forests, rivers, a pure windswept cleanliness, but he could not see it. He could only see the people walking through the grass. He could only see what was on their faces: hope and fear and determination, a furious ardency he could not put a name to. The wind grew louder around him. He understood that the wind in his dream was the sound of a spacecraft, departing for another world.

He awoke. It was still dark. He could still hear the wind from his dream.

He knew immediately that Catareen had died.

She lay rigid. Her eyes were closed. The orange no longer shone through the thin membranes of her eyelids. Simon put his hand on her small, smooth head. It was cool as a stone.

He wondered: Had she hastened her death in the hope that he

might still be able to get aboard the ship? Could a Nadian do something like that? It was impossible to say.

The ship. He might still have time to get aboard, then.

He ran from the room, down the stairs, and outside. He knew. Of
course he knew. Still, he shouted, "Wait."

The ship was one hundred feet or more above the ground, quivering as its reactor prepared to deliver the blast. It floated, humming. Its
three spider legs had been retracted. It was a perfect silver platter,
trembling as if it might flip over, girdled with green-gold porthole
lights. Centered in its underside was the circle of the reactor, deepening from blinding white to volcanic red. Ten, nine, eight . . .

Simon ran to the empty place where the ship had been. He
shouted, "Wait, please, wait." He stood shouting in the middle of the
scorched circle the ship had left behind. He knew it was too late.
Even if they could see him (they could not see him), there was no way
to bring the ship down again, no rope or ladder to unfurl.

"No," he shouted. "Please, oh, please, wait for me."

The reactor fired. Simon was consumed by red light, obliterated
by it. He was momentarily made only of light, blinded, shouting. It
was not hot; it was only bright. The reactor made a small sound, a mechanical cough, and then the ship hurtled upward so fast it seemed to
vanish entirely. By the time the red light had dissipated, by the time
Simon's sight was restored, it was already impossible to tell which light
was the ship and which was one of the nearer stars.

Simon stood looking up at the sky. He fixed on a moving light that
might have been the ship, though he could not be sure. The sky was
full of starlike lights that moved, that could have been flycraft from
Eurasia or secret weapons aimed at various enemies or alien ships
bearing pilgrims from one world to another. The sky was full of travelers. Simon remained under the stars and the points of moving light
shouting, "Wait, wait, wait, oh, please, wait for me."

When he was finished shouting there was nothing to do but go
back into the empty house. He returned to the bedroom. He lay
awake beside Catareen's body, which contained no trace of her. She
had departed entirely. Her flesh had joined the inanimate objects of
the room; it was no more than the chair or the lamp. He lay beside
the body until the room began to pale with the first light of morning.

By the time the sun was fully risen, he had dug her grave. He chose a place behind the farmhouse, in the shade of the tree they had looked at together through the bedroom window. When the hole was deep enough he went and lifted her body and carried it outside. She weighed almost nothing. In death, she was like a collapsed umbrella. He held her body carefully, with her head pressed to his chest, though of course it made no difference. As he carried her across the yard the horse nickered. It wanted to be fed.

Before he fed the horse he took Catareen to the grave, sat awkwardly on its crumbly edge, then slid down and laid her on the cool, moist earth. It didn't seem right to put dirt directly onto her face. He thought at first he would go back into the house for a cloth but decided instead to remove his shirt and drape it over her head. He thought she should have something of his in the grave with her, though of course it made no difference.

When her features were shrouded by his T-shirt he reached up, took a handful of earth, and spread it over her face. He worked carefully and gently. He added another handful, and another. He covered her handful by handful until she was entirely blanketed by earth. Until she had disappeared. Then he hoisted himself out of the grave and shoveled the rest of the dirt in.

The horse whinnied insistently. It needed to be fed. He went and fed the horse.

The sun was high by then. The heat of the day had begun. He was alone here, with the horse and Catareen's grave. The others were on their way to a new world, one that might be beautiful or might be barren.

He made breakfast for himself and washed the dishes. It was nine-thirty on a summer morning in an empty house on the outskirts of Denver. He walked onto the porch and looked at what was there. Grass and sky. A single finger of cloud, dissolving in the searing blue above the distant mountain range.

It was time to go.

He saddled the horse. He was drawn more to the idea of riding the horse than he was to the prospect of driving away in the Winnebago.

The Winnebago could stay here, in the heat and the silence. The sun would rise and fall and rise again on the truck and the house, on the scorched circle where the spaceship had been, on Catareen's unmarked grave.

He mounted the horse and rode out. He would ride west, he thought. He would ride to California. He would ride in that direction. He and the horse might die of starvation or the sun. They might be attacked by nomads and zealots. Or they might get to the Pacific. They might go all the way to the far edge of the continent and stand on a beach before what he imagined to be a restive, infinite blue. Assuming of course that the ocean was still untainted. There was no way of knowing, was there?

He rode west. He rode until the farm was out of sight, until he was no one and nothing but a man on a horse in a vast emptiness, a world of grass and sky. The horse walked steadily on. It was unconcerned. It was only walking. It had no idea about anything.

Simon and the horse would have to get across the mountains. What were they called? The Rockies. People had done that, though. People who were now long dead had ridden horses across these mountains and reached whatever waited for them on the other side. They had buried their dead. They had carried with them bowls that bore messages written in forgotten languages. They had carried memories of a pond or of a tree perfectly centered in an accidental view or of being left behind as others sailed away. They had harbored unreasonable hopes. They had built cities that rose and fell and might for all he knew be rising again.

The woman was in the ground. The child was on his way to another world. Simon was on his way someplace, and there might be nothing there. No, there was something everywhere. He was going into his future. There was nothing to do but ride into it.

A pure change happened. He felt it buzzing through his circuits. He had no name for it.

He said aloud, "The earth, that is sufficient, I do not want the constellations any nearer, I know they are very well where they are, I know they suffice for those who belong to them."

He rode on then, through the long grass toward the mountains.

Acknowledgments

As novelists go, I am not a particularly private or solitary individual. I tend to talk about work in progress with a small body of trusted friends, and have the good sense to listen to their ideas. I also show various drafts to various readers, and each helps to make the novel in question stronger and truer than I'd be capable of making it on my own.

I extend my deepest gratitude to Diane Cardwell, Judy Clain, Frances Coady, Joel Connarroe, Stacey D'Erasmo, Marie Howe, Joy Johannessen, Daniel Kaizer, James Lecesne, Michael Mayer, Adam Moss, Christopher Potter, and Derrick Smit. Also crucial readers, and much more than that, are my agent, Gail Hochman, and my editor, Jonathan Galassi. Marianne Merola sees to it that my books are well published outside the United States. Susan Mitchell, Jeff Seroy, Timothy Mennel, Sarita Varma, and Annie Wedekind have been heroic in their efforts to make this book look beautiful, to catch its errors of fact and infelicities of diction, and to convey it into the world.

The assistance and friendship of Meg Giles have been crucial in ways too numerous to mention.

I wrote the third section while staying at the Santa Maddalena Foundation in Tuscany at the invitation of Beatrice von Rezzori, whose generosity toward writers is nothing short of remarkable.

I relied for information on *Gotham: A History of New York City to 1898* by Edwin G. Burrows and Mike Wallace, published in 1999 by Oxford University Press; *The Historical Atlas of New York City* by Eric

Homberger, published in 1994 by Henry Holt and Company; *Walt Whitman: The Song of Himself* by Jerome Loving, published in 1999 by the University of California Press; *Walt Whitman's America* by David S. Reynolds, published in 1995 by Alfred A. Knopf; and the edition of Walt Whitman's *Leaves of Grass* published by the Library of America in 1992. Mike Wallace, coauthor of *Gotham*, was kind enough to e-mail me in response to certain questions regarding life in the nineteenth century. Although the reader will not learn about the underwear those characters are wearing, *I* know, thanks to Mike Wallace, and that helped me to more fully imagine them.

Finally I must acknowledge Ken Corbett, who not only reads passages as I go along, offers brilliant suggestions, and talks me through my fits of discouragement, but helps to create a domestic environment of discrimination, generosity, humor, scrupulous thought, and belief in the fundamental human obligation to try to do at least a little more than one is technically able to.